Dear Reader,

When Pocket Books brought three of the eight novels I'd penned under the name Deborah Martin back into print, I was ecstatic at the chance to revise and refresh my early works. I'm thrilled to now be adding *Windswept* to the list that includes *By Love Unveiled*, *Silver Deceptions*, and *Stormswept*. These early works set the stage for my career. First came the historical details, passionate action, and darker tones of my Deborah Martin novels. Then followed the sensual entanglements, witty repartee, and lighthearted spirits of my recent Regency series: The Sinful Suitors and The Hellions of Halstead Hall. Both romantic styles are infused with the sexy romantic liaisons my readers have come to expect in my works.

And now, long out of print, a revised *Windswept* is available once more from Pocket Books! In this tale, Catrin Price is haunted by a death curse that already took the man she married. The only way to break the spell is to buy back a druid chalice and drink from it before her marriage. But when Catrin redeems the chalice, she leaves a dead man in her wake, and now must prove her innocence.

Evan Newcome is on a mission to find the woman last seen with his dead friend. When he meets Catrin, passion blazes hot between them. Can the magic of true love overcome the secrets and lies and cloud of mistrust? In this all-new, thoroughly revised, powerful love story, I heightened the emotions of the story line, tightened the dialogue, and enriched the heart-pounding sexual tension between my two wounded, entangled characters. I hope you enjoy this new edition of *Windswept*, whether it's one of your past favorites or a new adventure for you to relish.

Happy reading!

Sabrina Jeffries

"ANYONE WHO LOVES ROMANCE MUST READ SABRINA JEFFRIES!"

—*New York Times* bestselling author
Lisa Kleypas

The Sinful Suitors

Sabrina Jeffries's delightful Regency series featuring the St. George's Club, where watchful guardians conspire to keep their unattached sisters and wards out of the clutches of sinful suitors.

THE STUDY OF SEDUCTION

"Lovely, poignant, and powerful."

—*Kirkus Reviews*

"[Sabrina Jeffries] knows what readers want and she delivers on every level, satisfying fans and garnering new readers."

—*RT Book Reviews* (4½ stars, Top Pick)

"Graced with pleasingly wrought characters who develop beautifully and a crafty villain you'll love to hate, along with clever dialogue and rapier wit, this compelling, deliciously seductive story takes the classic marriage of convenience to a new level and sets the stage for the next in the series. A delectable and rewarding read."

—*Library Journal* (starred review)

THE ART OF SINNING

"With every book, Jeffries grows into an even more accomplished writer whose memorable characters and unforgettable stories speak to readers on many levels."

—*RT Book Reviews* (4½ stars, Top Pick)

"Veteran historical romance author Jeffries launches her Sinful Suitors Regency series with two effortlessly crafted charismatic protagonists."

—*Publishers Weekly*

"*The Art of Sinning* is an endearing beginning to a new series, and showcases Jeffries's talents in making the reader swoon in delight."

—*Fresh Fiction*

**Also from *New York Times* and
USA Today bestselling author**

SABRINA JEFFRIES

STORMSWEPT

"The depth of [Rhys and Juliana's] emotions makes them believable characters, and their fast-paced story is intensely moving."

—*Publishers Weekly*

The Duke's Men

They are an investigative agency born out of
family pride and irresistible passion . . . and they
risk their lives and hearts to unravel any shocking
deception or scandalous transgression!

IF THE VISCOUNT FALLS

"A perfect conclusion to Jeffries's addictive quartet."
—*Library Journal* (starred review)

HOW THE SCOUNDREL SEDUCES

"Scorching . . . From cover to cover, it sizzles."
—*Reader to Reader*

"Marvelous storytelling . . . Memorable."
—*RT Book Reviews* (4½ stars, Top Pick, K.I.S.S. Award)

WHEN THE ROGUE RETURNS

"Blends the pace of a thriller with the romance of the Regency era."
—*Woman's Day*

"Enthralling . . . rich in passion and danger."
—*Booklist* (starred review)

WHAT THE DUKE DESIRES

"A totally engaging, adventurous love story with an oh-so-wonderful ending."
—*RT Book Reviews*

"Full of all the intriguing characters, brisk plotting, and witty dialogue that Jeffries's readers have come to expect."
—*Publishers Weekly* (starred review)

SABRINA JEFFRIES

WRITING AS
DEBORAH MARTIN

Windswept

Pocket Books

New York   London   Toronto   Sydney   New Delhi

Pocket Books
An Imprint of Simon & Schuster, Inc.
1230 Avenue of the Americas
New York, NY 10020

This book is a work of fiction. Any references to historical events, real people, or real places are used fictitiously. Other names, characters, places, and events are products of the author's imagination, and any resemblance to actual events or places or persons, living or dead, is entirely coincidental.

First Pocket Books paperback edition March 2017

POCKET and colophon are registered trademarks of Simon & Schuster, Inc.

For information about special discounts for bulk purchases, please contact Simon & Schuster Special Sales at 1-866-506-1949 or business@simonandschuster.com.

The Simon & Schuster Speakers Bureau can bring authors to your live event. For more information or to book an event, contact the Simon & Schuster Speakers Bureau at 1-866-248-3049 or visit our website at www.simonspeakers.com.

Manufactured in the United States of America

10 9 8 7 6 5 4 3 2 1

ISBN 978-1-4516-6555-0
ISBN 978-1-5011-3100-4 (ebook)

To my wonderful father, Jack Martin,
whose love of history and mystery shaped my career.
There's a little of both in this one, Daddy!

PROLOGUE

Catrin Price reread Lord Mansfield's note yet again: *Meet me at nine o'clock at the Green Goat. I shall reserve the private supper room at the back of the inn for you.*

But it was well after nine and he still wasn't here. For the first time since she'd embarked on this scheme, she wondered how wise it was to meet an English stranger in an inn.

Perhaps that explained the foreboding in her bones, poisoning her hopes for the evening. Ever since she'd left her lodgings, she'd had the uneasy sense of being watched. No doubt it was only her imagination, though. Her stalwart grandmother had always accused her of being scared of her own shadow.

Still, had Lord Mansfield chosen this seedy inn for a reason? Had he lured her here to steal her virtue?

Don't be absurd. He doesn't know what you look like, or if you're young or old. Why would he plot against a stranger?

Yet all her life, she'd heard terrifying stories of what

could happen to a Welshwoman from the country traveling alone in a huge English city like London. Although she spoke English well, she could sense people assessing her accent, trying to decide if she were an easy mark or no.

London oppressed her. It was too large, too crowded and noisy, and far too dirty. She missed the heather-carpeted moors of Wales, the mountains swept by bracing winds, and the tangled bushes of wild roses. Here she felt like a scared creature caught in a pen with gaolers whom she neither understood nor liked.

She fingered the sheaf of pound notes in her coat pocket. How she hated having to give it to some rich Englishman. She could use it for a thousand other things—new roofs for the tenants' cottages, an addition to the servants' cramped quarters, books for the charity school . . .

Still, this was more important. It would buy her freedom from the curse. Hope. And a future for her and the people who depended on her. For that, she'd pay any amount.

She drew out the diary that had brought her here, and the weight of the past settled on her like thunderclouds on Black Mountain. According to David Morys, the schoolmaster in Llanddeusant, it was over two hundred years old. Turning to the pages she'd practically memorized, she read again the ominous Welsh words:

To all women with the blood of Morgana in their veins. This is the tale of your inheritance, passed down from mother to daughter for generations. Heed its warning well.

On the wedding night of Morgana's daughter, while the Saxon merchant and Gwyneth stood before the priest at Llanddeusant, Morgana appeared in the doorway. Her eyes were glinting jewels and her hair a living flame as she called out her daughter's name.

Gwyneth was sorely tried, for she had run away with the Saxon in secret, hoping to keep her mother from learning of the wedding until it was too late.

But Morgana, called the Priestess of the Mists because she followed the ways of the ancients, had seen in a vision what was to occur on that night and had come to prevent the marriage.

Morgana stamped and swore. "Thou thinkst to marry this man, daughter? This abomination, this Saxon of low blood? Thou couldst have any Welsh prince of my choosing if marriage is thy desire!"

"'Tis not a prince I wish!" Gwyneth cried. "I love my merchant, and I will marry him!"

"He will take thee from the old ways!" the priestess protested. "He will corrupt thy mind and take thee from the truths I have shown thee!"

"He will not, my mother. I promise to remain faithful to thy teachings."

Morgana brought forth from the mists a bronze chalice of nearly two hands' breadth. Upon one side was a raven etched in bold detail, upon the other a warrior garbed for battle and a fair maiden arrayed in nothing but her own hair, which twined about her body like a snake.

Morgana offered the chalice to her daughter. "Thou must seal thy promise. Drink from this to show thou art my true daughter."

The merchant begged Gwyneth not to drink, for he feared Morgana might poison her daughter to keep her from the marriage. But Gwyneth drank, for she loved her mother and wished to honor her.

When every drop was drained, Morgana smiled. "Thou art my true daughter indeed. Thus I give thee this cup as a wedding gift to remind thee of thy promise. From this day forth, any woman of our lineage must drink from it on the night of her wedding to show that she honors the ways of her ancestors. It will give her the wisdom and beauty of the maiden and her husband the strength of the warrior, and her marriage will be blessed."

Her face grew dark as winter storms. "But be warned. If any woman of thy lineage doth not drink of the cup at her wedding, her husband shall die within three years of her wedding. Her sons shall be fruitless and her daughters as accursed as she until the day they marry and drink themselves of this cup."

The others gasped to hear the priestess's curse, but her daughter smiled. "It shall ever be so, my mother. The women of my line shall always honor thee and the ways of our ancestors."

Chills snaked down Catrin's spine. She wanted to believe that the curse was mere superstition. But after examining her family's past, she'd been forced to recognize that their troubles had begun only after her great-great-grandfather had sold the chalice in the seventeenth century.

To Lord Mansfield's family, from what she'd been able to learn. And Lord Mansfield's description of the chalice he owned perfectly matched the diary's. After years of searching, she felt sure she'd found the right one.

Pray heaven she had, for otherwise she could never remarry and risk subjecting another man to poor Willie's fate. Without it, she would have no heirs. She and her estate and all those who depended on them would have no future.

And she couldn't let that happen.

1

Carmarthen, Wales
June 1802

*E*van Newcome read the inscription on his father's gravestone: THOMAS NEWCOME. BORN JULY 3, 1741. DIED APRIL 25, 1802.

Nothing. Shouldn't he feel *something* besides a dull thud of hatred? Or the fear that clutched him in the dark?

Gritting his teeth, he noted the lack of an epitaph calling Thomas Newcome a wonderful father and husband. That surprised him, given that his older sister, Mary, always kept up appearances. From the moment she'd married her tailor husband and escaped their father, she'd acted as if her childhood had never been. Evan had assumed she'd willfully forgotten the past. But perhaps not.

Then again, perhaps *she* hadn't chosen the words on the gravestone. Perhaps his older brother had done so— dull-witted, ham-fisted Goronwy, who wouldn't have known what to write.

"Evan?" came a voice behind him. "Is that you?"

He turned to find Lady Juliana Vaughan standing there. She and her husband, Rhys, had rescued him from his abysmal home and sent him to Eton years ago. Just the sight of her banished his somber thoughts.

"Good day, my lady," he said with a smile.

She looked as pretty as ever, her forty-odd years only enhancing her natural beauty. Glancing down at the grave, she tucked her hand in the crook of his elbow. "I'm sorry about your father. You have our deepest sympathies."

He bit back the urge to say he hoped the arse rotted in hell. "Thank you."

Juliana searched his face. "I was surprised you didn't come home for the funeral, if only for your sister's sake."

"Trust me, it would have been harder for Mary to endure my obvious lack of grief. At least without me there, she could tell people I was abroad or suddenly taken ill." He paused. "What *did* she tell people?"

Juliana gave a rueful smile. "That you were suddenly taken ill."

"You see? I'm sure she was relieved I wasn't there to tell the truth about the bullying bastard."

She squeezed his arm. "Well, at least you've come now. You probably have matters you must discuss with your siblings."

"Yes." Although he'd arrived several hours ago, he'd put off going to his sister's. He dreaded the awkward task of explaining why he was staying at an inn instead of with her.

The truth was, he felt ill at ease in her home. No matter how hard he tried to make her feel comfortable, she always seemed conscious of the differences between them now, and it pained him to watch her and her husband struggle for conversation.

Staying with Goronwy was out of the question. It was too horribly familiar, watching Goronwy explode every time a meal was cooked wrong or one of the children crossed him.

Evan couldn't bear watching history repeat itself. Or being reminded that he, too, had a violent temper, that if matters were different and he had a helpless wife and children to lash out at . . .

Blood of his blood, flesh of his flesh. You are like him.

He shook off the bitter thought.

"That old gossip, Mrs. Wynton, told me you were here." Juliana shot him a sideways glance. "She said you were staying at her wretched inn. Surely you weren't planning to pass through here without even paying us a visit."

He smiled. "You know I'd never do that. But I left London so suddenly, I didn't have time to send a letter, and I didn't want to inconvenience you by showing up on your doorstep without warning."

"Don't be silly. You come here so seldom that it's sheer delight to have you. Do tell me you'll stay with us at Llynwydd. Rhys will be pleased to see you, as will the children." With a conspiratorial air, she leaned up to add, "Mrs. Wynton keeps a sloppy house, you know."

"You don't need to convince me."

"Good. Rhys is over at Morgan's, but we're having luncheon together at the Bull and Crown." She glanced down at the grave. "Come away from this place and join us. Will you?"

He nodded, letting her draw him from the cemetery. Perhaps being among friends would dispel his melancholy.

They walked together in a companionable silence. It felt good to be back in Wales. He'd forgotten how friendly the people were, how brilliant a blue the sky, how vibrant a green the forests that lined the roads. The wild sweetness of his own country roused a long-buried ache in him, to be in a place where every blade of grass seemed familiar. Wales was still his home, and he was astonished at how glad he was to walk the streets of crotchety old Carmarthen once more.

Soon they reached the tavern, where Rhys was waiting for Juliana, engrossed in reading a radical political pamphlet.

"Good morning, darling," Juliana said. "Look who I found wandering the streets."

Surprise lit the older man's face as he rose to clasp Evan's shoulders. "You wily scoundrel! Why didn't you tell us you were coming to town?"

Juliana flashed Rhys a dark glance. "He was at the graveyard."

"Ah, yes," Rhys said, sobering. "I'd forgotten about your father. I'm sorry."

"Actually," Evan said, "I didn't come because of that. I'm in search of the Lady of the Mists. I heard rumors of her as a child, so you two must know of her."

"Yes, but—" Rhys began.

Juliana cut him off. "Of course we know of the *old* Lady of the Mists." She shot Rhys a meaningful glance as she took a seat.

Rhys called a maid over and ordered food for the three of them, then sat down himself as Evan settled in a chair.

"How much do you know?" Evan grew sarcastic. "I've heard the legends, of course. She rides and shoots like a man, plays the harp like a goddess, and sings like an angel. It's a wonder she bothers with us mortals."

Rhys stared at Juliana, one eyebrow arched. "Yes, love, do tell Evan what we know about the Lady of the Mists."

Evan sensed some secret between them, but that was no surprise. He envied how they could still be so much in love after all these years.

"Why are you interested in the Lady of the Mists?" Juliana asked.

He wondered how much to say. "I don't know if you heard about the murder of my friend Justin."

"Yes, I remember reading about it in the *Times*."

Just then their food came, a substantial *cawl*, a roast leg of mutton, potatoes, and cabbage. Good Welsh fare that he couldn't wait to tackle.

Ever the hostess, Juliana dished the food onto plates and put one in front of him. "The *Times* said Lord Mansfield was robbed and killed by footpads. I'm sorry, Evan. It has been a year of losses for you, hasn't it?"

He nodded, though Justin's death had cut far more deeply than his father's. Years ago, Justin had braved the taunts of his classmates at Eton to befriend Evan. Justin had taught him how to defend himself from the snobbish young nobles and bullying merchants' sons without getting caught by the headmaster.

They'd remained friends at Cambridge, even after Justin

began living the reckless life of a young lord. He'd been the only one who could coax Evan from his books for a foray into London's gaming hells or a night of wenching, the only one who could make Evan forget for a while who he was and where he'd come from. And when Evan's engagement to a wealthy merchant's daughter had ended in disaster, it had been Justin who'd forced Evan to stop brooding.

How could the carefree devil be dead? It was unfathomable. Yet he was, and his senseless death left Evan with an unquenchable anger. "His death is why I've come in search of the Lady of the Mists." When they regarded him oddly, he added, "I believe she was the last person to see Justin."

As he ate some mutton, Rhys and Juliana exchanged glances.

"Why do you believe that?" Juliana asked.

"Because he met with her the night he was killed."

"And you think she had something to do with it?" Juliana asked in alarm.

He considered confiding his suspicions, but he wanted to know more of what had occurred first. "Not necessarily. But there's been little progress in finding his killers. I'm hoping she saw something that will help."

Juliana's face cleared. "I see. That's all right, then."

"I'm so glad you approve." He couldn't keep the sarcasm out of his voice. She was behaving strangely. "Tell me what you know about her."

"She's a widow," Rhys said. "It's a tragic story. Her husband, Willie Price, was killed on their wedding day in a freak accident."

Despite himself, Evan felt a twinge of sympathy. "That's awful."

"Yes," Juliana agreed. "But she has risen above it to make a place for herself in the world."

"We met her once when she visited Carmarthen," Rhys said. Suddenly he grunted for no apparent reason and shot his wife a sharp glance.

Evan dipped his bread in gravy. "What was she like?"

Before Rhys could answer, Juliana cut in. "She was as wonderful as the legends make her out to be."

"Of course, you probably already know she's the daughter of a knight and fairly well-off," Rhys said.

Evan blinked. He'd always thought of the old woman as classless, one of those unusual creatures on the fringes of society who in past times would have been termed witches. Why would a woman of such standing murder a nobleman?

"She's a bit of an odd one," Rhys added, ignoring his wife's scowl. "Despite her rank, she dabbles in all sorts of peculiar things."

"You mean, aside from the harp playing and shooting?" Evan quipped.

Rhys flashed him an enigmatic smile. "Yes. She writes, you know. You might have read her work. She studies the folklore and superstitions of the Welsh. Morgan and I have offered to publish her essays in one of our collections." He glanced at Juliana. "I think you'll like her a great deal more than you expect."

"Whether I like her is immaterial. I'd settle for knowing her actual name and how to find her."

"Oh, *that*!" Juliana brightened. "Her name is Catrin

Price, and she lives outside of Llanddeusant. I can tell you how to get to the village, and the villagers can direct you to her home. Her estate is called Plas Niwl, the Mansion of Mist. It's near Llyn y Fan Fach, the lake with the legend about the fairy who married a mortal. Their descendants are supposed to be the great doctors of Merthyr Tydfil."

He'd heard the tale. A merchant had fallen in love with the fairy after seeing her at the lake. She'd agreed to become his wife, bringing him cattle and gold as her dowry, but had promised to remain his wife only until the day he'd struck her three times. After years of marriage and four children, he'd done so, and she'd vanished, taking the cattle and gold with her.

Wise woman. Too bad Mother couldn't have vanished.

"You should see Llyn y Fan Fach while you're there," Juliana went on. "It's beautiful."

The wistful remark made him smile. Juliana held romantic notions about Wales. An estate named the Mansion of Mist near a renowned site of legend probably fired her imagination to new heights.

"I shall certainly try," he said. "But I won't have a lot of time."

"Does this mean you're not staying here long?" Juliana asked.

"I'm afraid so." He suspected that gleaning the truth from a wily old woman like Catrin Price might take patience . . . and a devious mind. He must approach this cautiously to avoid spooking her before he got what he wanted.

Juliana sighed. "While you're there, stay at the Red

Dragon. But you *will* pass through here on your way back to the coast, won't you?"

"Of course." Evan smiled. "And this time I'll give you fair warning."

"It doesn't matter. You know we always love to have you." A sly look crossed Juliana's face. "Although I wonder if the day will ever come when I welcome you *and* a wife to our estate."

With a groan, he pushed his plate away. "Don't start that again. I've already told you—no sane woman wants a tedious scholar for a husband."

"You are *not* a tedious scholar. You're a strong, handsome young man. Any woman would be proud to marry you."

Evan didn't bother to disguise his bitterness. "I know several women who'd disagree. My humble bloodlines disgust the gentry, and my education intimidates those of my class. I'm too Welsh for an Englishwoman, and too English for a Welshwoman. I'm cantankerous and stubborn and lacking in the charm that sweeps women off their feet." *I'm blood of his blood, flesh of his flesh.*

He forced back that thought. "In short, I don't suit anyone, and it's unlikely I'd find someone to suit me. And that's the last I shall say on the subject."

"Good," Juliana retorted, "because it's all nonsense. You're considered a genius for your linguistic abilities, your translations garner large subscriptions, and young men flock to your lectures at Cambridge. Humble bloodlines, indeed! Any woman worth her salt won't care about that. *I* didn't care a whit about Rhys's when he came courting." At Rhys's scowl, she added hastily, "Not that his bloodlines weren't perfectly respectable. But my father was hoping for a duke."

"Which would never have worked," Rhys confided to Evan. "Juliana is far too strong-minded. She would have made a duke miserable."

"Rhys Vaughan!" Juliana protested.

Rhys grinned. "But you make me perfectly happy, darling."

When Juliana gave Rhys an adoring smile, Evan felt a twinge of envy. "At least Rhys owned land. I haven't an acre to my name. No matter where I go or what I do, I'm still a tenant farmer's son of modest means. No woman will forget that simply because I've achieved success in certain circles."

"The right woman will," Juliana persisted. "You just haven't found her yet."

He didn't feel like arguing with her. "Perhaps you're right. But until that woman comes along, I'm happy to have friends like you and Rhys." He rose. "And if I'm to stay with you tonight, I'd best move my things."

Rhys flashed him a sympathetic smile, obviously aware of why Evan was hurrying off. "We'll meet you there with the carriage as soon as we're finished."

Evan nodded and walked out of the inn.

Juliana watched him leave, her heart tight with sympathy. She loved Evan as dearly as she loved her own children, and his unhappiness tormented her.

"He'll be all right." Rhys leaned over to take her hand. "Evan has survived many things, and he'll survive this."

"He needs someone. You know he does."

"Yes, but he'll have to find her himself."

"I swear I could kill the chit who broke his heart. He was even prepared to leave the university for her. How dare she make Evan fall in love with her, only to end the engagement for no apparent reason!"

"She must have had *some* reason."

"Don't defend her. I can't believe any woman would refuse Evan."

"And you're biased. Anyway, they obviously weren't well-suited, so aren't you glad he was saved from marrying her?"

"Yes, but now he's become a complete cynic about women. It isn't right."

"And you think that fooling him about the Lady of the Mists will help."

A startled expression crossed her face. "What do you mean?"

Rhys grinned. "You know what I mean, you little meddler. Why else wouldn't you reveal that the Lady of the Mists he heard about in childhood died two years ago, and that her granddaughter now holds that name? That this Lady of the Mists is a shy, bewitching miss liable to steal his heart?"

She sniffed. "If I'd told him that, he wouldn't have gone. He steers clear of bewitching misses these days. And it'll be even worse now that Justin is dead. At least Justin forced him to go out in society."

"So you're forcing him to meet Catrin Price."

Juliana scowled. "She's perfect for him—a scholar who's bright and kind and—"

"I thought you said she had turned aside every suitor who's come near her since Mr. Price's death?"

Juliana shot him a defensive glance. "She won't turn Evan aside."

Rhys laughed. "How can you be so damned sure?"

"A woman's intuition."

"And how can you be sure he'll like her?"

"Of course he'll like her. She's 'bewitching,' isn't she?"

At her peevish tone, Rhys smiled, then leaned over to give her a quick kiss. "Not as bewitching as you, *cariad*."

She melted, as always. In truth, it was a good sign that Rhys found sweet little Mrs. Price "bewitching." She only hoped Evan did, too. Because it would take a witch to storm his walled-up heart.

2

Catrin drew a deep breath, then dove into Llyn y Fan Fach. She came up sputtering, the water stippling her skin with goose bumps. She didn't mind. The cold revived her aching muscles after a morning of making candles.

With easy strokes, she struck out across the lake, enjoying the hush broken only by the faint swish of her movements. She swam enough to exercise her cramped arms, then stopped to tread water. Flinging her wet hair out of her face with one hand, she looked about her.

The mist clung to the surface of the water, shifting from one fantastical shape into another. Some days it made her think she saw the *Tylwyth Teg* in their fairy enchantment, playing harps and dancing. Or even the Lady of the Lake herself. Strange how it took only a heavy mist to make one's imagination run wild.

Unfortunately, the shapes she saw today were menacing, reminding her of her disastrous trip to London a week ago and her mad flight back to Wales. She muttered a Welsh oath. Coming to the lake hadn't been a good idea if it only fed her fears and frightening memories. She struck out for shore, headed to where she'd left her clothes.

She was so caught up in her thoughts that she didn't notice the man on shore until she rose out of the water far enough to expose herself to the waist. By heaven, who was *he*?

Tall and broad of shoulder, the man had one booted foot propped on a rock as he stared right at her, apparently as surprised to see her as she was to see him. His dark eyes moved inexorably down her face to her throat and then her breasts.

Oh Lord, she was wearing only her shift. Blushing furiously, she sank down to her neck. What was this stranger doing here? No one else ever came here this early.

Panic swept her. Should she swim to another bank? But then she couldn't get her clothes. Besides, he could still see her leave the water.

When he moved forward as if to catch a closer look, she cried, "Who are you, sir, to be spying on me?"

Shock made him halt. "You're real."

"Of course I'm real. What did you think?"

He shook his head as if to clear it. "For a moment . . . well . . . I thought I was seeing the fairy of Llyn y Fan Fach." A rueful grin transformed his serious expression. "But it's clear you're flesh and blood."

His accented Welsh, low and earthy, roused something unfamiliar deep in her belly.

"Normally I know better than to put stock in such

tales," he continued, "but when you rose out of the water through the mist as if by magic . . ."

"It's all r-right," she stammered, unable to look at him.

Strangers rarely came to this remote place. And there wasn't a soul to hear her cry out if the man hauled her out of the water and threw her down on the bank.

She stole a glance at him. He didn't *look* like the kind of man to do that. But neither did he look like the naturalists who trekked through the wilds with their expensive walking sticks and tour books.

His well-built body seemed made for hefting beams, but his face was that of an ascetic, dark and stern with the knowledge of years. His thick, wavy chestnut hair and lovely long eyelashes made him quite attractive, although his sober clothing marked him as unaware of it.

He'd been assessing her, too, but when she shifted her position, he averted his gaze. "I should apologize for intruding on your privacy. A friend of mine told me of this place, so I thought I'd take a look."

She wasn't sure she should converse with this giant, whose formal speech and bearing bespoke a learned man even while his mournful eyes hinted at knowledge beyond books. Still, she had little choice. Essentially, she was trapped.

"Do you live close by?" he asked.

Alarm skittered through her. "Why do you ask?"

He ventured a smile. "I'm not going to eat you, I promise. It's just that I'm looking for a place near here, and I thought you might direct me. The directions they gave in Llanddeusant weren't helpful."

His request was so innocuous and his voice so gentle that she relaxed. "If you'll let me dress, I can show you the way. I know the roads well."

"I'd appreciate that, actually."

When he stood there waiting, she blurted out, "Could you turn your back, please? My clothes are on the bank."

"Oh, of course," he muttered, pivoting away. "Sorry. I wasn't thinking."

Her eyes never leaving his back, she slid out of the water to snatch her clothes. Any minute, she expected him to whirl around and grab her. Fortunately, he was as courteous as he seemed, for he didn't so much as move.

She removed her wet shift and donned the dry one. Only then did she realize how transparent her wet shift was. What kind of woman must he think her? But then, she hadn't expected anyone to see her or she'd never have risked it.

As the silence stretched out, he cleared his throat. "I do hope it's not too far. Everyone in town had differing opinions about the distance."

"They're unaccustomed to strangers, and are likely to say things like 'go past the field with the cow in it, then turn left at the place where the trees grow thick.'"

"Or 'at the big rock.' When I asked how big the rock was, they told me, 'Oh, fairly big. You're not likely to miss it.'"

She smiled. "Did you find the big rock?" She put on her wrapping gown, then fastened it in front and picked up her stockings.

"I've passed seven 'big rocks' since I left Llanddeusant, each one bigger than the last. And not a one of them near an oak with a split trunk."

She froze. "Where is it you're going?"

"Plas Niwl. The estate of a widow named Catrin Price."

By heaven. He was looking for *her*. But why? And did it have anything to do with her disastrous trip to London?

As she drew on her stockings, she tried to make her voice casual. "I do hope you've informed Mrs. Price of your arrival. She's something of a recluse. If you haven't arranged a meeting ahead of time, she might not see you."

"I've heard about the Lady of the Mists riding, shooting, and playing the harp. But I hadn't heard she was a recluse."

The very mention of "the Lady of the Mists" struck her with dread. Few people outside Llanddeusant called Catrin that, and she'd only used the appellation once, when writing to Lord Mansfield.

But if this man knew what she was called, why was he spouting all this about riding and shooting? Everyone knew Catrin only rode the gentlest pony and was terrified at the thought of shooting anything. "Who's been telling you stories about . . . er . . . the Lady of the Mists?"

She slid on her slippers, then circled to stand in front of him. He wore a shuttered expression, and the full mouth that had seemed so friendly when he'd smiled at her now looked wary.

He clapped his hat on his head. "I've heard such tales ever since I was a boy in Carmarthen. She was spoken of with awe among the people there."

Oh, of course. He'd confused her with Grandmother, who'd worn the title like a regal cloak. And who'd filled out the cloak far better than Catrin ever could.

This could be fortuitous. If he was searching for an older woman of stalwart reputation and not a shy pedant like her, then he would never guess *she* was Catrin Price. Still, he would no doubt persist in his search until he learned the truth. Much as he intimidated her, she'd best find out why he was looking for her.

"I hadn't realized our local legend's fame was so widespread." Pasting a smile on her face, she gestured to a path up the hill. "This way. I assume your horse is up by the road?"

"Yes."

He followed her as she started up. They climbed in silence, the steep ascent making it difficult to talk. When they reached the top, she said in what she hoped was a conversational tone, "So you've come from Carmarthen?"

"Not exactly." He headed to where his horse grazed. "I haven't lived there in years. But the ship from London docks there, so I stopped to visit friends."

As he led his horse to the road, she froze. He'd come from London. Why was he here, asking after her? She tamped down her alarm. He could have a perfectly innocuous reason for wanting to see the Lady of the Mists.

Though she couldn't think of one.

He waited for her at the road. "If you could show me which way—"

"Why do you wish to see Mrs. Price?" she blurted out.

She cursed her quick tongue when interest sparked in his eyes. "I'm afraid that's private."

"I see." Her throat went dry. What private matter would entail his appearing on the doorstep of Plas Niwl without warning?

He watched her with a steady gaze. "Do you know her well?"

"Everyone knows Catrin Price."

"You said she was a recluse."

His suspicious words panicked her. "Until she grew infirm, she was quite sociable. But these days, she's too ill to venture from her bed, and probably will refuse to see you."

Forgive me, Grandmother. Grandmother had prided herself on being stout and healthy until the day she died.

"What sort of illness plagues her?"

Tucking a lock of hair behind her ear, she said the first thing that came to mind. "Um . . . gout." No, gout was for old men who drank too much. Besides, it wouldn't keep her from having visitors. "And heart trouble . . . and weak lungs."

Her capacity for deception was appalling. But she couldn't help it. If he'd come all the way from London to see her, it could only be for one reason.

His suspicion seemed to increase. "The poor woman is in dire straits indeed. It's a good thing I've come when I have, before she's in the grave."

By heaven, she hadn't discouraged him a whit.

There was only one thing to do. "Let me direct you to Plas Niwl. It's easy enough to find. Then I think I'll return to having my swim." There was another path from the lake up the hill, one that would put her at home long before he arrived, especially if he followed the directions *she* intended to give.

Trying not to look at him, she pointed up the road. "You travel another hundred paces until you come to where the road forks. Take the left fork."

"They told me in town to take the right fork."

Her breath stuck in her throat. "That's only if you want to go three miles out of your way. The best way is to the left."

His gaze on her was dark and intent, making her quake inside. Gone was the amiable companion of the road, replaced by a wary Welshman who looked as if he didn't believe a word she said.

"When you come to a bridge over a spring, you're close. You'll see a path, which will take you to the estate walls. Follow them around to the entrance."

That spot was on the far end from the manor house. He'd arrive at Plas Niwl a good half hour after she did, which should give her enough time to warn the servants to say she was unwell.

"Can I convince you to forego your swim to accompany me? It doesn't sound as if Plas Niwl is far."

Did she imagine his sarcasm? "Y-you really don't need me to get there."

"But a few minutes ago, you said you would show me the way."

His suspicions had obviously been roused. She must escape him!

Suddenly, a voice hailed them from down the road. In a panic, she looked to see a man headed toward them. She groaned. It was the pretentious Sir Reynald Jenkins, whose estate adjoined hers. He'd apparently returned from his annual sojourn to take stock of his many properties. No doubt he was coming to her with another enticement to make her sell Plas Niwl to him, even though she'd refused every offer.

He'd surely tell the stranger who she was; she must get away before he reached them! With any luck, her wet hair and the distance would keep Sir Reynald from recognizing her.

"I-I'm sorry," she stammered as she edged toward the path. "I have to go."

Then she fled, not even stopping when the wind gusted up to take her shawl.

"Wait!" cried the stranger, but she was already moving away as quickly as her skirt would allow.

Evan narrowed his gaze as the young woman vanished. If he'd been superstitious, he'd have thought his first assessment correct, for the Lady of the Lake was said to have spoken at length with her merchant suitor the first time she'd appeared to him, only to disappear seconds later.

But Evan wasn't superstitious. He picked up the shawl that had fallen, fingering the intricate lacework. Spirits didn't wear expensive shawls.

Besides, no spirit would have made his blood race or his loins harden when she'd emerged from the lake. Her wet shift had been a second skin outlining her breasts so that even the faint rose of her nipples had shown through.

He shouldn't have stared, but how could he not? High and firm, her breasts had been those of a woman obviously still young, yet mature enough to know the pleasures of the bedchamber. For an instant, he'd wanted to experience those pleasures with her. Very badly.

If she'd revealed any more of her thinly clad body, who knew what he'd have done? Probably acted like a Welsh raider of old, thrown her over his shoulder and carried her off. Even after it became clear she wasn't a seductive spirit, but a timid young woman, he'd desired her.

It had been years since a woman had aroused him so thoroughly; London had no one to compare. The mass of rich, black hair curling up around her shoulders as it dried . . . the red, red lips . . . that fair skin upon which her maidenly blushes were stamped so plainly . . . it was enough to make him curse himself for not getting her name.

And her eyes, which swallowed a man up! While she'd been in the water they'd been blue, but once she'd wandered near the purple heather, they'd turned periwinkle. Those and the trembling chin had given her the look of a startled elf.

The fashionable in London would consider her odd-looking, for she lacked the round features of the reigning classical beauties. Yet he was drawn to her otherworldly appearance. He must learn more.

With her shawl in hand, he strode back to where he'd left his horse and waited for the man who'd spooked his temptress.

The fellow halted his prancing mare. "Good day, sir." A heavy perfume clung to his dandyish clothing. "I say, didn't I just see you in town?"

"Yes. I stopped there to ask directions to Plas Niwl."

"You're in luck then. I'm going that way myself. I'm Sir Reynald Jenkins, and my lands border that esteemed estate."

"My name's Evan Newcome, and I'd be pleased if you'd show me the way. I was beginning to wonder if I'd find it at all." He mounted his horse.

Sir Reynald urged his mare into a walk. "Mrs. Price wasn't willing to accompany you?"

"What do you mean?" Evan asked as he followed. "I haven't met Mrs. Price."

"No? Ah, then the distance must have deceived me. I could have sworn you were talking to her just now by the path to the lake."

A coldness stole over Evan. "Begging your pardon, sir, but you must be mistaken. That woman couldn't have been more than twenty."

The man sniffed. "I believe Mrs. Price is closer to twenty-five. Black hair past her shoulders, blue eyes . . . much like the woman standing with you."

Clearly Sir Reynald didn't think he'd been mistaken. The coldness spread throughout Evan's body. "I don't understand. I thought Mrs. Price was an elderly widow. I've heard all manner of stories about her. Isn't she the one they call the Lady of the Mists?"

A smile twisted Sir Reynald's lips. "The women of Plas Niwl, including Catrin, have been called that for several generations. Catrin *is* a widow, as was her grandmother Bessie. In fact, it sounds as if you're looking for Bessie, whose reputation was legendary. Unfortunately, she died two years ago, so you're out of luck."

Evan stared ahead in stunned silence. No, it wasn't the grandmother he sought. The Lady of the Mists he wanted must be the enchanting woman he'd just met. No wonder she'd acted so strangely when he'd mentioned her grandmother's attributes. But why hadn't she set him straight?

Sir Reynald mopped his forehead with a handkerchief. "I do hope you're not one of those fools who come to Mrs. Price for knowledge of the ancients. Some claim she practices the dark arts, but the woman is no more a conjurer than that *consuriwr* in town, with his potions and divining rod. She's merely a chronicler of such practices."

Remembering how she'd looked coming out of the lake, Evan wasn't so sure. Had she lured Justin to his doom? Was that why she'd lied about her grandmother, obviously trying to deflect him from his visit? Was that why she'd avoided his eyes during their conversation? He'd assumed she was shy, but now he reconsidered that.

"Her writings about folk legends practically encourage the masses to continue with their absurd ideas." Sir Reynald wrinkled his nose with distaste, though his gaze on Evan was keen. "I can't believe they publish such nonsense, but her essays appear in journals. Don't you think it unwise to put such fanciful ideas into print?"

"Indeed." Wait, hadn't he recently read an article by a C. Price about the druidic origins of harvest traditions in South Wales? Druids—like the druid symbols on the chalice. A chill coursed down his spine. It had to be her.

And Rhys had said something about her essays. Evan straightened in his saddle. Rhys and Juliana had met Catrin Price. Why hadn't they corrected him when he'd spoken of her as old?

Then he remembered Rhys's reaction when Evan mentioned the Lady of the Mists' advanced age. And how Juliana had sung Catrin's praises.

He groaned. This was Juliana's doing. She'd been matchmaking again. That was what he got for not telling her the truth about his suspicions.

He remembered the night Justin died. Evan had met his friend just as Justin was leaving their favorite tavern. Justin had explained he was late for a meeting with a woman about a chalice she wanted to buy. He'd even shown Evan the letter from the woman, as well as the monstrous bronze drinking vessel with druidic symbols that had been in his family for years.

Justin had wanted money to pay his gambling debts, and he'd felt that the woman's offer was decent. He'd invited Evan to go with him, but Evan had declined, since he was meeting his publisher for dinner. But when his publisher hadn't shown up and Evan had decided to join his friend after all, he'd found Justin in an alley outside the Green Goat inn, stabbed to death.

Stricken with horror, Evan had called for the watch. They'd examined the body and discovered that the chalice and all Justin's money were gone. That had led to the constable's decision that the murder had been a simple case of footpads trying to rob a noble, then killing the man when he wouldn't cooperate.

Evan would have agreed, if not for one thing. The letter written by the Lady of the Mists was missing. She'd been the last person to see him and the one most interested in the chalice. Besides, it didn't seem likely that thieves would have bothered carrying off a box of such large size when the watch was about. Surely the money Justin had been carrying would have been sufficient to make the average thief happy.

Although Evan had pointed that out, the constable had scoffed at the possibility that an elderly woman would have come from Wales to plot Lord Mansfield's murder. But now that Evan knew that the Lady of the Mists was a young, devious Welshwoman, he wondered if the constable might reconsider.

The more he remembered her nervousness, the more his suspicions about her grew. When he and Sir Reynald reached the fork in the road and the man struck off in the opposite direction from the one Catrin Price had designated, Evan knew for certain she'd been trying to misdirect him.

If that didn't prove she had *something* to hide, he didn't know what did. He'd obviously alarmed her, even though she hadn't known who he was or why he was here.

Thus he wasn't surprised when they arrived at Plas Niwl and an elderly butler named Mr. Bos announced they couldn't see Mrs. Price because "the mistress is indisposed and unable to accept callers today."

Indisposed indeed. The chit was worried.

Evan had to resist the urge to stalk up the stairs to ferret the lying woman out. But this situation called for more finesse. He had no evidence that Mrs. Price had been involved in Justin's death. Without the letter Justin had been carrying, Evan couldn't even prove she'd gone to meet him. Since her real name had never been mentioned, she could easily claim that someone else pretending to be the Lady of the Mists had been there.

Before he could go to the authorities he needed proof, and to get that, he must lay her fears to rest. Otherwise, she'd never let him close enough to speak to her.

His eyes narrowed. Why not use Mrs. Price's interest in scholarly matters to flush her out? For once, his name and reputation could garner him more than a line of print in a dusty book.

Evan smiled at the servant. "I'm disappointed to hear of Mrs. Price's illness. My name is Evan Newcome. I've come from Cambridge to research a book about Welsh folklore. I thought I'd pay Mrs. Price a visit, since her essays deal with the same subject. I wish I could stay in Llanddeusant longer, but pressing matters compel me to return to London. You will tell her that I called, won't you? I'm staying at the Red Dragon if she should recover before I leave."

Sir Reynald was staring at him now, but all Evan cared about was making sure the servant noted his name. If the woman knew Welsh scholarship, she'd recognize it, and with any luck, she'd be interested enough to seek him out. Let her come to him. It was more effective than storming her defenses.

"I will inform madam of your visit." Mr. Bos cast a cursory glance at Sir Reynald. "And yours as well." Clearly the servant thought little of Sir Reynald.

With a sniff, Sir Reynald turned for the door. "Make sure you do."

Evan drew out Mrs. Price's shawl. "If you'd be so good as to give this to Mrs. Price. It's a small gift from one scholar to another."

"Certainly, sir," said Mr. Bos, taking the shawl with a frown that said he didn't know what to make of scholars bearing gifts.

The estimable Mrs. Price would know exactly what to make of it—that Evan had seen through her subterfuge. Along with the knowledge of his substantial reputation, it might prod her into meeting with him, if only out of guilt for having lied to a scholar paying a friendly visit.

Of course, she might choose to bury her head in the sand and stay away. If so, he'd find another way to approach her. But he wouldn't leave Llanddeusant until his questions were answered.

3

Catrin glanced up from her knitting as Bos entered. He crossed to the hearth to stoke up the fire with stiff movements that betrayed his pain.

"Is your arthritis causing trouble again?" she asked.

He straightened. "When the air is damp, I do find it more troublesome, but it's nothing for you to worry about, madam."

His haughty demeanor intimidated others, but Catrin knew better. Bos had been an upper butler for the Earl of Pembroke until his arthritis had made it difficult for him to perform his duties, and the tightfisted earl had cruelly turned him off without a pension. When her own butler had left in search of a more grandiose position, Bos had applied for the vacant post. And Catrin had given it to him, touched by the sad circumstances of his past employment.

What a wise decision. Bos maintained the household regimens that Catrin's late grandmother had established, relieving Catrin of the responsibility. Thank heaven, since she had always been dreadfully lax about discipline.

It was ironic, for if Bos had come to Plas Niwl a few years earlier Grandmother would have turned him away, pointing out the impracticality of taking on an arthritic servant who'd soon be too old for anything but a pension.

Of course, Grandmother had never needed anyone to maintain discipline. She had always possessed the iron will that made servants quake in their boots, whereas Catrin bent over backward to accommodate her servants.

She couldn't help it. Unlike Grandmother, widow of a viscount and a stern believer in class distinctions, Catrin couldn't bear to treat her servants as lackeys. They'd been her companions from childhood, her only family, since she had no other to speak of. She couldn't chastise them for petty infractions or condescend to them as if they were children.

So without Bos, the household would most certainly have gone on in a lackadaisical fashion, everyone doing as they thought best. Bos, however, made sure that the servants listened to him, if not always to her. Everything went smoothly, the work was always done, and Catrin even had the occasional rare moment to bury herself in another tome about ancient bardic rites and customs.

"May I fetch anything for you, madam?" Bos asked. "Perhaps you would like your shawl."

That reminded her of the afternoon's embarrassing events. "No. But sit down and stay for a bit, will you? The work can wait."

Without a flicker of expression, Bos did so, although the faintest "Ahhh" escaped his lips when he settled into the comfortable armchair by the fire.

"Tell me again what the stranger said."

"Mr. Evan Newcome, you mean. From Cambridge."

Yes. That had been where she'd made her first error—assuming he was from London because he'd come on the ship from there. But he wasn't. He wasn't even really from Cambridge. "He was raised in Carmarthen, you know."

Bos raised one white eyebrow. "Am I to assume you came by that bit of knowledge at the same time you bestowed your shawl upon the man?"

Catrin began to knit with a vengeance. "I didn't give it to him. I . . . I left it behind after he saw me swimming at Llyn y Fan Fach."

"Ah, yes." Bos's stern expression radiated disapproval. He probably knew that she swam in her shift, for Bos knew everything in the household, and Catrin had never found a way to hide her wet shifts from her maid.

Catrin's cheeks burned. "Although we spoke to each other at the lake, we did not . . . er . . . exchange names."

"I imagine not. Introducing oneself to a stranger when one is dressed in undergarments can be a trifle awkward."

Bos's bland reproof brought a small smile to Catrin's lips. "Yes, a trifle. But that's why I didn't know he was Evan Newcome." *The* Evan Newcome.

She'd heard all about the great man widely considered a genius. He could read, write, and speak ten different languages. His essays were published in prestigious journals. His books included a well-respected French grammar, translations of classical Greek and Roman texts, and an impressive discussion of the development of Celtic languages.

Until today, she'd assumed he was English. But she should have known he was Welsh from his perceptive, intriguing essays that perfectly described the elusive beauty of Welsh verse.

"Am I to assume that if you'd known who your companion at the lake was," Bos asked dryly, "you'd not have instructed me to tell him you were ill?"

An instant pang of conscience hit her. "That was awful of me, wasn't it? I do apologize for asking you to lie."

"Nonsense. If you do not wish to converse with an individual, I am more than happy to lie to keep that individual away." His voice softened. "I am well aware that you are . . . uncomfortable with strangers."

"That's not why I had you lie. When I first met him, I thought—"

She couldn't tell Bos the real reason Evan Newcome had alarmed her. She hadn't even revealed why she'd gone to London, nor what had happened there. He wouldn't approve. "It doesn't matter. I was obviously wrong. And now I'll look ungrateful for avoiding him, when he honored me by reading my essays and coming to speak with me about them."

How amazing that he was familiar with her work. She wished she hadn't been so hasty in her assumptions about his motives.

"There is no shame in being circumspect, madam. If you

still wish to speak to him, then you are perfectly within your rights. Merely explain that you were exercising caution, and I am sure he will understand why you avoided him."

She wished she shared Bos's conviction.

Bos cleared his throat. "Your little white lie becomes almost sensible under those circumstances."

"Little white lie?" Had Mr. Newcome told Bos how she'd led him down the primrose path by letting him think she and her grandmother were the same person?

"That you were sick." Bos's eyes narrowed. "He should understand why you were reluctant to greet a stranger who'd caught you in a state of undress."

"Oh yes." Unfortunately, Evan Newcome hadn't struck her as the kind of man who suffered being lied to without complaint. He'd left that shawl deliberately to show he'd found her out. A gentleman would have waited for a private audience to return the item and accept her apologies, but she suspected that Mr. Newcome's gentlemanly qualities were the merest veneer over a character more forthright—and perhaps more ungoverned—than a gentleman's should be.

"What do you intend to do about the situation?" Bos asked.

Catrin sighed. "I suppose I shall go to the Red Dragon and apologize to him for not seeing him when he came."

"Do so only if you truly desire to speak to him. If not, you have every right to continue pretending to be ill until he has left the shire."

Oh, how she wished she could. But it was one thing to avoid a painful confrontation with a constable; it was quite another to ignore the generous overtures of a respected scholar. She'd already insulted Mr. Newcome by lying to him. Now she must take her medicine and apologize.

At her silence, Bos rose. "Do you need any further assistance?"

"No. Thank you for all your insight."

Bos harrumphed. "I merely spoke your own thoughts, I am sure. You have an unerring instinct for the proper way to address troublesome situations."

She never knew how to regard Bos's pronouncements on her character. Was he being tongue-in-cheek or chivalrous? Either way, he couldn't possibly mean it. Her "instinct" for addressing "troublesome situations" was generally to run and hide, and she doubted Bos would consider that "proper."

Bos marched toward the door, his posture erect. "Shall I have a tray sent up or will you eat with the staff as usual?"

"A tray, please."

He frowned. "You do not intend to knit into the wee hours of the night again, do you? Mrs. Griffiths fell into hysterics when you didn't answer her knock yesterday morning. She was worried you had been kidnapped. It was only when I found you here—after a lengthy search of the house—that she calmed herself."

Catrin chuckled. "I suppose I did get carried away. I was afraid I wouldn't finish this blanket in time to give it to Tess as part of my wedding gift, but I think another hour or two will do it."

"Ah, yes, the wedding. Do you mean to attend the joyful event?"

Bos knew, as did all the staff, that she hadn't attended a wedding since her own had ended with the death of her husband. "I do," she said, avoiding his scrutiny. "Annie will never forgive me if I don't go to her daughter's wedding."

"I see." And with that, he left.

Catrin stared at the blanket made of the finest wool from their own sheep. She'd already embroidered the initials of Tess and her new husband. For the first time in five years, looking at a blatant symbol of a new couple's shared future didn't rouse her resentment. For the first time, she felt hope—thanks to the chalice.

She went to open the secret compartment built into the bookshelves, which she used as a safe. Right now it contained her two most valuable possessions.

The diary of her ancestress. And the chalice.

Looking at it gave her the same bittersweet thrill as on the night she'd bought it. From the moment she'd touched it, she'd known it would break the curse. The markings matched those in the diary, and her cursory examination led her to believe it was at least a few hundred years old.

She stared at the bronze etchings: the maiden with her cloud of hair, the stalwart warrior, and the raven, whose dark eyes seemed to glitter. A series of symbols ringed the edge, probably some druidic code. She didn't know how to interpret them. Lord Mansfield hadn't been able to enlighten her, either.

Lord Mansfield. She sank onto a nearby chair. The poor, poor man.

She still remembered breakfasting in a little English inn and reading the *Times*, only to discover to her shock that thieves had apparently robbed and murdered him a short while after she'd met with him.

No wonder she'd felt so uneasy that night that she'd gone out the back way. She'd even decided to return by coach to Wales, instead of waiting for the ship she'd booked passage on. For once, acting on her fears had been the right thing. She'd probably sensed the thieves watching the inn. Perhaps if she hadn't left through the back door, they'd have attacked her instead of Lord Mansfield.

A lump formed in her throat. She should have told the authorities that she'd been with Lord Mansfield right before he died, but the thought of enduring all their questions had terrified her. They might have misconstrued her presence there, especially if they'd learned how she'd used her appellation, "the Lady of the Mists," to lure Lord Mansfield.

Now she wished she hadn't. But she'd seen no other way to coax him to a meeting after his mother had refused to sell. As a result of her deception, he'd met her in a public place instead of at his home. And he'd been murdered.

No, the authorities wouldn't look kindly on her manipulations, especially if they learned that Lady Mansfield had been against the sale. They might even take the chalice from her. And for what? She'd seen nothing. She couldn't point them to the murderers.

At a sound in the hall, she shoved the chalice back into the compartment. This fear of being found out was absurd. One day she'd have to reveal she had it, if only to whomever she married. The whole point had been to make sure she could end the curse and have children to inherit Plas Niwl.

Now she had a chance to live again. Thank heaven, for the need to find a companion became more intense every day, and not just for practical reasons. To her mortification, she'd discovered she had strange urges and unfamiliar longings that came upon her late at night when she was alone in her bed.

Although she and Willie had never consummated their marriage, she knew a little of what went on in the bedroom. Now she thought about it more every day. And widows sometimes took lovers. But she couldn't imagine doing something so brazen, suffering more of the townspeople's whispers. Besides, she wanted a man who'd be hers forever, who'd look at her with longing in his eyes.

Unbidden, an image leapt to her mind . . . of a tall gentleman standing on the shore, his gaze moving over her with growing heat as it touched first her throat, then her shoulders, then her breasts—

Oh Lord. How could she even think of Mr. Newcome that way? He probably had a wife somewhere. And if not, he still wouldn't look twice at a country mouse like her, with scores of English noblewomen in his social circles.

Though he *had* looked twice—and more—when she'd emerged from the lake. No other man had ever stared at her as if he wanted to eat her up.

Her breath quickened. Would he stare like that tomorrow? By heaven, she hoped not, or she'd never be able to stammer out her apology. She'd make a fool of herself again.

Only this time, she'd never recover from the embarrassment.

4

*E*van sat in the common room of the Red Dragon, enjoying a leisurely breakfast without having to rush off to a lecture. The day stretched ahead of him, and it was all his.

As he sniffed the air redolent with the scent of wild roses and gazed out at the sun burning off the mist, he was glad he'd come here. He'd once hoped to spend his life in Wales, tending a little plot of land and poring over his books before sharing a bed with a loving wife.

A bitter sigh escaped him. What a pipe dream. He could only make a decent living through the universities. And his experience with his former fiancée, Henrietta, had taught him he wasn't meant to marry. Life as a gentleman farmer wasn't for him.

But he could still enjoy this visit. Llanddeusant was a lovely town set in the foothills of Black Mountain, a perfect place to get one's mind off one's troubles.

What's more, the Lady of the Mists had proven an intriguing puzzle. She was unlike any woman of her class he'd ever met, even Juliana. He couldn't wait for their next encounter.

He frowned. So he could learn more about Justin's murder. That was the only reason.

The congenial innkeeper's wife, Mrs. Llewellyn, came to clear the plates from his table. "Will that be all for you, sir?"

"Yes. The meal was excellent."

She beamed. "It's not often we have guests as distinguished as yourself. I do hope you're planning to stay a bit."

"I'm not sure how long." He gave her the same tale he'd given Mrs. Price's servant. "I'm doing research into local legends. That may take a few days."

"You mean legends like the story of Llyn y Fan Fach?"

"Exactly."

She plopped down across from him. "Well, I can tell you the whole thing." With that, the woman launched into the tale.

That gave him an idea. He waited until she mentioned that travelers still saw the Lady of the Lake, then said, "How odd. Yesterday I met a woman named Catrin Price, who gave me quite a start coming out of the lake."

"Did she now?" Mrs. Llewellyn said with a knowing smile. "I'll bet that's not all she did."

He blinked at her. Surely she didn't mean what he thought.

"Come now, I know Catrin's appeal. Half the lads in Llanddeusant watch her swim when she thinks she's all alone."

His temper flared at the thought of a herd of randy boys seeing what he'd seen. "Perhaps someone should tell her."

"Oh no, if she knew, she'd be mortified. She's painfully shy. She'd never go near the lake again, and I'd hate to deprive her of one of her few pleasures."

Shyness *would* explain her nervousness at the lake.

"So you saw her swimming, did you?" Mrs. Llewellyn asked slyly.

He couldn't believe he was having this conversation with an innkeeper's wife. He'd forgotten how frank the Welsh were. "Yes, but I wasn't spying on her. I merely happened along and saw her—"

"Naked as my nail."

"In her shift," he corrected.

"Which was next to nothing." She wagged a finger at him. "You saw her in her shift, and you got ideas in your head." He opened his mouth to retort, but she cut him off. "I know what goes on in a man's head—and his body—when he sees a fetching girl. And now you want to know all about her, don't you?"

Evan was thoroughly nonplused. Yes, he found the woman attractive. And yes, he had indeed felt a strong bolt of lust before he'd discovered who she was. But it didn't mean his interest in her was prurient.

But it might be better for Mrs. Llewellyn to think it was. "I did find the woman intriguing."

"Intriguing, eh? A good word for Catrin." A scowl darkened her brow. "Some people aren't so kind. They call her peculiar."

"Because she swims near naked in the lake?"

"Because folks don't understand a woman living alone, buried in her books and rarely venturing out . . . They think it's odd."

"But you don't."

She shook her head. "Catrin Price has endured enough tragedy to destroy a lesser woman. I'd think something amiss if she *weren't* odd."

"What kind of tragedy?" he asked, reminded of what the Vaughans had said.

"Her parents died before she was three, which is why her maternal grandmother raised her. And her husband died in an accident on their wedding day. A lot of tragedies, that."

It *was* a lot, wasn't it?

Mrs. Llewellyn leaned forward. "But don't believe the tales about her being a witch. She's not casting secret spells up there at Plas Niwl."

He couldn't hide his amusement. "People really say that?"

She scowled. "I know you university chaps consider yourselves too clever for such things, but there's those who hear of Catrin ordering books on druids and look at Willie's freakish death, then cast about for someone to blame."

"That's absurd."

"I agree. And it don't help that her father-in-law, the old bastard, encourages them. He blames her for his son's death. But the tale-telling isn't all his fault. When people don't understand someone, they make up reasons for why. And they don't understand Catrin's quiet ways . . . or her interests."

Sympathy welled in him. He knew what that felt like. "So she's an outcast."

"More like the village eccentric." A faint sarcasm entered her voice. "Even though her patronage keeps the charity school going, her land keeps the tenant farmers well-fed, and her generosity maintains our little chapel."

He thought of how Mrs. Price had at first offered to give him directions. That was the act of a generous woman, wasn't it?

A wry smile creased his lips. He was already making excuses for the woman, based only on the tales of an innkeeper's wife.

And the sight of her half-naked.

He bit back an oath. "Why are you telling me all this?"

"Because I want you to know her true character before you hear a lot of nonsense from superstitious fools. Especially if you're . . . er . . . interested in her."

Evan fought a pang of guilt at misleading Mrs. Llewellyn. But he couldn't tell her the truth. She'd go straight to Mrs. Price. "You said she had an interest in druids. Well, so do I. I'm planning a whole chapter on them. Could she tell me more about them?"

"Oh yes." Mrs. Llewellyn smiled, apparently pleased that her stories about her friend hadn't put him off. "Her grandmother made sure she had a fine education. She's a clever one, she is."

"Do you think she'd have any druidic artifacts? Daggers, or . . . perhaps chalices used in rituals? I'd like to put sketches of that sort of thing in my book." This fictitious book was growing to phenomenal proportions.

She considered the question. "I don't think so. She's never spoken of any."

"I suppose antiquities of that nature are difficult to come by. She'd probably have to go to London for them, and I don't suppose she travels much."

"She did go to London recently. Came back a week ago, she did."

Ah—so Catrin Price *had* to be the one who'd met with Justin.

"But she didn't tell me about buying anything," Mrs. Llewellyn went on, "although I heard she sold a painting to Sir Reynald for a hundred pounds before she left. Can you imagine? For a painting! But then, she's an heiress. She probably has a hundred paintings worth that."

"No doubt," Evan said dryly. Mrs. Llewellyn had apparently assessed his financial worth and decided that an heiress might tempt him.

Suddenly a pretty young woman rushed down the stairs. "Mama, you must come set these sleeves. I can't make them work at all! It'll never be finished before tomorrow!"

"I'm coming." Mrs. Llewellyn rose with a helpless shrug. "You must excuse me. My daughter's getting married tomorrow, and she's in a state. If you'll wait, we can continue our chat about local legends when I'm done."

As Mrs. Llewellyn trotted off, he considered the possibility that Catrin had *bought* the chalice. But a hundred pounds was half the amount she'd offered in the letter. Had she been unable to come up with the other half and thus decided to have the chalice stolen by footpads? Then again, why sell a painting to raise funds for the purchase?

Until now, he'd postulated that Mrs. Price had lured Justin to the inn with the aim of stealing the chalice. But the shy woman Mrs. Llewellyn described wasn't the type to engineer such a scheme. Although he didn't know how Mrs. Price's husband had died, everyone said it was an accident. Obviously she *had* wanted the chalice, but she *did* study druidic objects.

Still, why not write to Justin using her real name? Why not meet him at his home? What about the missing letter?

At the sound of someone entering the inn, he glanced up to find the object of his ruminations hesitating on the threshold.

A flush stained her cheeks, making his pulse quicken. She looked nothing as she had yesterday. Dressed fashionably in a morning gown, she was the very picture of a woman paying a formal call. It accentuated the difference in their stations.

Certainly, his body's response to her wasn't gentlemanly. With the swell of her breasts and her slender throat rising from a froth of lace and painted muslin, she resembled a delicious confection. And like the coarse creature he was, he wanted to devour her.

He shook his head. What was he thinking? No matter how enticing her looks, she'd acted suspiciously in London. She was a privileged woman who'd thought nothing of lying to him yesterday.

He rose to offer a sketchy bow. "Good morning. You seem fully recovered from your 'illness.'"

The stain on her cheeks deepened. "I-I suppose I deserve that. I behaved very badly yesterday. I've come to apologize."

"I trust you received your shawl?"

Her voice was the merest whisper. "Yes." She gestured to the chair Mrs. Llewellyn had recently vacated. "May I join you?"

"Certainly, Mrs. Price." He remained standing until she was seated, then settled back into his chair. "I *do* have the name correct, don't I?"

She flinched. "Don't you think you've rubbed it in quite enough?"

"Oh, I don't know. You haven't yet apologized."

"You haven't given me the chance!"

"True. Then again, I don't have to, after being misled and then turned away on your whim."

Her lips tightened. "Why are you making this so difficult?"

Because flustering her gave him a petty satisfaction that he didn't want to examine too closely. "I become cantankerous when I'm lied to."

"Will explaining why I lied make you less cantankerous?"

"Perhaps."

"Very well. I'm . . . I'm not good with strangers. I know it sounds silly, but when I heard you were heading toward Plas Niwl, I panicked and said a lot of nonsense to put you off because you made me nervous."

He could tell from her evasiveness that at least part of what she was saying was a lie. "I wouldn't have guessed it from the way you came up out of the lake wearing nothing but your shift."

Never had he seen a woman grow so red. "B-but that's

just it," she stammered. "After you'd seen me like that, I knew I could never face you again."

"So why are you here now?"

She met his gaze, looking miserably humiliated. "I told you. To apologize."

"That's a bald-faced lie. You wouldn't be here at all if I hadn't left your shawl at Plas Niwl to show that I knew who you were."

She stood abruptly. "I'm sorry. Obviously I under-estimated how much I offended you. So if you'll excuse me—"

As she turned away, he jumped to his feet. "Wait!"

She halted, her back to him.

He would get nowhere with the woman if he drove her away. "Please, Mrs. Price. Sit down. I promise I'm finished being a beast about yesterday."

"You have every right to be angry. It wasn't right of me to take advantage of your misconception about Grand-mother. I should have set you straight."

"Enough, I beg you. You've made your apology, and I accept it. All right?"

When she turned to look at him, her eyes misty with tears, he felt a stab of guilt. Softening his voice even more, he asked, "Won't you join me for tea?"

She hesitated, then pulled out the chair and sat down, folding her hands primly on the table.

"I'll fetch Mrs. Llewellyn and order us a pot," he mur-mured.

"That's not necessary. I just breakfasted. I don't need anything."

With a shrug, he took his seat. When she stared at her hands, obviously uncertain how to go on, he said, "I hope you're not going to get all skittish again. After all, we have much to discuss. You write essays on Welsh folklore, and I'm researching a book on the subject. We have a great deal in common."

For the first time since she'd entered the Red Dragon, she flashed him a brilliant smile, which fairly crushed his male defenses. "We really don't. I've only scratched the surface of Welsh literature, whereas you have mastered it."

The awe in her voice struck him with surprise. "So you recognized my name."

"Instantly." She ducked her head. "I've read many of your essays and three of your books. I even own a copy of *The Development of Celtic Languages.*"

Despite himself, he smiled. "I'm flattered."

"Oh no, 'tis I who am flattered, nay, astonished that you even know my name." She flashed him a timid glance. "When Bos said you'd read my essays, I could hardly believe it."

Deuce take it. "Actually, I have a confession to make. I'm not as familiar with your essays as I implied."

Instantly, that wariness she'd shown at the lake entered her expression. "But you told Bos—"

"I wanted to see you."

"Why?"

"You'll laugh when I tell you. I came to Wales to research my book on folklore, but when I stopped in Carmarthen to visit my friends, the Vaughans, they told me this intriguing tale—"

"The Vaughans?" Her face lost some of its wariness. "You know Lady Juliana?"

"Yes. She and her husband have been my friends for years." He couldn't bring himself to tell this well-dressed knight's daughter the whole truth—that his father had been one of Rhys's tenant farmers, that if it weren't for the generosity of the Vaughans, he'd be no better than a farm laborer right now.

A genuine smile lit her features. "The Vaughans are wonderful people."

"Yes." Then he added in a dry tone, "Of course, they were the ones who misled me about you in the first place."

"Oh?"

"We began talking about legends of the region, and Lady Juliana mentioned the Lady of the Mists. I'd heard of the Lady of the Mists all my life, so I made some comment about the old woman. Juliana got this peculiar look on her face and began going on and on about your advanced age. I should have guessed then that she was jesting with me, but I didn't. And she never set me straight."

"Why on earth would she do such a thing?"

He shook his head. "There's no telling with Lady Juliana. In any case, she told me about your writing and I remembered I'd read an essay of yours. She also suggested I see the lake. So I thought, why not take a jaunt up to Llanddeusant to see this old woman for myself? Perhaps I'll put her in my book about Welsh legends. Then when Sir Reynald told me *you* were the Lady of the Mists—"

"You became angry at me for having let you continue in your misconception."

"I also became intrigued."

Her eyes met his. Something passed between them . . . a frisson of awareness that shook him clear to his bones. Despite himself, he wondered what those eyes would look like glazed with passion . . . how that luscious mouth would feel under his.

Damn it all. He was here to find out what happened the night of Justin's murder, remember?

"So you didn't really want my help," she said, clearly disappointed.

"Not at first. But last night I realized it would be a good idea. You know the area. You know the local superstitions. Perhaps you wouldn't mind showing me around and helping me collect information." That gave him a perfect excuse for getting to know her and finding out all her secrets.

"Oh, I don't know. I'm not nearly the scholar you are. I might not—"

"Catrin!" exclaimed a voice behind Evan.

Both he and Mrs. Price stood as Mrs. Llewellyn hurried down the stairs.

Mrs. Price broke into a smile. "How are you, Annie?"

"Fine, fine." Mrs. Llewellyn hurried over, and the two women kissed cheeks. Then Mrs. Llewellyn held Mrs. Price at arm's length. "You look well." She cast Evan a sideways glance. "Doesn't she, Mr. Newcome?"

"Quite well," he said, relishing Mrs. Price's blush.

"You *are* coming tomorrow, aren't you, dear?" Mrs. Llewellyn asked Mrs. Price. "I know you generally avoid weddings, but—"

"I wouldn't miss it for the world."

"Good, good." Mrs. Llewellyn turned to Evan. "You should come, too, Mr. Newcome. A wedding is the perfect place to learn about our local legends." Mrs. Llewellyn cast Mrs. Price a sidelong glance. "And I'm sure Mrs. Price would enjoy having you accompany her."

Mrs. Price colored. "Oh, I doubt Mr. Newcome would want to—"

"I'd be honored."

"That's set then." Mrs. Llewellyn winked at Evan. "I'd best get back to Tess before she has another fit of nerves." She hurried toward the stairs, then stopped on the first step. "By the way, Catrin, David Morys may be here any moment. He promised to stop by and show me the verses he plans to recite for the wedding."

Mrs. Price's face turned ashen. "Thank you for warning me."

After Mrs. Llewellyn left, Evan asked, "Who's David Morys?"

"The schoolmaster." Mrs. Price glanced nervously at the entrance to the inn. "I'm sorry, but I must go."

"He must be a dreadful man to make you run off so quickly."

She forced a smile. "Not exactly. But if you'd be so good as not to tell him I was here, I'd appreciate it."

"May I know why?"

Averting her gaze, she murmured, "It's a personal matter."

Though he wanted to pry, he dared not alarm her. "You will let me accompany you to the wedding, won't you?"

A smile touched her lips. "If you wish, Mr. Newcome."

"Evan," he corrected her. "There's no point in standing

on formalities if we're to work together." When she blinked at him, he added, "You know, on the book. I'd still like you to help me."

"I'd be honored. And you must call me Catrin." She glanced again at the door. "Now I really must go."

"Good day, Catrin." He caught her gloved hand and lifted it to his lips, surprised by the strength in the small-boned fingers that curled around his. He brushed a kiss across the leather, wishing it was her bare skin.

When he released her hand, the color rose in her cheeks. "Good day, Mr. . . . er . . . Evan," she mumbled, and left.

He stared after her, wondering at the perverse impulse that had made him kiss her hand. Even knowing she wasn't as innocent and sweet as she seemed, he felt this absurd attraction to her. The whole time she'd talked, he'd wondered what it would be like to cover her mouth with his.

How would she respond? Would she tell him he was being too forward, as Henrietta had done the first time he'd kissed her? Or would she blush prettily and kiss him back?

Best he not try to find out. She might be shy, but she still hadn't sufficiently explained why she'd lied to him. And why would a shy woman travel to London and meet with a stranger in an inn to acquire a chalice that hadn't seemed worth the two hundred pounds she'd offered? It didn't make sense.

The woman was hiding something, and he intended to find out what. So he mustn't let his attraction to her stand in the way.

atrin's hand tingled as she left the inn, all because Evan Newcome had kissed it.

By heaven, if this was what happened after one brief encounter, how would she survive spending half the day with him tomorrow? Why had Annie suggested it?

She sighed. Because Annie was scheming to find her another husband. But a reclusive Welshwoman like her couldn't possibly attract a distinguished gentleman like Mr. Newcome—Evan.

He had to be a gentleman. He dressed like one, and his position at Cambridge bespoke someone with money and connections. Though she might be of equal station, she couldn't compare to the women in his circles.

At least her friend wasn't trying to match her up with David. Thank heaven Annie saw right through the handsome schoolmaster's dashing air to the cold-as-stone heart inside.

Unfortunately, when Catrin rounded the corner, she practically ran into him. She hadn't escaped soon enough.

"Catrin!" he cried. "I heard you'd returned. You've been back from London a week, haven't you?"

She ignored the chiding note in his voice. "You know how it is after one has been away, even for a short time. All the servants are in a dither about this or that and there's a great deal to do."

"I wouldn't know." He scowled. "I don't have servants."

As usual, David resented her moderate holdings. The second son of a squire in Merthyr Tydfil, he'd had the choice of becoming a merchant, a cleric, or a teacher. His dislike of "the vagaries of trade" and his hatred of the church had landed him a post at a Merthyr Tydfil school for a few years before he'd left abruptly to become headmaster of Llanddeusant's small grammar school.

Although he wasn't brilliant, his position afforded him a high status and provided him with a decent living. It also enabled him to move among the gentry and indulge his interest in Welsh poetry and antiquities. Yet he seemed continually to feel that it wasn't enough.

Which was probably why he persisted in courting *her*, despite her obvious lack of interest.

He took her arm in a disturbingly possessive gesture. "I'm glad I've finally met up with you. We need to talk."

"I'd like to, but I really must get home. Mrs. Griffiths is waiting for me to go over the household accounts."

"I've been waiting for you for four years. Can't you spare me a moment?"

She sighed. He was right. She'd let this go on long enough, even if she'd done so unwittingly. "Only if you walk back with me to Plas Niwl."

With a nod, he fell into an easy pace up the road beside her.

As they passed two young women, David drew admiring glances with his sculpted features and dramatic shock of dark hair falling casually on his forehead. Most of the local women thought him a gallant and poetic figure, and he cultivated that image.

Today, however, his eyes were fixed on Catrin. He only waited until they were alone before asking, "Did you get the chalice?"

A pox on him. If she told him she had, he would renew his suit, forcing her to reject him outright. Wouldn't a lie be kinder?

You lied to him before, remember? That's the coward's way out.

But she *was* a coward when it came to David. "I'm afraid not."

His jaw tensed. "That wretched Lord Mansfield refused to sell it to you?"

"It wasn't the right one. And you know it has to be to break the curse."

He fell into a brooding silence that made her wish she hadn't told him about the curse four years ago. But at the time, she'd thought it would be an easy way to put him off without hurting his feelings. Or his pride. She'd shown him the diary and told him about the curse and how she couldn't marry because of it.

She'd even let him examine the diary to determine its authenticity. It had seemed a good idea, since he knew more than she about antiquities. And when he'd confirmed it to be over two hundred years old and had agreed that she dared not marry, she'd assumed the subject was dead, especially since he actively courted other young women.

So she'd foolishly made the mistake a month ago of telling him she'd located the chalice, because she'd wanted to know whether he thought, from Lord Mansfield's description, that it could be genuine. Unfortunately, that had renewed his interest in her.

"Are you planning to search elsewhere?" he clipped out.

"I have nowhere else to look."

He stopped short. "Perhaps *I* could find it. If you'd let me peruse the diary again and review your family records—"

"No!" This was so difficult. She hated confrontations. But if she didn't discourage him now, she'd never persuade him to find someone else. "I knew the possibility of locating the right chalice was slim. If I'd had any idea you were still hoping for marriage between us, I would have quashed the idea at once. I doubt you want to marry me badly enough to sign your own death warrant."

"What if I said I didn't believe in your blasted curse? That I'd take my chances with it?"

"Can you really ignore four generations of dead husbands?"

He blanched. David had a decidedly superstitious bent to go along with his love of poetry and antiquities. He didn't live in the real world, so it was easy for him to believe the world wasn't real.

Suddenly his eyes darkened and he drew her close. "We don't have to marry." He bent his head. "You're a widow. You have a right to your pleasures."

Her heart faltered. "You forget that I'm a widow in name only."

"I didn't forget," he said huskily. "But if no one knows, it doesn't matter. No one would judge you for taking a lover."

"*Everyone* would judge me, because everyone knows! Willie died before we could even have our wedding night. So if I . . . if we . . ." She shoved him away. "I'm not the kind of woman to do what you want. Please, forget about me."

"I can't," he said brokenly. "I think of you all the time—your sky-blue eyes and your raven hair, the way your smile brightens a room and your lilting voice turns prose into poetry. I think of you alone at Plas Niwl, and I can't stand it. I want to take care of you, to look after you."

And my holdings, she thought cynically. "But I don't want you to die. Nor can I carry on a scandalous affair with you. Everyone already gossips about me more than I can bear. Find someone else, David. Until you do, I think it best we keep our distance from each other."

"Oh, you do, do you?" he said in an ugly tone, then caught her and brought his mouth down on hers.

Shock held her frozen. David had never kissed her. And she didn't like it *at all*.

She shoved at his chest, but he forced her flush against him, making her all too aware of his arousal. He thrust his tongue against her clenched teeth, and when she refused to part them and tore her mouth free, he began to kiss and suck her neck, holding her so close that her arms were pinned between his.

Frightened by his surprising strength, she struggled. Oh, why had she let him walk so far with her? Why hadn't she rebuffed him more ruthlessly?

When he slid his hand down to her behind, she kicked him, then bucked against him in a panic, bringing her knee up in an attempt to drive him away.

With a cry, he fell back and bent over double. She didn't know what she'd done, but she wasn't staying to find out. Lifting her skirts, she ran for Plas Niwl.

"I shan't relent, Catrin!" he called out. "Somehow I'll find a way around your curse, and then you'll marry me! You and I were meant for each other!"

She ran faster, praying he didn't come after her. All she could think was thank heaven she hadn't told him the truth about the chalice. Or she'd really have a fight on her hands.

~

Blackheart stood inside a deserted cottage near Llanddeusant, watching the path leading from the overgrown woods. When a shiver wracked him, he took a swallow from his flask, wishing the sweet burn of port were stronger.

If that fool David Morys doesn't have news for me today, he'll regret it. Catrin Price has been back for days now. He ought to know something.

When he saw the familiar lanky form emerge from the trees, he shoved the flask back in his pocket. Morys entered the dilapidated room, and Blackheart barked, "You're late."

Morys's expression turned mutinous. "Can't blame me for that. I just today got the chance to talk to Catrin Price. I came as soon as I could."

"What did she say about the chalice?" Blackheart considered Morys a posturing fool, but he had his uses. "Does she have it?"

Morys shook his head.

"What do you mean? Of course she does. That's why she went to London, isn't it?"

"She says it turned out to be the wrong one, so she didn't purchase it. She says she's given up the search."

Blackheart frowned. "Perhaps she's lying to avoid refusing your offer of marriage. The chit is woefully tenderhearted."

With a haughty lift of his chin, Morys faced down his interrogator. "Have you ever known a woman to refuse me? Especially one of Catrin's age, with an uncertain reputation and no prospects for a husband?"

"Who is also an attractive, wealthy widow wary of fortune-hunters. She might be a quiet sort, but she's no fool," Blackheart said.

That was how she'd evaded him in London: Somehow she'd sensed him watching her. With a canny nature worthy of her grandmother, she'd left the inn another way and changed her lodgings that very night. She'd even returned by coach instead of ship to elude him. Now she was back in her stronghold, surrounded by servants, making it impossible to discover where she might have hidden the chalice on her property.

Morys flushed. "It's not Catrin's money I'm interested in."

"Are you telling me you don't want to be a gentleman farmer, lording it over a substantial estate?" Blackheart gave a harsh laugh. "If so, then you lie."

"You don't have an ounce of passion in your veins, do you?" Morys growled. "That's why Father called you Blackheart, because there's nothing beneath your ribs but coal."

"And because I wouldn't forgive the debts he owed me. Or, should I say, the debts he *still* owes me, since you wouldn't have that position at the school if not for me."

Morys glanced away. "That's not true."

Blackheart chuckled. "Do you think they would have hired you here if I hadn't taken care of the mess you got into at your previous position, when that . . . passion you regard so highly prompted you to impregnate a student?"

A stony silence was his answer.

"As I recall, you didn't offer to make the girl your wife. In fact, I believe you were more than pleased when I had her blamed for some petty crime and transported to Australia before she could betray you. So don't talk to me about black hearts. Yours isn't exactly pristine, is it?"

"You may not believe this, but my desire to marry Catrin is pure. I love her. She's the only woman in this accursed town who appreciates the finer arts."

"She's also the only woman who *owns* the finer arts. And you covet them so badly, you can't even separate true feeling from greed."

"Think what you will." Morys tossed his head. "But I want Catrin—and everything that goes with her. And I will have her."

"How? Without the chalice, she'll never accept your suit."

With a scowl, Morys paced the study. "Surely there's a way to end that blasted curse! If I could only get another peek at that diary, I could find out where that chalice is and get it myself."

"I doubt that. I saw the diary, too, remember? *I'm* the one who proclaimed it to be genuine."

"If I'd known you'd take such an interest, I'd never have involved you."

"Too late for that. And I can get Catrin for you, if you get me that chalice."

"What is your interest in the blasted thing anyway? To keep her from remarrying? Because if so, I won't let you have it. I *will* marry Catrin."

"If it's true you only want her for 'love,' that's easy enough to arrange. Find the chalice, and I'll make certain you get what you want from her ... as well as the fortune you crave."

"I'll hold you to that. But how can I find it when she doesn't have it?"

"A woman like her wants a husband, so she won't stop looking for it. And when she finds it, I want you to know about it."

"Watching her won't be easy. She says she can't bear to be around me, knowing that my pursuit of her is hopeless." Morys stiffened. "But that won't last. She'll come around. I kissed her today, and she didn't resist until I went too far. I can tell she has some feeling for me."

Blackheart rolled his eyes. If that were true, she would have at least offered to make Morys her lover. The girl had clearly lied about her acquisition of the chalice to get rid of the man.

In any case, Morys would not relinquish his pursuit of her, which was all to the good. Blackheart could wait awhile for Morys to uncover more useful evidence or Catrin herself to reveal the truth. But if Morys wasn't successful soon, Blackheart would have to change tactics. Because he must have that chalice.

"I'd best go back now," Morys said.

"Fine, but I want to be kept better apprised of what occurs between you and Catrin. I want regular reports. Leave them here for me."

Morys gave a weary sigh. "I don't understand all this subterfuge. Why can't I just go to your estate and—"

"No! There must be no connection between you and me. I explained that when you first came to Llanddeusant. I don't want to lose everything I've worked for, if your past ever emerges and my part in covering it up is discovered."

Morys shot him a shrewd glance. "No, I don't suppose that would do."

Blackheart narrowed his gaze. "Don't use that threatening tone with me. The only way I'd be found out is if *you* were. Then you'd lose any chance at snagging Catrin. So you will keep this secret and do as you're told. I don't think your father will put up with any other mistakes on your part."

Anger glinted in Morys's eyes before he wisely masked it. "Whatever you say, sir."

Much better, my boy. Don't even consider taking me on. You wouldn't win. No one ever does.

6

As the wedding bells chimed and the couple rushed down the aisle with faces aglow, Catrin stifled a sigh. Five years ago, she, too, had left the chapel smiling, her husband on her arm. But the bells hadn't been tolling her happy future; they'd been foretelling her husband's tragic death later that day.

Though her grief had subsided to a dull ache over the years, today's celebration resurrected it. It didn't help that Sir Huw Price, her late husband's father, was here, too. As usual, he ignored her, but she was all too aware of his presence in the small chapel.

He'd been against the marriage from the beginning, hoping to find his only son a better match. When Willie had died, the light of Sir Huw's life had gone out. So he'd turned his anger and grief toward the only person he could blame. Her.

She understood it since, thanks to the curse, she already blamed herself. But that didn't make his hatred any easier to stomach, especially on an occasion like this, when she could have used his sympathy and support.

You mustn't dwell on it, she told herself as she rose from her seat. *It's time to put the past behind you and start anew.*

As the bride and groom left the chapel, Evan, who'd sat beside her during the ceremony, offered her his arm. She took it with a grateful smile, then turned to find David at the back of the church, watching as she and Evan moved down the aisle. She saw him scowl at the sight of her companion, but ignored him when his eyes bored into her as she and Evan passed.

Put the past behind you and start anew, she reminded herself.

Today she would enjoy herself and forget her troubles. She would eat and drink and dance. With Evan.

A blush stole over her as she glanced up at the stalwart Welshman. He'd been attentive through every aspect of the wedding, murmuring a question or two about certain traditions. There'd been something so intimate about those whispers and the feel of his breath brushing her hair.

How foolish of her to think of him like that. His presence here had nothing to do with her. Yet even David's assault yesterday hadn't dimmed her attraction to Evan, for she sensed that he was as different from David as Wales was from England.

Evan gazed down at her. "Did you enjoy the wedding? Sometimes you didn't look as if you did."

She managed a smile as they emerged from the church. "It was lovely. I only hope you didn't find it too dull."

"Quite the opposite. I'd forgotten how colorful Welsh weddings are. English ones are rather boring by contrast."

English ones—why, she still didn't even know if he was married. How could she ask without making him wonder at the question? "Do you go to many weddings?"

He glanced around as most of the guests set off toward the Red Dragon, where Tess's parents were hosting the wedding breakfast. "Not too many. Most of my friends are bachelors. University fellows aren't allowed to marry."

So he wasn't married. He *couldn't* marry. "Ever?" she asked, trying to ignore her ridiculous dismay.

"Ever. When a fellow decides to marry, he leaves the university to engage in another sort of work. As you might imagine, we lose fellows all the time."

He sounded so casual about it that she wondered if he'd ever considered leaving the university. She started to ask, but noticed that his gaze was now fixed on David, who stood a short way off.

"Who's that man there?" Evan asked.

With a groan, she tugged Evan toward the Red Dragon. "David Morys."

"The man you were avoiding yesterday? Mrs. Llewellyn told me he's something of a scholar. She thought I might find him helpful in my research. She was planning to introduce us when he came, but he was late arriving and I wanted to walk about the village, so I missed him. Is he as knowledgeable as she said?"

"Yes, although he knows more about poetry and Welsh antiquities than about local superstitions."

Evan cast her a searching glance. "That doesn't explain

why he's been scowling at me for the last hour as if I were the devil incarnate."

She sighed. "It's not you he's scowling at. It's me."

"I beg to differ. Although I'll admit he watches you incessantly, he only scowls when he looks at me."

"If you must know, I suppose he is ... er ... perturbed to see me with another man, no matter how innocuous the circumstance."

"Ah. A suitor of yours, I take it?"

"An unwelcome one. Unfortunately, he won't take no for an answer. That's why I've been avoiding him."

Evan's gaze probed her again, but she refused to acknowledge it. A plague on David! Must he act as if she were his personal property?

"Why don't you wish to marry Mr. Morys?" Evan asked. "He looks like a handsome enough chap, and if he's as learned as Mrs. Llewellyn claims, you ought to get along with him very well."

Oh, how to explain this embarrassing situation? She said the only thing she could think of. "We aren't suited to be husband and wife."

"I see." Evan's voice hardened. "I don't suppose a schoolmaster *is* an appropriate husband for a woman of your station."

"What?" Her gaze flew to his. "That's not it at all! If I loved him, I wouldn't care about his station."

Evan searched her face. "Then you're different from most women." He lowered his voice. "And I well understand why Morys pursues you."

Under his steady gaze Catrin colored, then glanced away.

By heaven, he was as smooth-tongued as David. So why did his words affect her so differently? Why did her heart quicken at his praise? Clearly she had a very foolish heart.

A voice behind them fortunately saved her from further embarrassing herself. "Good morning, Mr. Newcome, Mrs. Price. Lovely wedding, wasn't it?" When they turned to find Sir Reynald approaching, he added, "I see you two have finally met."

Belatedly, she remembered that Sir Reynald had witnessed her shameful behavior two days ago.

"Yes," Evan said, "Mrs. Price seems fully recovered. And by the way, Sir Reynald, you *were* mistaken about who that was on the path to Llyn y Fan Fach. As it turned out, it was only someone who *resembled* Mrs. Price."

Catrin's gaze shot to Evan's. He gave her the faintest smile, and her heart lurched. How considerate of him to protect her from embarrassment.

Even if Sir Reynald *did* look skeptical.

"Quite a resemblance," the middle-aged knight murmured, but he seemed content to say no more, so the three of them walked on together.

"How do you find our quaint country weddings, Mr. Newcome?" Sir Reynald went on.

"Not as quaint as the ones in Carmarthenshire. When I was growing up, anyone who could afford it raced to the wedding on horseback, with the groom and his men pursuing the bride and her guardian. Sometimes they raced to the breakfast, too. As I recall, it made for an animated procession."

At once, Catrin tensed.

Sir Reynald cast her a sympathetic glance before saying dismissively, "Oh, horse-weddings are much too dangerous. We don't have them here."

"It's a shame to put an end to the colorful practice on the slim chance that someone might get hurt," Evan persisted. "Besides, young men need an outlet for their energies. I must ask Mrs. Llewellyn why her daughter was so skittish as to not have a horse-wedding."

When Catrin bit back a sob, Sir Reynald said quietly, "Tess Llewellyn chose not to have a horse-wedding because Willie Price was killed at his. During the mad dash from the church to Plas Niwl, his horse stepped into a hole and sent him flying into a rock. He hit his head and died shortly after." Sir Reynald ran his hand over his thinning hair. "Ever since, couples here have been reluctant to follow the tradition."

"Good God." Evan's gaze shot to hers. "And here I am talking about— I'm terribly sorry, Catrin. I wouldn't have mentioned it if— I mean, I heard that your husband died in an accident, but—"

"It's all right," she murmured, staring ahead at the road. "You couldn't have known."

Sir Reynald seemed perturbed by the entire exchange and murmured something about finding a friend, then wandered away.

Evan covered her hand. "I *am* sorry. No wonder you were so quiet during the ceremony. It must have brought back terrible memories."

She squeezed his hand, grateful that he understood. "I . . . I have learned to deal with them."

But that wasn't entirely true. At night, sometimes, she couldn't sleep for reliving that horrible day . . . Willie galloping at breakneck speed behind her . . . his face flushing as he struggled to gain on the horse ridden by her and the old friend of the family playing the role of her guardian . . . the wind whipping her hair into her face as she leaned back to shout encouragement at Willie and laugh at his harried expression. Then the horse going down . . . Willie hurtling headfirst . . . the sickening crack of his head as he hit the rock.

She'd screamed and fought to turn her horse around. But they'd returned to find his with its leg broken and Willie lying motionless, blood streaming from his wound. She'd known instantly that he would die, although it had taken him two days to slip from unconsciousness into eternal sleep.

Poor Willie had never stood a chance. The curse had seen to that. Still, how could she have known? She didn't even discover the diary until after his death.

Fortunately, she and Evan had finally reached the inn, giving her an excuse to change the subject. "Here we are. I do hope you're prepared to eat a monstrous amount. Mrs. Llewellyn has probably been baking and roasting and boiling all manner of delicious things for two days."

To her relief, he made no more mention of Willie's death as they waited to greet the bride and groom at the door. And once they were inside, milling with the other guests, she relaxed, grateful to drop the subject of her late husband.

A fiddler was already tuning up, while two harpists set up their instruments. Roast beef and goose, mutton, turnips, cabbage, and potatoes covered the tables pushed against the walls to make space for the dancing. True to form, Mrs. Llewellyn was dashing about, directing servants. And in one corner, as was customary at Welsh weddings, the groom's father was recording each gift, mostly money or livestock, in a ledger that would be consulted to repay the gift obligation when it was the giver's turn to marry.

Catrin breathed in the warm air with a smile. At least the wedding breakfast wouldn't bring back memories. Thanks to the accident, she and Willie had never made it to theirs.

"Would you like a drink?" Evan asked. "It appears that Mr. Llewellyn has already opened the taps."

"That sounds wonderful. I'm parched."

For the next half hour they said little. Catrin was still a bit intimidated by Evan, and Evan seemed reluctant to speak. But there was no need, since everyone else was chattering away. Some recounted their own weddings. Others teased the bride and groom. All of them included her and Evan in the merriment, which touched her deeply, reminding her that plenty of people ignored the vicious rumors about her.

Trying not to look as out of place as she always felt, Catrin picked at her mutton and potatoes, but Evan ate with the lusty enjoyment of a farmhand. In fact, he seemed more at ease with the locals than she. He wasn't fastidious and didn't wrinkle his nose at the strong ale. He didn't complain about having to stand to eat. If it hadn't been for his fine clothes, she might have thought him just another laborer enjoying the festivities.

While the men talked about farming and husbandry, she kept quiet but paid close attention, for she often gleaned helpful advice from listening to farmers.

Suddenly she felt Evan's eyes on her. "Tell me about your estate," Evan said. "I thought I spotted pastures on my way to Plas Niwl. Do you raise sheep?"

"Mrs. Price has some of the finest sheep this side of Black Mountain," a laborer put in as he wiped his mouth on the back of his sleeve. He turned to her. "And how did you fare with the shearing this year, Mrs. Price?"

Evan's gaze unnerved her so much that she answered haltingly at first. But he joined the others in prodding her to speak, and before she knew it, she was talking with earnest animation about the shearing and wool prices and the feeding and care of sheep.

Evan asked particularly knowledgeable questions, and she soon forgot he was a scholar of amazing reputation. Instead, he became more like the farmers crowding the room than like David, who stood at the far end holding court with a bevy of females and looking down his nose at their uneducated male companions.

After she'd been talking awhile, one of the farmers said, "Why, Mrs. Price, you know as much about the sheep as your old granny. No wonder ye've been gathering a fine price for your wool these past two years."

The compliment meant more to her than anything David had ever said about her hair and eyes. And when she heard Evan murmur his agreement, her face flushed with pleasure.

When the music started, Catrin had to remind herself

that Evan Newcome wasn't another country Welshman, ready to dance a lively jig. No doubt he was accustomed to more sophisticated forms of entertainment.

She flashed him an apologetic smile. "I'm afraid there won't be a single minuet played here. I hope you don't mind."

He smiled as he held out his hand. "I know a jig or two from my boyhood. I'm a bit rusty, but I'll try not to tramp on anyone's feet. Shall we?"

Trying to hide her pleasure, she let him lead her to the floor.

She seldom got to dance, and now she realized how much she'd missed it. Fortunately, Evan proved far from rusty. Although she had to show him some of the steps, he was a quick study. Before long he was falling into step with everyone else, linking arms and kicking up his heels like any other native Welshman.

After three dances, her face was aglow. For the first time in years, she felt part of the community, and the smiles of Evan and the farmers helped her ignore the scowls of David Morys and Sir Huw. Even when she had to stop to catch her breath, her spirits remained high.

Until Sir Huw appeared at her side and bent down to mutter, "Why, if it isn't Mrs. Price, the merry widow."

Despite the stench of liquor on his breath, she tried not to panic. Her father-in-law had always intimidated her, but it was worse today, for she desperately wanted to avoid arguing with him in front of half the town. "G-good day, Sir Huw," she stammered. "I hope you're enjoying the breakfast."

"Not nearly as much as *you* seem to be." He leaned heavily on her shoulder. "No one'd ever guess you buried a husband not long ago."

"Five *years* ago," she reminded him.

"I guess that seems like a long time to be without a husband, eh? But it's an even longer time to be without a son." He scowled. "I suppose you think you ought to start looking for another husband. I see you've picked out a new prospect. Does he realize keeping company with you can be dangerous to a man's health?"

Startled, she stared up at him. "What do you mean?" He couldn't possibly know about the curse. Unless David had revealed it out of spite after what had happened yesterday.

"Come now, I'm not a fool." His voice rose, and she winced when the people nearest them turned to listen. "I can see the pattern. Your great-grandfather. Your grandfather. Your father." His black eyes smoldered. "And my Willie. All dead within a short time after marrying a Lady of the Mists. Think you I can't tell what all of you were after?"

"And what is that?" Anger rapidly replaced her embarrassment.

"Land. Each time the ladies marry, they insist upon a fine settlement that includes the right to keep Plas Niwl. And each time their husbands die, they have the freedom to run it as they wish. You married my Willie to secure your inheritance. Then you killed him so you could do as you pleased with it."

Tears welled in her eyes, especially when she noticed

people drinking up the conversation. It was so unfair! At least Evan was too far away to hear Sir Huw's drunken accusations. "Even if I wished it—and I don't—I could no more cause a man's death than I could make the sun rise. I have no such power! And I would never have hurt Willie, anyway. How could you think it?"

She tried to slip away, but he grabbed her arm, his face contorted with an anger born as much of grief as of liquor. "When I took a wife after Willie's mother died, I thought I could sire another heir, but my wife is barren." He shook her roughly. The music had stopped, and now everyone could hear him. "Barren, do you hear? And who is keeping her from giving me another son if not you, with your druid spells and enchantments?"

"Why on earth would I do that?"

Annie pushed her way through the crowd. "Here now, Sir Huw, what's this all about? Leave the girl alone. We're celebrating a wedding, and I'd thank you not to spoil it by manhandling women and spouting nonsense."

He shoved Annie aside, snarling, "It isn't nonsense. This . . . this witch shouldn't even be here. She's poison to all men, like her mother and grandmother before her."

He thrust Catrin against a wall, but before he could do more, Evan jerked him around, his eyes glittering dangerously. "Leave her be, unless you want to find yourself face-down in the gutter outside."

Sir Huw flushed. "Who do you think you are, sir, to threaten me? You stay out of this, or I'll take you apart! Go back to your dancing, so we can finish our discussion."

Evan's gaze shot to her. "Do you wish to continue talking with this mannerless lout?"

Mortified by Sir Huw's public accusations, she could only shake her head.

Evan faced Sir Huw with fists clenched. "It appears that your discussion is over, so I suggest that you do as Mrs. Llewellyn asked and leave Mrs. Price alone."

When Sir Huw bristled, Annie stepped in again, having fetched her husband and new son-in-law. "Come along, Sir Huw." Though her tone was cajoling, it was clear she would have Sir Huw carried forcibly from the inn if he didn't behave. "You haven't had any roast goose in capers yet, have you? It's my special dish, and I'll be insulted if you don't sample it."

He hesitated, looking from Evan to the scrappy little Mr. Llewellyn and then to the groom, a hulking farmer with hammy fists. Then his lips thinned, and he let Mrs. Llewellyn lead him away.

Catrin collapsed against the wall, unable to face the inquisitive eyes around her. A sudden dizziness assailed her and her breath came in quick gasps.

"Are you all right?" Evan asked.

"I . . . I think I may faint. I must get out of here." When she veered toward the side door, Evan caught her about the waist and led her through it, closing it firmly behind them to cut off the chorus of questions from other guests. With quick efficiency, he led her to a wrought-iron chair, which she dropped into. White spots appeared before her eyes as her stomach roiled.

"Put your head between your legs." He knelt beside her. "It will help."

She did as he said, and the dizziness and nausea lessened a fraction.

"Breathe deeply," he urged.

She was already sucking in great lungfuls of air. But she felt silly in the bent-over position. She lifted her head, then her stomach lurched once more, forcing her to clap her hand over her mouth for fear she'd disgrace herself.

"Not yet," he murmured. "Give it a moment."

"I-I've never done this before," she stammered into her skirts. What a coward he must think her. Grandmother would never have fainted. She would have cut Sir Huw into pieces with her sharp tongue, then had him thrown bodily out the door. "I'm not the f-fainting sort, truly I'm n-not."

"Don't worry about it." His voice was kind as he stroked her back. "Under the right circumstances, anyone can get light-headed. Besides, you scarcely ate anything and you've been dancing on an empty stomach in a crowded room. It's a wonder you didn't faint before."

She said nothing, but as she continued to breathe deeply and keep her head down, the fainting spell seemed to pass. Slowly she became aware of the chill in the air now that dusk was approaching.

Then other things caught her attention . . . Evan's hand rubbing her back with soothing motions . . . his leg only inches from hers as he knelt on one knee at her side . . . his breath feathering her hair.

Her awkward position was becoming uncomfortable, too. Fortunately, this time when she tried to sit up, her stomach didn't revolt. Yet he kept his hand on her back, his fingers still tracing circles on the silk of her gown while he watched her with obvious concern.

His kindness was too much to bear, especially after he'd been forced to subject himself to Sir Huw's insults. "I'm sorry I put you in such an abominable position."

"Kneeling at your feet?" His tone was light. "It's not so bad."

How could he joke about what had just happened? "N-no, I mean—"

"I know what you mean. Forgive my jest, but I thought it might cheer you."

"I can only imagine what you must think—"

He touched a finger to her lips. "I think you're a woman unfairly maligned and little understood."

His words only made her feel worse. After all, Willie's death had indeed been partly her fault, since she was accursed. "How can you say that when you don't even know me?"

When a tear trickled down her cheek, he rubbed it away with his thumb. Then he traced the rise of her cheek and the curve of her jaw until his thumb came to rest beneath her chin. "You're right." His voice grew husky. "I don't know you well at all. Perhaps it's time I remedy that."

She met his gaze, and her mouth went dry. He looked at her as if he could fathom the depths of her soul. Suddenly she realized how close he was, how intimate his thumb beneath her chin, how vibrant and rich his eyes in the dying light. He was close enough for her to feel his warm breath quickening on her face.

He leaned forward to touch his lips to hers.

His kiss bore no resemblance to David's. Light and undemanding, it was the merest whisper of a caress. She didn't know what instinct made her close her eyes and sway toward him, but for a moment, they were frozen like that, only their mouths touching.

Then he drew back, his face tautening with surprise before something more ancient shone in it. "So sweet. I need more."

The plain statement affected her as David's flowery phrases never had. So when he clasped her chin and his mouth covered hers in earnest, she melted.

She scarcely noticed the taste of mulled wine on his breath or the rasp of his whiskery cheek against hers. She knew only the heady pleasure of being kissed by a man who knew exactly what he wanted and how to get it.

His hand now stroked her neck as he plunged his tongue into her mouth in a bold caress of terrifying intimacy. His kiss was hungry, even voracious . . . a raw, real thing. He devoured her mouth with shameless satisfaction, his long, hard strokes seeming to say, *I know what dark urges you have in the night. I can fulfill them. I want to fulfill them.*

It ought to frighten her. Instead, it made her answer with a kiss equally bold, offering herself to him like a sacrifice to the ancient druidic gods.

She forgot about David and even Willie. This felt like the first time, the *only* time a man had touched her. The pleasure was too intense for words. A silky heat rose from her belly to fire her hunger until it was an aching pulse in her loins.

As he cradled her neck in his hand and ravaged her mouth over and over, she abandoned herself to the wild kisses, leaning into him to get more of them.

The next thing she knew, he was on the ground pulling her off the chair into his lap. His arousal pressed into her bottom, but instead of rousing her panic, it made her blood run even hotter. The dusky evening was sweet and secret, scented with summer flowers. She wanted to go on kissing him forever.

His kisses grew more fervent. With a groan, he rained kisses on her temples . . . her cheeks . . . her neck. Then he returned to plundering her mouth, stabbing deeply with his tongue until he'd reduced her to a puddle.

Only then did he tear his mouth from hers. "Good God, you're enchanting." He buried his fingers in her unruly curls. "I was right at the lake. You can't possibly be real."

"Oh, but I am." Without thinking, she laid his hand on her heart. "You see? My heart beats like everyone else's."

When his eyes glittered, she realized she'd actually placed his hand on her chest. Without taking his gaze from her, he slid his hand down to cup her breast through her gown. At her startled gasp, he covered her mouth with his again.

She forgot they were seated on the ground a few feet away from an inn full of people. She forgot that it wasn't yet dark, that anyone who came into the garden would see her nestled in Evan's lap. All she knew was that his kiss was the most glorious thing she'd ever tasted. And when he kneaded her breast with his palm until the nipple hardened into a tight, aching kernel beneath her silk bodice, she leaned into him with a satisfied sigh.

So engrossed was she in the wild, consuming sensations coursing through her body that she didn't at first register the sound of a door opening. But she couldn't miss the sharp intake of breath or the angry slam.

She didn't need to hear the hissed words "Unhand my fiancée, you bastard!" to know that the one person she hadn't wanted to deal with tonight had chosen this inopportune moment to seek her out.

David.

7

*E*van moaned as Catrin scrambled out of his lap. It took a moment for him to clear his head. Kissing and caressing Catrin had driven all thought of where he was from his mind.

But as his wits returned, he recognized the man standing there. David Morys. *Unhand my fiancée.* But hadn't Catrin said she'd refused to marry the schoolmaster?

Evan looked to Catrin, but her eyes were fixed on David. "I'm not your fiancée, and you know it!"

"But you *should* be! I won't stand by and watch some blasted stranger take advantage of you!"

Jumping to his feet, Evan prayed that the dimness of dusk would mask his heavy arousal. The last thing he needed was a jealous suitor on his back. Evan didn't like being caught in the middle, even if the woman involved *had* just been firing his blood to unbearable heights.

Her voice grew acid. "The man you're insulting is Evan

Newcome, the scholar from Cambridge who wrote *The Development of Celtic Languages.*"

As Morys's face registered fury, then resentment, Evan groaned. Why must Catrin throw Evan's credentials at the man? Weren't matters bad enough?

"He's here researching a book on folktales," Catrin added, "and he's asked me to help him with it."

Morys glared at Evan. "Why would a scholar of your vast reputation ask for the help of a woman who's written only a few measly articles for small journals?"

Catrin's flinch sparked Evan's anger. Hadn't the woman endured enough for one night? Deuce take them, some of these villagers were damned cruel.

Stepping between Morys and Catrin, he put on the superior air that used to cow even his father. "I'd heard you were an intelligent man, but apparently not. Mrs. Price has an uncanny gift with description, and her talent at retelling legends is astounding. I'm only surprised I'm the first to seek her expertise."

Morys's hands balled into fists. "Is that what you were doing out here? Seeking Catrin's expertise?"

"That's not your concern," Evan bit out. "Mrs. Price has made that perfectly clear."

Morys shifted his gaze to Catrin. "Don't you see what he's after? I know his kind, always looking for a quick tumble from a country girl who doesn't have the sense to know she's merely a night's entertainment!"

Evan's temper flared higher, and it took a massive effort to contain it. "Listen here, Morys—"

"*You* listen, you London bastard! I'll not have you mauling my Catrin—"

"I'm not *your* Catrin!" she cried. "You have no claim on me!"

"Because of the curse!" Morys retorted. "You said if not for that, you'd marry me!"

What the deuce was he talking about?

Catrin tipped up her chin. "That's not what I said. If you'll recall, I told you we weren't suited."

"Because of the curse," Morys insisted.

"What curse?" Evan said.

Morys sneered at him before glancing at Catrin. "You haven't told *him*, have you? Is that because you know he'd never marry you?" Then his expression turned stormy. "Unless you lied about the curse."

"I didn't—" Catrin began.

"Are you planning to make him your lover?" A muscle worked in Morys's jaw. "You kissed me, too, only yesterday, but you wouldn't make *me* your lover. You said you were worried about your reputation. Yet you're willing to play the whore for a blasted scholar?"

As shame slashed over Catrin's face, Evan's control over his temper snapped. He lifted Morys by the collar and thrust him against the wall. "How dare you call the lady a whore? Apologize! Or I swear I'll tear out your tongue!"

Morys shoved at Evan's shoulders, but the schoolmaster's slender body was no match for Evan's farm-boy physique. "Let me down, you fool!" Morys growled, twisting his torso in a futile attempt to get away.

Evan pressed his hand against the man's throat. "Not until you apologize!"

"Go to hell, you . . . you . . ." Morys started to choke as Evan increased the pressure.

Suddenly Evan felt Catrin's hand on his back. "Please, Evan, let's just go!"

God, how he wanted to ignore her.

But when he hesitated, she dug her fingers into his coat and whispered, "Please. I can't bear to see anyone hurt."

Damn it all to hell. She'd suffered a great deal this evening, and watching two men fight over her wouldn't help.

With a curse, he released Morys and stepped back, breathing hard as he throttled his temper into submission. "You're lucky Mrs. Price has a kind heart, for I would have dearly enjoyed thrashing you."

"Let's go," Catrin said, pulling on his arm.

He turned toward her, so he didn't see the fist come sailing at him until it landed on his jaw. "You bastard!" he barely had time to choke out before Morys launched himself at him.

Morys's weight sent them both to the ground. Evan's mind registered Catrin's scream, but his body reacted to the second punch Morys sent his way, blocking it easily and using Morys's momentum to twist the man beneath him.

Then the fight began in earnest. The schoolmaster proved quite a pugilist, his slender frame masking a lithe strength that enabled him to fend off some of Evan's blows and get in a few of his own as they rolled on the ground.

But no one was a match for Evan in a temper, and he

was furious. He hated men who insulted women or tried to bully them. He hated being punched when he wasn't looking. Worse, he hated knowing that Morys had kissed Catrin only yesterday. And the fact that he hated *that* infuriated him most of all.

As the rage swelled behind his eyes, he took it out on the schoolmaster, pummeling the man over and over. After a few moments, Morys no longer hit back, but lay curled into a ball on the ground, groaning as he tried to avoid the punishing blows.

"Stop it!" Catrin screamed, then caught Evan's arm as he brought it back for another punch. "That's enough, I tell you!"

When Evan hesitated, she hung on his arm with all her strength. "Please stop! Can't you see you've beaten him?"

The anguish in her voice reached Evan somewhere in the red haze of his anger, making him aware of where he was and what he was doing. He dropped his fists to his sides, puffing hard. As he surveyed the schoolmaster, he realized Catrin was right. He'd thrashed Morys thoroughly. The man was coughing and clutching his head as if to protect it from any more blows.

Evan's anger drained from him. Good God, what had he done? While the man had deserved a beating, he hadn't deserved to be nearly killed.

As always happened after Evan's temper got the best of him, shame stole over him, making his stomach lurch. If Catrin hadn't been there to stop him . . .

Morys rolled to his side, still coughing. Evan scanned him and prayed none of the man's bones were broken. But though the schoolmaster appeared soundly whipped, it didn't look as if he'd suffered any permanent damage.

"We must go," Catrin whispered. "We must leave him with his pride at least."

Evan couldn't fault her logic. He stood to dust off his trousers. Something wet trickled down his chin that he wiped away. And he couldn't see very well out of his right eye, which meant the flesh around it was probably swelling from another punch Morys had given him. Good God, he was a mess, wasn't he?

Catrin touched her hand to his mouth. "Your lip's bleeding."

"Only a little." He wiped away more blood and prayed she wouldn't pass out again. His former fiancée would have done so, and Catrin was more timid than Henrietta had ever been.

But Catrin surprised him. Though her face was ashen, she drew out her handkerchief and wiped his lip with a tenderness that made his breath catch. Then she touched the swelling above his eye. When he winced, she murmured, "You require tending."

He certainly did. At the very least, he needed a compress for the swelling. Pray heaven he hadn't cracked a rib or two. He didn't think so, judging from the lack of pain when he breathed. He knew exactly how a broken rib felt, having had several in his youth, thanks to Father's beatings. This felt different.

But his leg hurt, for when Morys had hurtled himself at Evan and they'd gone crashing to the ground, Evan had cracked the side of his knee on a rock.

"Come with me," she said. "I'll see you're taken care of.
You probably won't believe this, but I know a bit about
doctoring." She added softly, "I made sure I learned something about it after Willie's death."

He let her lead him away, trying not to show the pain
that each step sent shooting up his right thigh. But when
it became apparent she wasn't returning inside, he asked,
"Where are we going?"

"To my estate."

He stopped short. That was the last thing he needed
tonight . . . more time spent with sweet little Catrin. Despite everything that had just occurred, he still wanted her.
Badly. And acting on it wouldn't be remotely wise.

"You don't want to return to the breakfast looking like
that, do you?" she said. "It'll ruin Tess's celebration. And
since going through there is the only way to reach your
room upstairs, you don't have much choice. It's either go
home with me and get your scrapes and bruises tended,
or walk the streets of Llanddeusant until the celebration is
over, which may be hours from now."

He hated to admit it, but she had a point. And going
home with her might give him a chance to search the place
for the chalice or the letter. It would enable him to find out
more about why that drunken man at the reception had
accosted her. That is, if he could keep his hands off her
long enough to ask questions.

Still, it irritated him to skulk away from the scene like
a criminal. "What about him?" He jerked his head toward
Morys, who'd managed to sit up, though the effort had

given rise to a fresh set of moans. "Don't you want to take care of his bruises and scrapes, too?" *After all, yesterday you were kissing him.*

And how was it that the mere thought of her kissing Morys made him see red again?

Fortunately, she didn't seem to notice the jealous edge in his voice. "I'll go inside and tell Annie about David. She'll make certain he's tended to without creating a fuss." She nodded toward the alley. "You'll find my carriage out front. Mine's the one without a coachman. John's inside celebrating with everyone else."

When Evan merely stood there, she gave him a push. "Go on now. I'll be there in a moment."

She didn't stay to watch as he limped down the alley. Instead she disappeared inside, leaving him to stumble toward the front alone. As he headed for the carriage, favoring his right leg, he couldn't help smiling. Only Catrin would let her coachman join the celebration.

With some difficulty, he hoisted himself inside, then settled into a seat barely wide enough to accommodate his large frame. He propped his leg on the seat opposite him and winced at the pain that shot through it.

Had he really fought over her? Kissed her, despite all his warnings to himself? He still had the warm, sweet taste of her on his lips. Her skin had been soft as rose petals, pure pleasure to kiss, and her thick curls had twined about his fingers like satin ribbons. Was the skin—and hair—in other, more secret places of her body as lush? Would he ever know?

As he hardened again, he cursed. He'd lost his bloody mind. He couldn't think of her without wanting to bed her, just as he'd been unable to resist kissing her when she'd begun to cry.

A woman's tears had affected him profoundly ever since he'd been forced as a child to watch his mother sob after her beatings. Now that he was grown, he had this desperate urge to make any woman's tears go away. But he didn't usually do it by kissing her senseless. Then again, no one like Catrin, with her hesitant smile and her imploring eyes, had ever burst into tears in front of him.

Just thinking of her mortification after that drunken bastard in the inn had made his disparaging remarks roused Evan's protective instincts again. He could hardly believe what he was feeling for a woman he suspected of treachery. Yet despite knowing she'd acted suspiciously the night of Justin's death, he couldn't reconcile the scheming woman he'd expected with the shy, endearing one he'd kissed. How could she have had anything to do with the murder?

She couldn't have. He couldn't believe it.

The carriage door opened and Catrin climbed in and took the seat opposite him. He wondered if she'd had to suffer any embarrassment inside the inn, but if so, she kept it well hidden as she ordered her coachman to set off.

Once they were moving, she lit a carriage lantern and glanced at his propped-up leg. "Did you hurt it, too?"

"I knocked my knee on one of those boulders. It may only be bruised. Or I might have fractured it."

"Oh, I hope not. This is awful. And it's all my fault!"

He cast her a wry smile. "I think Morys had something to do with it."

"But he would never have come at you if he hadn't seen us . . . if we hadn't been . . ." She dropped her gaze. "It was wonderful of you to defend me. And I do appreciate all that nonsense you said about how good my essays were. I know it wasn't true, but it sounded lovely."

"How do you know it isn't true?"

She looked up. "Because you told me you only came here because of what the Vaughans said about me."

"But I *have* read one of your essays, and I found it to be exactly what I told Morys." Actually, he remembered little, but no one would wrench that confession out of him when his remark had clearly meant so much to her.

He hated the way she held him in such awe. It made him feel like an impostor. He was surprised she hadn't guessed the truth about him after how he'd laid into Morys. But if she ever did learn of his poor upbringing, she wouldn't be looking at him as she was now . . . with shining eyes and a smile that stopped his breath. No woman had ever looked at him like that before. Not even his former fiancée.

"It's all right," she murmured. "You don't have to pretend. I know you only sought me out because of confusing me with Grandmother. She was a fascinating woman; I can see why you would have been interested in her. I'm only sorry you had to be stuck with me instead."

Her gaze locked with his, and something twisted in his gut. "I want to study *you*. And I don't regret being 'stuck with you,' as you put it."

"But I've ruined every moment of your stay. I shouldn't

have come with you tonight. I should have known David would act foolishly."

The jealous words were out before he could stop them. "Especially when you were kissing him only yesterday."

"I *didn't* kiss him—he kissed me. There's a vast difference. I . . . I tried to make him stop, but he—"

"You mean the bastard forced himself on you?" Evan sat up straighter. "Now I wish I hadn't stopped beating him."

"Don't say that. And anyway, it would have done no good. He can't seem to understand that I can't marry a man I don't love."

"That's why you refused his suit? Because you don't love him?"

"Of course."

"But I thought you refused it because of some curse."

Alarm lit her eyes. "Some curse?"

"The one Morys kept blathering about."

She turned her face to the window.

"Tell me about the curse," he prodded. "*Did* you lie to get rid of Morys?"

"Not exactly."

When she said no more, he frowned.

"Is there a curse?" Evan persisted. "I think I have a right to know what story you told Morys that got him so angry over our . . . involvement."

She was silent a long time. When she spoke again, her voice quavered. "You'll think me mad."

"I already begin to think you're dangerous to be around."

"You sound just like my father-in-law," she said in a hurt tone.

He stared at her in confusion. "Your father-in-law?"

"Sir Huw. The man shouting at me inside the inn."

Evan crossed his arms over his chest. Mrs. Llewellyn *had* mentioned her late husband's father. "Sir Huw was the man who said you were poison?"

"Yes." She looked wary. "How much did you hear?"

"Not much. I didn't notice him badgering you until the music stopped and he shouted something about your making his wife barren."

"It's not true, you know." She stared him down. "All that stuff about my casting a spell on her."

"I didn't think it was." Remembering what Mrs. Llewellyn had told him about the rumors, he added gently, "I don't believe in things like spells and curses, and I certainly don't believe you cast a spell to send your husband to his grave or put a curse on Sir Huw's wife. Is that the curse Morys was referring to?"

"Sort of, but—" Her eyes went wide. "How did you know Sir Huw thinks I cast a spell on my husband, if you only heard him accuse me of making his wife barren?"

Deuce take it. Ah, well. The damage was done. "Mrs. Llewellyn and I chatted about you. She told me that Sir Huw, among others, thinks that . . . well . . ."

"I put some enchantment on Willie." She sounded wounded. "I know what they think, but I didn't expect Annie to pass on such gossip."

"She wanted to set me straight before I heard the gossip from anyone else. But she made it perfectly clear that it was all balderdash."

"Did she tell you I'm not the first woman in my family to be accused of such 'balderdash'? Did she tell you I'm descended from a long line of women who've all sent their husbands to early graves?"

How many was that? "Of course not. She merely said you'd had a great deal of tragedy in your life."

She sucked in her breath. "Tragedy. I suppose she does look at it that way. But everyone else believes that the Ladies of the Mists marry their husbands for their wealth, then send them to their dooms with a spell or two."

"They're just superstitious fools. You shouldn't take their words to heart."

"Oh, but I do." Her gaze shot to his. "You asked about the curse. Well, Sir Huw wasn't entirely wrong when he said we are poison. The female line of my family has been cursed for some time."

He couldn't prevent an indulgent smile. "Surely you don't believe that."

Her lips tightened. "I know it sounds ridiculous. I don't consider myself a credulous person, either. Although I enjoy collecting folktales, my interest in them has always been academic. But even the wildest story has a grain of truth. And sometimes the evidence of supernatural events is incontrovertible."

"What evidence?"

She tilted her chin up. "My great-grandfather and my grandfather and my father all died within three years of marrying. In every case but Mama's, the women outlived their husbands by many, many years. As I am doing now."

Despite his avowed disbelief, a chill shook him. "Four

men? One after the other? Good God, that is a strange coincidence. How did they die?"

"My great-grandfather died at sea, my grandfather was accidentally shot on a hunting trip, and my parents' carriage went over a cliff. And you know about Willie." She straightened her shoulders. "All the deaths were accidental, and all the men except Papa left behind wealthy widows. A few had sons to inherit, but since the sons never produced children, the widows always left Plas Niwl to their daughters rather than entail it."

"That's a wild tale. And you truly believe those men died because of some curse?"

She stiffened at his condescending tone. "I'll admit that at first I was skeptical, but after looking at my family history, I had to accept the veracity."

"Then why did it only start after four generations?"

She flashed him a defensive look. "It was only four generations ago that the female descendants stopped drinking from—"

When she stopped short, his heart sank. "Drinking from what?" he prompted, though he knew the answer. A chalice. A druidic chalice.

Turning pale, she glanced out the window. "Oh, look. We're here. Come, let's get your leg tended to, shall we?"

As the carriage jerked to a halt, he gritted his teeth. There was no way he was leaving here tonight until he got her to talk about the chalice.

But ten minutes later, as he sat in a kitchen chair while Catrin, Bos, and a housekeeper named Mrs. Griffiths hovered over him, he wondered how he could get Catrin alone again to question her.

"We need to have a look at his leg," Catrin said as she put a cold compress on his eye. "He's not sure if it's broken or bruised or what."

"Then you will have to ask the gentleman to remove his breeches, madam," Bos said.

Catrin went crimson. "Of course. I suppose you should look at it, then. Mrs. Griffiths and I will leave."

"That would be advisable," Bos said, looking down his nose at Evan.

Evan took umbrage at being the object of the man's contempt. "Now see here, you should leave the tending of my leg to a physician." *Or at least someone more competent than a butler, anyway.*

"As you wish, sir," Bos said.

"Really, Evan," Catrin said, "you should let him look at it. He knows more about such things than I do. Bos was the upper butler for the Earl of Pembroke, and one of his duties was to care for the earl whenever he was wounded while hunting or riding, which apparently was often. The earl is a dreadful rider, I'm afraid."

Bos said nothing, although he obviously disapproved of his mistress's frank disclosure of his former employer's faults. And her use of Evan's Christian name.

It occurred to Evan that getting Bos alone might be useful. If the butler had previously worked for an earl, Catrin's household represented a sad drop in his fortunes. Though Evan didn't have much blunt to spare, he certainly had enough to bribe a butler. And judging from the man's cold demeanor, Bos harbored little affection for his mistress.

"All right," Evan said. "If you think it's best."

In seconds, he and the butler were left alone.

Bos turned his back to Evan. "Remove your trousers, sir, if you will."

Feeling awkward, Evan did so, then sat back in the chair. Propping his leg up on a stool, he pulled his drawers up enough to expose his knee. "I'm ready."

Bos cupped Evan's kneecap and moved it around. "Does that hurt?"

"No."

He pressed lightly on the flesh around the kneecap.

"Ouch!" Evan cried out. "*That* hurts."

Bos examined the spot, then straightened. "I would venture to say it is merely a bruise. Its position near the kneecap is what makes it painful for you to walk, but by tomorrow, you should feel more fit. If you had indeed fractured a bone, I believe you would be experiencing pain in an entirely different area."

It had taken Evan all his effort to keep a straight face during Bos's cold recitation, but now he ventured a smile. "Thank you."

"You may don your clothing, sir. I shall fetch the mistress."

"Wait!" Evan jumped to his feet, quickly pulling on his trousers. "I'd like to apologize. I see that I misjudged you."

"If you say so, sir."

"I can see you're a competent butler, an asset to Mrs. Price's household."

Bos stared suspiciously down his long nose. "I certainly hope so."

Evan reached into his coat pocket. "And I want to offer you something for your services."

Bos's face remained perfectly bland. "That will not be necessary, sir."

"Nonsense. I know it's customary to offer a vail." Evan withdrew a sovereign from his pocket and held it out to Bos.

Although the amount was larger than necessary, Bos showed nothing as he took the sovereign. "Thank you, sir."

"I'd be willing to double that sum if you answer a few questions about Mrs. Price."

Bos fixed him with a steely gaze. "I beg your pardon, sir." If possible, his voice was even chillier. "For no amount of money would I be willing to discuss my employer."

Evan was taken aback. Usually servants delighted in talking about their masters, especially when money was involved. Justin used to bribe maids to tell him what presents their mistresses liked.

"It's nothing personal," Evan protested. "I'm just curious about—"

"Then you must ask Mrs. Price yourself, mustn't you?" His tone was decidedly clipped. And protective.

Obviously Evan had misjudged the situation, though it oddly relieved him to know that Catrin inspired such loyalty in her servants. "I'm sorry if I offended you, Bos."

The butler merely turned for the door.

"There's no need to mention this to your mistress," Evan called out as Bos left, but the butler didn't even acknowledge the statement.

"Deuce take it!" He'd handled that badly. And when Catrin entered alone, looking anxious, he feared he knew *how* badly.

She dipped a cloth in cold water. "Sit down." When he did, she placed the cool compress on his eye. Then she dipped another cloth in a pot of steaming water and used it to cleanse his cut lip, her fingers shaking so badly that he couldn't stand it anymore.

He caught her hand in his. "Why are you suddenly afraid of me?"

She wouldn't look at him. "Bos said you asked questions about me and wanted him not to tell me."

"Only because I'm interested in you and your strange curse." That was partly true, after all. "You roused my curiosity, then refused to finish the story, so I thought perhaps Bos would tell me."

"Bos doesn't know. Only David does."

"You told Morys, but you won't tell me?" When she remained silent, he added, "Since Morys mentioned it in front of me, I assumed it wasn't such a dark family secret. *He* seemed perfectly willing to talk about it."

As he'd hoped, his implication that he could always ask Morys had the desired effect. She went to stare out the open door leading to the kitchen gardens.

The moon rose beyond her, encasing her head in a halo. God, he'd never met a woman who intrigued him more . . . or roused his hunger so thoroughly.

She spoke in a monotone. "The curse is chronicled in a diary I found four years ago. It states that if any female descendant of a certain druidess refuses to drink from a chalice she gave her daughter at her daughter's wedding, then that descendant's husband will die within three years of the marriage and any sons will be unable to have children. I am one of those descendants."

At last. She was finally telling him about the chalice. "I assume you refused to drink from the chalice at your wedding. Because you didn't know about it?" He knew the answer, but had to hear her say it.

"I didn't know, but even if I had, it wouldn't have made a difference. My great-great-grandfather sold it years ago."

That meant it had belonged to her family before it had belonged to Justin's. "Who was it sold to?"

She stiffened. "That hardly matters, does it? It's no longer in the family, so the curse is in effect."

"Yes, but you could get it back, couldn't you? Then you could put an end to the curse." He held his breath, waiting to see what she would say.

She was silent a long time. "I tried that, which is why David is so upset. He'd been waiting for me to return from London with the chalice that I thought I'd located. But the man in London who'd promised to sell it to me . . . never showed up. So I was left without a chalice, which means the curse is still in effect. That's why I refused David's suit."

Her words thundered in his ears. She'd never even met with Justin. Justin had been murdered on the way to meet her, and the thieves had stolen the chalice. Then she had come home, and that was that.

It was just as he'd begun to suspect. She'd had nothing at all to do with the murder. Why had he assumed early on that she must be involved, when her explanation made so much more sense?

Because of the missing letter. Still, it had been ludicrous of him to base his suspicions on something so flimsy. The letter could have fallen out in the struggle. For all he knew, Justin had kept it with the chalice and the thieves had taken it. In any case, she wouldn't have told him about going to London to buy the chalice if she'd had anything to do with the attack on Justin.

God. What should he do now? Tell her the truth—that he had come to Llanddeusant only to find out about Justin? No, he couldn't. She was already hurt that he wasn't interested in her scholarly work. He couldn't hurt her further by admitting he'd lied to her about everything.

He must continue this pretense of gathering material for a book on folk legends, if only for a few days. Then he could leave and get on with his life.

"Now you know all about me." She faced him. "Now you know why I am considered a poison to men."

The ache in her voice tore at him. He recognized it well, for he, too, had spent years on the outside of society looking in, always the subject of speculation, rumor, and sometimes hatred. He knew what a vast, lonely world that was.

Sympathy flooded him, so intense that he rose from the chair and went to her. When she dropped her gaze, he slid his arm around her waist. "I don't consider you a poison."

Then he took her mouth with his.

8

*O*uch!"

Startled by Evan's cry, Catrin drew back, her surprise becoming concern when he gingerly touched his bruised lip. "Oh no, you're bleeding again!"

"It's nothing to worry about."

"Nonsense, you should sit down and let me put some salve on it."

That would give her a chance to gather her wits. As he took a seat, she fetched a bowl of salve that she kept for emergencies, and tried not to think of what she'd just done.

She'd let him kiss her again. Thank heavens he'd stopped or she'd have found herself in another disastrous embrace. She couldn't bear another of his shattering kisses, not when she'd just lied about the chalice.

If he hadn't cornered her with questions about the curse, she wouldn't have had to lie at all. A pox on David for making it impossible to keep the tale secret.

"I don't need salve," Evan grumbled.

"Yes, you do. It'll lessen the swelling and stop the bleeding."

She smeared the stuff on his lip, but he took the bowl and tossed it to the floor. When she turned to get it, he pulled her onto his lap. Then groaned as she landed on his hurt knee.

"Stop that!" she scolded, wriggling out of his grasp. "You're hurt, and you're only making it worse."

With a rakish grin, he drew her between his legs. "So why don't you kiss it and make it better?"

As she stared at all the bruises he'd gained "defending her honor" like a knight out of a Welsh legend, a thrill coursed through her. Yet David was right—Evan wasn't the man for her. He'd seen her half-naked at the lake and thus considered her a loose woman. And now that she'd given in so easily to his first kiss, he meant to take advantage. But she wasn't what he thought.

"Kiss me, Catrin." His eyes smoldered with a frightening hunger.

That she desperately yearned to satisfy. "It'll hurt you."

"Not as much as holding you and not kissing you hurts me." He dragged her onto his uninjured knee.

"Don't," she said weakly, but he nuzzled her neck, and the whisper of his mouth over her skin sent a wild shiver through her. The only thing keeping her from giving in entirely was the scent of camphor from the salve, reminding her of his injuries. "You mustn't."

"Why not?" He nipped her earlobe, stirring her very blood.

Making her despair. "You're used to women who think nothing of giving themselves to men. You merely see me as a diversion."

"Damn it, I'm not some smooth-tongued seducer. But I can't ignore that you're as attracted to me as I am to you."

As he tongued her ear, desire shot through her, confirming his assertion. "What I feel . . . for you doesn't matter."

"It matters to me."

This was going too far too fast, and in entirely the wrong direction. She tried to rise, but he clamped his arm about her waist to stay her.

"I won't hurt you. I just want a kiss, that's all."

"I know, but—"

He stopped her mouth with his, and this time he didn't protest the pain. She should tear her mouth away. Leave the room. Stop this madness.

But she couldn't. Because his lips explored hers without demanding anything, shaped hers with such exquisite tenderness and warmth that it cast rippling waves of heat through her body.

What could one kiss hurt?

So when he ran his tongue along the seam of her lips, she let him tease her mouth open. A groan erupted from him, and he drove his tongue deep, kindling flames in her. The coppery taste of his blood made her hesitate, but he wouldn't let her withdraw. He caught her head in his hands to hold her still for his kiss.

And oh, what a kiss it was, as enticing as the waters of Llyn y Fan Fach and just as fraught with danger. Yet she slipped into the depths without a thought, letting him plunder her mouth, immerse her in the treacherous waters of seduction.

He hardened beneath her bottom; she softened everywhere. Soon his hands were roaming her waist and ribs, then traveling higher, until his thumbs skimmed her breasts. When at last they touched her nipples, she shuddered from sheer pleasure.

Then berated herself for giving in so easily.

She tried to draw back, but he murmured, "Don't. Not yet."

"The servants will wonder what we're doing."

"I don't give a damn. And I don't think you do, either."

As he dragged his open mouth down into the hollow between her breasts, her hands crept up to clasp his shoulders. And when his rough tongue swept the upper swell of her breast, she dug her fingers into his muscles.

"I-I should care . . ." she whispered. "I *should*."

Yet when he tugged the silk down to bare one breast, then closed his mouth over her nipple, she could no more pull away than plunge a knife through her heart. The sweet swirl of his tongue, the way he flicked the nipple, built the ache in her to a hot, urgent need. As he sucked hard, she clutched his head and gave herself up to that wicked mouth. She wanted it *so badly*, wanted to feel his mouth there and everywhere. On all her hidden places.

How mad was that? Yet she reveled in the madness, especially when his hand slipped beneath the silk to cup her other breast, kneading and teasing it until she thought she might explode.

"Evan . . . oh, dear Evan . . ." she whispered as she arched back to give him better access to her breasts.

"You are . . . so adorably soft," he rasped as he filled both hands with her breasts. Then took her mouth again.

This time his kiss was ravenous and showed no sign of pain. *She* was the one feeling pain, a sharp hunger that gnawed at her most private places, making her ignore the taste of blood and return his kiss with more enthusiasm than sense.

Only when his hand left her breast to move down and slide her gown up her legs did the depths of her insanity dawn on her. She was letting a man seduce her!

It took all her will to drag her mouth from his. "Please don't do this."

With a noise half-moan and half-growl, he tried to seize her lips again, but she jerked her head to the side and clamped her fingers around the hand that swept up her thighs. "Evan, you must stop. I don't want you to . . . I can't . . ."

"Let me make love to you," he said in a throaty whisper. "Please—"

"No!" Taking him by surprise, she pushed him back and scrambled off his lap. "I can't do this."

He stared at her with eyes glittering as his breath came heavy and hard. "Why not?"

She drew her gown up to cover her breasts. "It's . . . it's not right."

"The hell it isn't." He rose from the chair. "I want you. You want me. What's wrong with that?"

"We're not married!"

He went very still. "You're looking for marriage?"

"Yes!" Then she realized that her words contradicted what she'd just said about the curse. "I mean, that's what I *would* want, if I *could* marry. Of course, with the curse, I can't—"

"Right, the curse." Did she imagine it or did he seem relieved? He stepped toward her. "So there's no problem. You can't marry, and I can't marry. We're perfect for each other."

I can't marry. The words echoed hollowly in her head, dashing all her hopes.

She'd been thinking of Evan as a suitor. What kind of fool assumed that a man like him would relinquish a prestigious position as a fellow at Cambridge to marry a country sparrow like her?

Somehow she made her voice sound normal. "I know you said you're not allowed to marry. But surely you intend to marry someday, don't you?"

"No. Never."

That startled her. "Why not?"

"I have my reasons." The clipped words made it clear he didn't intend to reveal them. "So if neither of us is seeking marriage, then you and I can—"

"I can't simply leap into bed with a man who thinks no more of it than of eating a fine meal."

"Good God, what gave you that impression?"

"You said you don't intend to marry."

"That doesn't mean I consider lovemaking akin to a 'fine meal.' I intend our . . . friendship to last longer than that." His eyes glowed obsidian in the candlelight of the kitchen. "And be quite a bit more enjoyable. You and I would make wonderful lovers." He gave a mocking smile. "It's quite the thing for widows to take lovers these days, or hadn't you heard?"

"But I couldn't! I want . . . I want . . ." *I want a husband.*

His mouth formed a hard line. "What *do* you want that I can't give you? What am I lacking that your previous lovers had?"

"Previous lovers?" she squeaked. This was worse and worse. "I've *had* no previous lovers! I'm a virgin!"

He stared at her with narrowed eyes. "I realize that your husband died on your wedding day, but . . . Are you telling me you and he never indulged yourselves before you were married? Or that in five years of widowhood, you haven't taken a single lover?"

A blush stained her cheeks. "Never."

"I suppose I should have realized that. But you're twenty-five and passionate, and I just assumed—" He lowered his voice to a husky murmur. "Don't you think it's long past time you took one? Don't you get lonely?"

"Of course! But I can't have what I want: a husband to comfort me at night, children to inherit Plas Niwl and care for my tenants and servants." *I can't have it with you, anyway.* She forced calm into her voice. "And I won't take a sordid substitute."

His eyes blazed. "I promise you, lovemaking between us would *not* be sordid."

The way he looked at her, as if he could offer her secret delights beyond her ken, threatened to incinerate her misgivings. "You mustn't say things like that!" She straightened her shoulders. "Just go, Evan. Please, go away and leave me be."

"Very well, I'll go. But I'm not leaving you be." He cast

her a dark smile. "You promised to help me with my research, remember?"

"You don't care about that. You only asked me to help you because you wanted to . . . to . . ."

"To seduce you?" he said dryly.

She nodded.

"I never said that."

"But it's true, isn't it?"

A muscle twitched in his jaw. "No. Despite what you think, I'd like your help."

Even if he meant it, she couldn't give it to him now. It would mean being constantly in his presence, all the while knowing he wanted her, and it was pointless, for she'd never let him make love to her when he didn't desire marriage.

She came up with the only excuse she could think of. "But I've done a terrible job so far. Tonight I was supposed to make sure you learned things at the wedding, and instead I got you embroiled in two fights."

"I didn't mind what happened tonight." The low thrum of his voice made it quite clear what parts of the night he didn't mind.

She didn't know what to say. She couldn't very well back out if he truly wanted her help.

When she stood there in confusion, he said, "I'll be here tomorrow morning at nine. I'm told there's a man living near the top of Black Mountain who claims to be descended from the Lady of Llyn y Fan Fach. Since I intend to make the trek up there, we must get an early start."

She couldn't believe he simply assumed she'd do as he asked.

"Make sure you wear something for walking," he added with a faint smile.

That snapped her out of her astonishment. "Why do you need me if you already know what you're going for?"

He held her gaze. "I need you to get me there, of course. Mrs. Llewellyn says you know Black Mountain like the back of your hand. And I'd enjoy having your company. Climbing mountains is lonely work."

Frantically she searched for a good reason to refuse. "What if I have matters of the estate to take care of tomorrow?"

"Then I'll postpone my trip until you can accompany me." He leaned forward, resting his fists on the table. "But be assured of this. I'll return every day until I get what you offered me." His gaze drifted to her mouth and then farther, to her throat and her breasts. "*Everything* you offered, but are too afraid to admit."

While she was still reeling from that bold statement, he murmured, "Don't forget. Tomorrow at nine." Then he left the kitchen.

Catrin sank into a chair, her pulse a maddening thud in her ears. What on earth was she to do? He'd implied that she'd offered him her body, but that wasn't true! Just because she'd let him kiss her ... and fondle her breasts ... and ...

A blush stole over her. She couldn't blame him for misunderstanding her. If not for his cold words about matrimony, she'd probably have let him lay her out across the table and take her right there like the scandalous creature everyone believed her to be.

Worst of it was, she still wanted him to. No matter how much she told herself it was wrong, she couldn't banish the swirling images of Evan sucking her breast . . . touching her thighs . . . bending her back over his arm so he could—

She shook her head to clear it. She mustn't allow these fantastic imaginings to consume her. It was fruitless to think of Evan that way when he wanted only one thing, the very thing she should reserve for her husband.

Bos entered the kitchen, cooling all her heated thoughts. "Mr. Newcome asked to borrow a horse. In light of his injuries, I offered to have the carriage return him to his lodgings, but he insisted upon riding. He said he would give back the mount in the morning, so I allowed it. That *is* what you wish, is it not?"

She frowned. Evan was making sure he had a reason to return. "That's fine."

Bos stared at her. "Are you well, madam?"

She rose to pace the kitchen. "No, I am not."

"Mr. Newcome did not harm you, did he?" Bos said in alarm.

"Not exactly." She sighed. "Oh, Bos, I don't know what to do with the man."

"Must you do anything at all with him?"

"Yes. I owe him, I'm afraid. For lying to him and then landing him in not one, but two fights on my behalf tonight."

"On your behalf?" Bos regarded her with narrowed eyes. "Do you mean to say that the gentleman's wounds were received while coming to your rescue?"

"I'm afraid so."

For the briefest moment, he looked taken aback. Then

he smoothed his features into his typically haughty ones. "That does alter matters. It almost makes me regret giving Medea to the gentleman for a mount."

"You didn't!" Her heart leapt into her throat. "Why, Medea is liable to run him right off the edge of a cliff! You know she's impossible to manage! Why did you do that?"

For once, Bos appeared distressed by her criticism. "You came home with a gentleman who had obviously been in a fight. He then tried to pay me to betray your confidences. Surely you can understand why I thought it prudent to discourage future visits."

She sank into a chair. "Sometimes I don't know whether to kiss you or throttle you."

"I take it that you did not wish me to discourage him?"

"No . . . Yes . . . By heaven, I don't know."

Bos stiffened. "It seems to me that if the gentleman has upset you to such an extent that you no longer know your own mind, perhaps you should not see him again." Then, as if realizing that he had offered unsolicited advice, he added, "Of course, the entire affair is none of my concern."

She raised her eyebrow. "Which is why you gave Medea to Mr. Newcome as his mount."

"A lapse in good judgment, I now realize."

"No. You were only protecting me from a man who appeared to be dangerous." *Who* is *dangerous*, she amended. "The trouble is, I don't know if I want to be protected from him."

An awkward silence followed. She glanced at Bos, who looked as if he'd rather be anywhere but here, listening to her deepest thoughts. Unfortunately, Bos was the only one she could talk to. And tonight, she desperately needed someone to give her perspective on this situation.

"I . . . I like him," she said. "I like him a great deal."

Though Bos's expression remained bland, the tips of his ears reddened. "And does the gentleman share your . . . er . . . feelings?"

"I don't know." It was true. She couldn't fathom what Evan felt. One moment he claimed he had a more than cursory interest in her, and in the next, he insisted he would never marry.

But would he say differently if she'd told him that the curse was no longer in effect? Or was that wishful thinking on her part?

Now that she'd lied about the chalice, she didn't know what to do. If Evan truly had no desire to marry, then there was no point in revealing that she was indeed free. There was no point in continuing in any "friendship" with him.

On the other hand, if he knew about the chalice . . .

"Bos?" she asked.

The servant stood rigidly at attention. "Yes, madam?"

"Please sit down. You make me nervous standing there like a statue."

"Then I shall leave you to your ruminations."

"Don't go. I need your advice about . . . about something personal. I don't know where else to turn."

It was comical to witness the two sides of Bos warring with each other—the butler side protesting that it was inappropriate for a servant to listen to the personal woes of an employer, while the human side argued for compassion.

She could tell when the human side won, for Bos lowered himself into a chair. "I will endeavor to advise you as best I can, madam. Please proceed."

Without looking at him, Catrin recounted the entire tale of the chalice . . . how she'd discovered its significance and whereabouts, how she'd gone to London to acquire it, how Lord Mansfield had been murdered shortly after selling it to her, and how her lies about it had affected both David and Evan.

Bos merely uttered a "Hmm" or an "I see" here and there. When she finished, she looked at him, wondering if she'd find condemnation in his eyes. Instead she found compassion.

"I wish that you had confided in me sooner."

"Why?"

"Because I would never have allowed you to go to London. I would have insisted that you let me go in your stead." His lips tightened. "To think that you might have been murdered . . . or worse . . . by those ruffians. Only good fortune—and good instincts—saved you from that. You shouldn't have gone alone, madam. You must never do such a thing again."

His concern so overwhelmed her that she had to fight back tears. "You don't think I'm mad for wanting to acquire the chalice? Or believing in the curse?"

"I have no opinion about the curse. *You* believe in it. That is all that matters."

She swallowed hard. "You don't think I was wrong to lure Lord Mansfield to that inn under a false name and try to circumvent his mother?" Her voice dropped to a whisper. "You don't think it's my fault the poor man was murdered?"

"Indeed not!" Bos's look of outrage warmed her. "I would say you acted admirably to solve a knotty problem. You are certainly not to blame for the deplorable criminal element in London."

"But I should have told the authorities I was there. If they ever find out Lord Mansfield went to meet the Lady of the Mists, they may send someone after me."

Bos stared at her. "I begin to comprehend your recent actions. Was your fear of having the authorities come in search of you what prompted you to shy away from Mr. Newcome when you first encountered him? Did you suspect that he might have come from London for such a purpose?"

"Actually, yes. He did come shortly after I left there, and he asked about the Lady of the Mists." She smiled. "But later he explained how he'd heard about me from the Vaughans, and it turned out to be nothing more than coincidence."

"Hmm."

"Truly, Bos, that's all it was. Why would a scholar of his reputation act like a constable, looking for the woman who'd met Lord Mansfield before his death?"

Bos scowled. "The more appropriate question is why a scholar of his reputation would travel all the way from Cambridge to meet a woman whose endeavors as a scholar are not . . . shall we say . . . on the level of his own."

"I know, I know," she said without rancor. It wasn't as if she hadn't tried to launch more ambitious endeavors. But the work of a woman without a university degree was largely disregarded.

Besides, to do any serious research on Welsh folktales

would have meant leaving Plas Niwl and seeking out strangers to tell her about particular customs. The very thought of doing such a thing terrified her.

"All right," she said. "We've established that he can't be interested in my work. But he didn't come here to seek *me* out. The Vaughans implied that I was Grandmother, so he decided to research her for his book. He found me instead."

"And is now researching you. Is that it?"

"I suppose you could put it that way."

"Instead of gathering his folktales, he is waiting on your leisure . . . accompanying you to weddings . . . fighting battles for you—"

"He went to the wedding so he could hear folktales," Catrin protested.

"Oh, indeed. And did he hear any?"

"Well, no, but—"

"Madam, I believe you are allowing your interest in this man to overwhelm your good judgment. I find it highly suspicious that only a week after your return, a man should come to 'research' you, as it were."

Bos had a way of making it *sound* suspicious. But he was wrong about Evan. "I don't believe he came here for any other reason, or he would have been put off by what I told him this evening."

Bos's eyes widened. "Surely you did not confess to him the same things you confessed to me."

"I told about the curse, but I lied about the chalice. I said I never bought it, that Lord Mansfield never showed up."

"I see you have not entirely lost your wits," Bos remarked.

"In any case, if Evan *were* trying to find out something about the murder, he'd have taken what I said tonight to mean I wasn't involved, and he'd be planning to return to Cambridge. Instead, he's coming here tomorrow. Why, he practically demanded that I go with him to speak to that descendant of the Lady of Llyn y Fan Fach who lives on Black Mountain. So you see, he really is researching a book, and he truly does want my help."

"Perhaps. Nonetheless, I find all of this highly disturbing." Bos rose. "Here is my advice, madam. You should avoid any future encounters with the gentleman. You were right to refuse to see him the first time, and you should follow that course from now on. Involvement with the investigation of that earl's murder could do you naught but harm, and you must protect yourself."

Catrin agreed with Bos, though for different reasons. She didn't think Evan had come to spy on her. But it was clear he wanted to take her virtue. And if she continued in his presence much longer, she'd let him. What a mistake *that* would be. It would involve her in a sordid affair that could only end in scandal. And illegitimate children.

She groaned. "I *want* to avoid him. But he's very persistent. He says he'll come here every day until I agree to accompany him, and I . . . well, I'm not like Grandmother. I don't know how to send a man packing."

"There is no need for you to send him packing, madam." Bos straightened his perfectly straight cravat. "I shall make certain Mr. Newcome refrains from bothering you further. You leave him to me."

9

So this is hell, Evan thought as he prodded his horse through the mist up the now familiar path to Plas Niwl. *Burning for Catrin with no chance of quenching the flames.*

Both days he'd tried to see her, he'd been rebuffed by that bloody butler. The first day Bos had told him she was closeted with her solicitor. The next day he'd said she was indisposed. When Evan had refused to leave until he saw her, Bos had instructed the footmen to escort him back to Llanddeusant.

Evan could have fought them, but what would have been the point? Even if he'd seen her, she'd have been surrounded by her watchdogs, and he wouldn't have been able to talk any sense into her . . . to touch her . . . to kiss her.

Why was he behaving like such a fool? A hundred times, he'd considered leaving, especially after he'd discovered she couldn't have been involved with Justin's murder. But every time he closed his eyes, he tasted her on his lips and felt the silken texture of her skin. Her soft voice intruded in his waking thoughts, and she tormented him in sleep with hot, wanton dreams.

And it wasn't just her body he desired. He liked talking to her. He liked prying opinions out of her, uncovering the complex woman beneath the shy facade. He'd anticipated spending days in her company, sharing ideas . . . and intimacies. Now that he'd been denied the chance, he wanted to take it.

It was madness. It couldn't go anywhere. But perhaps if he spent more time with her, he could shake this strange obsession. And she burned as much as he did. It was absurd for them not to enter the flames together.

Catrin excelled at protecting herself by avoiding what was most frightening, and God knew he understood about escaping into one's private world. But this time he wouldn't let her. Which meant he must sneak into Plas Niwl and find Catrin himself.

A grim smile on his face, he spurred his horse on. The mare he'd borrowed from the Vaughans wasn't nearly so skittish as that deuced Medea Bos had given him to ride three days ago. Apparently Bos had intended to wreak some petty vengeance on him, but it had been worth his madcap ride down to Llanddeusant to see Bos's face the next day when Evan brought Medea to a halt outside Plas Niwl.

Just as he was thinking that a ride through the night with Catrin would be wonderful, he emerged from a thick patch of fog to find two horses tethered to a tree. Perhaps he'd caught Catrin out trying to avoid him again.

He followed the path that wound through the thick woods. As he topped a hill, he heard a male voice complaining about "imbeciles and fools." Then he came upon Sir Reynald, with a man he didn't know. Behind them was a large dolmen, two upright stones supporting a third to form a table.

Wisps of mist swirled about it, giving it an air of frightening mystery, and at its foot was a dead animal. A bull, he conjectured, though he couldn't be sure, since the head and genitals had been removed and the hide pierced in several places.

He let out a shocked gasp, and the two men whirled to face him.

"Ah, Mr. Newcome," Sir Reynald said. "I thought you might be one of the scoundrels who did this, returning to the scene of the crime. Do come see. You shall probably find this evidence of insanity in our county quite intriguing."

"What in God's name is it?"

The man next to Sir Reynald muttered, "It's those idiots in Llanddeusant who dabble in druidry. They think the dolmen was once an altar, so they come here to perform their sacrifices under cover of darkness. But one day I'll catch them at it, and I'll take a pitchfork to the lot of them!"

Sir Reynald raised an eyebrow. "Mr. Newcome, meet Mr. Parry, Mrs. Price's groundskeeper. We are standing on Plas Niwl land."

"Aye," said Parry. "They're trespassing. And butchering fine animals."

"This is the second of my cattle they stole and butchered," Sir Reynald said. "Do you know what price a bull like that fetches at market? And he had several more years of stud service in him. Now this. If I ever catch them, I'll strangle the lot."

"Now you see why I dragged you from your bed to show you this, sir," Parry said. "We must find a way to put a stop to it."

"Does it happen a great deal?" Evan felt as if he'd stepped back a few centuries in time. He couldn't tear his gaze from the mutilated bull.

Druids, no less. Iolo Morganwg and the Gwyneddigion Society in London arranged meetings of the Gorsedd and wore white robes to call upon the ancient bards for inspiration, but animal sacrifice? Somehow he couldn't see Morganwg butchering a bull.

Yet here in this desolate place, with Black Mountain scowling down on them and the mist floating through the clearing, he could too easily believe that druids in long white robes had come in the night to perform strange rites.

"It happens every so often," Parry was saying. "I've waited for them many a time, but I can't seem to predict when the devils will appear."

"Mrs. Price and I must lay a trap for them," Sir Reynald said. "I'll speak to her at once."

With a start, Evan remembered the tale of the chalice. Could Catrin have had something to do with this?

He snorted. The very idea of meek Catrin presiding over such butchery was ridiculous. Even if she were given to performing rituals, she'd use less violent means . . . and her own livestock.

"You can't talk to Mrs. Price until tomorrow," Parry said. "She's at the mill in Craig y Nos to see about the wool prices. She left 'bout two hours ago and won't be back 'til evening."

Evan groaned. He should have known she'd do something like that to avoid him. The woman was driving him mad. "Do you know which road Mrs. Price took?" he asked Parry. "I need to speak with her today."

"Aye, I can direct you to where she is. With a good horse, you ought to catch up to her."

Excellent. She wasn't escaping him this time.

~

Catrin sank down beside her Welsh pony, who munched grass with utter contentment. It wasn't Little Boy's fault that he'd developed a saddle sore. It was hers for letting her mind wander while she'd saddled him.

"A pox on you, Evan Newcome." Keeping away from him should have ended her imaginings, but it had only made them worse. Last night, she'd awakened to her own hand caressing her breast as she'd pretended it was *him* fondling her.

Which was why she'd taken this ride. She'd hoped that another day away from Evan would lessen her wild imaginings. Yet not only had she failed in evicting him from her thoughts, now she was stuck out here. She really had only one choice—to lead Little Boy home.

Unfortunately, now that Little Boy was lunching on the fine grass by the road, he wasn't about to move. She drew an apple from her provisions and held it under his nose.

"Here's a treat, my poor dear. I'll not mount you, but you must come along home with me. I can't leave you here."

The pony nuzzled the apple. Slowly, she backed up, cooing to him. "Come on then, Little Boy. Come with me, and you shall have this apple."

She was so intent on enticing him onto the road that she didn't hear a horse come up behind her until a familiar male voice rumbled, "I wouldn't listen to her if I were you. She's notorious for reneging on her promises."

"Evan!" She couldn't hide her relief. "What are you doing here? However did you find me?"

With a wry frown, he dismounted. "Why? What had you instructed dear old Bos to tell me today? That you'd run off to America? That the *Tylwyth Teg* had taken you to fairyland?"

"You . . . you haven't talked to Bos?"

He shot her a cold glance. "No. I talked to your grounds-keeper, who was more forthcoming." He gestured to her pony. "What's wrong with your mount?"

"Poor thing has a saddle sore. I was in too much of a hurry to leave. I guess I didn't tighten the girth properly."

He examined the pony. "You can't ride him, you know."

"That's why I'm *trying* to lead him home."

"We can lead him home together. You can ride with me."

The thought of doing that quickened her blood. Unfortunately. "There's no need. You go on, and I'll just walk home with Little Boy."

"Not bloody likely." His gaze warmed on her. "Admit it. I've caught you now. You can ride with me or walk with me, but there's no way in hell you're going to avoid me this time."

She sighed. Since walking all the way back to Plas Niwl didn't appeal to her, it looked as if she'd be riding with him.

Still, once she was seated across his saddle with her shoulder against his chest and her bottom nestled in his lap, she wasn't sure how she'd endure the ride. She was all too aware of his corded thighs and his strong arms bracketing her body. Of his face close enough to kiss.

By heaven, what was wrong with her? He'd made it perfectly clear what sort of "friendship" he wanted, and it wasn't what *she* wanted at all.

"How much longer had you intended to avoid me?" he asked.

"I don't know what you're talking about. I've simply been busy with matters of the estate."

His voice dropped to a husky rumble. "You mean, busy inventing matters of the estate to keep you from seeing me again."

She stared at the mist-shrouded road. Must he always be so forthright? Must he always make her feel guilty?

"Is that why Morys was so angry with you? Because you gave him just enough of a taste of you to whet his appetite, then withheld the feast?"

She glared at him. "I never let David touch me like that! I never wanted him to . . ." She trailed off as she realized how much she'd admitted.

His gaze dropped to her mouth. "Never wanted him to what? Make love to you?"

"I didn't say that."

"But you were thinking it. Admit it, Morys was angry because you let me take liberties that you'd never allowed him. Because he knew you wanted me . . . and that infuriated him."

"I don't want you."

"Oh?" Nuzzling her hair, he kissed the tip of her ear. His breath tickled her skin, then warmed it until the heat spread clear to her toes.

"I don't," she repeated, trying to convince herself.

"Shall I prove that you do?" He nipped her earlobe, scattering pleasure through her.

"Certainly not."

But Evan was already halting the horses. Before she could make another protest, he'd tucked the reins under her thigh, freeing his hands so he could turn her face up to his. He trailed one hand down her jaw to her neck, and she could feel the imprint of every finger splayed over her throat.

Then she was drowning in the soft kiss he pressed to her mouth. On a sigh, she parted her lips and he drove his tongue in deep, claiming her the same way he'd claimed her dreams, without apology or remorse.

He shifted her so that she lay tucked in his arm, half-reclining across the horse. The position forced her to cling to his neck, which meant she couldn't easily push him away.

Not that she wanted to. She'd lain alone three long nights anticipating this kiss, and her good sense wouldn't deprive her of what her body wanted. Thus when he slid his hand inside her bodice to cup her breast, she made no murmur of protest, but arched up against the hand that caressed and teased the soft flesh exactly as she'd imagined in her dreams.

Only when she moaned low in her throat did he draw his mouth from hers, his eyes glittering with triumph. "Tell me you want me, sweet girl. Tell me you're not afraid of me."

When she stared up at him, wide-eyed and dazed, he thumbed her nipple and added, "There's nothing wrong with wanting me, Catrin."

Suddenly she realized where they were. Good heavens, anyone could come along and see them!

With a cry, she wriggled free and slid off the horse, then snatched up Little Boy's fallen lead rope and hastened down the road.

Evan prodded his horse into walking beside her. "Catrin," he said in his low, commanding voice.

"Just leave me alone."

"You don't want that."

"I do!" But it was a lie. What she wanted was for him to court her, and he'd already made clear he didn't intend to do that.

"You're merely afraid to let your perfectly normal urges overwhelm you. It's fear that makes you avoid me, that keeps you from taking a lover or marrying again after all this time."

"I can't marry because of the curse."

"You know in your heart that the curse is a lot of nonsense. But you've convinced yourself it's true because you're afraid."

She shook her head. She believed in the curse because it was real. Of course, she had the chalice now, so it didn't matter, but he couldn't know that.

"You're afraid to let a man close for fear he'll uncover the wanton side of you that you're so ashamed of."

"I'm not a wanton!"

"I didn't say you were." His voice thrummed with emotion. "But neither are you the passionless drone you think you are, or the quiet, cowardly creature you show to the world."

"You don't know what I am."

"I do. Despite how you try to hide from everyone who might see your supposed character flaws, I know you're stronger than you think."

There was too much truth in his words, curse him. She increased her pace.

So did he. "It's not cowardice that keeps you from hurting people, but compassion. You're bright and beautiful and remarkable. You have nothing to fear. Any man would be delighted to have you as a companion."

"I don't want to be a man's companion. I only want to live my life in peace." With a husband who loved her.

Why couldn't he see her as a wife? If she was as "remarkable" as he claimed, why didn't anyone want to marry her? David wanted to, but only because of her property. He'd made it quite clear that he thought little of her intelligence.

Sometimes she suspected even Willie had married her only to strike back at his overbearing father. He'd liked her well enough, to be sure, but he hadn't been in love with her.

And Evan? He claimed to see her finer qualities, yet he had no desire to marry her. Even her property didn't tempt him. Then again, he was probably from some fine family and needn't ever worry about such things. He was only interested in her body, and while that was flattering, it wasn't enough to tempt her into throwing her future away.

She was so caught up in her thoughts that she'd gone several feet before she realized Evan was no longer at her side.

"Stop!" he called after her. "There's someone on the road ahead!"

She looked up. Someone *was* approaching, and with great haste. Evan rode up beside her. "Mount the horse behind me. We must be able to flee if the man proves to be foe rather than friend."

But now the man was too close for escape. Besides, he looked more like a solicitor than a highwayman.

"Good day to you!" he called out, and Evan muttered an oath. The red-faced fellow halted his horse, then fixed her with shrewd gray eyes. "I say, you wouldn't happen to be Mrs. Catrin Price, would you? I was told you might be on this road."

"Who wants to know?" Evan asked.

The man drew out a handkerchief and mopped his jowly face. "The name's Archer Quinley. I've come from London to ask Mrs. Price a few questions."

Catrin's heart pounded. So they'd found her, had they? In a way, it was a relief. At least now she wouldn't have to spend her time looking over her shoulder.

Mr. Quinley drew a folded paper from his coat pocket. "Lady Mansfield hired me to look into her son's death. Here's the letter her solicitor sent, setting forth what she wanted done."

Evan tried to take the letter, but with a shake of his

head, Mr. Quinley looked at Catrin. "You *are* Mrs. Price, aren't you?"

"You don't have to answer that," Evan said.

She ignored him. It was one thing to avoid the authorities, but quite another to openly refuse to cooperate. And why did Evan seem unsurprised to hear that an investigator wanted to ask her questions about a murder? "Yes, I'm Catrin Price."

Mr. Quinley handed her the letter. As she scanned it, she noted that Lady Mansfield had immediately assumed a connection between Catrin's first letter to her about the chalice and her son's mysterious murder.

Then a line caught Catrin's eye. She had to read it twice to be sure she wasn't mistaken. As pain engulfed her, she read aloud the words, "My son's friend, a respected scholar by the name of Evan Newcome, has already told the constable that a woman going by the name of the Lady of the Mists met with my son on the night of his murder. I suggest you focus your investigation on this woman, who I'm sure must be Catrin Price. She may have seen something which could lead to the apprehension of my son's killers."

Catrin stared at Evan, her heart plummeting. It had all been lies, every single moment they were together. And his guilty expression confirmed it.

"You didn't come here to research a book, did you?" she said in a hollow voice. "You didn't seek me out because you'd read my essay."

He cursed, but didn't avert his gaze. "No."

That's when her world crumbled.

10

"Mrs. Price?" Mr. Quinley asked. "Are you all right?"

Hardly. Here she'd been thinking Evan was interested in her, if only for her body, but he hadn't been interested in her at all . . . not for her body or property or even help with his book.

His book. Hah! He'd probably made that up to gain access to her so he could ask his questions. He'd lied and misled her, treated her as if her feelings didn't matter. How dared he?

"Catrin—" Evan began.

"Mr. Quinley, meet Mr. Evan Newcome," she bit out. "He's been conducting his own investigation. A pity you came along so soon; he'd almost dragged the entire story from me. But now I'm sure he's pleased to relinquish his onerous task to you."

"Catrin!" Evan said more firmly. "This isn't what it seems."

She continued addressing her remarks to Mr. Quinley.

"I'm sorry you had to travel so far, but I'm more than happy to answer your questions. I'd have been more than happy to answer Mr. Newcome's . . . *if* he'd ever asked any."

It wasn't entirely true, but it felt good to say it—and to watch a guilty flush rise to stain Evan's cheeks a dark red.

Mr. Quinley fidgeted in his saddle. "Are you telling me that this fellow here is Lord Mansfield's friend, the scholar?"

She nodded. It suddenly occurred to her why Evan hadn't been forthcoming. Because he'd actually thought she'd had something to do with his friend's murder. For the past few days, he'd conversed with her, defended her . . . kissed her, all while believing that she'd taken part in a brutal crime.

The thought made her stomach roil. She swayed, and Evan was off his mount and at her side in an instant.

"I'm so sorry—" he began as he took her arm to support her.

She snatched her arm away. "Don't you *dare* touch me! After everything you said and did, you have no right."

Mr. Quinley was off his horse now, too. "Perhaps we should pull the horses off the road and stop for a bit." He cast Evan a suspicious glance. "Mrs. Price looks as if she's had a shock."

She shook her head, though she fought to keep from collapsing. This was no time to be weak. Neither of these men were friends. She must keep her wits about her, or she'd find herself carted off for a crime she hadn't committed.

"I'm fine, Mr. Quinley." Straightening her shoulders, she forced a smile. "But we *should* probably pull off."

Mr. Quinley nodded. "There are some trees over there. Why don't we sit, and you can tell me what you know of what happened the night of Lord Mansfield's death?"

"Certainly." She turned for the trees.

Evan did, too, but Mr. Quinley stopped him. "Sorry, sir. This would be better done without you, since you seem to upset the young lady."

"No need," Catrin said. "I've nothing to hide from Mr. Newcome."

With a shrug, Mr. Quinley led his horse off the road and tethered it. As she started to do the same, Evan caught her arm, speaking in Welsh so the investigator couldn't understand. "I know you're angry, and I don't blame you, but—"

"I told you not to touch me." She met his gaze coolly. "Bad enough that you pretended to care about me when you were only spying on me. Don't make it worse by continuing the pretense."

With a stricken expression, he tightened his hold. "Oh, my darling, it wasn't a pretense—"

"Stop it!" How stupid did he think she was? And what did he mean to gain by going on like this? "If you don't, I swear I'll—"

"Is everything all right here?" Mr. Quinley asked, with a glance at Evan's hand on her arm.

"Everything's fine." She tugged her arm free of Evan's grip. "It will be even better once we get this over with."

As she and Evan tethered their horses, she fretted over what to say. She couldn't tell the truth; everything she'd done in London would seem questionable. She was the last person to have seen Lord Mansfield, and she'd been mysterious in setting up their meeting. Even if she explained why, she couldn't explain the instinct that had made her flee the inn.

Besides, she'd told Evan that she'd never met with Lord Mansfield. If she said otherwise now, Evan would reveal it to Quinley, and both men would find her conflicting stories suspicious.

So she must give Mr. Quinley the same story she'd given Evan, and continue in her lie that she'd never met Lord Mansfield. Otherwise, they'd not believe anything else she said.

Besides, if she told the truth about the chalice, Mr. Quinley would tell Lady Mansfield, who would no doubt demand its return. Then Catrin would be back where she'd started—without a husband or hope of a future.

When she faced the two men, her mind was set. Now if only she could sound convincing, when all she wanted was to crawl into a hole and never come out.

What would Grandmother do? Brazen it out.

Usually thoughts of her grandmother's capabilities made Catrin aware of her inadequacies, but today, they helped. She imagined Grandmother fixing her steely-eyed gaze on Mr. Quinley. He *was* just a man, after all. And Catrin had a good reason to lie—not only to save herself from jail, but to save her lands from confiscation and the people she depended on from losing their positions.

But what about Evan? Could she lie to him?

She squared her shoulders. He'd lied to her without a thought. From the moment he'd spun his tale about wanting her help with a book, he'd given up his right to the truth. He deserved to be lied to.

And she'd have no trouble giving him his just deserts.

~

Evan's stomach knotted as Catrin sat down on the hard ground, ignoring the coat he'd spread out for her.

She was enraged. He'd never seen her like that before, and it tore at him to know he'd provoked it.

But what made it worse was the pain he glimpsed behind the anger. She was sure of his perfidy. And with Quinley here, he couldn't explain that once he'd come to know her, he couldn't believe anything bad of her. He must find a way to make her listen. But how?

Quinley began the interrogation. "Why didn't you use your real name when you approached his lordship?"

Good question. Evan had wondered that, as well.

"Lady Mansfield refused to sell the chalice to me," Catrin said, "so I was afraid that if I told her son my real name, he'd tell his mother."

That made perfect sense. Justin's mother was miserly. Although the chalice probably hadn't mattered a whit to her, once she'd learned that someone else wanted it, her first instinct had no doubt been to pray she could find an even better buyer. Evan had to admire Catrin's resourcefulness in using her appellation of the Lady of the Mists to entice Justin to meet her. It had obviously worked.

As she answered Quinley's questions about the chalice, Evan's spirits sank. She told Quinley the same things she'd told *him* when she'd thought she could trust him. She even told the investigator about the curse and why she'd wanted the chalice.

Although Evan had already decided that Catrin couldn't be guilty, it still pained him to hear how blameless she was, for it made his subterfuge with her even more unconscionable. He could easily remember their last night together: how she'd told him about the chalice in such innocence and revealed her belief in the curse, which she'd apparently told no one else about but Morys. Evan had been given the chance to tell her the truth about his own motives then, but hadn't.

The knot in his stomach grew hard as stone. She would never forgive him. And he couldn't bear that.

Quinley licked his pencil. "So you never met with Lord Mansfield?"

"Sadly, no." Her voice shook as she met the investigator's too-keen gaze.

She was suffering, and she wouldn't even let Evan comfort her.

Quinley flipped through his notebook. "Nothing I've learned so far either proves or disproves your assertion, Mrs. Price. The innkeeper and his wife admit to having directed you to the room where you were to meet his lordship, but they never saw Lord Mansfield enter."

The investigator shot her a veiled glance. "Of course, if Lord Mansfield arranged for the private room as you told me, then he would have known which room to go to, and he wouldn't have needed to make his presence known."

"Yes," Evan put in, "but surely someone would have seen him and remarked upon it."

"Denizens of such places tend to mind their own business, sir." Quinley stared at Evan as if trying to assess his interest. Then he returned his attention to Catrin. "I'd like to know why you left London without seeking to discover why Lord Mansfield hadn't kept his appointment with you."

Catrin colored. "I didn't need to discover it. The next morning the murder was in all the papers, and I read about it."

Quinley's eyebrow quirked up. "Didn't you consider that you had information of relevance to solving his murder?"

"I did. But I hadn't seen anything. I didn't know anything." Her voice lowered. "And to be truthful, I was afraid to come forward. I didn't know if anyone knew about our meeting, and I thought it best to leave it that way. I suppose that sounds awful, but it's the truth."

Those few words explained so much. Alone in an unfamiliar city, Catrin had probably been terrified at the thought of going to a constable, especially when she had no new insights to offer.

But while her words increased Evan's feelings of guilt, they apparently piqued Quinley's interest. "I suppose you couldn't have known that Lord Mansfield carried the last of your letters in his coat pocket. That is, unless you had something to do with the removal of the letter."

The look of surprise on Catrin's face was so genuine that Evan groaned. His poor darling didn't even know what Quinley was talking about, which only further confirmed her innocence.

"I don't understand," she said.

"It's simple, madam. When Lord Mansfield left his club, after showing your letter to Mr. Newcome here, he proceeded straight to the inn. We can only assume he had the letter on him when he was murdered. Yet none was found on him. I must admit I can see no reason for thieves to take it, whereas I can see any number of reasons for you to do so."

"You mean, only *one* reason, don't you?" Catrin's voice sounded hollow. "That I murdered him and wanted to hide the evidence of our meeting."

Quinley seemed surprised by her straightforward assessment. "That could be one interpretation of the events, yes."

When the blood drained from Catrin's face, Evan's temper flared. "This is absurd! The letter could have fallen out in the scuffle, or Justin might have left it in his carriage."

"He didn't take a carriage," Quinley said. "As you may recall, he walked."

"Still, that doesn't prove anything," Evan bit out.

"You seemed to think at one time that it did," Quinley said pointedly.

Evan groaned, especially when he noticed Catrin grow even more ashen. He'd started all this, and God help him, he wished he hadn't. If he'd known she'd turn out to be a sweet, shy lady instead of the greedy schemer he'd thought . . .

Somehow he had to get Catrin out of this mess. The investigator's evidence against her was flimsy at best.

Quinley leaned forward. "Have you anything to say,

Mrs. Price?" His voice was deceptively gentle. "Any idea where the letter might have gotten to?"

She shook her head. "I wrote the letter, Mr. Quinley, but that's all."

"And you know nothing about what happened to Lord Mansfield the night you were to meet with him?"

"No!" Her eyes brimmed with tears. "But I *am* sorry he was murdered."

With grim satisfaction, Evan noted Quinley's discomfort. The man wasn't blind. Obviously, he was beginning to realize that Catrin Price wasn't the sort of woman to arrange a man's murder. Still, would that be enough? Quinley had no evidence against her, but that didn't always matter in English courts.

A rumbling sound came from down the pockmarked road, and a carriage hastened toward them. Evan knew it was Catrin's because of the man whose head was stuck out the window. Her watchdog, Bos.

Catrin rose as the carriage halted.

Bos leapt out. "I have come to fetch you home, madam. There's an emergency, I'm afraid."

Alarm suffused Catrin's face. "What kind of emergency?"

"The kind only you can deal with. I would rather not speak of it here."

For once, Evan was pleased Bos took his responsibilities so seriously, since the "emergency" was clearly a way to get Catrin out of Quinley's clutches. When the investigator had gone to Plas Niwl, Bos must have been alerted to the fact that a stranger was causing trouble for his mistress.

It didn't surprise Evan that the butler had taken it upon himself to rescue Catrin.

But Catrin was apparently oblivious to Bos's ploy. "We'll have to tether Little Boy to the back of the carriage. He can't tolerate a rider just now."

"There's no time for that," Bos said. "I shall send a groom back for him."

Turning to Quinley, Catrin asked, "May I go now, sir? I've told you everything you wish to know. And as you see, I have pressing duties at my estate."

"Yes, you may go." When she murmured a quick "thank you" and headed for the carriage, Quinley called out, "But I may think of other things I need to ask. You will be at home, won't you?"

"Of course," she said as Bos helped her into the carriage. She stuck her head out the window. "Rest assured, Mr. Quinley, I'm willing to help you in any way I can." Then, without sparing even a glance for Evan, she told the coachman to go, and they were off in a cloud of dust.

With mixed emotions, Evan watched her carriage depart. On one hand, he was pleased to see her escape Quinley's questioning. On the other, she was once more inaccessible, surrounded by her servants and her fears.

He didn't realize how much his feelings showed until Quinley said in an acid tone, "Next time, sir, you should leave the investigating to professionals."

"What's *that* supposed to mean?" Evan snapped.

"That you're obviously inexperienced at eliciting the truth from an unwilling subject, especially a pretty widow."

Evan gritted his teeth. "I came here as convinced as you that she'd had something to do with the murder. But only a fool could learn what I have and persist in believing her guilty."

"And what have you learned?" Quinley drew a pipe from his pocket and began filling it. "Or have you gone over so fully to the young woman's side that you aren't willing to say?"

Evan was rapidly losing patience. "I'll tell you whatever you wish to know, but none of it paints her guilty." He drew a deep breath. "First of all, she is indeed shy, enough to be afraid to face a magistrate."

Quinley lighted his pipe with a nonchalant air. "Yet that 'very shy' woman traveled alone to a strange city and agreed to meet a strange man in an inn without knowing a single thing about his character."

"Because she wanted the chalice very badly. She truly believes in that curse. She even refused to marry the local schoolmaster because she thinks marriage to her is a death sentence. You should talk to him. He's thoroughly convinced of her belief in it. As am I."

Quinley regarded Evan with narrowed eyes. "You're saying she was so desperate for that chalice she'd have swallowed her innate shyness to obtain it."

"Not desperate enough to have a man murdered."

"What if she was unable to meet Lord Mansfield's price? I began my questioning this morning in Llanddeusant and discovered that she recently sold a painting for a hundred pounds, probably to ensure she could purchase the chalice. Yet that is only half of what she offered Lord Mansfield.

What if she couldn't raise the other half? What if he'd refused to sell it to her for less, so she had it stolen?"

Evan rolled his eyes. "Even if she's lying and her meeting with him went as you say, she could hardly have arranged to have footpads attack him between the time he left the inn and the time he reached the alley down the street. And surely you don't believe she did the deed herself."

"Of course not. But we have no idea how long Lord Mansfield remained in the inn before he ventured into the street. Nor do we know if Mrs. Price had anyone with her. She might have brought two companions along for the very purpose of relieving Lord Mansfield of the chalice if he didn't agree to her price."

Uttering a frustrated sigh, Evan stared off down the road. "Then why kill him? Why not just have him robbed?"

"Because he would know who'd done it."

He tried to imagine Catrin hiring footpads and stationing them outside the inn so they could accost Lord Mansfield—or not—according to her signal. The idea was ludicrous. It wasn't in her character. He knew it, and any number of people in Llanddeusant could attest to it.

Of course, there were the few who would claim she cast spells and created havoc, people like her father-in-law. He could only hope Quinley was too good an investigator to listen to such hogwash.

Then it occurred to him that he had evidence in Catrin's favor. "Before you arrived, Catrin told me about the chalice and her trip to London to acquire it. If she'd murdered Justin, why would she have told me, a stranger, about her attempts?"

Mr. Quinley's drew deeply on his pipe. "That is indeed curious. I take it she didn't know of your part in the investigation?"

"No. She believed me when I said I was in Llanddeusant doing research." Evan leaned forward. "And consider this—her stories to you and to me were the same, yet when she told me of it she didn't know who I was. If she'd acquired it, why not say so while she was being so open?" Evan smiled in triumph. "Because she doesn't have the chalice. Only the innocent are open about their actions."

"Actually, that's not true," Mr. Quinley said with a puff on his pipe. "Guilty men—and women—often feel compelled to confess. Their dark deeds eat at them until they spill out the truth at unwarranted moments. We catch many a criminal because of an unwise word spoken to friends."

"Oh, for God's sake, she's not a criminal. Surely you could tell that." When Quinley shrugged, Evan's exasperation turned to fear for Catrin. "So what will you do now?"

"I've done all I can, since I have no hard evidence against her. But I shall report my findings to Lady Mansfield and the constable in London. If they choose to pursue the matter further, they may. In the meantime, I shall spend the rest of the day questioning the townspeople of Llanddeusant before I leave on the morrow."

"What do those you've already questioned say?"

"A few claim she's a witch. I suppose such nonsense is to be expected in Wales." He shot Evan an arch glance. "But most hold the woman in high regard, probably because she lends her assistance to charitable institutions."

Evan hid his relief. "Does that count for anything with you?"

A puff of smoke escaped Quinley's lips. "Of course. It will go in my report with everything else, including your observations. I'm merely trying to get at the truth. And unlike you, I'm not easily swayed by soft words and sweet looks."

Evan ignored the insult. "Just be sure you *do* get at the truth. Because if you hound Mrs. Price to jail on the basis of nothing but a few conjectures, I'll find a way to prove your incompetence. Though that may not sound like much of a threat, I do have friends in positions of power. More than you, no doubt."

Quinley didn't even bat an eyelash. "You'll do what you feel you must. But if I were you, sir, I'd hesitate to place my trust in even a woman of Mrs. Price's standing. Women are natural deceivers. Remember, 'twas sweet-faced Eve who tempted Adam to sin . . . and Adam's lust brought about the downfall of man."

Evan snorted. "As I recall, the serpent tempted Eve first, and he was decidedly male. And if God hadn't wanted Adam to lust, why did He create Eve in the first place?"

That bit of unorthodox theology must have taken Quinley aback, since he said not a word as Evan stalked off for his horse. But Evan could feel the man's gaze on him, and much as he hated to acknowledge it, he knew he should heed Quinley's cautious words.

Catrin had taken hold of him. It frightened him how badly he wanted her, and how quickly he'd come to believe her version of what had happened in London. Yet he couldn't help but think her innocent, for to think anything else meant forsaking his instincts, which told him she was falsely accused.

He ought to leave her alone. He'd already hurt her too much. He would never convince her that everything he'd said to her wasn't a lie.

But a glance at Catrin's pony decided him. He must see her again, convince her that he believed in her. Though he feared that might prove even more difficult than convincing the investigator of her innocence.

11

*R*ain drummed against the window in Catrin's study. She watched the fat drops slide, and wished they could wash her traitorous thoughts away.

No matter how much she told herself she was well rid of Evan, soft thoughts of him intruded. He'd come to her defense so gallantly that night at the wedding. He'd given both Sir Huw and David a piece of his mind, and then he'd comforted her with the tenderness of a lover. He'd kissed and fondled her and offered to make love to her. Had that all been a sham? Or was it as he'd tried to tell her this afternoon—that things were not as they seemed?

She pressed her head to the glass. What was she to do? How could she drive him from her mind?

With a sigh, she went to open the secret compartment and stare at the chalice. Had gaining it been worth it? This afternoon's discussion had reminded her of how high that cost had been. Lady Mansfield had lost a son. Evan had lost a friend. She'd been lied to and manipulated and—

A knock at the door drew her from her thoughts. "Yes?"

"May I have a word with you, madam?"

Dear, sweet Bos. "Come in," she called out as she closed the compartment.

Bos came in looking uncomfortable. "I am sorry to disturb you, madam, but we have a problem with Mr. Newcome."

In the height of her anger, she'd told Bos everything about her interview with Mr. Quinley, including Evan's betrayal. To Bos's credit, he hadn't said, "I told you so," but he'd been as irate as she.

"What about him?"

"He wishes to see you, I'm afraid."

His words shattered all her attempts at calm. "He's here? Downstairs?"

The merest raise of his eyebrows demonstrated Bos's surprise. "Not downstairs. Did you think I would allow the man entrance into the house after what he did to you?"

She tried to hide her disappointment. "Oh, I see. You sent him away. That was the right thing to do, of course."

Bos's lips tightened. "I attempted to send him away, madam, but he refused to leave. That is why we have a problem."

As it dawned on her what he was trying to tell her, she ran for the window. "You mean he's sitting outside in the rain?" She rubbed away the condensation on the window and peered out, but it was too dark and the rain too heavy to see much.

"Precisely. I had assumed that the mountebank would

leave when the storm worsened, but he is still rather stubbornly sitting on the entrance steps."

"How long has he been there?"

"Nearly two hours. He says he will not leave until he is allowed to converse with you."

Two hours! Lightning tore across the sky, and she jumped. "We can't leave him out there. It's dangerous! He might be struck by lightning!"

"One can only hope," Bos said dryly.

"Bos!" She lifted her skirts and strode to the door.

"You must admit it would solve your difficulties if Mr. Newcome were to . . . shall we say . . . expire of natural circumstances."

She circled around Bos when he tried to block her path. "Oh yes, that would certainly help. Then Mr. Quinley could blame me for *two* deaths."

Bos followed her as she hurried down the hall. "Surely you do not intend to let him enter the house."

"I shan't leave him out in the rain to catch his death of an ague." She hastened down the stairs. "I could never forgive myself."

Bos struggled to keep up with her. "Then let me fetch him in and see that he is cared for. You need not deal with him. He can stay here until the storm ceases, and then I shall send him on his way."

"Yes, on crazy Medea, no doubt." She stopped short to look back at Bos. "I appreciate your concern, but if I let you take care of him he'll probably find himself boiled in oil."

Bos shrugged. "If *you* care for him, madam, you may

find yourself in the gaol. After all, he came to Llanddeusant to discover how to have you arrested."

"Don't you think I've told myself that? But I can't let him perish in the storm, either. It would make me no better than him."

Bos sighed. "You are too kindhearted. It will be your downfall."

"No doubt." When Bos looked forlorn, she added, "Don't worry, I won't let him hurt me again. This time I know what he really is. I'll make sure he's taken care of, then leave him in the servants' capable hands. All right?"

"Whatever you wish."

She ignored his skepticism. As she headed for the door, she called out to the footman to fetch the maids and tell Mrs. Griffiths to start boiling water for a bath and stoke up the fire in the Red Room. Then, pausing only long enough to let Bos help her into her hooded coat of oiled twill, she rushed outside.

It took her a few moments to find Evan, since the rain blinded her. Then she spotted him seated at one end of the steps, with his back against the marble in a futile attempt to protect himself from the driving rain. She hastened to his side.

He'd drawn his knees up to his chest and was curled into a ball against the rain that beat relentlessly against him. When a pang of guilt hit her, she cursed it. The man deserved such treatment. It wasn't as if she'd asked him to sit out in the rain like a fool.

Nonetheless, as she went to tug at his arm, untold relief

washed over her when he lifted his head and murmured, "Catrin? Is that you? Have you taken pity on me at last?"

"Come inside," she urged. "You mustn't sit here."

He glanced up at her window. "I thought you'd left the window because you'd grown bored with witnessing my suffering."

"Don't be absurd." She pulled on his arm again. "I didn't realize you were out here, or I'd have told Bos to let you in at once."

This time he stood, a hulking form against the lightning. "All this time, I'd supposed you were punishing me. Since I deserved it, I had no quarrel with it."

His self-deprecating words struck her hard. "Come inside where it's warm. You must be freezing."

Through chattering teeth, he managed to say, "It's not so bad. I've been through worse."

"They're preparing a warm bath inside." She led him up the steps. "My servants will get you into the bath before you take your death of a chill."

"Your servants? You will have no part in it?" He halted at the top. "If you mean to send me inside and disappear, I'd rather stay out in the rain. At least here I can watch you in the window."

"Oh, you . . . you fool!" She yanked at his arm, but he didn't move. How could he be so stubborn even when soaked to the skin? "You can't stay out here in this weather!"

"I must talk to you, Catrin. And until you're willing to let me, I'll stay anywhere I bloody well please."

She considered leaving him, but she couldn't. "Fine. You

may talk to me, but it won't make a difference." She planted her hands on her hips. "*Now* will you come inside?"

"I am at your command. As always."

By the time she'd gotten him into the house, her cloak was soaked through. Ignoring Bos's scowl, she told a footman to take Evan to the Red Room and get his clothes off him.

"I shall attend to it," Bos said, placing a hand on the footman's shoulder.

"Bos—" she began in a warning tone, but he murmured, for her ears only, "I promise not to boil him in oil. I think, however, that someone with a firm hand should make sure this is managed properly."

But Catrin knew that what Bos really meant was "make sure Mr. Newcome doesn't run loose through the house."

"Catrin?" Evan said as Bos took his arm and gestured to a footman to take the other. "You said I could talk to you."

"Yes, of course," she told him as the two men dragged him away. "As soon as you're more . . . er . . . comfortable, I'll be there."

Surely the man didn't think she would watch him be undressed and take a bath, did he? That was carrying things a bit far, even for him.

After arranging for a footman to lend Evan some clothes, she found Mrs. Griffiths, who assured her that the bath would be brought up to the Red Room momentarily.

As her servants scurried off to follow her commands, Catrin paced the hall. What was she to do? She'd have to let Evan speak his piece. Yet how could she listen to him when she wasn't sure if it was lies or truth? He'd lied to her from the beginning, the wretch!

Though she'd lied, too. Was *still* lying. But it wasn't the same. She'd lied to ensure a future for herself and her tenants and servants. He'd only lied to . . . to . . .

To discover who'd murdered his friend. She thought of Lady Mansfield's letter. Evan had been Lord Mansfield's closest friend. When she thought of the horrible manner of the man's death, she could understand why Evan had gone to such extremes to unmask the killer.

Almost. His urgent need to find a murderer didn't excuse his methods. If he'd been suspicious of her, why not say so? Why not come right out and ask her questions, instead of playing his terrible games . . . making her think he had an interest in her, making her like him?

Nothing he could say excused that. Besides, he knew everything now. Why hadn't he returned to London with his newfound knowledge and left her alone?

By the time Bos came to inform her that Evan had completed his bath and wished to speak to her, she'd made up her mind—she would give him the audience he'd requested, but he'd have to have Bos present.

As she'd expected, Bos was more than happy to oblige. He was obviously as uneasy as she about her speaking to Evan at all. Nor did her uneasiness improve when she and Bos entered to find Evan wearing only a shirt and a snug-fitting pair of breeches.

A blush stained her cheeks. "I thought a footman loaned you clothing."

Evan shrugged. "This is the best he could do. Your housekeeper says it will take a few hours to dry my clothes, so you're stuck with me until then, I'm afraid."

"I see." By heaven, this would be harder than she'd thought. He looked so different without his fine clothes, more like an adventurer. His wet hair slicked back from his face and his grim expression lent him a dangerous air that made him at once more frightening and more tempting.

This wasn't the Evan Newcome who'd spoken cordially to her of Celtic languages and Greek poetry. This was the Evan who'd beaten David Morys to the ground . . . and who'd kissed her with wild passion in the kitchen.

She clenched her fists. She mustn't think of that!

Somehow she managed to make her voice coldly formal. "You said you wanted to talk to me."

Evan winced. Then his gaze flicked to Bos, who stood rigidly beside her. "Not with your watchdog here. I want to talk to you alone."

She tossed back her head in a gesture that she hoped looked confident. "Whatever you have to say can be said in front of Bos."

"You promised to hear me out," he said through gritted teeth.

"I didn't promise that our discussion would be private."

Evan's eyes narrowed. "If you don't send him away, I'll be forced to remove him myself."

When she gasped, Bos said coldly, "I should like to see you try, sir."

"Stop this!" she protested. "Mr. Newcome, you wouldn't dare pick on an old man—"

"I am not an old man, madam," Bos said in outrage. "I am perfectly capable of taking care of myself in matters involving fisticuffs."

"You see, Catrin?" Evan cast her a dark, mocking smile. "Bos and I can settle the matter easily. And I shall try not to hurt him too badly."

"A pox on you both!" she cried. "All right, Mr. Newcome. You shall have five minutes. But Bos will be right outside the door, do you hear?"

Evan shrugged. "If that's what you want."

Bos wasn't so amenable. "Really, madam, I cannot believe you would allow this scoundrel to intimidate you. We should both leave."

"I can't. I promised to let him speak to me, and I must keep my promise."

"But madam—"

"Please go, Bos," she said. "I just want this over with."

His gaze shifted to Evan, and she feared this might end violently. Then he sighed. "As you wish. But I shall be close by if you need me."

"Thank you." As soon as he'd passed through the doorway, she shut the door and whirled on Evan. "You are a bully!"

Her words seemed to strike a chord, for anger flared in his eyes. "So I've been told. Still, it seemed the only way to get you alone."

"And why was that so important? This afternoon, you succeeded in finding out everything you sought to learn. What more can you want from me?"

"I want you to understand why I behaved so abominably. And I want to apologize."

"There's no need." She turned away. She was so very cold. Shivering, she moved to the fireplace to hold her icy hands to the flames. "I understand what you did. You wanted to find out who murdered your friend, and you assumed that I did it, so you came here to spy on me. It's perfectly clear."

She felt him come up behind her, and she groaned. By heaven, if he so much as touched her, she'd crumble.

But he didn't. Instead, he began to speak in a low tone. "There's more to it than that. It doesn't excuse my actions, but I want you to know why I stooped so low." He drew a ragged breath. "Justin—Lord Mansfield—and I have known each other since I was twelve, so his death hit me very hard."

She clamped her eyes shut, wishing she could do the same with her ears. Hearing the pain in his voice couldn't fail to touch her sympathies.

"The constable treated it as a simple case of thievery," Evan went on, "but I knew more than he did. Justin had shown me your letter—and the chalice—before he left to meet you, and I'd found it curious even then that you hadn't signed your real name. Justin treated it as a lark, so I didn't think any more about it. He invited me to go with him, but I had another engagement. When my companion didn't show up, I walked to the Green Goat on the chance I might still find Justin there."

Catrin faced him with dread over what he would say next. He was so close she could see the lines about his mouth and the growing horror in his eyes.

He sucked in a breath. "The moon was bright that night, you may recall. When I passed the alley near the inn, I saw what looked like a body and went to investigate."

Her heart sank. "Oh, Evan, it was you who found him?"

He went on, his face grim. "There was a . . . great deal of blood, of course. Seven stab wounds will do that."

His breath came quickly. She couldn't help laying her hand on his arm.

But he didn't seem to notice. "I called for the watch. I told them what I knew of why he was there, and they searched the body, but didn't find any money or the chalice, so they assumed he'd been murdered in the course of a robbery. But I found the whole thing very strange."

He swallowed. "He'd gone to meet a mysterious lady who wouldn't sign her real name. And the letter she'd sent, which he'd carried on his person, was gone. Though I tried to believe the constable when he said the Lady of the Mists couldn't have had anything to do with it, the thought that I knew something that might lead to justice for my friend plagued me, until at last I decided to come here. I didn't even tell his mother. I didn't want to upset her. That's why I didn't know who you were when I came. Everything she told Quinley about you after hearing of my suspicions from the constable . . . I didn't know any of that."

"All you knew was that I was a murderess," she whispered, her throat tight.

He shifted his gaze to her. "Nay, I wasn't such a fool as to leap to that conclusion. But I did have some vague idea that you might have . . . I don't know . . . had the chalice taken from him so you wouldn't have to pay for it."

She gaped at him. "You thought I hired men to rob and kill him?"

"Yes." When she gasped, he added, "I know it sounds

far-fetched, but it's not as strange as it seems. Quinley still considers it a possibility."

The blood drained from her face. "What do you mean?"

His eyes were steady on her. "After you left this afternoon, Quinley informed me that he found your story . . . suspicious. He thinks you might have had the chalice stolen . . . perhaps because you couldn't offer Justin as much money as you'd said and Justin had refused to take a lesser offer."

"But I ga—" She stopped short, her heart pounding. "I *had* the two hundred pounds. Why would Mr. Quinley think otherwise?" By heaven, she'd nearly revealed that she'd given the money to Lord Mansfield. She must be more careful.

"Quinley's been talking to people in town. He knows you sold a painting to raise a hundred pounds to buy the chalice, and he wonders where the other hundred came from."

She stiffened. "He should have asked me. I would have told him it came from the hard-earned rents of my tenants." Terror filled her. "The same tenants whose livelihoods he'll jeopardize if he arrests me."

"He won't." There was assurance in his voice . . . and determination. "I made sure he knew you didn't have the chalice. I pointed out that you'd told me everything when you didn't even know who I was. I think I convinced him it was a sign of your innocence."

Catrin turned away, sure that her guilt must be blazing in her face. If Evan ever learned that she *did* have the chalice . . .

Then the enormity of what Evan had done for her

struck her. "Why did you try to convince him I was inno-cent? You didn't have to."

"Of course I did." There was distress in his voice. "I'll admit that when I first came here, I believed you'd played some part in the murder. And when you were so evasive at the lake, I was even more convinced. I was afraid to confront you with my questions, because I thought you might flee. That's why I pretended to need your help with a book . . . so I could be around you."

Her gaze shot to his. "So you could spy on me."

"Yes. I can't deny that."

With a sob, she tried to move past him, but he clasped her shoulders. He went on relentlessly, his lips so close she could feel his breath on her cheek. "Then things changed." His voice dropped. "The more time I spent with you, the more I wanted to be with you. And I could no longer believe you'd had any part in Justin's murder."

She glanced up at him. "Then why did you go on lying?" She didn't attempt to hide her tears. "For pity's sake, you let me think I was worthy of your attention, when all the time you were merely trying to find out what I knew."

He dug his fingers into her shoulders. "Deuce take it, Catrin, you *are* worthy of my attention."

"You didn't intend to write a book about folk legends, did you? That was only one more way to soften me so I'd tell you what you wanted to know. You probably never even read my essay." All her insecurities rushed in. "You must have thought me such a fool to actually believe you'd go one foot out of your way to visit me . . . to care about my opinions . . . to—"

"I *did* care." He looked stricken. "I *do* care. Don't you see? That's why I couldn't tell you the truth, once I realized you were innocent. I knew it would hurt you. And that was the last thing I wanted."

Unable to bear his pity, she averted her face. "I-I'm not a complete coward, you know. I could have borne the truth."

"I didn't say you're a coward." There was no contempt or condescension in his voice. "If I've learned anything about you, it's that you're brave about things that matter. You do what must be done. But even brave women have feelings, and I couldn't bear to wound yours. If anything, *I* am the coward. I knew if I told you the truth, you'd hate me, and I couldn't bear having you hate me. As you do now."

"I don't hate you. But . . . but you didn't have to take your game so far. You didn't have to pretend to desire me or—"

"Good God, you're mad if you think I'm that good at pretending." He turned her face to his, his eyes glittering as he moved his gaze slowly over her. "Surely you could tell I wanted you, that every time I kissed you, I could hardly keep from tearing your clothes off."

His words shocked her. Since this afternoon, it hadn't occurred to her that his sensual overtures had been anything but part of his "mission" to find the truth. Could he mean what he said? Or was it one more way to spare her feelings?

Steeling herself against the desire she surely imagined in his face, she tried to pull away, but he slid his arm around her waist to draw her close.

"Does it frighten you to hear that?" he said hoarsely.

"Because it bloody well frightens me that I desire you more than I've ever desired any other woman."

Oh, how she wanted to believe him.

"Why do you think I came here tonight?" he persisted. "I didn't have to wait in the rain and pray you'd give me the chance to explain." He fixed her with eyes as tempestuous as the storm he'd left. "But I couldn't bear not seeing you again." He rubbed his thumb over her lower lip, sending a traitorous tingling through her. "I couldn't stand the thought of never touching you or holding you or kissing you . . ."

He said the last words on a breath, giving her full warning he was going to kiss her again. Yet she seemed incapable of doing anything but waiting for his lips to touch hers.

And when they did, a shudder broke over her, the shudder of a person finally given exactly what she wants. Her eyes slid closed as she parted her lips and let him drink of her mouth in a slow, sensuous kiss that stole her breath . . . her strength . . . her will.

It was probably only seconds before he drew back, but it felt like an eternity. When it was over, she felt confused. How could her body betray her by accepting the kiss of a man who'd sought to have her arrested?

He must have wondered the same thing, for he pressed his forehead to hers and murmured in an incredulous voice, "You truly don't hate me."

She had no earthly idea what to say.

"I know I had no right to that kiss," he whispered, "but I've spent three sleepless nights remembering that time in your kitchen and wanting you. I couldn't help myself."

And wanting you. The words echoed through a heart already torn by all he'd said to her.

"Catrin?" he murmured, his mouth so very close to hers. "Can you ever forgive me for lying to you?"

With a groan, she left his embrace to go stand by the window. No matter how much her mind told her he'd behaved in an ungentlemanly manner, her heart urged her to consider what she would have done in his place. If Bos had been murdered, she'd have told any number of lies to search out his killer. And she'd only known Bos two years, whereas Lord Mansfield had been Evan's friend much longer.

"Catrin?" Evan hadn't moved from his stance by the fire. "Can you forgive me?"

She knew what her answer must be. "I suppose I can."

He let out a breath. "Thank you."

Then she felt him move to stand behind her, but she didn't realize how close until he stroked her hair, which had tumbled down when she'd removed her cloak. He swept the mass aside, then planted a kiss on her bare shoulder.

Desire slammed into her, panicking her. It was one thing to forgive him, but quite another to let him stay here to kiss and caress . . . and do things that might lead to other things.

"Now that you have my forgiveness," she choked out, "you . . . you can leave here with a clear conscience."

He nuzzled her hair. "I don't want to leave. And you don't want me to, either."

Her traitorous body trembled. "That doesn't signify."

"Doesn't it?"

He turned her to face him, and they stared at each other in silence. His hands rested on her waist, but he made no attempt to do more. Still, the light in his eyes promised so much, reminding her that he'd been the only man to capture her desires, to transform her into a wild woman with one long kiss.

A knock at the door made them both jump. Evan dropped his hands, though he kept his gaze locked on her.

"Madam?" called Bos through the door. "It has been more than five minutes. Shall I come back in?"

Catrin froze, unable to tear her gaze from Evan. He made no sound, yet fear that she might send him away flickered in his eyes.

"Madam?" Bos's voice now held a note of urgency.

"I hear you." Oh, what to do? She didn't want to end this moment with Evan. And if she said, "Yes, Bos, we're finished here," it would be over.

"I'll make this easy for you," Evan said in a low voice. "If you call your watchdog back in, I'll leave and never disturb you again." His eyes burned into hers. "But if you send him away, I *will* make love to you. I'll lay you down on that bed there and show you all the desire that's built in me from the day I saw you emerge from the lake."

The clear promise in his words, in his eyes, roused her like nothing ever had.

"Those are your only two choices," he went on. "I can't continue in this in-between state, spending every night wanting you. If I cannot have you, then I must leave. It's up to you."

She sucked in an aching breath. He asked so much . . .

too much . . . offering only the pleasures of a moment. After it was over, she'd be spoiled for any other man. She might even find herself with child.

So she should chide him for his arrogance and send him away. She should flee as fast as her legs would carry her. And yet . . .

Night after lonely night stretched ahead of her. What good was it to be able to marry when no other man affected her as Evan did? What did it matter if he spoiled her for another, when she didn't want another?

She called out, "Bos? Come in, please."

Pain slashed over Evan's face. Then Bos entered and Catrin said, "I no longer require your services this evening. You are dismissed."

Evan stared at her disbelievingly as Bos sputtered, "But madam, do you mean you wish me to leave you alone with this—"

"You are dismissed," Catrin said more firmly, unable to tear her gaze from Evan. *Please, Bos, for once behave as my servant and not my guardian.*

A long silence ensued. She thought she could hear every drop of wax hitting the sconces.

Then Bos sighed. "As you wish, madam." And he left, closing the door behind him.

12

*E*van could hardly believe it. They were alone. Despite his lies, she'd chosen him.

"Good God, Catrin." He stroked her face. "I thought when you called Bos in—"

"If I hadn't let him see I was unharmed, he wouldn't have left."

"I'm glad you sent him away." He trailed his fingers over her blushing cheek. She was his now, *his* by her own choice. "I don't know what I would have done if you'd sent me away instead."

"I should have. I shouldn't have even agreed to see—"

He kissed her, muffling any further protests. He wouldn't let her have regrets, not tonight. Drawing her close, he plundered her mouth, relieved that though her mind still vacillated, her body knew exactly what it wanted. She looped her arms about his neck and pressed against him with the guilelessness of a woman who had no idea how much she was about to relinquish.

Her innocence. And though she believed she couldn't ever marry and thus would never need it, he felt a stab of guilt at what he was going to take from her.

That didn't last long once his body responded to her nearness, her sweetness, her untutored enjoyment. Never had he held a woman whose passion mirrored his, who made him feel driven and hot and eager to do anything to experience her pleasures.

With Catrin, desire was a golden promise of fulfillment. She was so entirely his. When he smoothed one hand over the lovely curve of her hip, then up her waist to cover her rounded breast, she groaned and arched into his hand like a seagull lifting its body into the wind.

It fired his memory of how she'd looked emerging from the lake, her rosy nipples showing through her shift. He wanted to see her like that again. Or better yet, bared entirely, so he could stroke her thighs and the lush cleft between them.

Instead, he contented himself with exploring every secret of her warm, wet mouth as he kneaded her breast through her clothes. Only when he had her trembling did he move his lips down to her collarbone, planting open-mouthed kisses everywhere. Pushing down the neck of her bodice, stays, and shift, he found her breast with his mouth and drew hard on the pebbled nipple.

She dug her fingers into his shoulders. "Oh, *Evan* . . ."

The eager whisper drove him on until he had her breasts bared and was lavishing attention on one delicious crest, then the other, reveling in how she twisted her body blindly against him in the urgency of her need.

His need was just as urgent. He wanted to bury himself deep, to feel her legs clamp about him. Oh, the wicked things he wanted to do with her . . . taste her everywhere . . . have her taste him . . .

And he'd do them all eventually, but he must be careful with his darling. She wasn't used to passion. The last thing he wanted was to frighten her off.

He drew his hand from her. Her closed eyes and parted lips inflamed him. "I want to see you naked. Will you let me?"

Her eyes flew open. "I . . . I don't know. I have no idea what I should do."

With a low chuckle, he turned her around to undo the buttons and ties that held her gown closed. "Don't worry. I know exactly what you should do."

She went still as he pushed her gown off her shoulders. "I know you do. You've probably done this with countless women."

"Not countless." He dispensed with her stays, leaving her wearing only her shift. Seeing her like that made him grow unbearably hard. "And no one I've ever wanted as much as you."

He turned her to face him and cupped her cheek, feeling the heat of her blush against his palm. "Would it help if I let you take *my* clothes off, too?"

Her eyes went wide. "That would make it worse! Oh, Evan, I shouldn't do this! It's wrong!"

"Does it feel wrong?" He tugged loose the ties of her shift, then dragged the muslin slowly off her shoulders until she stood there naked.

"Yes ... no ..." She trailed off as he raked his gaze down her body ... to the pert breasts ... the trim waist ... the slender hips.

Her blush spread over her when his gaze reached her triangle of silky hair. She tried to cover herself with her hands, but he caught them, murmuring, "Please, let me see all of you. I've dreamed of it in the night, my darling."

The endearment seemed to affect her, for although she ducked her head, she let him hold her hands aside and made no move to stop him as his gaze drifted down over her long legs, with their well-turned calves encased in stockings.

A faint hint of lilacs lingered, reminding him that she was of a higher class ... one that bathed daily in lilac-scented water and wore clothes of finest muslin.

As a boy, he'd watched her kind come and go from Llynwydd. He'd marveled at their beautiful garb and clean scent, for on the farm, he'd worn only rough wool and homespun and had been lucky to bathe once a week.

Now, of course, he could have baths whenever he wanted and dress in fine clothes and mingle with the beautiful people he'd admired from afar. But a voice inside always whispered that he was naught but a farmer's son pretending to be something better.

That voice clamored at him now, telling him he had no right to this exquisite woman with her blushes and innocence ... no right to take a knight's daughter to bed.

Firmly, he squelched the voice. Catrin didn't care about his rank. And she wanted him. That was all that mattered.

He bent on one knee to untie her garters, then removed

both her stockings and her dainty shoes. He stroked up the inside of her thigh, feeling her quiver. "Does it feel wrong to have me touch you like this?" His throat felt raw with his need. "Because it feels right to me. I've lain awake every night since we met, wondering if your skin could be as soft as it looked, or your legs so lovely."

He rose but kept his hand on her thigh, moving it higher until he was stroking the skin so close to her thatch of curls that they brushed his hand.

When he covered the hair with his palm, she gasped, but he gave her no time to protest. He took her mouth again, this time more roughly and thoroughly to distract her as he ran his finger along the silken folds.

She was so damp and warm that he moaned in sheer pleasure. She might be nervous, but she wanted him, thank God.

When he began to tease and rub her, he thought she'd jump out of his arms, but as he caressed her more boldly, she groaned and pushed against him.

"It feels right, doesn't it, darling," he murmured against her lips.

Catrin scarcely knew what to answer as he moved his hungry mouth to her breast, sucking at it with delicious fervor. It did feel right . . . and wonderful and thrilling. His mouth roused aches she'd never felt, even in her lonely bed.

Such magical fingers, too! When one delved inside her, she shuddered at the outrageous intimacy. But as he continued to fondle her, smoothing her fluid warmth over her skin until she tingled all over down there, her shock turned to an absolute pleasure so stunning, she thought she'd die.

No one had told her it would be like this. On the night before Catrin's wedding, Grandmother had termed lovemaking a "sometimes pleasant duty," but had warned there'd be pain the first time. Catrin could easily see how, for she couldn't imagine anyone planting something inside her the way her grandmother had described.

But there was no pain yet, just a consuming need that made her fist her hands in his shirt, then flex her fingers against his linen-draped muscles.

She wanted to touch those muscles more fully, to stroke his bare chest. Feeling a bit foolish, she pulled loose the ties of his shirt. She'd never undressed a man before and wasn't sure how, but the moment he felt her hands, he helped her, drawing back only long enough to tug his shirt over his head. Then he jerked his breeches, drawers, and hose off. And he was naked, too.

Holy God in heaven. His was not the body of a scholar, though she'd guessed as much from the fine figure he'd always cut in his swallow-tailed coat and snug breeches. But how had he gained such muscular shoulders and arms? Or the broad chest with its trickle of hair passing down between more of those well-defined muscles to a lean waist and then down to . . .

She yanked her gaze back to his face, blood flooding her cheeks.

"Am I the first man you've seen naked?" he rasped.

She bobbed her head.

"Then perhaps you should do more than look." With a dark smile, he took her hand and placed it on his chest.

The thought of touching him shot a thrill through her.

She ran her fingers down the sculpted flesh and the ridges of his stomach, marveling at how firm he was. When she moved her hand over his belly with its shadowed navel, his muscles bunched and tightened, and he shuddered.

She stopped, but he groaned and moved her hand lower until it actually rested on his jutting member. Somehow, his hand over hers, pressing her against him, freed her to explore him with all the curiosity she'd been embarrassed to admit. As she stroked the silky skin and ran her finger over the rounded tip, he uttered a ragged sigh.

Then she made the mistake of looking, and she froze, her hand still on him. So this hard shaft was to go inside her? But how? It was too big. It would surely cleave her in two!

In a panic, she jerked her hand from him, but he caught her fingers, lifting them to his lips and kissing them one by one. "Has anyone told you what lovemaking is about, what a man does to a woman in bed?"

Unable to look at him, she nodded.

"Then you probably know that it hurts the first time."

She nodded again, more insistently.

He rubbed her hand against his cheek. "I assure you the pain is fleeting."

Shaking her head in disbelief, she tried to back away, but he caught her head in his hands, forcing her to stare into his fathomless eyes.

"I wouldn't lie to you about this, not even to gain my own pleasure. It will hurt at first, but you must believe me when I say the pain fades quickly. And after that, you'll enjoy it. I'll do whatever I can to make sure that you do."

As she stared at him uncertainly, he brushed kisses on her cheeks, her nose, her brow. "*Everything* I can, I swear," he added in a husky voice. Then, before she could say another word, he lifted her in his arms and carried her to the bed.

She kept her eyes fixed on him as he laid her down. She didn't know how to contain her fear, and she wanted to protest that she hadn't really meant him to do this at all. But she couldn't. Besides, if she said no, he would leave, and she didn't want that, either.

He seemed to recognize her fears, for he lay down beside her and began to caress her body with soothing strokes. "You must tell me what feels good and what doesn't. You must help me find your pleasure places."

She turned her face away, feeling exposed and embarrassed, but he covered her breast with his hand. "This is no time for shyness, darling. Outside of the bedroom you may be reticent, but here, with me, you must be bold. How else will I know how to please you?"

He thumbed her nipple in teasing circles, his voice dropping to a sensuous murmur. "Does this please you?"

When she remained silent, he started to pull his hand away, but she covered it and pressed it to her breast with a mute look of entreaty.

He resumed his caresses. "Yes, you needn't use words. Let your body speak for you."

What he said unleashed her reluctance. There was something less shameful about speaking to him in touches, drawing his hands to all the places of her body that had burned for him in the middle of the night.

And he obliged her every wish. When she pulled his head down, he took her mouth again, with tender delicacy at first and then with more ardor, plunging his tongue inside to mate with hers. When she timidly pushed his hand below her waist, he needed no more provocation to run his hands over her belly, but he soon found places to caress that she'd never dreamed were so sensitive . . . her navel . . . behind her knees . . . inside her thighs to coax her legs apart so he could settle his hard body in the juncture.

That in itself gave her an unexpected pleasure only enhanced when he settled his hand there, rubbing between her legs until she thrust her hips boldly against those maddening fingers in an urgent need for more.

She could tell he wanted more, too, for his hand shook as he caressed her, and a sheen of sweat broke out on his forehead. But he was patient and slow, only slipping his finger inside her when she prompted it by widening her legs.

"That's it, darling," he murmured against her lips. "Open yourself for me. Let me in."

She clutched his shoulders, moaning her delight as his fingers drove inside the tight passage, deeper and more intimately until suddenly, he lifted his body slightly off hers. Then it was no longer his fingers there but something harder, bigger, inching up insistently inside her.

Her haze of pleasure shattered. Panicking, she bucked against him as if to throw him off, but that only succeeded in driving him farther inside her. Then he came up against something and paused.

She gazed at him in wide-eyed fear as the feeling of invasion intensified. "Evan? Are you sure that this is the way?"

He gave her a strained smile. "I am quite sure."

His arms were tense as they bracketed her body. He seemed to be controlling himself only with the greatest effort. Though she appreciated his concern, it didn't lessen the strange feeling that she was his captive, her thighs widened to receive him . . . her breasts pressed beneath his chest . . . and that hard part of him delving into her as if to reach her soul.

He would never let her go, his glittering eyes seemed to say, and his hard mouth, too, as he bent to take her mouth in a long kiss.

Then he gave a hard thrust that planted him fully inside her. There was indeed pain, but it wasn't the terrible one she'd feared. Instead, a fleeting feeling, as of something small tearing inside her, came and then was gone.

She wiggled her hips, curious to see if that was all, and he seemed to take that for an invitation, for he drew out and drove in again, his mouth devouring hers. He was marking her as his, and she felt it in every thrust of his hips, every stab of his tongue.

And she *wanted* to be his, she discovered, as his movements began to warm and then excite her. She didn't understand why the feel of him inside her sent hot, melting pleasure spreading throughout her body, but she didn't stop to think on it. She simply let the enjoyment overtake her, push her on and up toward some height she could only glimpse.

"Ah, darling, you feel so good," he muttered against her mouth, scattering kisses over her cheeks and jaw. "You can't know . . ."

"I . . . I can . . . I do . . ." She met his thrusts, at first timidly and then with abandon. He felt wonderful, as if he belonged inside her, as if she'd been waiting all her life for him to join her in this incredible dance.

He plunged deeper and harder and faster, each thrust carrying her higher, like a runaway coach racing up the slopes of Black Mountain. The brush of his taut belly against hers, the tantalizing look of hunger in his face, the delicious slide of him inside her made her insensible, until she no longer thought of anything but opening to him, pushing against him more and more and more . . .

The world exploded. "Oh, *Evan!*" She grasped him close as wave after wave of bliss inundated her. "Yes, oh, yes!"

"My darling!" he cried out and drove into her with one mighty thrust. Something warm and liquid filled her as they strained against each other. Then he sank against her body. "My sweet . . . darling . . . Catrin . . ."

He lay atop her, twitching a little as she shook beneath him. Then, as her body calmed, she dropped into a contented peace, warmed by the feel of him against her and the aftermath of what they'd just shared.

After a moment, she felt him nibble her earlobe. "Are you all right?"

At the sound of his voice, so calm and normal, her innate shyness reasserted itself and all she could manage was a nod. Then it hit her. She'd done it. She'd given her innocence to Evan, despite all the reasons she shouldn't have. By heaven, she was a ruined woman.

Yet she didn't feel ruined. She felt alive and full of joy. Was this what she'd missed all these years? No wonder widows took lovers. Once they'd tasted this, they weren't likely to want to abandon it.

Then again, she couldn't imagine sharing this with anyone but him. It wouldn't be the same; she was sure of it.

Evan slid off to lie at her side, resting one hand on her belly as he propped his head up on the other. "Was there very much pain?"

"Only a little."

"Good." Not looking at her, he traced circles around her navel. "And was I right? Did you end up enjoying it?"

His uncertainty gave her a start. Didn't he know? He always seemed so sure of himself.

That drove away her shyness. She stared up at the features she'd come to know so well. "It was the most wonderful thing I've ever felt."

When he met her gaze, his eyes shone. "I've never had that with any other woman." He dropped a kiss on her nose. "But from the moment I saw you, I knew it would be special."

Special, she thought with a little stab of disappointment. Yes, it had been special for her, too, and so much more. Now what was to happen between them? What would he do? Leave her? Stay?

She didn't want to ask and ruin the pleasure of the moment. But as he covered her mouth in a tender kiss, only one thought played through her mind.

After this, what next?

13

As the first streaks of dawn brightened the room, Evan slid from the bed. Years of getting up at dawn on the farm had made him an incurable early riser. But Catrin slept blissfully, her lips curved in a secret smile and her hair scattered across the pillow like crushed ebony silk. Though he ached to twine each curl around his fingers, he didn't want to wake her. She needed the rest.

He shouldn't have taken her the second time, sore as she must have been. Yet once hadn't been enough for him . . . nor her, either, judging from her enthusiasm. He bore marks on his shoulders where her fingernails had dug into him as she'd writhed and cried out her enjoyment.

The memory aroused him again, damn it. But he must give her body a chance to adjust. Despite her passion, she'd been a virgin. The thought doused his arousal like a cold bath. He'd never taken a woman's innocence. Now what was he to do about it?

After finding his freshly pressed clothes on a stool outside the door, he dressed quickly. He needed to think, and he couldn't do it here, with Catrin looking so luscious. He'd want to touch her . . . kiss her . . . make love to her again. He'd best find somewhere quiet, where the servants wouldn't notice him.

As he slipped from the room, his mind raced. One thing was certain—he couldn't simply walk away. How could he endure never again being with her or talking to her or holding her?

He walked down the hall to the stairs. Why did she affect him like this? Though he couldn't deny the appeal of her elfin looks and lithe body, he'd met women more beautiful. But none had made him feel like a king.

Women of her class had always been aware of his unsuitability. In London society, he'd been classed as "Justin's friend, a genius but a farmer's son." A man had once described him as "not a bad chap really, if he weren't a penniless Welshman. You know what I mean."

What he'd meant was "an immoral scoundrel who'd as soon steal your sheep as buy them." How did that popular English rhyme go? "Taffy is a Welshman, Taffy is a thief." It didn't matter that Evan's work was highly respected, that he behaved like a gentleman, that he had lofty friends. As soon as he came around any gentleman's daughter, his background was all that mattered.

Of course, Catrin knew nothing of that. Was that why he wanted her, because she represented the unobtainable? Perhaps he simply longed to have someone like him for who he was.

No, he didn't think so. Even before he'd known who she

was, she'd intrigued him. Catrin emanated a captivating blend of intelligence and shyness. She was bright but didn't know it . . . pretty but uncertain of her appeal . . . wealthy but didn't care.

What was more, she'd grown up in the same limbo as he, never quite fitting in and trying to hide how much it mattered. Watching her bravely navigate those treacherous waters brought out all his protective instincts.

That was the trouble. Now he felt responsible for her. He ought to offer marriage, even if she refused and clung to her ridiculous belief in that curse.

God, but she would make a marvelous wife. Not only would she be the rare woman who understood his work and his absorption with it, but she would be perfect in every other way . . . considerate, passionate . . . refined.

Just like Henrietta had been.

His smile faded as he hurried down the stairs, remembering the night Henrietta had broken with him because of what she'd seen him do in a temper. But at least he hadn't harmed *her*. What if he ever lost his temper with shy, delicate Catrin and . . . and hurt her? It would destroy her.

It would destroy *him*. No, marriage wasn't wise . . . to Catrin or anyone else. Besides, Catrin didn't expect or want him to marry her. She truly believed in that bloody curse.

So what other choices were there? He couldn't, *wouldn't*, end their liaison. She'd crept into his heart, and he couldn't tear her out. But could he stand being her sometime lover, coming here when he could, living from visit to visit as he carried on his real life in Cambridge?

No. Yet the only other choice was to persuade her to return with him.

He paused at the bottom of the stairs, glancing around at her well-appointed manor. How could he ask her to leave all this to live in a scholar's lodgings, sneaking about like a pariah? That wasn't for Catrin.

He headed toward some doors that looked as if they might lead to a parlor, where he could be alone.

There was one choice he hadn't considered: He could give up his position as fellow and live here with her. He snorted. Right. Ask her to be considered a whore by all who knew her and to bear him bastard children. Even if she agreed, he could not.

He opened a door and found what appeared to be her study. A half-knitted shawl lay draped across a delicate writing table with spindly legs and a fragile chair that would probably collapse under Evan's weight.

Even the bookshelves had feminine touches. Curious to see what kind of books she preferred, he scanned the titles. Scholarly works. Tomes about myths and legends. And she did indeed have a copy of *The Development of Celtic Languages*. That made him smile.

Suddenly he came to a shelf slightly out of kilter. When he pushed on it, it swung in a fraction. A secret compartment, of all things. Who'd have thought Catrin would have such an archaic safe—if she even knew it was there.

He pushed it in all the way. The shelf slid open on well-oiled hinges, and sunlight glinted off something metal. When the shelf shuddered to a stop, he stared at the object, his blood running cold. Before him sat a massive bronze chalice.

Memory slammed into him, of the night Justin had been murdered and had shown him the chalice Catrin wanted to buy. *This* chalice.

"Oh God." He picked it up to examine it, praying he was wrong and knowing he wasn't. He'd have recognized the hideous vessel anywhere. It had the same strange etchings, the same unusual coded letters.

A sense of betrayal sliced him so deeply, he reeled. If Catrin had the chalice, then she had indeed met with Justin. More importantly, she'd lied about it, so convincingly that he'd abandoned his suspicions.

His sweet, shy Catrin wasn't what he'd supposed at all.

The ramifications so overwhelmed him that at first he didn't hear the door open. But when a soft voice said, "Evan?" he whirled around, the chalice still clutched in his hand.

She looked like an angel in her white wrapper, with her raven curls in a tangle on her shoulders . . . her lips full and red . . . her eyes still dazed from sleep.

But she wasn't an angel—a fact that was confirmed when she caught sight of what he held and went pale as death.

That drove a stake through his gut. "Come in and close the door," he commanded. "It's time you and I had an honest discussion of what happened in London."

~

Catrin's heart pounded as she crossed the threshold. This was horrible. "I know what you must be thinking, but—"

"Shut the door!" he hissed.

She did as he said. How would she ever explain this?

He shook the chalice at her, his eyes glittering like the coals of hell. "This is the chalice you claimed you didn't buy from Justin."

She swallowed hard. She'd never seen Evan like this. Even when he'd fought David, he hadn't been so angry. "Yes. You know it is."

With a curse, Evan hurled it across the room, knocking a painting off the wall. She jumped back a step. By heaven, what would he do?

She heard steps running down the hall toward the study, but Evan didn't even seem to notice.

"Let me see if I've assessed the situation correctly." He advanced on her in a fury. "Obviously, you lied about failing to acquire it."

Unable to speak, she backed away. Facing David's anger had been bad enough, but facing Evan's was like staring into the open mouth of a dragon.

He swept his arm across her writing desk, sending papers and quills and an ink bottle flying. Then he pounded his fist on the cleared top. "Answer me!"

"Y-yes. I lied."

"Did you also lie about never meeting Justin? Did you actually buy this from him? Or did you have it stolen before he could reach the inn?"

That sparked her temper. "Now see here, you know I could never do such an awful thing!"

"Yesterday I knew it." Gritting his teeth, he approached her. "But that was before I learned how easily you lie."

The unfair words tore her apart. "How dare you! You lied to me from the moment you came here."

"I was trying to get at the truth. You, on the other hand, were covering up a crime, which is ten times worse than what I did!"

"A crime?" How could this man have spent such a beautiful night with her and then accuse her of . . . "What are you saying? That I *murdered* your friend?"

The word "murder" seemed to bring him up short. "I don't think you drove the knife in yourself." He took a shuddering breath. "But you could have hired someone else to murder him. Either you had him waylaid before he reached the inn, or you sent men after him when your meeting didn't work out as planned." His gaze hardened. "You wanted that chalice badly. I've known that all along."

She reeled from him in shock. The man was *serious*. "You're insane." She must escape him and his crazy accusations. Turning for the door, she tried to open it, but before she could, he slammed it shut.

Then he turned the key in the lock and pocketed it as he faced her. "Insane? I was insane to believe you innocent! I ignored all the questionable evidence and listened to you when you claimed you'd had nothing to do with it!"

His voice grew bitter. "Even Quinley said I was a fool to believe you, but I was so . . . bloody enamored of you that I . . ." He speared his fingers through his hair. "I even threatened to use my influence to have him dismissed for incompetence if he tried to arrest you. What an ass I made of myself!"

That he'd defended her to Quinley gave her pause. She watched as he paced, his eyes haunted. He *didn't* believe this horrible thing about her. He couldn't. He was angry and confused right now because he'd found the chalice, but once his anger passed he'd realize she was innocent. He must!

A timid knock came at the door. "Madam? Is everything all right in there?"

Evan's head snapped around as Catrin recognized the voice of one of the maids. His hard gaze dared her to call out for help.

She considered it; he was behaving like a crazed beast. Yet somewhere in his anger, Evan knew the truth about her. She had to help him find it, make him see she could never have done this dreadful thing.

But she must tell the maids something or they'd fetch Bos to open the door. Catrin forced calmness into her voice as she called out, "I'm fine. I accidentally knocked over something. Go tell Mrs. Griffiths to see about preparing breakfast, and I'll summon you if there's a problem."

There was a moment of silence outside the door, then whispers as servants conferred. But seconds later, she heard footsteps moving away. Thank heaven.

Evan cast her an insolent look. "You're good at lying, aren't you? I wonder what your servants would say if they knew what you'd done. Would your precious Bos strive to protect you if he knew the truth?"

She refused to let him see how his words lacerated her. "Bos already knows what happened in London."

Evan blinked. "Everything? What you did to acquire that chalice?"

"I'll tell you exactly what he knows." She strove for calm. She would never convince Evan if she lapsed into hysterics. "He knows I traveled to London with two hundred pounds. He knows I went to the Green Goat to meet Lord Mansfield. I felt uneasy in the road outside the inn." She drew a steadying breath. "After I purchased the chalice from Lord Mansfield, some instinctive fear of danger made me leave through a back door and return to my lodgings."

A muscle worked in his jaw. "So you lied to Bos, too."

Tears burning her eyes, she moved closer. "I didn't lie. That's exactly what happened, and the only difference between what I told you at first and what I'm telling you now is that I did meet with your friend and buy the chalice. But everything else is the same. I swear I never did anything wrong."

Needing a connection to him, she touched his arm.

"Take your hand off me!" he hissed, jerking back as if he'd been burned.

Desperation clawed at her. "I didn't have anything to do with Lord Mansfield's murder! You must believe me!"

"How can I?" His face filled with pain. "Everything shows your guilt. The missing letter . . . the lies to me and Quinley . . . the way you fled London without a word to anyone about your meeting with Justin!"

"I don't know what happened to the letter, but I fled London because I was afraid everyone would jump to the same conclusions you are!" She gripped the top of a chair. "I admit I lied about buying the chalice from your friend. But when he left, I swear he was whole and healthy and in possession of two hundred pounds!"

Whirling away, he crossed the room. "Then why didn't you tell me the truth about this monstrosity?" He kicked it. "If you were so bloody innocent, why did you lie even when you didn't know my purpose here?"

That wretched lie again. As usual, she'd been afraid to risk revealing too much of herself to anyone. And her reticence had served her ill.

"I didn't mean to tell you about it at all," she said. "I feared from the beginning that you might be an investigator come from London to find out what had happened. I didn't want to take any chances."

"The guilty fear taking chances, not the innocent. And the innocent don't lie. They don't run." He gestured to her safe. "They don't hide things in secret compartments."

Remembering how betrayed she'd felt yesterday when she'd discovered his deception, she could understand his anger, but it didn't alleviate the knot of hurt festering in her belly. After everything they'd done . . . after all the sweet things he'd murmured last night, how could he think so ill of her?

"The innocent can still be afraid," she whispered. "People are sent to prison on little more than supposition sometimes. Don't you think I realized how my presence at that inn looked in light of Lord Mansfield's murder? Don't you understand why I had to protect myself?"

He scooped up the chalice. "I don't even understand why this bloody thing is so important to you." As he held the drinking vessel up, sunlight glittered off the bronze. "For God's sake, it's not even worth the money you paid!"

"It's worth *more* than that to me. Without it, I can't marry and have children—not if I want their father to see them grow up. I can't ensure the future of my tenants and servants. Women of property may be rare, but they have the same responsibilities as men of property. They must have heirs to maintain the property when they're gone."

He cast her a hard look. "So you made sure you gained it at any cost."

"Not at the cost of seeing anyone hurt!" Frustration gripped her. "Did last night mean nothing to you? After that, how can you think me capable of murder?"

His eyes met hers, and she glimpsed his turmoil. Then he wrenched his gaze away. "Last night you shared every intimacy a woman can with a man, knowing that you'd lied to me. Last night you made me beg forgiveness for *my* lies when yours were far worse." He sucked in a ragged breath. "You aren't the woman I thought. I no longer know *what* you're capable of."

She went to his side. "That's not true. Deep in your heart, you know my true character. I'm sure of it!"

He fixed her with a glittering gaze. "You think because I desire . . . *desired* you, you can make me dance to your tune, that my cursed attraction to you will blot out everything. But it won't."

She laid her hand on his chest. "Please, Evan, you must—"

"I won't listen to more of this, do you hear?" He grabbed her hand and jerked her up close to him. "You can touch me, you can murmur your soft, false words, but it won't work. I won't be made a fool of anymore!"

In his eyes shimmered a vast darkness, like in bottomless lakes rumored to hold demons in their depths. She'd glimpsed that darkness a few times and known there was an edge to his seemingly easy accord with life, but she'd never had to look into it so deeply. Clearly there was more to his distrust than anger over her lies, or determination to avenge his friend's death.

If she could only pull him out of that all-encompassing darkness. "I'm sorry for not telling you before, but you know what a coward I am."

"A coward." The cool distance in his tone struck fear in her. "Who marched off to London all alone to gain her property, who did whatever it took to make sure she could marry again."

He let the chalice fall with a thud at her feet. With in-drawn breath, he lifted his hand to stroke the side of her face. But though his touch was almost a caress, his expression was hard.

"I should have listened to Quinley," he murmured. "I should have listened to all those who termed you pretty and deadly. But I've always been taught to revere and pro-tect women like you." His tone grew brittle. "I've spent a lifetime apologizing for what I am to your kind, but I can see it's a habit I must break."

"What do you mean, 'your kind'? How am I any differ-ent from you?"

His face grew even fiercer. "I'm a farmer's son, unfit to kiss your boots and certainly to bed you." He dragged her against him until she could feel every muscle in his un-yielding body. "But that doesn't mean I'm blind. Even I can see the corruption lying at the core of your beauty and gentility."

His words took her aback. His being a farmer's son was

of no consequence to her, but it was obviously of great consequence to him.

She struggled to find words that might reach him through his darkness. "It's true I'm not the kind of woman to revere. But I know none who is, no matter what her class. Like you, I'm simply trying to muddle through life as best I can, and I make mistakes. I made several in the past two weeks, but none so heinous as you seem to think."

When he shut his eyes as if to close her off, she lifted her hand to stroke his hair. "Must I be either angel or devil? Can't you see I'm just a woman, as fallible as everyone else?"

He groaned. His head moved infinitesimally against her hand as if to meet her caress. Then, with a low curse, he thrust her away. "You are not 'just a woman.'" His eyes snapped open. With a frankness bordering on insolence, he let his gaze trail down her thinly clad body, and despite her fear, desire rose again in her belly. How could he still affect her, even after the terrible things he'd said?

When he spoke again, his voice shook, but whether with anger or desire, she couldn't tell. "I don't know what you are yet, but you could never be 'just a woman.'"

They stood frozen. She could hear his tortured breathing, and the wild light in his eyes made a shiver ripple over her. "So what happens now?" she asked.

"Quinley is staying at the Red Dragon. We'll take the chalice and you'll tell him your new version of what happened. Then he'll have to decide what to do with you."

Terror gripped her. When he bent to pick up the chalice, she grabbed it at the same time he did. "You can't do this to me! I'm innocent!"

He lifted one eyebrow, his gaze so cold it froze her heart. "Then you'll have no trouble convincing Quinley of that, will you?"

She couldn't believe he would drag her before Quinley on the basis of nothing but his wild suspicions.

Tugging the chalice free of her numb fingers, he went to look out the window. "You have two choices. Call for your servants and have them throw me out, in which case I'll tell Quinley everything, and leave it to him to have you dragged from your home. Or go with me to Llanddeusant of your own free will and tell him what you've told me."

He glanced at her. "No matter what you choose, I *will* make sure Quinley hears the story."

"You mean, your distorted version of the story!" She approached him, heedless of how her wrapper had fallen open to expose her shift. "After last night, how could you do this?"

Paling, he stared at her. Then his gaze moved down her throat to the swells of her breasts that showed above the edge of her shift. He swallowed convulsively, one of his hands tightening on the chalice as his hungry gaze moved lower.

Then, with an oath, he stalked past her to the door. He unlocked it. "For God's sake, go put some clothes on. I'll give you ten minutes to dress while I see to the horses. If you're not down here when I'm ready to leave, I'll leave without you." He paused. "But I'll be back. And I'll have Quinley with me." Yanking the door open, he strode from the room.

Catrin drew her wrapper closed with shaky fingers.

He'd left her no choice. She couldn't let him go to Quinley alone with his mad suspicions. Nor could she risk having Quinley come here, forcing her servants to either defend or hide her. She had to go with Evan.

She wanted to cry, to rage against his unfairness. She wanted to nurse the devastating wound Evan's accusations had inflicted on her pride . . . her heart . . . her soul.

But she had no time for that. So she pulled her wrapper tight and squared her shoulders, tamping down the pain.

He was in for a surprise if he thought he could bully her into a jail cell and destroy everything she held dear. She couldn't afford to be a coward anymore.

She was the Lady of the Mists and the descendant of a druidess. She would not go without a fight.

14

*E*van rode toward Llanddeusant with grim purpose. He didn't need to look over to know that Catrin was keeping up with him. After all, he'd won the first half of the battle by getting her to come with him.

How she'd convinced the servants that nothing was amiss he didn't know, but he didn't really care. She excelled at lying.

He stole a glance at her, then regretted it. Good God, how did she manage to look so angelic on another of her gentle ponies? It wasn't just her gown of spotted muslin or her lace-trimmed spencer. It was the delicate blush of her cheeks, as pink and fragile as the satin lining of her bonnet. It was the trembling of her lips as she set her face stoically forward. She made him feel like a monster.

Deuce take the woman! What right had she to look like an affronted goddess? His fists tightened on the reins. She ought to look like a murderess, instead of sitting so proudly, her very manner proclaiming her innocence.

His knee bumped the bag that held the chalice, and he grimaced. She'd been desperate to obtain it, desperate to make sure she could marry someone—anyone.

Yet she'd refused Morys's suit, even after she'd gained her precious drinking vessel.

The thought brought him up short. It *was* odd she would go to such lengths, then refuse the one man in Llanddeusant most suitable to be her husband.

I can't marry someone I don't love, she'd said. A strange sentiment for a woman whose blood ran cold in her veins.

Except when she was in his bed.

And that was another thing. Why had she let him bed her? It made no sense. She should have sent him away, secure in the knowledge that she'd escaped detection.

He groaned. He mustn't think about it anymore or he'd go mad. Best to leave the sorting of truth from lies to Quinley. At least the investigator could be objective.

To his relief, they'd reached the Red Dragon. At last he could give her to someone else. If he spent more time brooding, he'd start making excuses for her.

When they rode into the inn yard, the ostler rushed out to take his horse, casting a speculative eye on him and Catrin. "Good morning, sir. Mrs. Llewellyn has been in a tizzy worrying about you. With the storm last night, she thought you might have lost your way or fallen into a ravine."

Evan forced a smile. "I did lose my way, but Mrs. Price was kind enough to give me shelter for the night."

He dismounted, slinging the bag with the chalice over one shoulder as the ostler helped Catrin down from her horse. When Evan led her into the inn, she murmured, "Thank you for lying to the ostler. I already have enough problems with my reputation."

Her gratitude irritated him. "I didn't do it to save your reputation. But I can't have the town up in arms about the stranger who has come to hand Mrs. Price over to the authorities."

She stiffened. "I forgot that the courteous Evan Newcome of these past few days has been replaced by a madman bent on vengeance." Then she swept through the door ahead of him.

He followed at a leisurely pace, eyes narrowing. So she had claws, did she? Well, she'd best keep them sheathed if she wanted to enlist Quinley's sympathies.

He surveyed the common room, expecting to find Quinley eating breakfast, but no one was there. Mrs. Llewellyn swept in from the kitchen, wiping her hands on her apron. She beamed as she caught sight of him and Catrin together. "Good day, both of you. The ostler tells me that—"

"I've come to speak to Mr. Quinley," Evan bit out. He wasn't in the mood for polite conversation. He wanted to be done with this whole nasty business.

Mrs. Llewellyn blinked. "But . . . but he left."

A chill stole over Evan. "What do you mean, he left?"

"This morning, early. Said he didn't want to miss the ship from Carmarthen."

"How long has he been gone?"

Mrs. Llewellyn watched him warily. "More than two hours."

"Deuce take it!" Evan expected to see triumph on Catrin's face, but she merely stared woodenly into space, as if no longer caring what happened.

With a twinge of guilt, he told the now scowling Mrs. Llewellyn, "Thank you. Then I'll be leaving, too." He drew out some coins. "This is for my lodgings, and there should also be enough to send my belongings on to Cambridge. I don't have time to pack."

"You're going after the man, are you?" Mrs. Llewellyn asked.

Catrin eyed him coolly, clearly waiting for his response.

"Mrs. Price and I are both going after him." Evan went to Catrin's side. "Come on. We'll have to ride like the devil if we're to catch up to him."

"My pony can't possibly keep up such a killing pace."

"Then you'll ride with me." He certainly wasn't leaving her behind. And though riding double might slow them, at least it would ensure she didn't try to escape.

Still, the thought of having Catrin in his arms for a day's ride to Carmarthen bloody well terrified him—even if it was the only way to ensure that he got her to Quinley before Quinley boarded the ship.

"Mrs. Price is going with you to London?" Mrs. Llewellyn asked in shock.

Damn. He hadn't thought of how this would look. All Catrin had to say was that she didn't want to go, and Mrs. Llewellyn would rise to her defense.

So it surprised him when Catrin said, "Mr. Newcome and I need to speak with Mr. Quinley. If that requires going to London, then I suppose we shall."

Mrs. Llewellyn's eyes narrowed. "Does this have anything to do with all the questions the Quinley fellow asked about you last night?"

Catrin colored. "Yes."

"He said you might have been involved in a murder and a theft. Of course I told him that was nonsense." Mrs. Llewellyn paused, then shot Evan an accusing glance. "Come to think of it, Mr. Quinley asked me about a chalice, just as you did, Mr. Newcome, the first time we spoke."

Evan tightened his grip on the bag he carried, but before he could answer Mrs. Llewellyn, Catrin said with an edge to her voice, "Mr. Newcome and Mr. Quinley are anxious to learn the truth, Annie. That's why Mr. Newcome insists that I speak with the investigator."

"That Quinley told me he'd questioned you yesterday, so why are you running after him in a rush today?" Annie glared at Evan. "Surely, Mr. Newcome, you don't think our Catrin had anything to do with this crime, do you?"

Catrin shot him a questioning glance.

He ignored it. "This is none of your concern, Mrs. Llewellyn. We're leaving now, and you have no say in it."

But as he took Catrin's arm, Mrs. Llewellyn stepped forward to clasp Catrin's other one. "She don't have to go anywhere she don't want. I don't know what made you up and decide our Catrin could take part in a murder, but I'll not let you carry her off to be hanged for no good reason."

The word "hanged" stopped him in his tracks. He hadn't considered what would happen to Catrin if she was found guilty of conspiracy to murder.

Hanged. The very word blew an ominous wind through him.

Catrin patted Mrs. Llewellyn's hand. "It's all right. Mr. Newcome is only doing what he believes he must. I'm going with him because I want to clear my name, and I can't if I stay here. Don't worry; it will all come right in the end. But your loyalty means a great deal to me."

Mrs. Llewellyn reddened. "Oh, Catrin, I would never have told Mr. Newcome a word about you if I'd known he would use it in this despicable manner. I can't bear to think—"

"We have to go." Evan couldn't take much more; he had to escape all these people who thought well of Catrin. It was having a very telling effect on him.

"But you must take provisions," Mrs. Llewellyn said. "You don't know how long it will be before you catch up to Mr. Quinley, and you both look as if you could use some breakfast."

"We're leaving now," Evan said sharply, and led Catrin out the door.

As he explained to the ostler that he and Catrin would both be riding his horse, he tried to ignore the mention of hanging. Damn it all, if Catrin were guilty, she deserved to be hanged. And if she were innocent, the truth would out.

For some reason, that didn't make him feel any better.

Evan and Catrin had just mounted his horse when Mrs. Llewellyn rushed out to thrust a bundle into Catrin's hands. "Here's a bit of cold mutton and a loaf of bread." She shot Evan a fierce glance. "The girl has to have something."

"Thank you," he managed to say.

Seconds later, they were on the road. At first, he concentrated on keeping up a punishing speed so they could overtake Quinley. But when after an hour's hard riding they hadn't spotted the investigator, Evan was forced to let the horse slow its pace.

By then the silence between him and Catrin had become painful. Nor did it improve matters that every jounce of the mare made Evan dramatically aware of Catrin's thighs draped over his and her face inches away. Their ride had tugged a few tendrils of hair free, which tickled his cheek whenever the wind blew, and her lilac scent eddied between them. Once, he even caught himself breathing deeply to take it in.

God help him. He tried to concentrate on what he'd say to Quinley, but he could only think of the slender woman whose luscious bottom nestled between his legs. Had it been only last night that he'd tasted every lovely inch of her, that he'd thrust into her, relishing her wanton cries of pleasure?

The memory made him so hard he doubted he'd ever again find satisfaction for his desires. How could he know fulfillment with any other woman after Catrin had shown him what mutual enjoyment really was? Damn her!

By now she should have collapsed under the strain, admitting the truth with tears and pleading, begging him not to bring her to the authorities. But ever since they'd left, she'd remained strangely calm. How could she, when her world was falling apart? And why did it make him feel like the basest man alive?

"That was a noble scene you played in the inn," he

snapped, determined to break her silence. "You were quite the tragic heroine. Unfortunately, I know the whole story, so I'm less inclined to think you a saint."

"No, you'd rather think me a thief and a murderess, which is why we're taking this madcap journey. You do nothing by halves."

"If you don't want to be regarded as a murderess, my dear, don't behave as one."

He knew he'd struck a nerve when she flinched. "You didn't think me capable of murder yesterday. Tell me, who was the woman who taught you that fine facades always hide treachery? Who of my 'kind,' as you so nicely put it this morning, convinced you that a woman of position and wealth can only be a saint or a sinner, never something in the middle?"

He thought of Henrietta, so amiable and sweet until she'd decided he was beneath contempt. Damn it, Henrietta had never betrayed him. If anything, he'd betrayed her. "What makes you think this has to do with another woman?"

"I'm trying to understand how you could make love to me with tenderness at night, then pronounce me a murderess the next morn."

"My reaction is normal, given that your deception was wholly unexpected."

"It couldn't have been, or you wouldn't have hidden your purpose for coming here. You must have been suspicious of me from the beginning." She sucked in a deep breath. "Perhaps you never lost those suspicions. Perhaps you merely pretended to lose them last night, because you wanted to bed me before you packed me off to the authorities."

"Damn you to hell! You know I meant every word of what I said last night! I thought you a . . . a . . ."

"An angel," she finished for him. "The question is, what made you suddenly decide I was a devil?" She lowered her voice. "Why would my foolish mistakes so blind you to my true character, if not because some other woman betrayed you before?"

"Not that it's your business, but the only other women of your class I've known *were* angels. Lady Juliana, who essentially saved my life. And my former fiancée, who'd never contemplate an act of such deception as you perpetrated."

She blinked. "You were once engaged to be married?"

"Yes." He stared off at the grass-carpeted slopes. He shouldn't have mentioned Henrietta, but he'd had enough of Catrin's foolish suppositions. "We didn't suit."

"Ah. So *she's* the one who made you distrust 'my kind.'"

"Absolutely not." He clenched his fists on the reins. "Henrietta broke off our engagement because of something *I* did. I well deserved her disdain."

"Why? Did you distrust her, too?"

He avoided her unswerving gaze. "Yes. I behaved like a jealous fool once and scared her off. But Henrietta didn't deserve my distrust. You do."

Her lips tightened as she stared at the road. "What will you do if we don't reach Carmarthen before Quinley sails?"

"Perish the thought."

"Will you take me to London then?" she persisted. "Will you drag me across the country in your thirst for vengeance?"

"It's a thirst for truth." He looked grim. "And the only

way to find out what really happened is to present Quinley with the new evidence and see if he can corroborate your story."

"Or prove me wrong." She stiffened against his arm. "What if he decides I'm as guilty as you think? They *will* hang me, you know."

There was that horrible word again. She was using it on purpose to unsettle him. Unfortunately, it was working. "If you're innocent, you needn't worry."

She laid her hand on his chest. "How can you, a Welshman, have such faith in English law?"

His gaze shot to her. Her eyes were as dark as the night waters of Llyn y Fan Fach, and her fear struck an answering fear in him.

The English had always been quick to judge harshly, even with their own people, but when the offenders were Welsh or Irish or Scottish, it took little evidence to gain a conviction.

"What if you're wrong?" she whispered. "What if everything happened as I said? Once you give me to Quinley, it will be out of your hands. He was an English lord. I'm a Welsh nobody. Even if they find no witnesses or evidence, they'll convict me, because they have no one else to blame."

A vivid image of a hooded man lowering a noose about Catrin's neck sprang into his mind. Good God, how could he endure seeing her hanged? He forced himself to remember how Justin had looked lying in his own blood, but the picture blurred next to the one of Catrin on a scaffold.

He cursed her for playing on his fears. "Stop talking of

hanging. We're merely presenting the facts to Quinley. He might decide you're telling the truth."

"I don't see how, when you've already tried and convicted me, based on nothing more than lies I told to protect myself from men like you."

Her fatalistic words chilled him to the marrow. What if he *were* wrong? What if she merely *had* been afraid to tell the truth in the beginning?

The refrain tormented him as he urged the horse into a gallop. *What if?*

He couldn't go on the entire journey this way or he'd go mad. He must fall back on what had kept him sane as a child, through his father's beatings. Literature. Other people's words to drown out his own thoughts and feelings.

Tacitus. Something from the histories.

So while the horse rocked beneath them and Catrin's scent assailed him, he tried to think of himself anywhere else as he recited in his mind, *Etiam sapientibus cupido gloriae . . .*

~

Annie paced the common room after Catrin and Mr. Newcome had left. Who'd have guessed the man was a betraying wretch? After how he'd brooded over his inability to see Catrin the past few days, Annie had assumed he'd taken a fancy to the girl.

Then there was the thrashing he'd given David Morys. After that, she'd assumed that Mr. Newcome's pursuit of Catrin was honorable. She'd never dreamed he'd been planning to carry the poor lass off. And under suspicion of committing murder, no less!

Something must be done about it. But what? Mr. Llewellyn, bless his soul, wouldn't approve of her getting involved. And the only person who'd presumed to fight Mr. Newcome was—

Of course! David would be willing to stop this. He'd wanted to marry the lass, after all.

Her mind made up, she rushed to Llanddeusant's school. She found David at his desk, poring over a pile of papers. "Mr. Newcome has taken Catrin off!"

"What?"

"You know that investigator who was here yesterday asking questions? He thinks she had something to do with a murder in London, and apparently Mr. Newcome is the one who set the man on her. I'm not sure of the details, but Catrin and Mr. Newcome showed up at the inn this morning, looking for the investigator. When I told them the man had already left for Carmarthen, Mr. Newcome said he and Catrin were going to follow him. Then he rode off with her on his horse!"

The blood drained from David's face. "Did she want to go?"

"I don't think so. I think she felt she had no other choice."

With a curse, David opened a desk drawer and pulled out a flintlock pistol.

"Good Lord, what are you doing with a pistol?" Mrs. Llewellyn asked.

"It was my father's." He stuffed it in his coat pocket along with a bag of powder and shot.

"What are you planning to do with it?"

"Get Catrin back, of course." He rounded the desk.

"But if you shoot Mr. Newcome, they'll come looking for you next!"

"I won't have to shoot him. If I wave this pistol in his face, he'll give her up, don't you worry. That bastard won't be so smug when looking down the barrel of a flintlock." He donned his hat and gloves, then left the study.

She ran after him. "Yes, but what will you do once you wrest her away? They can simply send someone else here after her."

He paused, and the coldness in his black eyes made her shiver. "And what would *you* suggest?"

"I . . . I don't know. Go with her to London, I suppose, and make sure they treat her fairly."

"If she makes it to London, no one will treat her fairly. You can be sure of that."

He stalked across the schoolroom, and she hurried after him. The pistol worried her. She didn't want David to *kill* anyone, even Mr. Newcome. She held her tongue until they were out of earshot of the students. "Perhaps you shouldn't take the pistol. What if you get into a fight and he wrests it away from you?"

That was the wrong thing to say. "He won't." A muscle worked in his jaw as he saddled his horse. "I'll take care of this problem. I'll get Catrin back, make no mistake." He mounted the horse and gathered up the reins. "Once I'm through with Newcome, that bastard will rue the day he was born."

Then, with a click of his tongue, he rode away.

Annie stared after him, feeling uneasy. A jealous man with a pistol could be dangerous. Had it been wise of her to arouse his fury?

She only prayed he knew how to use the gun properly and could indeed intimidate Mr. Newcome merely by threatening him with the weapon.

Because if not, they might be carrying Catrin home in a coffin.

atrin stared ahead at the road. She could feel every virile, unyielding inch of her tormentor. His arm occasionally brushed her spine and his hard chest pressed against her shoulder. She couldn't escape the memory of how that chest had felt beneath her splayed fingers, how that thigh had parted her legs so—

A pox on the man! Couldn't she forget what they'd shared?

Never. It was all she'd thought of for the last few hours, since they'd spent the day in total silence.

Normally she welcomed silence, her haven from Grandmother's harping and the neighbors' whispered comments. But this silence was a brutal chasm stretching between them, and there was no way to breach it.

A tear snaked down her cheek, and she wiped it away furiously, praying he hadn't seen it. She'd tried to lose herself in the sunlight skipping off the rain-speckled rocks, and Black Mountain looking more like a benevolent regent than a scowling tyrant. But the beauty seemed to mock her, for who knew how long it would be before she experienced it again?

Another tear trickled down her cheek, and she didn't bother to wipe it away. Despite the scenery, the ride had been long and tiring. Evan was obsessed with reaching Carmarthen before Mr. Quinley left. There'd been nothing to eat but the mutton and bread Mrs. Llewellyn had given them, which they'd devoured hours ago, so now Catrin's stomach rumbled continually.

But Evan showed no signs of hunger. That was what had made the day most horrible—Evan's eerie control. She might have thought him carved of oak, so stiffly did he suffer her nearness. How could this cold statue have made love to her with fire and fury?

Well, she'd had enough of his brooding. Night was falling, and they were nowhere near Carmarthen. Surely Mr. Quinley had already boarded his ship. How long did Evan intend to continue this?

"Where are we?" she asked.

"Two hours from Carmarthen."

The rumble of his voice hit her hard. She struggled to hide her emotions. "You intend to go on even after dark."

"I intend to go on until we reach Carmarthen."

"But surely it's dangerous at night, with highwaymen and—"

"There's never been a highwayman on this stretch of road. Rhys Vaughan makes sure of that."

"We're near the Vaughan estate, then?"

"Llynwydd. Yes." His words were clipped, but she could hear the weariness beneath them. "We just passed the drive leading to it."

She craned her head to look past his shoulder. In the dying light, she could just make out a road cutting off from the main one. "Don't you want to stop and visit?" She didn't know if she could stand two more hours of being so close to him . . . and so very, very far.

"I want to reach Carmarthen on the slim chance that Quinley is still there."

"Yes, but the Vaughans would at least have food."

"We'll eat in Carmarthen."

That was the last straw. Before he could realize what she was doing, she grabbed the reins out of his hand and began to turn the horse back the way they'd come.

"Deuce take it, what are you doing?" he growled.

"I'm hungry and tired, and I'm not moving another inch without food."

"You'll do as I say!" he bit out, snatching the reins from her.

"Don't be so stubborn!" She fought to regain control of the horse. "You know quite well that the ships set sail before sundown. There's no reason to continue this journey without sustenance or rest!"

They were both so intent on their struggle that they didn't hear the hoofbeats until a voice called, "Ho, there! Stand to!"

Catrin froze. "I thought you said there were no highwaymen on this road," she hissed as the rider approached.

With a low oath, Evan tried to reestablish control over his horse, but by the time he had, the man who'd hailed them had caught up to them.

When Catrin saw who it was, relief flooded her. "Thank heaven, it's only David."

Evan slipped his hand around her waist in an oddly protective gesture. "What the deuce is *he* doing here?"

"I don't know."

David scowled as he took in how Evan held Catrin pressed to his chest. "You've led me a merry chase today. My horse isn't used to such hard riding."

"So why did you follow us?" Evan snapped.

"Because I couldn't let you carry Catrin off. I've come to bring her home."

Evan's body tensed against hers. "What makes you think she wants to go home? She rejected you once already, you know."

His jealous tone shocked Catrin. She'd assumed he no longer cared.

"I know everything, Newcome," David bit out, "so stop pretending that this is some elopement. You're taking her off to be hanged. So I'm sure she'll be more than happy to come with me."

"She's not going to be hanged, and she's certainly not going anywhere with you," Evan stated as he urged the horse into a walk.

David rode up ahead to block the road. To Catrin's shock, he withdrew a pistol and pointed it straight at Evan's head. "I'm afraid you don't have a say."

With a curse, Evan halted the horse.

"David, you can't mean to use that!" Catrin cried.

"Get off the horse, Catrin," David said. "I won't risk shooting you."

"I don't want you to shoot anyone!"

"Get off the horse." This time the command came from Evan.

She glanced up into his stony face. "Wh-what?"

His eyes never left the pistol. "I don't know if Morys can use that thing, but I can't risk him hitting you."

Yet he would apparently risk being shot himself. "I'm not getting off. He'll kill you!"

Next thing she knew, she was sprawled on the ground. Evan had pushed her off and was now dancing his mare away from her.

She sprang to her feet, terror gripping her. Now David would surely fire. Lunging forward, she grabbed Evan's leg.

"Deuce take it, Catrin!" Evan said as he tried to shake her loose. "Let go!"

David swung the pistol back and forth, his face ashen as he gauged the shot.

If only Evan had a sword or a pistol or—

Something hard swung against her arm—the saddlebag containing the chalice. If she could just get close enough to hit David with it . . .

Hooking one arm firmly around Evan's leg, she slid her free hand into the saddlebag to withdraw the chalice, praying that David wouldn't notice. Fortunately, he was too busy watching the mare swerve from side to side.

"Move away from him, Catrin!" David growled. "Blast it, I can't get a clear shot with you there!"

Frantically, Catrin tried to think of a plan. Grandmother would have managed some spectacular maneuver to get David's weapon away and protect Evan. All she could think of was to get behind David and hit him with the chalice. But he'd have to dismount, and how on earth would she coax him into doing *that*?

With a wary eye on both men, she let go of Evan's leg and headed for David. "I'll go with you! Just don't shoot Evan!"

"The bloody bastard deserves to die!" David spat.

She tried to sound soothing. "But it'll be worse if you kill him. If we let him go, they won't come after us. It won't be worth tracking us into the mountains."

She hardly knew what she was babbling; she only prayed it would keep David from shooting until she could get him off that horse.

It didn't help that David was suspicious. "You'd run away with me? I thought you didn't want me."

"That was before I knew what a . . . a low bastard Mr. Newcome would prove to be. And before you so bravely came to rescue me."

Evan's eyes were the color of black ice as he watched her edge closer to David. "Running away again, Catrin? Afraid that this 'low bastard' might get the truth from you eventually?"

She ignored his cutting words, sidling ever nearer to David. Her heart thundered in her chest, but she kept moving, slow and easy so she wouldn't spook David's horse. A step to the left. A half-turn. Another step. David couldn't watch both her and Evan, and as long as he kept his eyes on Evan, she might reach him.

"Tell me, Catrin," Evan said bitterly, "was Morys one of the men you took to London with you? He seems awfully eager to use that pistol in your defense."

"What's he talking about, the men you took to London?" David asked. "I thought you went alone?"

Mentally, she cursed Evan. "Of course I went alone." She forced tears to her eyes. It wasn't hard to do under the circumstances. "You don't know what a beast Mr. Newcome has been. He's been saying all these awful things . . ."

David steadied his aim again. "The bastard! I'll kill him!"

"No!" She took the last few steps to his horse and grabbed the reins. "Please, just take me away." She managed a petulant pout. "If you shoot him, I won't run away with you. In my situation, I can't risk being linked to a known murderer."

David held his free hand down to her. "Come on up, then."

Clearly he thought to have her safe in his grasp before he shot Evan. She must get him off that horse! "You'll have to dismount and help me. I can't climb up by myself."

David looked at her, then at Evan. *Please, God*, she prayed, her fingers clammy on the chalice. *Please let him be certain enough of my incompetence to believe me.*

"Oh, very well." Keeping his eyes trained on Evan, he slid to the ground with the pistol still clutched in his hand.

In that moment, when he was slightly off balance, she swung the chalice with all her might down on his head.

Then everything happened at once. David growled, "What the hell?" as he turned toward her. At the same time, Evan rode up to vault from his horse onto David. The two men crashed to the ground, struggling for the pistol as she screamed and circled them, trying to find an opening to hit David again.

Suddenly there was a thunderous noise and Evan fell back, clutching his shoulder. "Evan!" she screamed as the horses bolted.

David rocked back on his heels to stare down at his smoking pistol, and a murderous rage consumed her. Without stopping to think, she struck David with the chalice over and over until he keeled over senseless.

A moan to her right jerked her from her fury. She dropped the chalice and ran to where Evan sat on the ground, his hand splayed over his coat as if to halt the red stain spreading across the wool.

"Oh Lord, Evan!" She knelt to stare at the blood seeping through his fingers. She'd failed! David had killed him!

Then she heard him choke out a word that sounded like her name. He lifted a face wracked with pain to her.

"Please don't die!" She opened his coat to examine the wound. "You can't die!"

Evan focused his gaze on her. "I . . . I don't think . . . it's fatal. And that bastard Morys might hurt you if you don't—"

"Hush." Pressing her fingers to his lips, she glanced over to where David lay slumped on the ground. "He can't do anything. But we've got to get you help."

He clutched at her arm as she struggled to drag his coat off. "The . . . the pistol," he rasped. "Must get the pistol . . . first. Before he can . . . use it on you."

Tears coursed down her cheeks. Thanks to her, his lifeblood was draining away, and all he could think of was protecting her. "He won't. He doesn't want to hurt me."

He winced as she tugged his coat sleeve off his right arm. "He might . . . want to . . . now that you hit him . . . over the head."

"I'm not worried about that." She pulled the other sleeve off as gently as she could. "You said Llynwydd was half a mile away. Do you think you can walk that far if I support you? I'm afraid we've scared off the horses."

With a groan, he dug his fingers into her arm. "Get . . . the pistol *first*."

"A pox on that thing!" Then she heard another groan. She turned to see David lift his head.

"The pistol!" Evan hissed, his lips drawn from the pain.

She rushed to the pistol and snatched it up as David slumped back down with a moan.

Hurrying back to Evan's side, she gave it to him. He opened the chamber. "Deuce take it, he's used . . . the one shot."

"Of course he's used the one shot! It's buried in your shoulder!"

Evan looked up at her, then swallowed twice. "Catrin . . . you must get . . . another ball."

"Another ball?" she said uncomprehendingly.

He raised the pistol an inch.

"Oh yes, for the pistol." She glanced over to find David stirring once more. Hurrying to his side, she turned him onto his back. Then she searched his pockets until she found a bag containing the balls and powder.

Swiftly, she returned to hand them to Evan. Though his rigid mouth showed the pain it caused him, he reloaded the gun and gave it to her.

"What am I supposed to do with this?" she cried as she held the hateful thing in her hands.

"Catrin . . ." growled a voice behind her.

She whirled to find David struggling to his feet. Her heart beat triple-time as she moved in front of Evan.

David rubbed the back of his head. "What happened to me?" He caught sight of the chalice lying near him. As she watched helplessly, he picked it up.

"This is it, isn't it?" He turned it over in his hand. "It has to be. It's exactly as you described it. You hit me with it, didn't you?"

"Yes."

"You've had it all this time."

No point in denying it. She nodded.

Anger suffused his face. "You deceitful bitch. You lied to me! You *hit* me!" He stepped forward. "I'll make you regret that. You and Newcome both."

Her hands shook as she raised the gun. "Stay back, David!"

A taunting smile crossed his face. "It's already been fired."

"Evan reloaded it." Keeping the pistol trained on him, she picked up the bag she'd taken from his coat. "See? And I *will* shoot you if you come any nearer."

His handsome features hardened into a nasty mask. "You wouldn't dare!"

"I won't let you hurt either of us. I'll shoot if I must!"

With a snarled oath he took a step forward, but she cocked the gun as she'd seen him do earlier. Pray heaven that the dusk concealed how her hands shook.

He halted to scowl at her, then at Evan. "Come, now, you can't think I'd hurt you. As for Newcome, how can you defend the man who'd see you hang?"

"How can I let him die by the side of the road?"

David sneered. "He'd let *you* die."

"Perhaps, but it doesn't matter. I can't do it."

David stared at her, face sullen. "I tell you what. Come with me and we'll send someone back to help him."

"You should . . . do as he says," Evan choked out behind her.

"Don't be a fool. I'm not leaving you." Her arms began to ache from having to hold the pistol so steadily on David. Evan was losing blood. She must get David away from here, but how? What would Grandmother have done?

Whatever it took. "Listen, David." She forced herself to sound calm. "I don't know why you want me to come with you, when I don't care for you, but—"

"It's only your infatuation with this bastard that keeps you from seeing we're meant for each other," David put in.

"No! And it's pointless for you to try persuading me to go with you. I'm not leaving Evan. So hunt up your horse and return to Llanddeusant, before I tire of holding this pistol and shoot you in the leg." She lowered it until she was aiming at his crotch. "Or somewhere more important. After what you just did, I'll have no compunction about leaving you here to die."

Paling, he glanced from her to Evan, then down at the chalice in his hand. "Very well, then, I'll go. But you'll regret sending me away when he dies of his wounds and they blame you for his murder. What will you do then? You'll need me to tell them the truth. So I'm not going far, I promise. I'll be close by, waiting for when you come crawling to me."

He held up the chalice. "Besides, I have this. You'll come to me, if only to get it back." Then he turned and walked off.

"No!" she cried. "You drop that chalice, David! Drop it now!"

But he kept walking. A pox on him! He knew that while she might shoot him to protect Evan, she'd never shoot him over the chalice. And she dared not leave Evan to go after him.

She watched despairingly as David headed off after the horses. The minute he disappeared over a hill, she uncocked the pistol and went to Evan's side. "We must get you away in case he returns."

Unbuttoning his waistcoat, she peeled it back to examine the wound. The light was almost gone and she could see little to nothing, but she could feel the blood against her fingers. Ignoring the fear gripping her, she moved her fingers over his shoulder until she found the place where the ball had gone in.

It seemed high enough to have missed his heart and lungs, but she couldn't be sure. A person could only learn so much from talking to apothecaries and surgeons. She couldn't get the ball out in the darkness, but perhaps she could stop the bleeding.

Trying not to move him unnecessarily, she unknotted his cravat and folded it into a pad, then held it against his shoulder to stanch the blood. She glanced around for something to keep it in place and put pressure on the wound.

Her scarf! She drew it off and threaded it under his arms and around his shoulder, tying it tightly.

"Catrin." He covered her hand with his. "The walk to Llynwydd . . . is too long. I won't make it . . . even with your help." He sucked in several deep breaths. "You . . . must go. . . and fetch someone."

"I can't leave you here unprotected!"

"Give me . . . the pistol . . . and help me move . . . off the road." He glanced up at the sky. "It's getting dark. No one will find me."

She wanted to argue, but he was right. He had no chance if she didn't move swiftly, and she couldn't do that with him so badly wounded.

She buttoned his waistcoat over the wadded-up cravat and her scarf, hoping that would provide added pressure to slow the bleeding. Next, she donned his coat so she wouldn't have to carry it and stuffed the pistol in the pocket, along with the bag containing the ball and powder.

She moved behind him to clasp him under the arms. Oh Lord, she would never be able to lift him. Fortunately, he had enough strength left that between her frantic tugging and his halting attempts to rise, she could maneuver him to a stand.

Looping his arm over her shoulder, she supported him

with her body as she clasped him around the waist. Then they began the long, tortured walk that took them off the road and into a wide field.

"Find a tree to . . . prop me against," he groaned.

She spotted one about a hundred paces away. Praying he could make it that far, she crept doggedly forward, though he shuddered with pain at every step.

Her right arm and shoulder ached from the effort of supporting him. She could feel him growing weaker, for he leaned more heavily on her. Only sheer force of will drove her to the tree. Though it required a few more torturous steps, she half-dragged, half-carried him around to the side away from the road.

Then she lowered him to the ground as gently as she could manage. He slipped through her grasp and fell the last few inches, landing on the ground with a grunt of pain.

"I'm so sorry, Evan." She knelt beside him. "Are you all right?"

"I'll . . . survive," he said. "Give me . . . the pistol."

She pressed it into his hand. Then she put his coat around his shoulders and tried to make him comfortable.

Loath to leave him, she slid her hand inside his waistcoat, checking to be sure the wadded cravat was still in place. "I'm so sorry about this, Evan. If not for me, you'd never have been shot."

He covered her hand. "If . . . not for *you* . . . I'd be dead."

Tears stung her eyes. He could still die, out here alone in the night. "It's such a mess. But I swear I'll do my best to get you out of this alive."

She started to rise, but he gripped her hand. "Tell me

something . . . before you go. Why didn't you . . . leave with him when . . . you had the chance?"

"I couldn't let you die—"

"Why . . . not?" He drew in a ragged breath. "I was taking you . . . to London against your will . . ." Guilt tinged his words. "I was risking . . . *your* life. You had the right . . . to risk mine."

That he really believed she would have left him to die tore at her. "What you and I did together last night . . ." She swallowed. "It may have meant nothing to you, but it meant something to me."

He clutched at her hand. "Ah, Catrin . . . I wish last night had . . . meant nothing. Then I wouldn't have been . . . in hell ever since it . . . happened."

He angled his head up to hers, and though she couldn't see his features, she could feel his difficult breathing on her cheek. Had he been in hell today? She wouldn't have guessed. But she'd certainly been in hell, and there promised to be no salvation in sight until she saw him safe.

Afraid she'd betray how much she cared, she turned away. "I-I have to go now, before you lose any more blood."

But he clung to her hand a moment longer. "Thank you." He rubbed her hand against his roughly whiskered cheek. "For looking after me."

The gesture was so intimate, it made her throat constrict. Why must he turn her inside out when she least expected it? "I have to go now," she choked out and extricated her hand.

It took every ounce of her will to leave him lying there

against the tree, knowing that when she returned he might be dead.

No! She wouldn't let him die. She'd already watched that happen to one man she cared for. She was *not* going to watch it happen to another.

She paused to memorize every facet of the landscape, praying she could find the spot again. Then she turned and rushed into the darkness.

~

Juliana and Rhys Vaughan had just sat down to dinner when their youngest footman burst into the dining room. "Excuse me, sir, but there's a madwoman out here begging to speak with you and Lady Juliana."

Rhys stifled a smile at James's tendency to exaggerate. "A madwoman?"

"She says you know her and she gives her name as Mrs. Catrin Price, but she looks a terrible sight. You want me to send her away?"

What was Catrin Price doing here? And did this have anything to do with Evan's visit to her?

Rhys rose. "Don't send her away. Of course we'll speak to her."

They found Mrs. Price pacing the hall, her face distraught. As she whirled toward them, Rhys could almost understand why James had thought her a madwoman. Blood was spattered all over the poor girl's gown. Her hair was a disordered mass, and her eyes shone with a wild light.

"Thank heaven you're home! I don't know if you remember me, but—"

"Of course we remember you," Rhys said. "But what in the devil has happened?"

"Evan has been shot. You must help him. You must send someone—"

"Evan Newcome?" Juliana asked.

"Yes!" Mrs. Price turned to Juliana with a pleading expression. "He said you were his friends."

"Where is he?" Rhys asked.

"Up at the road, close to the entrance to your estate. I had to leave him, because he couldn't make it this far with his wound."

Juliana paled. "How badly is he wounded?"

"Very badly, I'm afraid. The ball is lodged in his shoulder and he's lost a great deal of blood, although I think it missed his vital organs." Mrs. Price gripped Rhys's arm. "If you don't hurry—"

Rhys was already drawing on his coat and barking orders, calling for a wagon and horses and telling the footman to send to Carmarthen for a surgeon.

Juliana drew on her coat. "I'm going with you."

"No, you're not," Rhys said. When she flashed him a mutinous glare, he added, "I don't know who shot him or if they're still lurking. Besides, you need to get a room ready and find someone on the estate to help patch him up. It'll be hours before the surgeon arrives."

With a curt nod, Juliana hurried off to find the housekeeper.

Rhys turned to Mrs. Price. "Let's go."

They hastened down the steps to where two saddled horses already awaited, along with a wagon drawn by a cob. Once they were mounted, Rhys took off like a shot, praying that the girl was as good a horsewoman as her grandmother and could keep up with him. Because he needed her to tell him where Evan was.

Evan was like one of his own sons. To think of him lying alone and wounded made Rhys's gut wrench.

Mrs. Price matched his pace and they soon left the wagon far behind. Then they reached the spot where the drive to Llynwydd met the main road. She went only a few feet farther before she halted her horse and dismounted, peering into the shadowy land bordering the road. "I left him propped against a tree." A note of fear entered her voice. "We have to find him before David returns."

"David?" Rhys asked as he dismounted.

"The man who shot him," she explained. "He said he'd be back."

Rhys wanted to ask more, but she'd already left the road to enter a field. He made out a tree silhouetted against the night sky and rounded it in time to see her kneel on the ground. Then he spotted a large figure slumped against the trunk.

When the wagon lumbered onto the road, he rushed back to fetch the groom driving it. It would take two men at least to get Evan into the wagon, and he was grateful the groom had brought a stable boy along.

By the time he returned, Mrs. Price was rocking back and forth, rubbing Evan's hand in hers as she sobbed, "Please, Evan, wake up! Please don't die and leave me!"

Rhys knelt beside her to grope along Evan's neck until he found a pulse. "He's not dead yet," he said reassuringly. "Bring that light here!" he called out, and the groom approached with a lantern.

When he saw Evan's face, so bloodless in the glow of the lantern, he feared the worst. Pushing aside Evan's coat, he caught his breath. The shirt was soaked with blood. They must get him back to Llynwydd at once.

Rhys was relieved to hear his friend moan when he, the groom, and the stable boy lifted Evan. At least he was still enough in this world to feel pain.

Evan was a giant of a man and they had to struggle to carry him to the wagon. Once there, Rhys helped Mrs. Price into it, then climbed up beside her while the stable boy scurried off to collect the horses. As the groom started the wagon moving toward Llynwydd, Mrs. Price pulled Evan's head into her lap.

Rhys watched with interest as she stroked the hair from his face, whispering that he must not leave her yet, that he could not die, that they would have him fixed up fine if he could just hold on.

"Tell me, how did he come to be shot?" Rhys asked.

She looked up, her face blank, as if she hadn't even realized he was there. "It's all my fault!"

"I doubt that," he said soothingly. "You mentioned that a man named David shot Evan. Who is he?"

"David Morys." She wiped a tear away. "Schoolmaster in Llanddeusant."

This grew increasingly curious. Odd enough that Evan should have been near Llynwydd with Mrs. Price, though from how Juliana had tried to throw them together, it shouldn't surprise him. Still, Evan had left only a week ago.

"Why did a schoolmaster shoot Evan?" he asked, praying she wouldn't collapse into tears before he could get the entire story. If this Morys fellow was running loose shooting people, Rhys wanted to be prepared. Besides, focusing on finding Evan's attacker kept him from thinking about that bloodstained shirt and the wan face of his friend.

"It's complicated, and I promise to tell you all of it eventually, but I . . . I can't talk about it right now."

"I understand." He reached over to pat her hand. "Under the circumstances, your first concern has to be making sure Evan lives. Nonetheless, I must know if this David Morys would come to the estate after either of you."

"He might. The only way I got him to leave was by threatening to shoot him with his own pistol."

"Good God," Rhys said, incredulous. "Where is it?"

She pulled the weapon from Evan's coat pocket. "I never want to see another as long as I live."

That made him smile. "I imagine not." Rhys tried to envision the shy Mrs. Price facing a man down with a pistol but couldn't. She had obviously changed considerably since he'd met her. Juliana would be surprised.

"When David was leaving," Mrs. Price went on, "he said he'd be back. I think he assumed we had nowhere to hide. That's why I had to pull Evan off the road. I was afraid David might find him before I could return."

Rhys gaped at her. "*You* pulled him off the road? Alone?" Why, she was a little slip of a thing!

"He could still stand, but I had to support him while we walked. I was afraid I wouldn't make it." She lifted her face to him. "I . . . I couldn't let him die."

Rhys took her hand as they neared the squire hall. "You did well, Mrs. Price. If he comes through this, it will be largely due to your efforts."

In the lights blazing from the house he could see tears fill her eyes again. "If it hadn't been for me, he wouldn't be in this predicament."

"Nonsense. It sounds as if it was this Morys fellow's fault entirely."

She hid her face. "Oh, but you don't know . . ."

The wagon halted at the foot of the entrance. As servants scurried down the steps, followed by an anxious Juliana, Rhys squeezed Mrs. Price's hand. "He'll be all right. He's in good hands here. Evan's strong. He's survived many things in his life, and he'll survive this. So don't worry about him. All right?"

She managed a smile. "I hope you're right. I couldn't bear it if . . . if . . ."

Rhys shared her sentiments entirely.

16

*L*ayers of mist clung to Evan like damp cotton, dragging him into a swamp. He flailed his arms. The mist swirled tighter . . . closer . . . It suffocated him. He sucked in air, but it was fetid and poisonous.

Bone-chilling cold. Alien and clammy, drowning him in a terrible black emptiness.

"No . . . No . . . Please help . . . me," he choked out.

"I'm here," came a voice out of the mist.

A gentle voice. Catrin's. He stopped flailing and turned. Only Catrin could part the dangerous vapors.

I must find her. She's here, somewhere, my Lady of the Mists.

"Catrin!" he croaked out as the mist wrapped his legs in spidery tendrils.

Then he saw her, cocooned in a halo of light. His Catrin, coming to him with a smile.

"It will be all right." She held out her hand. "I'm here. Everything will be fine."

He strained against the blackness threatening to swallow him up, then strained toward Catrin. The cold trickled out of him, seeping away like vapor that vanished in her light.

He fought the pull of the mist. His shoulder ached from the effort of reaching for her, of fighting. But he ignored it. Catrin would rescue him from the darkness if he could only reach her. But his shoulder ached so much . . .

Her hand closed around his . . . warm, supple fingers and strength greater than his own . . . stealing into him, heating him. Relief rushed through him as he gripped her hand.

Suddenly the mist faded, and he realized he was lying on his back in a soft bed. His mouth was dry and hot, but his skin was drenched in cold sweat, making his breeches and shirt cling to him. His shoulder throbbed. He tried to move it, but discovered it was bound in bandages, as was his arm, which lay on his chest beneath the loose shirt.

"It will all be fine," came a hoarse whisper from somewhere to his right. "It has to be. You can't die. You can't!"

His eyes fluttered open, and he was disoriented. Sunlight streamed through the windows of a lavishly appointed room, and Catrin gripped his hand, pressing it against her pale cheek as anguished tears slid down her face.

Dark smudges under her eyes attested to a lack of sleep. Her hair was a wild mass of tangled curls, and her gown was stained and creased.

She looked like an angel.

Suddenly, everything came back to him. Catrin crowning Morys with the chalice. His own fight with Morys. The pistol going off and Catrin struggling to save him. Their torturous walk to the side of the road that had ended with him alone, staring at the sky and wondering if he was going to die.

He obviously hadn't. He glanced at his arm. It must be in a sling, since the left arm of his shirt hung down empty from his shoulder. Someone had patched him up very well.

His eyes widened as he stared at Catrin. How had she gotten him here? And where was "here"? He remembered her talking about getting him to Llynwydd. Had she managed that? Was that where he was?

Licking his dry lips, he tried to speak. Only a pitiful rasping noise escaped his lips, but it was enough to draw Catrin's attention.

She lifted her head to look at him with glistening eyes. "Evan?"

He swallowed, then croaked, "Good . . . morning."

Shock filled her face, then she flashed him a brilliant smile. "You're awake . . . and alive and—" Tears streamed down her face. "When you had such a bad fever last night, I thought—by heaven, it doesn't matter. Nothing matters now that you're all right." Then her face fell. "You *are* all right, aren't you? I know you must be in pain, but—"

"I believe I'm through the worst of it." He flexed his legs and his unbound arm experimentally, pleased to discover he'd maintained control of his other limbs. "As you said, there's pain . . . but everything seems intact."

With a sob, she clasped his hand to her chest. "I'm so sorry about David's shooting you. I keep getting you hurt."

"Doesn't matter." He squeezed her fingers weakly. "Nothing matters but . . . that you're here and . . . I'm here. Safe."

A devastating smile lit her face. He tightened his grip on her hand, then ran his thumb over her knuckles. Her fingers were so delicate and dainty, the skin so soft. Something flickered in his mind, something about a mist and a hand held out to him, but thinking about it made his head hurt, so he stopped.

Besides, it felt wonderful just to hold her hand, to feel her warmth against the cold clamminess of his skin. It seemed as if he'd wandered in the darkness for an eternity, waiting to hold this hand. "How long . . . have I been here?"

"Two nights and a day. The surgeon removed the ball successfully, but you'd lost a great deal of blood and you didn't awaken." Her mouth tightened. "Last night during the storm, you were so still and your fever so high that I feared—" She squeezed his hand. "We've all been frantic with worry."

"We?"

"The Vaughans. You're at Llynwydd. Don't you remember?"

Running his tongue over his parched lips, he murmured, "Some. Not all." He remembered asking her why she'd stayed. What had she said? Because their lovemaking had meant something to her, even if it had meant nothing to him.

And he had thought to give up the beauty of lovemaking with Catrin, simply because . . .

Other things came back to him then—all the accusations he'd thrown at her, all the lies she'd told him. Justin's murder seemed a lifetime away now. Strange how none of it mattered so much anymore.

He was alive and whole. He hadn't perished by the side of the road. Catrin hadn't left him, even when it had been to her advantage to do so. She'd nearly killed herself to save him. Surely that proved her innocence.

"Evan," she whispered, drawing his attention from his unsettling thoughts. "Mr. Vaughan and Lady Juliana are beside themselves with worry for you, so I must tell them you're awake. It will only take a minute. All right?"

He nodded, though he watched her leave the room with a spurt of panic—the same panic he'd felt when she'd left him propped against the tree. The menacing darkness had clawed at him, reminding him of nights as a boy when his father's fury and beatings had driven him to hide in the woodshed, when he'd lain in the dark hearing rats scrabble along the floor as he waited for morning and the abatement of his father's anger. He'd struggled to stay conscious enough to use the pistol if Morys came back.

But his struggles had been fruitless, for somewhere in that horrible night, he'd slipped into unconsciousness and a black morass of—

He wouldn't think of it now. He was safe and among friends. The darkness was banished, and Catrin was here. Everything was right with the world.

A need not to look helpless and weak assailed him, and he struggled to push himself into a sitting position. That was all he managed before the door opened and Lady Juliana thrust her head inside. With a little cry, she rushed into the room, followed closely by Rhys and Catrin.

Evan noticed that Catrin stood back, watching as Lady Juliana fussed over him and Rhys teased him about being a "damned sight too big to carry." It took all of Evan's will not to call Catrin to his side. After what had happened, he needed her even more than before. He needed to feel her warmth, her strength, her will. Yet he knew that Rhys and Lady Juliana would make much of his urge to have Catrin at his side, and he didn't want to embarrass his darling.

Instead, he turned his gaze to the squire. "I'm afraid I lost the horse you loaned me, old chap."

Rhys laughed. "As if I care. But you didn't lose it. She showed up at the stables yesterday, a little ragged and weary, but otherwise whole."

"Good."

"The surgeon said your shoulder would heal well if you lived through the fever and loss of blood." Lady Juliana settled her hip on the bed. "You should be fine now, thank heaven."

"Yes, thank heaven," Rhys echoed. "I don't think the university could stand to lose an instructor of your caliber."

Lady Juliana rolled her eyes. "He doesn't give a whit about the university. *He* would have been destroyed if something had happened to you. He's paced the floor ever since he and Mrs. Price brought you back in the wagon."

As Rhys smiled at him, a lump formed in Evan's throat. It was good to have such loyal friends. "Thank you, all of you, for looking after me."

Lady Juliana patted his hand. "Yes, well, it's not over yet.

You must get your strength back. You need lots of rest and plenty of food in that bottomless pit you call a stomach. I'm having Cook prepare some broth for you right now."

"Sounds wonderful," Evan murmured.

"We shouldn't tire you too much, so we'll let you rest for a while."

She turned toward the door, but when Catrin did the same, he blurted out, "Will you stay, Catrin?"

"Of course," she said, her eyes bright as she stepped toward the bed.

But Lady Juliana checked her with one hand. "Evan, you need rest. And so does Mrs. Price. She hasn't slept since she and Rhys brought you here, except for dozing in that chair." She pointed to a chair that looked uncomfortable as hell.

"If Evan wants me to stay with him—" Catrin began.

"No, it's fine," Evan broke in. Good God, he was such a dolt. Of course she needed rest. "I am indeed . . . quite tired. I think I shall sleep awhile."

Catrin cast him an anxious glance. "Are you sure? If you need me, I'll stay."

He looked at the weariness evident in her slumped shoulders and the worn lines about her mouth, and cursed himself for not thinking sooner of what she must have been through. She had eaten next to nothing the day they'd been on the road. Thanks to him, she hadn't had a good night's sleep in days. And she'd probably drained her strength in her struggle to get him here.

The enormity of what she'd done struck him. After he'd threatened to turn her over to the magistrate, she'd saved his life at great personal hardship. It was amazing. *She* was amazing.

And tired. "I'll be fine," he said, keeping his eyes averted from Lady Juliana, who watched the interchange with interest. "Truly, I do need sleep."

Catrin nodded but laid her hand briefly over his. "If you want me, just call." She lifted her hand as if to stroke his cheek, then drew away. "I'm so glad you're doing better. Sleep well."

Long after she and the others were gone, he thought about her aborted gesture and wondered how she felt about him now. She must have cared some for him to save him from Morys. But was it merely the kind of caring one showed to another human being, or was it a sign of something deeper?

Had he so alienated her affections with his accusations that he would never again feel her hand against his cheek? God, he hoped not.

~

Blinking back tears of relief, Catrin followed the Vaughans to the stairs. Evan was going to make it.

Lady Juliana insisted that she eat something, and Catrin was too tired to protest, so she let them lead her to the dining room.

Though her joy at seeing Evan well seemed to have roused her appetite, the prospect of sharing a meal with the Vaughans unnerved her. The only words she'd spoken to them since she'd arrived had concerned Evan's condition. Despite Lady Juliana's attempts to get her to sleep or eat,

Catrin had refused to leave his side, for fear he would wake up and no one would be there to help him.

Now she felt like an outsider in this house where everyone knew Evan so well—not only the Vaughans but the servants, too. When Evan's sister, Mary, had joined Catrin at his bedside yesterday, Catrin had learned why Evan was so close to the Vaughans. They'd paid for his education and treated him like a son for twenty years. They'd seen in Evan what no one else would have taken the trouble to see—a genius who only needed nurturing to blossom.

No wonder they'd been so distraught. No wonder they were kind to her for saving his life. She swallowed the lump in her throat. If they knew how responsible she'd been for his near death, they wouldn't be so kind to her.

She sighed as the Vaughans ushered her to the table, their expressions so considerate and friendly. As she'd left his room, Evan had looked at her with such tenderness it had made her heart beat faster. It was the same way he'd looked at her the night he'd made love to her.

Had he forgotten why they'd been traveling this road? Or was he simply feeling a temporary gratitude that would fade as he grew stronger? She almost didn't care, she was so happy to see him alive and well and smiling at her like a man who has found good fortune at last.

"Why don't you sit here by me?" Lady Juliana said, patting the chair next to her. "Cook has prepared enough food for an army."

As Catrin sat down, she scanned the Vaughans' tired faces and realized they were probably as weary and hungry as she. They, too, had waited through Evan's frightful fever, and they, too, had missed meals and sleep to be sure Evan was cared for.

"Where are the children?" Mr. Vaughan asked his wife.

"Owen was up before dawn to go into town for me, and Margaret is still asleep, but they'll join us for lunch." She cast Catrin a kindly look. "I think, however, that our guest won't be there to meet them, since she'll probably spend the next several hours sleeping."

Catrin looked down at her plate. "Yes, if Evan doesn't need me."

"He can do without you a few hours," murmured Lady Juliana, though Catrin could feel the older woman eye her with curiosity.

The food came then, blessedly ending attempts at conversation. Eggs and sausage had never tasted so good, nor simple baked bread so exotic.

When they'd eaten, Mr. Vaughan leaned back with a sigh of contentment. "I tell you, Mrs. Price, there is nothing so wonderful as a good meal when one is starved."

"I'll have to agree with you there, sir."

Lady Juliana said gently, "Except perhaps for a good night's sleep when one is tired."

Mr. Vaughan turned serious. "I know Mrs. Price needs a long rest. But before we send her off to bed, I must ask her a few questions." He looked at Catrin. "If that's all right with you."

With a sigh, she nodded. The time had come. Ever since she and the squire had carried Evan here, she'd waited for him to question her more thoroughly.

"A man calling himself Mr. Price showed up here yesterday."

For a moment, she simply stared at him, bewildered. "Mr. Price?"

"I suspect it was David Morys, since he asked for you and Evan."

Fear clutched at her. "What did he say?"

Mr. Vaughan cast her a shrewd look. "That his wife, a pretty woman named Catrin, had run off with a mountebank from London, and he wanted to know whether they'd stopped here. He said the mountebank had stolen his pistol."

"That wretched liar! I assure you I'm *not* his wife!"

Mr. Vaughan smiled. "Yes, I know. I figured that the likelihood of your having married two Mr. Prices was slim. Obviously, your Mr. Morys was lying. He must have realized you'd use your real name to gain help, and he couldn't very well pose as your husband with a different last name."

A shudder wracked her. "What did you tell him?"

"That I hadn't seen the couple, of course. I did remark that a coach passes this way late at night on its way to Carmarthen, and perhaps you had taken it."

"Very quick thinking," Lady Juliana said. "That particular coach goes on to other parts before returning to Carmarthen. It will be days before he can speak to the driver and find out that the man didn't pick up Evan and Mrs. Price."

Mr. Vaughan nodded. "And that storm we had yesterday ought to slow him down even more. The roads are still treacherous. Besides, once he learns that Evan and Mrs. Price didn't take the coach, he'll no doubt assume they made it onto a ship to London. With luck, his pursuit will end there."

"I think it will," Catrin said. "I don't think he'd try to follow us to London." Catrin flashed Mr. Vaughan a grateful smile. "Thank you so much for misdirecting him. After what he did to Evan, I never want to see him again."

Mr. Vaughan steepled his fingers. "I can well understand that." He drew in a deep breath. "I hope you don't mind if I ask why this Mr. Morys is going to so much trouble to find you. You said you'd tell me the whole story eventually, and now that Evan is doing better . . ."

"Of course." How much should she say? How much would Evan want him to know?

"When Evan stopped here on his way to Llanddeusant, he mentioned that you might have been the last person to see his friend Justin alive. Evan said he was on his way to question you. Can I assume all of this is related to that?"

If Mr. Vaughan knew that much, there wasn't any point in keeping the whole truth from him. "Yes."

She began to relate the whole story, leaving out only the real reason she'd wanted the chalice. All she said was that it was a family heirloom she'd thought to regain. She also left out her physical relationship with Evan, but apparently they deduced that, for Lady Juliana began to regard her with a knowing gaze.

But when Catrin came to the part about Evan's finding the chalice and accusing her of duplicity, she dropped her eyes to her plate, unable to see their condemnation.

She could hardly finish without tears, especially when describing David's shooting Evan. Then she ended with, "And that's why David is after us."

The long silence tormented her. At last she lifted her head, only to find Mr. Vaughan looking speculative and Lady Juliana intrigued.

Mr. Vaughan cleared his throat. "That's a very interesting tale. You say Evan was carrying you to London to be questioned by this Mr. Quinley?"

She nodded.

"Because he thought you might be part of some sordid conspiracy to murder his friend." Lady Juliana snorted. "Men! They always look at the 'evidence' and never their hearts. I should have known Evan was as bad as the rest, jumping to conclusions based on the flimsiest of facts."

Catrin gaped at Lady Juliana, surprised to find an ally.

Mr. Vaughan raised an eyebrow at his wife. "I don't think these are the flimsiest of facts. Perhaps you're letting your own . . . ah . . . past experiences color your assessment."

Lady Juliana drew herself up with a haughty glare. "Perhaps. But a guilty woman wouldn't risk death to save the man who planned to have her arrested. Nor would she stay by his side when she could run off and leave him to die."

"No, of course not," Mr. Vaughan said. "But when Evan accused Mrs. Price, he didn't realize she was going to come to his rescue so valiantly. So you can't blame him for his suspicions." He cast Catrin a solicitous glance. "In any case, I think we've discussed this enough. Mrs. Price looks as if she might fall asleep in her chair if we don't allow her to retire."

"I agree." Lady Juliana smiled at Catrin. "I know you haven't spent much time in it, but you do know where your room is, don't you?"

"Yes." Catrin rose, more than happy to end the discussion. "And please let me know if . . . if Evan calls for me."

Lady Juliana's eyes sparkled. "Of course, my dear."

Then Catrin started for the stairs, weary in every muscle. When she reached her room, directly across from Evan's, she hesitated, wondering if she should check on him. But she didn't want to risk waking him.

Instead, she entered her own room to discover that a beautiful night rail had been left for her on her bed. Then a knock came at the door before a cherry-cheeked maid bustled in with two footmen carrying an empty tub.

"Good morning. My name's Sally. Milady said you'd be wantin' a bath. And I'm to be your maid while you're here."

"A hot bath sounds lovely, thank you," Catrin murmured, tears welling in her eyes. Lady Juliana must be the most thoughtful woman in Wales.

As the servants prepared the bath, Sally turned to Catrin. "Milady has chosen a few gowns she thinks you might be able to wear with a tuck or two."

It would take more than a tuck or two to make any gown of the voluptuous Lady Juliana fit *her*. But at least she wouldn't have to wear her own bloodstained one anymore.

A few minutes later, immersed in hot water up to her chin, she considered how many things one took for granted—sleep, clean clothes, baths, good food. With a lurch, she realized that if she *were* arrested for Lord Mansfield's murder, she would lose such simple things.

What was to happen to her now? Once Evan was well and able to travel, would he continue in his purpose? Surely the fact that she'd stayed by his side would sway him to believe in her at least a little.

All at once, the pain she'd been fighting so hard to ignore hit her. Evan had thought her a criminal, a monster. How could she bear it if he still insisted on carting her off to the magistrate?

She had no choice but to go. Escaping into the hills, the solution she'd posed to David, was farcical, since it would still mean losing her lands and condemning her tenants to an uncaring owner. At least if she went to London and spoke in her own defense, new evidence might be found to exonerate her.

But what if Evan decided to believe her? She would return to Llanddeusant, of course, and go on with her life. Evan would probably go on to London, and . . . and . . .

The pain of separating from Evan sliced through her. He'd made it clear he didn't want to marry. And now that David had stolen the chalice, she couldn't marry anyway.

It was so unfair! The only man she wanted to marry thought she was a criminal, and the only man she *could* marry without risking the curse wanted to treat her like a whore.

Feeling defeated, she stepped from the tub and dried off. She couldn't think about this right now or she'd go mad. She must sleep and prepare herself for whatever awful things were thrown at her next.

Donning the nightdress, she slipped between clean sheets. Time to gather her strength, as Grandmother had done when she'd lost first her husband and then her daughter and son-in-law. There was no longer any place for reticence in her life.

That was her last thought before she drifted off to sleep.

avid roamed the streets of Carmarthen, searching for his quarry. Catrin and Newcome had escaped him on a blasted coach, of all things. But they had to be around Carmarthen; it was the closest port.

Glancing down at the bag in his hand, he gave a grim smile. At least he had the chalice. And Catrin wanted it. So when she came to him for it, he'd make her agree to marry him before he gave it to her.

Perhaps Catrin and Newcome had left the coach before they reached town. That was worth pursuing. He should start questioning people in the cottages on the outskirts, then work his way in.

He sauntered along the road back to Llanddeusant, but there seemed to be only forest along it. As he rounded a bend he thought he heard a rustling behind him, but when he whirled to look, he saw naught but the muddy road.

As he turned back, he nearly jumped out of his skin. Blackheart stood in front of him, blocking the road.

"You frightened me half out of my wits!" David cried. "What are you doing here?"

When Blackheart approached, David fought to hide his panic. If Blackheart noticed the bag with the chalice, he'd take it. David couldn't let the bastard have his only hope of getting Catrin back.

"I told you to keep me informed of all developments between you and Catrin," Blackheart said. "Then I had to hear from Mrs. Llewellyn that you'd taken off for Carmarthen without telling me your plans."

"There was no time. I had to catch up to them."

Blackheart examined his well-manicured fingernails. "Mrs. Llewellyn said that Newcome and the London investigator suspect our shy little Catrin of killing Lord Mansfield. That she sent you off to rescue the chit." He glanced up, his eyes cold. "Obviously you were unsuccessful, or Catrin would be with you."

"Actually, I did catch up to them. I shot the bastard. He'll succumb to his wounds soon enough."

Blackheart's eyes narrowed. "What did you do? Leave him for dead? And what about Catrin?"

David glanced away from Blackheart's contemptuous expression. "She and Newcome . . ." Blast, he hated having to tell the old man of his humiliation. "They escaped me. That's why I'm here. I'm trying to find them."

Blackheart gave a bark of laughter. "How did a woman and a wounded man escape you when you had a pistol on them? They got it away from you, did they? Christ, what a fool you are."

He stiffened. "They're in Carmarthen somewhere. I'll find them."

"You'd better. Catrin must lead me to that chalice." As David instinctively tightened his grip on the bag, Blackheart caught the movement. "Unless, of course, you managed to retrieve it after you shot Newcome." He gestured to the bag. "Give it to me." When David hesitated, Blackheart stepped closer and added, with menace in his voice, "I'm not an idiot. I know you have it."

"But I need it to make Catrin marry me!"

Blackheart's laugh seemed to rustle the very leaves in the forest. "Cross me now, and you risk losing her forever. All I need do is tell her of your peccadillo with that student in Merthyr Tydfil, and she'll choose to be a widow all her life rather than marry you."

Helpless anger surged in David. Devil take Blackheart, he would always get what he wanted!

With a sigh, David handed the sack over. To his surprise, Blackheart strode into the forest with it.

David hurried after him. "Where do you think you're going?"

Blackheart only stopped when he'd reached a spot well hidden from the road. "I want to examine the chalice to make sure it's the right one, and I'm not going to risk doing that where anyone might see." He drew it from the bag and held it up to the light. His unholy smile made David shiver.

"*Siprys dyn giprys dan gopr,*" Blackheart muttered as he ran his fingers over the markings.

The words sounded like no Welsh David had ever heard. As Blackheart continued to murmur nonsensical phrases and stroke the chalice, David grew uneasy.

When he shifted his feet, Blackheart started, as if he'd forgotten David was there. He fixed David with eyes brightly burning. "So you thought you could keep it from me, and force Catrin to your side with it. Ignore my claim."

"What claim? You have no more claim than I. Besides, why can't we both have it? I only need it long enough to court Catrin and marry her. You can have it after that."

With a scowl, Blackheart came toward David. "What makes you think I want you to marry Catrin?"

David backed away. "Even . . . if your aim is to k-keep her accursed," he stammered, "she'll do anything to get it back. She'd certainly give herself to me for it. That's all I want . . . Catrin in my arms for one night—"

"Liar! You want her to marry you so you can get your hands on her land. That's why you tried to hide the chalice from me in the first place."

"No!" David cried, alarmed by the menace in Blackheart's face. "I would have given it to you, I swear! Once Catrin and I were married . . ." He trailed off as Blackheart pulled a dagger from his coat.

David's heart faltered. Judging from the strange markings and S-shaped blade, it was an antique weapon. And Blackheart clearly meant to use it on him.

"No, no! You don't understand—" As Blackheart advanced on him, David shook his head. "You wouldn't have gained the damned thing at all if not for me!"

"True, but you've served your purpose."

David took another step back, only to find himself against a tree. He threw up his hands. "You can have the chalice! Take it with my blessing! I'll go my way and—"

"Tell Catrin where it is." Blackheart's eyes flickered like ghastly lights in his stony face. "But I can't have you link me to it. My possession of it must remain utterly secret, and that's impossible with you alive."

Blackheart paused to let his words sink in. In that instant, David darted from between the man and the tree, whirling back toward the road. Dear God, Blackheart planned to kill him! He was completely mad!

David weaved through the trees, his heart pounding in his ears. If he could only reach the road . . .

A sharp pain tore through his back, knocking him to his knees. "Oh God," he cried as pain radiated outward and something warm soaked his shirt.

In a panic, he tried to rise, but a savage kick from behind sent him crashing down. Fear clutched at his gut as he crawled blindly forward, but a foot came down on his back and he heard a tearing sound just as another awful pain wrenched him and blood gushed forth.

With surprising strength, Blackheart kicked him onto his back, and David stared up in disbelief. Blackheart held the dagger, sheathed in blood. David's blood.

David tried to raise his arms to cover his face but couldn't make them work. He could barely feel the dry brush scratching his palms.

"Your poor father," Blackheart said as he casually knelt on David's belly with one knee, causing David a fire of pain. "To have his younger son set upon by thieves while running to the rescue of a damsel in distress. A fitting end to a disappointing life, is it not?"

The disapproving face of his father loomed in David's mind. Then, inexplicably, it became the face of the schoolgirl in Merthyr Tydfil whom David had debauched and abandoned. He could see her pretty cheeks drenched in tears as she'd stood trial for the crime his father and Blackheart had blamed on her. He saw her pale when the sentence of transportation was announced.

With a sob, David closed his eyes. He didn't want to die thinking of that. He would think of Catrin, of her shimmering eyes and soft lips.

But as Blackheart brought the dagger down into David's chest over and over, all David could see was the face of the young girl in Merthyr Tydfil. It was the last thing he saw before the light died.

~

Muted light from the setting sun spilled into Evan's room, rousing him from a deep and satisfying sleep, his first in three days. This time it took only seconds for him to realize he was at Llynwydd.

His shoulder still ached and his head still throbbed an insistent beat, but he felt a bit stronger, thanks to the broth and cider Juliana had forced him to drink that morning. He also had less trouble maneuvering into a sitting position.

God, he was hungry. That was to be expected, since he'd had little to eat in the last few days. And it was a good sign that he was feeling better. In fact, he was eager to leave his bed, to flex his muscles.

With his uninjured arm, he pulled the bell to call for a servant. To his surprise, scarcely ten minutes passed before Rhys himself entered. As soon as he saw Evan sitting up, he smiled and settled into a chair near the bed. "A servant said that you rang. I thought for sure he was mistaken, but I decided to check. And here I find that Mr. Lie-Abed is awake at last."

Mr. Lie-Abed, indeed. Rhys's concern seemed inversely proportional to the amount of teasing he subjected Evan to. Evan had to admit he preferred Rhys's way of dealing with the crisis. Juliana's fussing embarrassed him.

"I'm awake, alive, and starving," Evan said, matching Rhys's light tone. "I want a real meal tonight, not broth."

"One day's rest, and already you think you're cured. I'll admit, however, that you sound stronger. This morning you could barely wheeze your demands. That's promising."

"Enough to gain me a joint of mutton and a pudding?" Evan asked hopefully.

Rhys laughed. "You don't waste any time recovering, do you? Juliana will be delighted. She has peeked in here ten times today, convinced that your protracted sleep must indicate a relapse. Only your snores and healthy color kept her from sending for the doctor again."

"I'm surprised she didn't take my snores for moans of agony and bring the doctor in anyway," Evan grumbled. "Sometimes your wife is overly diligent in seeing to my health."

"Someone has to be, when you go about the country throwing yourself at madmen with loaded pistols."

Evan met Rhys's now serious gaze with surprise. "Catrin told you what happened? What did she say?"

"That she knocked a certain Mr. Morys over the head with a family heirloom, thus enabling you to launch yourself at him and his pistol."

"Did she also tell you why Mr. Morys was there in the first place and why we were on our way to Carmarthen?"

Rhys fixed him with a steady gaze. "She said you were taking her to talk to an investigator who believes she had a part in Lord Mansfield's murder."

Evan couldn't tell whether Rhys approved or disapproved of his actions. "She must have told you about the chalice, too."

"You mean the one she bought from Lord Mansfield?"

"Yes. Did she mention her reasons for wanting it?"

"She said that was the family heirloom she clobbered Morys with."

Evan gave a faint smile. He could hardly expect her to tell the Vaughans about the curse, since it sounded so unbelievable. Then again, he was surprised she'd told them everything else.

What did her candor mean? Deuce take it, what did *any* of it mean? Why had she fought so hard to save him? Why had she chosen him over Morys, the one man who would have done his best to keep her from being arrested?

"Tell me something," Rhys said, breaking into his thoughts. "Do you really suspect her of involvement with Lord Mansfield's death?"

Evan stared at his longtime friend, trying to assemble all the evidence that had pointed to her complicity. None of it seemed very convincing now. "I suppose I did once. Two days ago, I was almost sure of it."

Leaning back, Rhys eyed him with interest. "And now you're not?"

"I'm not sure about anything anymore." Evan laid his head against the headboard. "I'm not sure why Catrin saved my life or why she sent Morys packing when he only wanted to help her. I'm not even sure why she explained the situation to you and Juliana, especially when it reflected badly on her."

A long silence ensued, punctuated only by the beat of the clock in the hall.

"If I might venture an opinion," Rhys said, "it seems that Mrs. Price's lies and her fleeing the scene are understandable, given her shyness and her lack of experience in dealing with London officials. And I find it hard to believe a woman like her would go to such lengths merely to acquire a family heirloom."

Evan stared up at the ceiling, thinking of the ugly bronze object that had caused so much grief. "Yes, well, the chalice is . . . more than that. She thinks she has pressing reasons for acquiring it."

"Pressing enough to have a man robbed and murdered?"

Evan thought of Catrin's kindness to her servants, her generous spirit, her willingness to put aside her natural reticence when it was necessary . . . like when she'd saved his life.

That one act had transformed his entire image of her.

Or had he had the right image from the beginning? Had he merely allowed his rage at her lie about the chalice to blind him to her true character? The Catrin who'd saved his life was not the Catrin he'd imagined plotting to steal from Justin.

He turned an unsettled gaze on Rhys, who awaited his answer. "I'm not sure anything in this world could compel Catrin to hurt someone."

"Except a threat to your well-being," Rhys said dryly. "She certainly routed Morys, didn't she?"

Evan smiled. "You should have seen that pompous bastard's expression when she hit him. He never for one moment expected it." He shook his head. "I never expected it. When I handed her the loaded pistol and told her she'd have to defend herself, she looked as if I'd asked her to handle dog dung with her bare hands."

His smile faded. "But she did it to save my life, paying me good coin for the bad I'd given her." He didn't remember much about her confrontation with Morys, but he did remember her standing with that cocked pistol, willing to defend Evan to the death if Morys didn't leave.

Why had he been so ready to think that Catrin had conspired against Justin? The woman who'd risked her life to save him, who'd shown courage and kindness time and again, couldn't be part of such a horrendous act.

"You're in love with her," Rhys said, breaking into Evan's thoughts.

Evan stared at his friend as the statement thundered in his ears. *Was* he in love with Catrin? Was love this feeling of being in a permanent state of waiting for her return? Or the crushing ache he'd felt when he'd believed her guilty of involvement in Justin's murder? Was love what had made their ride from Llanddeusant a torment unmitigated even by his absurd attempts at reciting Latin?

Or what made him cringe whenever he thought of the difference in their backgrounds?

"If I am in love," Evan said morosely, "Fate has certainly played a devilish trick on me. She has wealth and rank and can marry anyone she wants, especially now that she has—"

Wait, what *had* happened to the chalice? Evan tried to remember if she'd picked it up, but everything from that time was hazy. She and Morys had discussed it. That was all he'd absorbed. Still, she'd had the pistol, so she would never have let Morys have the chalice.

"Now that what?" Rhys asked.

"Nothing. But you see what I mean, don't you? A woman like Catrin Price with a man of my background? It's impossible."

"Not if she loves you." Rhys leaned forward. "I would never have thought to marry an earl's daughter, but Juliana proved that a good woman doesn't care about such things. And you've just been telling me what a good woman Mrs. Price is."

"That's the trouble. Catrin is *too* good for the likes of me."

Henrietta had been a good woman, too, and after witnessing his violent side, she'd recoiled. Still, hadn't Catrin seen him at his worst that day in her study? Was it possible she could come to love him?

Evan considered telling Rhys about his fears, but couldn't bring himself to reveal his dark urges to the man he respected more than anyone. "In any case, I don't even know how she feels about me."

"You could ask her."

Evan's smile faded. God, he'd be devastated if he asked and she spurned him. "I don't know, Rhys." He sighed. "But perhaps I will."

Rhys took one look at his expression and rose. "I'm sorry. It wasn't right of me to meddle. I'm becoming as bad as Juliana, tormenting you with questions when all you want is a joint of mutton." Rhys was back to his light tone, for which Evan was grateful. "I'd best go downstairs and see to getting you some sustenance. Juliana will take a stick to me if I leave you starving."

He walked to the door, then paused. "Oh, I almost forgot to tell you. That Morys fellow came here looking for you and Mrs. Price yesterday."

Evan scowled. "What did you tell him?"

"I sent him on a wild-goose chase. He won't be back for a while, so don't worry about him."

"Thank you. One of these days I must figure out how many centuries it will take me to repay you and Juliana for everything you've done."

"Nonsense. You're a friend. You owe us nothing." Rhys opened the door and grinned. "I take that back. Give us an autographed copy of your next book, and we'll be content."

Evan managed a smile as Rhys walked out. Then he lay back against the pillow. The muddle in his head was giving him a great deal more trouble than the pain in his shoulder. His thoughts twisted and turned, always returning to one place. Catrin, the woman who'd entranced his soul.

And yes, the woman with whom he was wonderfully, horribly in love. What was he going to do about her?

Marry her. That was what people did when they were in love. It was the only way to keep her.

But did he dare? Even if she'd have him, could he risk seeing his marriage degenerate into one like his parents', where love was twisted up with explosive violence and loathing? Memories assailed him of his father's vicious temper and subsequent tearful apologies . . . his claiming to love his wife even though he beat her and their children regularly.

Father and Mother had both claimed to love each other. Yet what Evan felt for Catrin wasn't violent. The only time he'd come close to hurting her physically was when he'd thought she was lying, and he'd resisted the urge.

He couldn't imagine striking her because she spilled his glass of wine or spent too much on a gown or talked too loudly in church, all things for which his father had beaten his mother. He certainly didn't want to make Catrin fear his moods and cringe whenever he raised his voice. The idea of Catrin watching him with constant wariness repulsed him.

And children. Oh God, if he ever had children with Catrin, he'd never hurt them. He'd cherish any child that came of their union.

For the first time in his life, hope flickered within him. Perhaps he wasn't like his father. Yes, he'd lost his temper in the past, but he'd never hurt anyone he loved or anyone more helpless than himself. And he especially couldn't imagine doing so after his near brush with death. Life was too sweet to waste in anger.

It had made him realize something else, too. He needed Catrin. He wanted her for the rest of his life, and there was only one way to ensure that—marriage. He must ask her to forgive him for his deplorable lack of faith in her earlier.

But first, he would explain what she was taking on if she agreed. It was only fair to let her know of the dark possibilities, of the violence that simmered in his breast. Once before, he'd tried to hide it from the woman he wanted to marry, and that had ended disastrously.

This time he'd do things differently, tell her everything, even if it meant that she refused him. He only prayed that she didn't.

18

As the last slivers of daylight crept in splintered designs across the rich carpet, Catrin paused outside Evan's room. Should she go in, or wait until she'd heard from a servant that he was awake?

She glanced down at the simple muslin gown Lady Juliana had loaned her. It hung on her, and Catrin wished she had the curves to fill it out. Despite all she and Evan had gone through, she had this inexplicable need to look beautiful for him.

Oh well. Evan would have to settle for clean and presentable.

The sound of footsteps made her whirl to find a maid coming toward her with a tray of food.

"Good evening," Catrin said. "Is that for Mr. Newcome?"

The young woman nodded. "The master says he wants dinner." She glanced doubtfully at the tray, which was heaped with plates holding bread and cheese and a joint of mutton. "If you ask me, this is too much for a sick man, but the master laughed at Cook when she tried to tell him so, and milady isn't here just now to set him straight."

"I suppose it can't hurt to offer it," Catrin said. "But if you don't mind, I'd like to bring it in myself."

"Certainly, miss." The maid handed over the tray, then opened the door.

As Catrin slipped inside, she found herself suddenly reluctant to face Evan. What would she do if he'd returned to his suspicions? Staring down at the tray, she said, "I waylaid the servant and stole your meal. I hope you don't mind."

"Only if you don't intend to give me any of it."

The rumbling amusement in his voice made her look up to see him sitting on the edge of the bed. She dragged in a sharp breath. He looked so wonderful in his breeches and the large shirt covering his bandaged shoulder and arm. Despite everything he'd been through, his color was better, and he smiled at her with such devastating effect she could only smile back.

As he pushed himself to a stand, her smile vanished. "What are you doing?" She set the tray down and hurried to his side. "You shouldn't be up yet! You'll hurt yourself!"

Laying his free arm about her shoulder, he leaned on her. "I'm really much better. And I don't want to eat in the bed like an invalid."

"Yes, but—"

"You're not getting me back into that bed just now, Catrin, so don't even think about it." He did seem stronger, for he barely put any of his weight on her as they headed toward the table where she'd set the tray. "Besides," he continued in a husky voice, "I don't mind struggling out of bed when it allows me to hold you."

The tender note in his voice was painfully familiar. She looked up to find his eyes burning with a fire she'd never thought to see again. She couldn't breathe or move.

Apparently neither could he, for they'd come to a complete halt. He turned toward her, dropping his good arm from her shoulders to her waist so he could pull her close. When he brushed a kiss to her forehead, she let out a sigh and slipped her arms about him.

"Catrin," he whispered. "I've been thinking about doing this ever since I woke up."

"So have I."

He nuzzled her temple. "You haven't been cursing me for hauling you across the country on the basis of my foolish suspicions?"

She pulled back to stare at him uncertainly.

His eyes filled with remorse. "I've been the greatest fool. I must have been mad to think you were involved with Justin's murder. I know in my heart you'd never do such a thing."

Relief hit her so swiftly that she erupted into tears.

Looking stricken, he pressed his lips to her cheek. "Please don't cry, darling. I've made you cry enough. I don't ever want to make you cry again."

Darling. That made her tears flow even more freely. "I'm s-sorry," she stammered, wiping the tears away. "I just didn't know what to expect. I feared that once you got better, everything would go back . . . to how it was before."

His voice dropped to an aching whisper. "You mean, when I let my stupid anger blind me to what should have been obvious from the start—that you could never commit a crime? When I sat on a horse, holding you in my arms while every step closer to London tormented me? God, it nearly killed me to think I'd never kiss you or caress you or make love to you again."

She lifted her gaze to his, scarcely daring to believe his words. "But you were so . . . cold that day. I thought you'd dismissed me totally from your mind."

"Only a eunuch could have done that, and I'm no eunuch." He grimaced. "I don't know how you can ever forgive me for the things I said and the wretched way I treated you. I didn't even bother to consider your version of events. Morys recognized one thing, at least. I deserved to be shot for how I behaved."

His remorse so touched her that it blotted out her earlier hurt. "It wasn't entirely your fault. I did lie to you. And it's easy to see why you might have thought I'd—"

"No, it's not easy to see." His eyes glittered like gems at the bottom of a night stream. "I behaved like a deuced idiot. It was one thing to be angry at your lie, but I carried it too far."

His breath came quickly now, as if it took all his strength to speak. "After my tantrum, I should have stopped to consider the absurdity of my accusation, instead of hauling you off like a common criminal. If I'd used half a brain that morning, I wouldn't have gotten myself shot later and put you in danger."

She cupped his face in her hands. "And if I hadn't been

such a coward and told you the truth in the first place, none of it would have happened."

"Coward?" His voice held a note of incredulity. "You saved my life! Morys would have killed me if it hadn't been for you."

"Yes, but if not for me you wouldn't have—"

"Enough. If it makes you feel better, I'll lay some of the blame on you, but only so we can forgive each other and put it behind us." He splayed his hand across the small of her back. "Besides, I can think of a hundred more important things to do just now than fight over who was more guilty of getting me shot, especially since I survived it."

The look in his eyes drained the breath from her lungs. Understanding...caring...desire...all shone forth where once there'd been nothing but condemnation and hurt.

"In fact," he rasped as his gaze trailed to her lips, "I can think of one very important thing I want to do just now." Then he brought his mouth down on hers.

Such a kiss he gave her, sweet and light, like whipped cream, the kind of kiss befitting a vow to abandon the past. She'd almost forgotten how snugly his lips fit with hers. And how easily he could make her blood leap and race.

He drew back, his eyes wide and wondering. "How could I have ever thought to give this up ... to give *you* up?"

This time when he kissed her, his mouth began a ravening possession that sent wild shivers over her skin. His tongue mated with hers in a mesmerizing rhythm, as if he had an unquenchable thirst for her, as if he sought to find the very secret to her soul.

She knew she shouldn't let him kiss her. There was no point to it. He wouldn't offer her marriage, and even if he did, she couldn't marry without the chalice.

But he needs me right now, she told herself as he enveloped her in his scent and taste and essence. *I can't turn him away.*

And she needed him, too, to wash away the terror of the past few days. She strained against him, wanting to feel more of him, and he drew her so close, she could feel his arousal through his breeches.

"Oh, Catrin," he murmured against her lips, "you see what you do to me? I've barely left the sickbed and I want you beyond endurance."

His words were a splash of cold water, reminding her of where they were and what he'd been through. She drew back. "You shouldn't be standing like this."

"I want to hold you." He brushed kisses over her cheek. "I *need* to hold you."

"You can hold me while you're sitting down. I'm not going anywhere, I promise." Not yet, anyway. She needed more time with him.

With a groan, he let her lead him to the chair, but as soon as she had him seated, he tugged her into his lap and buried his face in her neck. "You were right; this is much better."

He kissed a path along her collarbone to the cleft between her breasts. Closing her eyes with a sigh, she clasped his shoulder.

Then she felt the bandages beneath his shirt. By heaven, what was she doing? He shouldn't even be out of bed!

"No, Evan." She pushed his head from her breast. "For heaven's sake, you've only just recovered. You need time to regain your strength. I'll die if you fall ill again. It nearly killed me watching you languish from that fever."

His eyes darkened as he gazed at her flushed cheeks, her half-parted lips, her gaping bodice. "Good God, I don't know how I'll wait."

She turned her face away for fear she'd burst into tears if he said many more seductive things like that. He leaned forward to kiss her, but she slipped off his lap.

As he stared at her, his breath coming hard and his eyes gleaming, she planted her hands on her hips. "You should eat some of this food you called for. It'll help you recover your strength."

Apparently sensing the change in her mood, he watched her solemnly. "I'll eat, don't worry. But first I have things to talk to you about. Important things."

Oh no. Although he'd said he believed her now, he probably still wanted her to tell the constable what she had or hadn't seen, and she couldn't bear the thought.

"We'll talk after you eat," she said brightly. "You really should get some sustenance in you."

He arched an eyebrow. "You certainly want to hasten my recovery."

"You were the one who asked for food." She went to the tray and looked at it. "Still, I don't know what possessed Mr. Vaughan to send you so much. There's even a joint of mutton."

"Don't you touch that joint of mutton," Evan warned. "In a few minutes, I shall eat the entire thing. I might even make you feed me, since you obviously think I'm not strong enough to lift a fork."

When she looked at him askance, he grinned. Then he reached over and took her hand. "But right now, I need to talk to you."

"If this is about Quinley and the investigation and—"

"It's not about that. If I took you to London to speak to Quinley now, I can't predict the outcome, so I can't risk it." When she blinked in surprise, he said gently, "You saved my life. What kind of man would I be if I made you face those hostile men who don't know you—who might jump to the wrong conclusions?"

"But what about your friend's death?"

"You said you had nothing to do with it, and I believe you, so that leaves only one possibility: He was murdered by thieves. So there's nothing you can add to the investigation, but much you'd risk by speaking out. And there it stands."

She slumped in relief.

"But that's not what I wanted to discuss." He drew her to stand between his splayed legs, then nodded at his knee. "Will you sit with me again?"

Out of consideration for his weakened condition, she sat at his feet instead.

With a sigh, he laid his hand on her head. "Do you remember the night you first told me about the chalice?"

She tensed. "The night I lied to you, yes."

"And the night we talked about marriage."

That wasn't what she'd expected. Why was he bringing it up now, when nothing had changed, especially since she no longer had the chalice?

"Yes," she said. "You told me you couldn't marry because of your position at Cambridge."

His lips tightened into a thin line. "That was a lie, I'm afraid." When her eyes widened, he added, "I mean, it's true that university fellows aren't allowed to marry. But that wouldn't stop me. I'd simply leave the university to do something else." He gave a faint smile. "Be a schoolmaster in a town like Llanddeusant, for example."

"Oh, of course," she said with a trace of bitterness. "I'm sure you'd prefer the scintillating conversation of scruffy children to the boring intellectual stimulation of Cambridge."

"University fellows are more like children than you'd think." He stroked her hair absently. "They're just as likely to snub someone who's different. They're jealous of anyone more successful, and like children, they can be inordinately cruel, except that their sophisticated minds enable them to find more subtle ways to ostracize the unusual . . . the brilliant . . . the misfit."

When he glanced away, she realized with surprise that he spoke of himself. She'd assumed that a genius would be perfectly at home at Cambridge, but she'd forgotten he was also a Welsh tenant farmer's son. She well understood what it meant to be a misfit in one's community. With a pang of sympathy, she rested her cheek on his knee, unsure how to comfort him.

"Intellectual stimulation doesn't feed the heart, Catrin. Leaving Cambridge wouldn't trouble me in the least, I assure you."

She chose her words carefully. "Then why did you tell me you couldn't marry?"

He glanced down at her. "Do you remember what I said about Henrietta, my former fiancée?"

She nodded. She shouldn't let him tell her this, especially if it was leading to a discussion of marriage. But she wanted to hear it all.

"I'd known Henrietta for years when I became enamored of her. Her father was a rich Welsh merchant who admired my books and was pleased when I offered for her. We even made plans for me to work with him in his business."

He stared off across the room. "One night I found Henrietta alone with a man. He was holding her close, and I . . . went insane with jealousy. I jerked him away and began hitting him while she screamed and begged me to stop. Of course, that only made it worse, for I thought she was defending her secret lover."

A shadow crossed his face. "She was defending her cousin, whom she hadn't seen in several years. I'd come across them just as she was hugging him . . . as she would hug any cherished relative who'd just returned from the war."

His gaze met hers. "In my fit of temper, I broke his nose and bruised him badly." He let out a heavy sigh. "She was furious. She called me a beast and ended our engagement, and that was that."

Catrin gaped at him. After he'd hinted at the terrible thing he'd done to make his fiancée hate him, Catrin had imagined something much more horrible. "You mean, she ended it because you made a mistake?"

"No." He tipped her chin up with one finger. "Because she saw for the first time what I really was. Unreasonable. Ill-tempered." His lips tightened. "Violent. I couldn't blame her for breaking the engagement. She was refined and beautiful and civilized, and I was exactly what she'd called me—a beast."

"Oh, but you're not!" she cried, wishing she could tear the word from his memory. "One slip does not make you a beast. Besides, many men would do the same if they saw their fiancées in what looked like compromising positions!"

"I doubt it. Another man would shout a little. He might even challenge the man to a duel, withdrawing the challenge once he realized the circumstances. But a civilized man never loses his temper to the extent that he beats someone to a bloody pulp without even knowing the situation."

"But you've learned from what you did, haven't you? I doubt you would do it now."

"I don't know if—"

"I know," she broke in. "I know you're not a beast."

He stroked her jaw with the back of his hand. "What a prickly little minx you are, so fierce in my defense even when what I did was inexcusable. Perhaps you're right, and I'm not quite the beast Henrietta thought."

He brushed her hair back from her face. "Even though you're of similar wealth and station, you're nothing like her. She was always just so: every hair in place, every word proper, the epitome of perfection . . ."

"No, that's not me at all," she said with a trace of envy. "I am definitely imperfect."

"Thank God. Perfection is for statues, not for people with whom you wish to share your life. Perfection doesn't feed the heart, and after a while it can be bloody intimidating." His eyes bore into hers. "You, my darling, are perfectly imperfect and warm and full of surprises. I wouldn't trade a thousand Henriettas for one of you."

He'd barely given her the chance to revel in the sweet statement before his face hardened. "Anyway, that's why I told you I couldn't marry. I've always been afraid of what might happen if I ever . . . lost my temper with a woman I cared for. I couldn't bear the thought of striking a woman, and the fear of doing that has kept me from taking a wife."

"But you lost your temper with *me* the day you found the chalice, and you didn't strike me—although I'll admit you wreaked havoc on my study." She rested her arms on his knees. "If ever you had provocation, it was then."

"I've told myself that." Anguish filled his face. "Still . . . Good God, Catrin, you don't know how quickly I can lose my temper. Nor how . . . violent I can be when I do. I'm terrified of what I might do." He gazed down at her. "Especially now that I've found someone I want to marry . . . someone I love."

Her heart twisted. Marriage to Evan would be heaven . . . until the day she watched him die because of the curse.

She rose and turned away, trying to conceal her turmoil. He didn't believe in it, so it didn't matter to him. And if she encouraged him, he'd seduce her into believing it didn't matter to her, either.

But it did. Deep inside, she knew it was real. She couldn't marry without the chalice. These past few days had been bad enough, but if she ever had to watch him die, knowing it was her fault, she couldn't bear it. Not when she loved him.

A groan escaped her lips. She loved him with all the breath in her body. Her friendship with Willie paled by comparison. Watching Willie die had been heart-wrenching, but watching Evan die would split her in two.

So she must give him a firm refusal. No explanation, no soft words of regret, just a no. That was the only way to make him see how impossible it was. She wouldn't make the same mistakes with Evan that she'd made with David. No more evasions.

Oh, but how could she stand to tell him no?

At her long silence, Evan broke into her thoughts. "I know I'm not much of a prize. I can bring nothing to a marriage but myself and my willingness to work hard. Yet I'd like to try. I—"

A knock sounded, and they both started. Catrin whirled toward the door, thankful for the reprieve.

But Evan cursed under his breath. He couldn't believe this. Here he'd been in the midst of telling Catrin how he felt, and some idiot had come to spoil it. "Go away, I'm resting!" he shouted.

But the door swung open and Lady Juliana breezed in. "Resting, indeed. Your sister's here and—"

She broke off as she caught sight of him in the chair and Catrin standing a few feet away. "I'm sorry, I didn't realize you had company."

"I brought Evan his tray," Catrin said.

Evan tried not to scowl, but it was hard. Catrin seemed suddenly distant, and he could only hope it wasn't because of what he'd said. He wanted to finish their conversation. He wanted to know how she felt about marriage.

Lady Juliana eyed the untouched tray with raised eyebrows. "I see your appetite hasn't yet returned. I'll call and have a servant take this away."

"Touch that tray, Juliana, and I'll bite your hand off," Evan said. "I called for that food, and I intend to eat it."

"Is that Evan?" came a familiar voice from the doorway, and he looked up to find his sister standing there.

A wave of feeling gripped him. Mary, his sweet Mary. He'd missed her more than he knew.

Tears welled in her brown eyes, and she hurried to his side with a little cry of joy. "Oh, Evan, look at you! You're ... you're ..."

"He's nearly back to his old self," Lady Juliana finished. "Ordering people about and scowling at everyone."

Mary wiped away tears as a smile spread over her ruddy face. "As long as he's awake and breathing, I don't care if he orders me about."

"It's good to see you," he whispered, his own eyes growing misty.

What he'd been through had made him appreciate his family more than ever. He rose, ignoring a flurry of protests from the three women, and pulled his sister close.

She hugged him, though he noticed she was careful not to press his bandaged arm and shoulder. "Oh, my dear boy," she whispered, "I can't tell you how glad I am to see you well. And standing up, no less!" Drawing back to look at him, she said, "I feared I'd not see you again in this life, and here you are, looking quite fit for a man who's been shot."

"You must thank Catrin for that. She saved my life." Still leaning on his sister, he angled his body toward Catrin. "I'd like to introduce you to—"

"Oh, we've already met," Mary said brightly, casting Catrin a shy glance, "haven't we, Mrs. Price?"

When Catrin nodded, Evan stared at Mary. "You were here before?"

"Oh yes, while you were so bad off with the fever," Mary said. "Mrs. Price and I kept vigil over you until I had to go home and see to my own family. She and I became rather cozy." She squeezed him with a smile. "I told her all about the scrapes you got into as a boy, and she told me what a hero you were to throw yourself in front of that madman with the pistol."

It was all Evan could do to keep his expression even. He dared not let Mary see how her matter-of-fact words alarmed him. Which scrapes did she mean? The times he'd stolen plums from the Llynwydd orchard before being caught by the gardener and then rescued by Juliana? Or the punishments his father had inflicted?

He didn't think Mary would speak of the latter, but at the very least, she must have revealed that his father had been a mere tenant farmer to the Vaughans. He'd planned to tell Catrin himself eventually, but he'd thought that if he first told her how much he loved her, the other wouldn't matter so much.

Now he wondered if her unsettling reaction to his talk of marriage signaled that it did indeed matter. She might have decided that a man like that, especially one with the violent nature he'd described, wasn't a man to marry.

And though she was probably right, he couldn't bear it if she rejected him. He tried to catch her eye, but she refused to look at him, causing more dread to build in his chest. Had he completely misread her kisses, the way she'd melted in his arms, the sympathy she'd shown him when he was telling her about his broken engagement? Had he misunderstood everything?

"In any case," his sister was saying, "it appears as if our vigilance has been repaid, for here you are, looking much better. Don't you think he looks well, Mrs. Price?"

"Yes." She glanced at him, then cut her eyes away.

That one movement spoke volumes. And he feared what it said.

"Oh dear," Mary exclaimed. "I'm forgetting about everyone who's waiting for me downstairs. Goronwy is here, and I brought Robert and the girls. They're all eager to see you. Do you think you can endure a few more visitors?"

Somehow he managed a smile, even though he felt as if a hollow chasm was opening up beneath his feet. "By all means, tell them to come up."

She beamed at him. "Wonderful. I'll hurry down and fetch them. I'll be only a moment." Then she hastened out the door.

Deprived of her support, he felt a little weak, but it was Juliana who came to help him back to the chair, not Catrin. And when he sat down and released a heavy breath, he looked up to see Catrin headed for the door.

"Where are you going?" he asked, his throat feeling raw and tight.

She paused at the door, not looking at him. "To my room."

"Don't leave." He was begging and he knew it, but he couldn't let her go. If she left, it meant that his talk of marriage had alarmed her. It meant she didn't want him. "Please stay and meet the rest of my family," he said, knowing it was a shameless ploy and not caring.

But even that didn't work. She met his gaze, then said in gentle tones, "I don't think that would be wise. I wouldn't want to intrude."

"It's not an intrusion."

She looked on the verge of tears, and shook her head. "I'm sorry, I can't stay." She stiffened, as if gathering her courage. "I shall be in my room if you wish to speak to me later."

"Why can't you stay?" Juliana asked, clearly puzzled by the strange interchange.

Catrin left without answering, but Evan didn't need words to know what her answer was. She knew he was going to ask her to marry him. And she was going to refuse him, so she didn't want to meet his family or further the connection with him in any way.

He'd lost her, and he wasn't even sure why.

"Evan?" Juliana said. "What's going on? What happened between you and Catrin just now?"

He closed his eyes, marshaling his resources to endure the pain. "Nothing."

"If this is about Justin's murder—"

"Deuce take it, no!" He glared at her. "I'd be an idiot to still believe she had any part in that after she saved my life, wouldn't I?"

"Then what—"

"It's none of your concern. Good God, haven't you meddled enough?" When Juliana stiffened, he instantly regretted his words. "I'm sorry, I shouldn't have said that."

She leveled a wounded gaze on him. "How have I meddled? What have I done to make you snap at me?"

He bit back another angry retort. Juliana had been a second mother to him, and he wouldn't hurt her for anything in the world, but her questions were driving him mad. "Nothing. I shouldn't have said anything."

"No, I want you to tell me what terrible thing I've done!"

He glared at her. "Well, for one thing, you let me believe that the Lady of the Mists was an old woman. I've had plenty of time to think about that, and I've finally figured out why."

Juliana's anger seemed to dissipate like smoke in a sudden rain. Now she looked nervous. "Oh? And what did you decide?"

"You wanted me to meet Catrin without any prejudgment." His voice grew hoarse. "You thought I'd take one look at her and be lost, and then it wouldn't matter if she was the Lady of the Mists. It wouldn't matter what part she had in Justin's murder."

Juliana just stood there, quiet, waiting.

"And you were right," he said bitterly. "You know me so well. I lost my heart to her the second I saw her." He lifted his anguished gaze to her. "But you forgot to take her feelings into account. You assumed she would fall in love with me, too. Well, I hate to disappoint you, but she didn't."

"What? That girl sat by your bedside night and day, crying and praying that you'd wake up, not eating, not sleeping . . . Merciful heavens, Evan, how much more proof of her feelings do you need?"

"I need her not to leave when I start talking about our future." He gave a shuddering breath. "Before you came in, I was on the verge of asking her to marry me. She knew it, and that's why it 'wouldn't be wise' for her to stay and meet the rest of my family. She's planning to refuse me, and it would have been too hard for her to meet them, knowing what she intended."

"I don't believe that." Juliana planted her hands on her waist. "If that girl isn't in love with you, then I'm deaf and blind. If you could have heard the way she spoke of you, the way she fretted over you—"

"Yes, but that was *before* she found out from Mary that I'm only a tenant farmer's son by birth!" He couldn't stand hearing Juliana talk about how well Catrin spoke of him. "And before I told her why my engagement to Henrietta failed. Now that she knows I wouldn't make a good husband—"

"Men are such fools!" Juliana said with an expression of disgust. "When it comes to love, do you think women care about things like position and money?" She came up to lay her hand on his shoulder. "Catrin is a wonderful woman, and I don't believe she cares at all about your background."

"Then why did she flee just now? A woman in love would have remained with me until I got the words out."

"Perhaps, perhaps not. But I wouldn't assume she's rejecting you. If she really means so much to you, go find out what's troubling her, instead of sitting here sulking."

He glared at her. "Thank you for your unwanted advice, but I know Catrin better than you do."

With a shrug, she headed for the door. "Fine, do as you wish. Give up on the one woman who suits you and cares for you." She stopped in the doorway to fix him with a haughty glance. "But don't blame me for your broken heart. I don't regret meddling, and I believe I picked the right woman for you. I just underestimated your ability to hold on to her." Then she stalked from the room.

Evan let out an explosive curse. He should never have told Juliana what had happened between him and Catrin. Deuce take her, she was wrong! Catrin had obviously stayed by his bedside out of an overdeveloped sense of guilt for what had happened to him. If she'd been in love with him, as Juliana claimed, she wouldn't have left when he'd started talking about marriage.

He settled into the chair with a scowl. This was one time Juliana would be forced to acknowledge that she'd made a mistake.

Unfortunately.

19

After Juliana's talk with Evan last night, she'd tried not to meddle. She'd done nothing when Mrs. Price had sent down a message saying she was too tired to come to dinner. She'd kept her peace when Evan spent the evening brooding in his room and not eating any of the food he'd called for so eagerly.

She'd even restrained herself from acting when a servant told her this morning that Evan had called for a bottle of brandy in the middle of the night, "to dull the pain in his shoulder and help him sleep." Hah! She knew exactly what pain he wanted to dull, and it wasn't in his shoulder.

But now that Sally stood here telling her that Mrs. Price was preparing to return to Llynwydd and wanted her old clothes back, Juliana had had enough.

She rose. "Thank you, Sally. I'll take care of it."

"What are you going to do?" Rhys asked as Juliana turned for the door.

"Talk some sense into Mrs. Price."

"Maybe you should keep out of it," Rhys warned. "Let the two of them work out their problems."

She glared at him, her irritation with Evan getting the better of her. "I'm surprised you noticed that they were having problems, or even that they were interested in each other. Men are usually stupid about such things."

Rhys raised an eyebrow. "Not always. And yes, I've noticed that Evan turns into a puddle of mush around Mrs. Price. And vice versa, I might add."

"Turning into puddles of mush is all very well, but at the moment, those two puddles are being stubborn, and I think it's time a third party made certain they don't go their separate ways and live the rest of their lives in misery."

"You're the third party, of course," he said dryly.

"Don't even think of trying to stop me." She shot him a quelling glance. "I left it up to them yesterday, and they bungled it. Now it's time to see that matters come out right." She paused, then added, "Oh, and you'd best prepare to go to town."

"To town?" He looked blank. "Why?"

"Because when I get through with them, they'll need some privacy. So we're going to Carmarthen for the day. The whole family. Margaret has been begging for a new dress and Owen has been itching to visit with Edgar now that he's home from university, so we might as well get that done."

After that pronouncement, she swept from the room. Although she heard Rhys laugh behind her, the fact that he didn't try to dissuade her meant he knew she was right. Something must be done about this situation.

When she reached the hall between Evan's and Mrs.

Price's rooms, she hesitated, but it was clear which one she must work on first, since saying her piece to Evan last night had done no good. So she knocked on Mrs. Price's door.

When Mrs. Price opened it, her face reflected her surprise. "Good morning, Lady Juliana."

Juliana took one look at Mrs. Price's tears and knew she'd made the right decision. "May I come in?"

Dully, the woman nodded and stepped aside to let Juliana enter.

Juliana closed the door. "Sally told me you want to leave this morning, so I thought I'd see if everything is all right."

Turning away, Mrs. Price said in a strained voice, "Everything . . . is fine."

"I can tell. Your eyes are the color of poppies, a sure sign that matters are going well."

Mrs. Price stiffened. "Please, Lady Juliana. I prefer not to talk about it."

"Very well. But I thought you should know that Evan is sitting in that room across the hall, convinced that you won't marry him because of his lowly background."

There. She'd meddled to the highest degree, and she didn't care.

This time it took Mrs. Price several minutes to speak, but Juliana could tell she was crying. "It's better that way," she whispered.

Juliana's temper rose. Merciful heavens, the woman was as stubborn as he was. "You can't let Evan go on thinking he's not worth marrying, especially if you have some other reason for refusing him!"

"As I said, I don't wish to discuss it."

"Oh, but I do. Sit down, Mrs. Price."

"I will not di—"

"Sit down!" Juliana ordered.

Mrs. Price started, then dropped onto the bed with a mutinous expression.

Juliana crossed her arms over her chest. "Evan is like a son to me. I shan't stand by and watch him suffer for no good reason. So I'm going to tell you some things about that young man that I've never spoken of to anyone, even him." She sucked in a heavy breath. "When I'm through, you may do as you wish: Break his heart, suffer in silence, I don't care. But first, you will hear me out."

The woman merely gave her a stony stare.

"Evan Newcome is an incredible man," Juliana said, "but you must have already realized that. And yes, he's the son of our tenant farmer Thomas Newcome, who passed away this year." When a flicker of sympathy shone in Mrs. Price's eyes, Juliana added, "But in case you pity Evan for losing his father, don't. The man regularly beat him, and would have kept him out of school and ignorant if Rhys and I hadn't intervened."

Mrs. Price's rigid composure cracked a little.

"Evan has never spoken of what he suffered," Juliana continued, "but I saw plenty of evidence of it during the years I tutored him. He used to come to lessons covered with bruises. Several times he had black eyes that he claimed came from fights with other boys. The first one appeared when he was only seven, so I was suspicious of that explanation, especially since his father rarely gave him time to play with other children."

As Mrs. Price's face filled with horror, Juliana hardened her voice. "And then there was the time Evan broke his ribs 'falling out of a tree.' He wasn't yet eleven, and could climb like a monkey. Oddly enough, when his mother came to tell me he wouldn't be coming to lessons, she was also sporting a black eye.

"In fact, he was often not the only one in his family with bruises. His mother . . . his sister . . . his older brother . . . I saw all of them with injuries at one time or another."

Mrs. Price's shoulders began to shake.

"You met Mary," Juliana went on relentlessly, "so you know what a dear she is. But that little dear didn't shed a single tear at her father's funeral. And Evan's brother . . ." Juliana glanced away. "Let's just say that Goronwy's family wears a good many bruises, too. I guess it's difficult to grow up in a household like the Newcomes' and not learn the wrong things."

She swung her gaze back to Mrs. Price. "But Evan rose above all that. Despite his wretched father, he fought to wrest an education from a system designed to keep out the Welsh. Evan made something of himself, and that takes a very strong and brave man. But he still believes what that horrible man beat into him—that he's unworthy of love. And if you walk away from him—"

"Please, no more!" Tears streamed down Mrs. Price's face. "You don't understand. I'd be honored beyond words to marry Evan. But I can't, and he knows why!"

"Does he?"

"Yes!" She clenched her fists. "He knows I don't have the chalice anymore!"

Juliana gaped at her. "That family heirloom you went to London to get from Lord Mansfield? What in the name of God does *that* have to do with anything?"

Mrs. Price swallowed. "It's a long story, and you'll not believe it."

Juliana sat down on the bed and took Mrs. Price's hand. "You don't know that. Why don't you tell me?"

For a moment, Juliana thought Mrs. Price would refuse. Then the woman began speaking in a low murmur. "There's a curse on all the Ladies of the Mists. If I marry without drinking from that chalice on my wedding day, my husband dies. That's why Willie and my father and grandfather and great-grandfather all passed away within three years of their weddings. That's why I went to London to purchase the chalice."

Staring off into space, she whispered, "But David Morys took it, and he'll never give it back. So if I marry Evan, he'll die." She fixed Juliana with a dark gaze. "I can't watch Evan die the way I watched Willie die. I can't!"

Juliana felt as if someone had punched her. This was a new development entirely. All this over some chalice? "But Evan didn't mention a curse—"

"He knows about it; he just doesn't believe in it. Yesterday, when I realized he was going to ask me to marry him without taking the curse into account, I didn't know what to do. I knew he'd pursue me until I gave in." She ducked her head shyly. "I can't resist Evan when he . . . I have no will at all where he's concerned."

Juliana bit back a smile. She'd known she was right about Mrs. Price's feelings.

"So I decided to refuse him without explanation. But I never got the chance, and after you came in and he wanted me to meet his family, I couldn't meet them, knowing I was about to turn him down. I did tell him to speak to me later, but I confess I was grateful he didn't. I suppose Evan guessed what I was about to do. I don't know why he acquiesced, but I'm content to let matters lie. I shall simply leave and let him get on with his life."

"But how can he? He thinks you have contempt for what he is . . . or was."

Mrs. Price swallowed. "That will pass. If I remind him about the curse, he'll never let the matter drop. And if he presses me into marriage, he'll die. So I must avoid that at all costs."

It was all so medieval. And had four men in Mrs. Price's family really died after three years of marriage?

A chill swept her that she shook off. Even if such a curse existed, there must be a way around it. And if anyone could find it, Evan could.

"Now you understand," Mrs. Price said, a catch in her throat. "So you must help me leave."

Juliana squeezed her hand. "Yes, of course. I shall go see about having your clothes brought and a horse saddled for you."

Mrs. Price nodded, but as Juliana left, she heard the woman weeping. Grimly, Juliana headed across the hall. Evan must be reminded of this curse business. She suspected he'd welcome her meddling for once.

She tapped on his door.

"Who is it?" a voice snarled on the other side.

She smiled. He was clearly unhappy enough to end this foolishness. "It's Juliana," she said in a low voice. "I must speak to you."

She heard him mutter an oath. "Go away! I'm . . . I'm getting dressed!"

Nonsense. He'd summoned a servant earlier to help him dress. She tried the knob. It was unlocked, thank heaven.

"I'm coming in," she said, in case he truly did need the warning, then entered the room. As she'd suspected, he was fully clothed.

"Can't a man have any privacy around here?" he growled.

"You'll have all the privacy you want an hour from now." She noted the half-empty brandy bottle and the filled glass in his hand. "That's what I've come to tell you. Rhys and I and the children are going to Carmarthen for the day. We may even spend the night, depending how long it takes us to finish our business."

"Fine," Evan bit out. "Have a wonderful time. Now if that's all—"

"Mrs. Price is planning to leave today, as well."

That got a reaction; his fingers clenched his glass. "Where's she going?"

Juliana shrugged. "Back to Plas Niwl, I suppose. I didn't ask."

A distinct bitterness crept into his voice. "I hope she has a wonderful time. I hope you *all* have a wonderful time."

Barely suppressing an oath, Juliana said, "One more thing. What's all this business about a chalice and a curse?"

He gave a heavy sigh. "She told you about the curse?"

"She says that's why she won't marry you."

He whirled on her. "Then she lies! She has her bloody chalice now, so the curse is no longer a problem!"

Aha. So *that* was the source of the problem! "Oh, but she doesn't have it. That Morys fellow stole it while she watched over you with the pistol."

The astonishment spreading over his face shifted rapidly to fury. He swore and stalked past her.

Heaving a relieved sigh, she watched as he crossed the hall, threw open Mrs. Price's door, and entered.

Juliana strode blithely down the hall. If they couldn't carry it on from here, she washed her hands of both of them. But she had a sneaking suspicion that all would be well.

~

When her door slammed shut, Catrin jumped. She hadn't heard it open, and she whirled away from the window, wondering if Lady Juliana had returned.

Then she came face-to-face with a glowering Evan. "You . . . you shouldn't be here. You're not well enough to—"

"I'm much better than one would expect, given that I spent the last fifteen hours barely able to sleep or eat. I did manage to drink, though it merely reminded me that even liquor can't dull some pains." His gaze burned over her swollen eyes and red nose, and his scowl faded. "Answer one question for me. Did Morys take the chalice?"

"Of course he did. You saw him."

"For God's sake, I was half-conscious when that happened! I dimly remember you two discussing it, but by that point I could barely see, and all I could hear was the blood roaring in my ears!"

"I thought you knew." She dragged in a breath. "I thought you were ignoring the fact that it was gone, since you don't believe in the curse anyway." Obviously Lady Juliana had told him the truth. Catrin wanted to be angry at her, but she couldn't.

"Yesterday when we were talking, you didn't bring up the curse," he said, his voice tight with emotion. "Why? Or did you indeed have some . . . other reason for not wanting to discuss marriage?"

She should do as she'd planned and simply tell him she didn't want to marry him, didn't love him more than life. But faced with his pain—and remembering all Lady Juliana had told her—she couldn't bear to hurt him more.

When he'd told her about his violent nature, she hadn't known it came from years of abuse, of witnessing a marriage fraught with violence. She hadn't known how deep his scars were, how much he hurt. Lady Juliana had certainly done her work well. Catrin couldn't stand to heap new suffering on him.

"The only reason I could *ever* have for not wanting to marry you is the curse." She stared out the window. "And I knew you . . . wouldn't accept the curse as a reason, so I let you think whatever you wanted."

As he came up behind her, she held her breath, wishing he'd go away and leave her alone. No, she didn't want that, either. Oh, how would she ever bear this?

"So you don't care that I'm a tenant farmer's son," he murmured, "that I have a temper, that I'm not fit to kiss your dainty little foot?"

"Of course I don't care! Besides, I'm the one who's cursed."

"It doesn't matter to me." He slid his good arm about her waist and drew her against him. "You were absolutely right—I refuse to accept the curse as a reason not to marry you." He pressed a kiss against her hair that tore at her heart. "And I do want to marry you, to be part of your life at Plas Niwl, whatever part you see fit to allow. I want to spend every night in your arms, to see you grow big with my child. No curse will keep me from that."

Every word was a glittering promise dangling out of her reach. She'd known he wouldn't relinquish her easily, yet she still felt powerless before the force of his will. "Please don't say these things to me. Nothing can come of it."

He dragged her around to face him. "Tell me you don't want the same, and I'll let you go—even if it means spending the rest of my days alone, wanting you." When she tried to glance away, he caught her chin and made her look at him. "Say you don't love me, and I'll end this now."

Oh, unfair. She couldn't lie about that, and he knew it. *You are too, too cruel, my love.* "It doesn't matter if I love you—"

He swore. "That's not what I asked. *Do you love me?* Tell me one way or the other!"

She stared at the man who'd endured a hellish childhood and a lonely adulthood, who'd defended her from David even while thinking she was a criminal . . . who'd become more precious than life to her. It wasn't in her to lie to him anymore. "There's no point to saying this, but I do love you. You know I do."

Then he was kissing her as if she were his only answer to living. And Lord help her but she gave herself up to him without protest, twining her arms about his waist, letting him do whatever he wished so long as she could kiss him forever. One kiss, she told herself, and then she'd make him see sense.

Oh, but that one kiss! His brandy-scented mouth tempted her to taste more and more, and his thrusting tongue marked his possession of her. The force of his need—and her own—alarmed her.

As if he sensed that, he stroked her neck with a silken touch, like a rider soothing a skittish colt. But when he slid his fingers along her collarbone to the neckline of her gown, she backed away, only to come up against the window seat.

Pressing her down onto it, he bent to kiss her again.

"No, Evan, we can't . . . we mustn't . . ."

"We will."

He kissed a path from her ear down the slope of her neck, turning her insides to liquid. When he dragged her gown down to bare her breasts and his mouth seized one to work its magic, she clutched his shoulders, anchoring him to her.

"That's it, my darling," he murmured. "Show me your sweetness . . . let me love you." He tugged at her nipple with his teeth, sending shocks of pleasure through her, weakening her will even further.

This is insane. I can't let him do this. In the end, they'd both lose.

"Stop it!" she cried. "This won't change anything. I can't marry you."

Black eyes glittering, he loomed over her. "You can and you will, if I have to abduct you to be sure of it."

She curled her fists against his chest. "It was torture enough watching Willie die, and I didn't even love him. But I love *you*, so if I watch you die . . . I can't bear it. And without the chalice, I know you *will*!"

"I won't. Now that I have you, I won't allow it."

Tears flooded her eyes. "A pox on you, it's not a matter of choosing!"

Her distress seemed to affect him at last. He caught her fist and kissed it until her fingers uncurled. "If you're so sure of the power of your curse, my love, then we'll get the chalice back. All I have to do is take it from Morys."

"Oh, certainly," she said sarcastically. "I'm sure David will be delighted to hand it over to his rival so you can marry me. He'd destroy it first."

"Then we'll go to the authorities and charge him with theft."

"And he'll tell them how I came by it, how I'm suspected of taking part in a murder. Is that what you want?"

He scowled. "All right, I'll take it from him by force."

She gripped his hand. "That's what I'm afraid of. You'll try that, and he'll shoot you. Only this time he'll kill you. You'll be dead before we even marry."

"There are many kinds of death, my love. If I don't have you, I'll still die, just not physically. Oh, I'll continue to teach and write my books, for I know nothing else. But I'll find no joy or purpose in it. My life will be over."

He stroked her cheek with the backs of his fingers in a gentle caress. "And if you consign me to *that* death, I promise to rub your face in it for the rest of your life. I'll become a schoolteacher in Llanddeusant, right under that deuced

Morys's nose, and I'll either provoke the bastard until he kills me or I'll pine away before your very eyes. What will you do then? Will you close yourself up at Plas Niwl to avoid the sight of me grown pale and thin?"

His voice dropped to a whisper. "Will you lie in bed wanting me, all the while knowing I'm only a mile away, wanting you? If I come and sit outside in the rain, will you tell Bos to let me in? Or will you watch out the window and know I'm thinking only of you, that my every breath is for you, that I'm slowly dying with want of you?"

She closed her eyes. "You . . . you wouldn't do all those things."

"I would."

"You'd find another woman to love."

"I wouldn't." He kissed her eyelids. "You underestimate me if you think I'd give you up without a fight. Even last night, when I was convinced you didn't want me, I was already trying to find a way to *make* you love me. I'd already decided I'd rather spend a short, torturous time with you than an untroubled eternity without you."

She opened her eyes to find him staring at her so sincerely that she couldn't doubt his words. "I could be your mistress. We could live as husband and wife without ever marrying. Then the curse couldn't touch us."

His eyes hardened. "Live in sin in Llanddeusant? Where people already gossip about you? You'd raise our children as bastards and subject them to the same whispers and veiled glances you and I have suffered all our lives?" When she paled, he went on relentlessly. "Or perhaps you'd hire a manager for your estate and travel with me to Cambridge.

Of course, I'd have to hide you from the prying eyes of my superiors."

She groaned, and he growled, "No, that wouldn't work in a university town. So we'd have to live in London, where I could travel to Cambridge with ease, always hiding the existence of my mistress. Or I could leave the university entirely and claim we're married. But we could never be comfortable in London, and you know it. We're Welsh, we're peculiar . . . we're the kind of people invited to social occasions out of curiosity."

The truth was painful, and she turned her face in a futile attempt to avoid his harsh words.

"You spent a few days in London," he went on fiercely. "Did you enjoy it? Did you long to live amidst the grime and misery? Because I hate the refuse in the streets, the black grind of poverty, and the corrupt nobility. I don't want to raise my children there."

He turned her face toward him. "I want to raise them in a community where I have *some* friends. With my wife. I know I said I'd be your lover, but that was when I thought I dared not marry. I don't feel that way now."

"Every choice you give me is awful," she whispered. "What am I to do?"

"You're to trust me. We'll find a way around the curse. We'll get the chalice back, I swear it. But we must do it together."

"I . . . I don't know what to do anymore."

A dark smile lit his face as he drew her gown up her legs. "Then let me show you what you'd be missing if you refuse me, my darling."

He parted her legs with his muscled thigh and pulled her forward until her privates rested against it. Dragging his knee over her, he watched with clear satisfaction as she sucked in a breath, then another and another. He repeated the caress until she was damp and aching.

"My Lady of the Mists," he whispered. "You know you want me. That's all that matters."

He slipped his hand beneath her skirts to fondle her warm, wet softness. Another gasp escaped her and he caught it with his mouth, then trailed openmouthed kisses down her throat. His tongue darted out to taste her wherever his mouth touched, leaving fire in its wake.

It was too much pleasure to bear. With a sigh, she clasped his shoulders. This time when he sucked her breasts, she arched her head and closed her eyes to soak up every moment. But he broke off far too quickly, dropping to the floor to kneel between her legs.

Her eyes shot open as he bared her patch of ebony curls to his hungry gaze. "What are you doing?"

"Making you burn, my darling girl," he said. "Making you burn."

Then he parted her curls and pressed a most intimate kiss to the soft petals between her legs. Every part of her body leapt to life at the incredible touch of his tongue, and when he caressed her with his mouth, finding all the places where she ached for his touch, she whispered, "Good Lord . . . *Evan* . . ."

His mouth was both fire and frost, arousing, then soothing, then arousing again. As his tongue darted inside her, she clasped his neck with a drawn-out moan, leaning back to give him better access.

By heaven, how *amazing*. It had never occurred to her that mouths could be used like this. Heat and want built within her in equal portions, making her move against him to get more and more of his mouth.

Then it left her, and she sagged against the window, feeling unfulfilled and ravenous. He stood and pressed between her legs, using his hand to continue the caresses he'd given her with his mouth. And all the while he watched her.

"Do you want more of this, sweet Catrin?" He stroked her roughly, then found the hard kernel that seemed to be the center of her pleasure and thumbed it until she cried out at the surge of molten wanting that poured over her.

As her body shuddered, she buried her face in his shoulder, ashamed to admit that she did indeed want more. She felt his every stroke to the depths of her soul, and each seductive touch shook her.

Then he slid one finger deep inside, eliciting a gasp from her. "Do you like that, my love?" His voice was hoarse with his own need. "Do you want to see what it can be like between us when there's no pain, when there's love instead of mistrust?"

"Yes," she whispered, unable to help herself. "Oh yes."

"I want to bury myself inside you. Will you let me?"

He was already unbuttoning his breeches, and she realized with a little shiver of horror and fascination that he intended to take her right there, against the window in broad daylight. "Evan . . . someone might see . . ."

"No one will see." He dragged his breeches and drawers down far enough to expose his rigid shaft. "No one's home. The Vaughans have gone to town."

He caught her beneath one knee, then pulled her toward him until her bottom rested on the edge of the window seat and his shaft nudged her wet heat.

She glanced over her shoulder. "But the servants—"

"—are not standing outside staring up at your window," he finished for her. "And in any case, they'd see nothing but your respectably clothed back."

"But Evan—"

"Hush," he growled, spreading kisses in her disordered hair. "I need you so badly . . . and with my arm in a sling, the conventional position will be hard to manage." He nipped her ear. "Please . . . if you want me, do as I say."

"You know I do," she said with a groan.

"Then guide me in, love."

It took her a second to understand what he meant, but though she blushed, she did as he asked, intoxicated by the thought of having him inside her again. There was some shifting of bodies, and the position was a bit awkward, but when he drove in deep, she forgot all that.

"Good God, Catrin . . ." he said as his breath quickened. "You are . . . oh, my love, you're exquisite."

When he bent her back against the window and began to move, an urge more basic even than hunger had her looping her arms about his neck and curling her legs behind his until she was fully open, aching to feel him buried inside her.

Evan could scarcely believe it when he felt her clamp her

thighs about his hips. He'd won this part of the battle, at least. As long as he kept her wanting him, he had a chance to break down her fears about their marrying.

She shifted to allow him to sink even farther inside her, and he groaned. God, she was heaven . . . so tight and warm. The sensation of entering her body was beyond anything he'd ever felt, and he knew it was because of who she was . . . the kindest, most generous woman he'd ever known. She hadn't cared about his past. And he wouldn't let her regret giving herself to him.

Anchoring her with his good arm, he bent his head to taste her mouth the way he knew she liked as he thrust into her.

He could feel the tension build in her body as she writhed against him with undulating movements that drove him mad. Pray heaven he could restrain himself long enough to let her find her release, for this was his only way to keep her, to "secure her soul."

With one hand in a sling and the other holding her, caressing her breasts was impossible. Instead, he used his mouth on her lush lips, her delightful ears, her enticing neck, nipping and sucking and kissing all the places he thought would thrill her, all the places he adored.

Then the animal in him took over. He'd been without her too long and she felt too good. Soon he was losing himself in her, driving her hard, trying to immerse himself in her sweetness as he rode out the storm.

She didn't seem to mind, for she clamped her legs about him and strained to join her body more closely to his, making mewling sounds that brought him to the edge of sanity. "Catrin . . . my love . . . my life. . ." he whispered as he quickened his pace.

Holding back became impossible as she ground her hips against him and his need for her built to mind-numbing heights. So when her thighs tensed around him and she cried out, he exploded into her in a shattering release, joining his cries to hers as her spasms wrung him dry.

Afterward, it took some time for the thundering of his blood to subside and his muscles to relax. He clutched her close as if to fuse her to him, and when she laid her head limply on his shoulder, he began to feel a painful throbbing near the site of his wound.

Still, he was loath to move. Having her body draped around his was the utmost in contentment, and if not for his waning strength, he could have stayed there forever.

He managed to wait until she stirred against his chest before he pressed a lingering kiss to her reddened lips. "What do you say, love? Shall we move to the bed? I confess I got little rest last night, and I can think of nothing more perfect than sleeping in your arms."

His words seemed to draw her out of some enchanted place, for she gazed up at him with a start. "But it's daylight and . . . and the servants will wonder."

He laughed. "For a woman of your rank, you have the most extraordinary concern for what the servants might think. Trust me, these servants are most discreet. And I suspect that Juliana ordered this part of the house off-limits for the day anyway."

Blushing, she trailed her fingers down his chest. "Surely you don't think she was encouraging us to . . . to—"

"Make love? Of course she was. I assure you that the Vaughans don't make a practice of running off to town when they have guests."

"She's a very unusual woman, isn't she?" Catrin ventured.

"No more unusual than you, my darling." When she seemed pleased at that statement, he added, "And I want to spend the day and most of the night making love to my unusual woman."

"You wicked man!" she scolded, but she didn't protest and even helped him to unhook her gown, then draw it off.

"This isn't how it's usually done, you know." He pulled off his drawers and breeches, then somehow managed to get his shirt off over his head. "Most people undress *before* they make love." After dragging off her shift, he led her to the bed. He lay down, then pulled her on top of him with a smile. Naked and splayed across his body, she looked like a goddess, and he hardened once more.

He nudged her legs apart with his thigh and watched as her eyes widened. "I'm not finished making you burn." He ground his hips up against her, letting her feel his burgeoning arousal. "By the time I get through with you, you'll be begging me to marry you."

He teased her nipple until she gasped. "*Begging*, I tell you."

Either that or he'd be dead, and not from her bloody curse, either. She was enough woman to send a man to an early grave.

Oh, but he'd die happy.

20

In the middle of the night, Catrin awakened with a start. She'd dreamed that the Vaughans had discovered her and Evan together and had thrown her out. The shame lingered, and she glanced over at Evan, sleeping peacefully at her side.

How could he feel so little guilt about consorting with her beneath the very noses of his benefactors? It was true that the Vaughans weren't in residence, but who knew when they might return? The servants had insisted that they often stayed overnight at their town house in Carmarthen, but Catrin still felt uneasy about the scandalous things she and Evan were doing here.

Not him. He had kept her in bed most of the day.

It surprised her how much she'd enjoyed being on top of him. Once she'd lost her embarrassment at being so blatantly exposed to his gaze, she'd liked having control. Oh, the things he'd shown her! No wonder he'd been amazed that she hadn't sought a lover before. She'd never dreamed what she was missing . . . the wonderful cresting pleasure of being in the arms of the man she loved.

When they'd gone down to dinner and heard their hosts were staying in Carmarthen for the night, that had given Evan license to behave even more shamelessly. As they'd sat beside each other, he'd fondled her under the table!

And though terrified of discovery, she'd found the most awful thrill in it. Then she'd fought fire with fire, slipping her hand inside his breeches to clasp him. She'd meant it only to tease him, but when she'd tried to withdraw her hand, he'd murmured, "Leave it there, love." By the time the next course had come, he'd been hard as iron. They'd made short work of their meal, so aroused they'd barely made it up the stairs to bed before falling upon each other.

What a beautiful, glorious night.

Now he was sleeping. Such an angelic face. No one would ever guess the fierceness of his passions . . . or the mischievousness he hid beneath his scholarly facade. Last night at dinner, it was as if he'd wanted to draw her into a conspiracy of desire, where she chose him over the strictures of society.

That had been an easy choice. All her life, she'd been gossiped about for things she hadn't done. It was nice, for once, to do something that merited gossip . . . and get away with it.

But stolen caresses were one thing; a lifetime of flouting convention was another. So that left only one choice: She must get the chalice back. Alone. If Evan was involved,

David would never give it back to her. But if she approached him on her own, she might get him to return it.

And the sooner the better. Once the Vaughans returned, getting away without being noticed would be near to impossible.

Slipping from the bed, she dressed swiftly. She had to write a note, for she couldn't leave Evan wondering where she'd gone. And she'd have to saddle a horse herself without rousing any servants.

Where should she look for David, though? Carmarthen? No, by now he would have heard they weren't on the coach, and would have given up his pursuit to return to Llanddeusant.

So that's where she'd go. With any luck, by the time Evan found her note and came after her, she'd have already regained the chalice.

She had to try. Because Evan had been absolutely right. There *were* other kinds of deaths, and a lifetime without him would be one.

~

The throbbing in his shoulder awakened Evan. To his surprise, sunlight streamed through the window. Good God, it was late. It wasn't like him to sleep past dawn. Must have been all that lovemaking with Catrin.

Where was she, anyway? No doubt she'd gone down to breakfast without him, afraid he might assault her under the table again.

When that memory made him hard, he groaned and got out of bed. Sadly, there'd be none of that today. Rhys and Juliana were returning. Catrin would spend the day trying to fool them into thinking that he and she were well-behaved. He would spend the day wanting her.

Was that to be his continual state? Did married people ever tire of desiring their partners? He certainly hoped it didn't continue to be this intense, or he'd be exhausted for the rest of his life. He wanted to make love to her night and day. He wanted to make love to her right now.

But he'd have to find her first. Unfortunately, he'd need help dressing, but Catrin would die of shame if he called for a servant to come to *her* room and help him. Grumbling, he pulled on his drawers, gathered up his clothes, and dashed across the hall. He'd be glad when he didn't have to sneak about, when he could make love to her without worrying about propriety.

While a servant helped him dress, Evan asked, "Have the Vaughans returned?"

"No, sir, but we expect them any moment."

Evan stifled a groan. It had been too much to hope that they'd stay in Carmarthen and give him more time with Catrin. "I suppose Mrs. Price is already up and about."

"I don't believe so, sir. I believe she's still in her room."

What? Why would the man think Catrin hadn't arisen?

After the servant left, Evan checked her empty room. He tried to remember if she'd mentioned anything about her plans for today, but they'd both been so caught up in each other that they hadn't spoken of it. He'd been afraid to press her too much about marriage, confident that they would work it out when he was fully recovered. Now he wished he hadn't been so hesitant.

He went downstairs, hoping to find someone who'd seen her, then discovered that the Vaughans had returned. Rhys was speaking with the butler, looking solemn.

"You're back earlier than expected," Evan said. "Where's the rest of the family?"

"Everyone else is eating breakfast. We left in too much of a hurry for that." Rhys lowered his voice. "I had to come back and let you know of the latest disturbing development in this mess with that schoolmaster. Early this morning, he was found murdered in the forest outside Carmarthen."

Shock kept Evan speechless.

"Apparently, it happened after he left here." Rhys headed for the drawing room. "When they found him, he'd clearly been dead awhile. They weren't sure who he was, but when I heard the description, I took a look and recognized him."

"You're *sure* it was him?" Evan asked.

"Yes."

They entered the drawing room and Rhys closed the door. "Everyone in Carmarthen assumed he was killed by thieves." He fixed Evan with a worried gaze. "But I couldn't help noticing that he'd been stabbed repeatedly. Like your friend Lord Mansfield."

Evan shuddered. "Oh my God."

"Yes. Apparently nothing of value was found on the body . . . like a chalice, for example."

Evan felt as if he'd been poleaxed. Morys must have been murdered for the chalice. Perhaps Justin had been, too. He remembered what Catrin had said about her uneasy feeling that she was being watched. Perhaps her feeling hadn't simply been the result of her fearful nature.

Someone *had* been watching her, waiting for her to gain the chalice so they could steal it from her. And when she'd eluded them, they'd assumed that Lord Mansfield still had it and assaulted him.

But who?

"Obviously," Rhys went on, "this chalice is dangerous to one's health. You saw it. Is it valuable enough to kill someone for?"

Evan shook his head. "Until now, I thought its only value lay in its ability to end the curse on Catrin's family."

"Ah yes, Juliana told me about that. You don't really believe in it, do you?"

"No. But Catrin does." Evan's eyes narrowed. "And perhaps someone else does, too. Someone who knows she won't marry without it."

"Is there anyone who'd want to keep her from marrying?"

Evan tried to remember who'd been most vocal in their disapproval of Catrin. "Perhaps her father-in-law, Sir Huw Price. He blames her for his son's death. He might steal it just to thwart her. He's a nasty fellow, but I can't see him committing two brutal murders."

Rhys frowned. "I suppose we'll have to talk to Catrin and see if she thinks her father-in-law would go to such lengths. She could also tell us if Sir Huw was gone from Llanddeusant while she was on her trip. Where is she?"

"I don't know. When I woke up, she wasn't in the bed."

"In the bed?" Rhys said with a raised eyebrow.

For probably the first time in his life, Evan was at a loss for words. "Well, she . . . I mean, we . . . deuce take it, Rhys, isn't that what you expected?"

Rhys smiled. "*I* didn't expect anything, but Juliana seemed rather certain that she'd pulled off the match of the century."

"Yes, well, half of the match seems to have disappeared," Evan grumbled. "The servants told me she hadn't arisen, but I knew she *had*. So where the deuce is she?"

"She probably went out to the gardens early. I'm sure we'll find her."

But they were met in the hall by Juliana, who waved an envelope at them. "I saw this on the salver. It's addressed to Evan."

With a sinking sensation in his stomach, Evan tore the envelope open. As he scanned it, he groaned.

"What is it?" Rhys asked.

"Catrin has gone to Llanddeusant to get the chalice from Morys. She says she knew I'd do something foolish to get it back, and she thought it would be easier for her to convince Morys to give it to her if I weren't around."

He crumpled the note with an oath, then turned to Rhys. "I'm afraid I'll have to borrow a horse again."

"You shouldn't be riding, with your shoulder still on the mend."

"I shan't sit here wondering what kind of trouble she's getting into," Evan bit out. "I know Catrin. She may be timid, but when something matters to her, she turns stubborn. They won't have heard about Morys's murder yet. When she discovers he hasn't returned, she'll start looking for him, and she might run afoul of the murderer."

"Then I'm going with you." Rhys turned to Juliana. "Can you manage without me?"

"Of course."

"There's no need for that," Evan said. "I'm sure I'm worrying for nothing. I'll probably find her at Plas Niwl, waiting for Morys to return to town so she can convince him to give her the chalice."

"And if you don't? You're still recovering, and you don't know what you'll come up against. The man who took the chalice has committed two murders to get it. What if it's Catrin he's after, and the chalice is just a means to gain her?"

"Good point." Much as Evan hated to take Rhys away from his family, he *was* worried. And he could use the help. "Very well. I accept your offer." He flashed Juliana an apologetic glance. "Sorry. I hate to take Rhys off like this."

Rhys called for horses to be saddled, then laid a reassuring hand on Evan's shoulder. "She can't have been gone long. If we hurry, we might even catch up to her before she reaches Llanddeusant."

Evan nodded. But the more he thought about those two murders, the more fear gripped him. Because if something happened to her, he didn't know how he'd survive it.

21

ight had fallen by the time Catrin reached David's study at the school, only to find it empty, just as his house had been. Where was he? He couldn't still be searching for her and Evan, could he?

She heard the door to the school open. Perhaps that was him now. But the man who came through the door wasn't David. It was Sir Reynald Jenkins.

He seemed as startled to see her as she was to see him, but then he broke into a broad smile. "Why, Mrs. Price, what a pleasant surprise. You've returned from your long journey, have you? The whole town has been talking about that dreadful Mr. Quinley's ridiculous accusations. I do hope your presence here means you're finished with all that?"

"Yes." Why was Sir Reynald here? He'd never shown an interest in the school before.

"So you escaped Mr. Newcome?" When she blinked at him, he added, "Mrs. Llewellyn has told us all about how he whisked you away. It was appalling."

"Mr. Newcome decided he made a mistake."

"Interesting. How did you convince him to believe you?" He cast her a knowing smile. "Then again, I think I can guess."

She fought a blush. How dared he insinuate such a thing? And how much had he heard about her and Evan through the gossip mill?

She didn't want to know. "I'm sorry, sir, but I have to go."

Sir Reynald's smile abruptly vanished. He closed the door to the study. "I am afraid I can't let you do that, Mrs. Price."

A warning rang in her mind. "Why not?"

"I already know what happened between you and our foolish Mr. Morys. Your presence here indicates that you survived that ordeal none the worse for wear. But I must confess to being curious about how Mr. Newcome fared. Morys seemed convinced he had dealt the man a fatal wound."

She was stunned, not only by what Sir Reynald had learned, but also by the change in his manner. Sir Reynald had always struck her as something of a fop, but now he looked purposeful and bold and . . . and threatening.

"So you've talked to David," she said. "Where is he?"

"It's not David that interests you, is it?" Sir Reynald remarked in a lazy tone. "It's the chalice." He unknotted his cravat and drew it off.

The strange action, combined with his words, started the blood pounding in Catrin's heart. She backed away. "How do you know about that?"

"From your ancient diary, of course. Morys brought it

to me for authentication. That's when I began watching you and waiting for you to find the drinking vessel. You see, although I found the curse intriguing, what interested me most was the chalice." He fixed her with an unnerving gaze. "I don't suppose you realize its significance, do you? Aside from its role in your family curse."

Unable to breathe, she tried to fathom what he was saying.

"The warrior, the snake-wrapped maiden, and the raven are emblems of a sect of druids that practiced during the early Middle Ages, long after the original druids vanished from the shores of Brittany. Artifacts from their sect are sometimes confused for artifacts from the earlier druids."

When she gasped, he added, "You didn't know I shared your fascination with such matters, did you, my dear? Of course, we have different reasons for our interest. You're attracted to the druids' oneness with nature, their belief in the spirits of the forest."

Reaching into his waistcoat, he withdrew a curved knife. "I, on the other hand, am intrigued by their darker beliefs. They understood what religion today has lost sight of. There's power in blood . . . the blood of the innocent *and* the guilty, sacrificed for the good of society."

She stared at the knife, her every muscle going rigid with fear. "Y-you're wrong about the druids. There's no evidence that they practiced human sacrifice. Some scholars claim that the Roman Church created those tales to discredit them."

"That's absurd. Any fool who studies the Mabinogion and the culture of the ancient Celts recognizes that the shedding of blood was central to their faith." He frowned. "But enough of this. I've always known you're much too tenderhearted to agree with me."

He stepped toward Catrin and lifted the knife to her throat. "Turn around."

She was too shocked to move. What did he want from her that he would use a knife to get it?

"Do as I say, Catrin, and I shan't hurt you. Now turn around and put your hands behind your back."

Trembling violently, she complied, afraid to find out what he'd do if she didn't. "Why do you want to hurt me?" she whispered as he grabbed her hands and wrapped his cravat around them.

"I don't." Yet he twisted the cravat into a painfully tight knot.

How she wished she hadn't left Evan so hastily! And where in God's name was David? She'd welcome his appearance now.

Leaning over her shoulder, Sir Reynald drew the scarf from her neck. As he paused to stare down the front of her gown, his breath whispered over the upper swells of her breasts. "It would be a shame to waste such loveliness on Morys or Newcome. But I recognize its worth and will treat it with the tender care it deserves."

The implications of that made her shudder. With a sinking heart, she felt him kneel to secure her ankles with the scarf. When he drew it tight and knotted it, she swayed, unable to keep her balance.

He rose and slid his arm about her waist, then rasped in her ear, "I'm sorry to truss you, but I don't think you'll play your proper role in tomorrow morning's drama unless I do."

"What drama?"

"I'd intended to look for you after I searched Morys's desk for any notes he might have left lying around that pointed to his association with me. But Fate has dumped you in my lap. Now I won't have to delay the ceremony until Samhain."

With a shudder, she recognized the name of the Celtic festival that fell in October, when cattle were slaughtered in preparation for winter.

"I can hold it at dawn tomorrow," he continued. "As the sun rises for the solstice, the day of its greatest power, we'll be joined in a union to eclipse all others. We'll be married at the altar, Catrin, and then we'll drink from the chalice."

He *had* the chalice? "Married?" she choked out, uncertain whether to be relieved or horrified by the prospect.

"Yes. I know you would never willingly marry me, but I've planned for that. After we're wed by a priest of our druid sect I'll take you to my estate, where you'll have a room of your own."

An involuntary shiver rippled over her. "You mean to keep me prisoner."

"Until you've sired my child and given me a true descendant of the druids to imbue with the knowledge of the ancients. What happens next is up to you. You can remain married to me and experience the power of the druids as your ancestress Morgana meant it to be. Or you can die. Either way, I shall have what I want—our child and your property, with the altar that stands on it."

He must mean the dolmen. So he was one of those strange men who crept onto her estate late at night to sacrifice birds and animals.

A shudder wracked her. "Kill me, and you'll never get my property."

"I'll be your husband, so it will be mine legally. Of course, I'll have to explain that you married me in secret, then fell ill and died, but no one will question that. The Ladies of the Mists have done stranger things. And I will, after all, have a will and testament in your own hand to prove me rightful owner."

"You'll never get that from me."

"Oh, but I will. Do you think you can resist any torture? I doubt it. You're not made of the same stuff as your doughty old grandmother, are you?"

Torture? Terror gripped her so powerfully that her every muscle went weak. All this about druids and true descendants and altars . . . The man was mad! Why had she never guessed it?

Because he was so crafty. But his plan couldn't succeed. Evan knew she was here and he would come after her. He would find her.

How? He won't know where to look for you, and he doesn't realize that Sir Reynald is so treacherous. You certainly didn't.

Then she remembered what Sir Reynald had said about watching her and waiting for her to find the chalice. A chill sliced through her. "You followed me to London. It wasn't thieves who murdered Lord Mansfield. It was *you*."

Surprising her with his strength, he set her on David's desk so she faced him. "Of course. When Morys told me why you were going to town, I knew I finally had my chance to get both you and the chalice. I followed you to that inn, and when I saw a nobleman enter with a large box under his arm, I settled down to wait until you came out with it. But you didn't emerge. I waited for you as I watched him walk out and stroll down the street, but still you didn't appear."

His eyes narrowed. "So I accosted him and asked where you were. Unfortunately, he was decidedly uncommunicative, and when I persisted, he put his hand on his sword hilt." He shrugged. "I don't like it when people threaten me. I made sure he didn't have the chance to draw."

Catrin shuddered, remembering what Evan had said about Lord Mansfield's brutal death. Sir Reynald truly was beyond reason if he could murder with so little cause. And he seemed to revel in it, for his face wore the expression of a boy pleased at his own naughtiness.

"Afterward," he boasted, "I took the letter and money he had." He gave a cruel laugh. "It was rather amusing to steal back the hundred pounds I'd paid you for that painting and make a profit on it, besides."

His voice hardened. "But it didn't compensate for the loss of the chalice. I'd thought to catch up to you at your lodgings, but you evaded me, so I had no choice but to wait until you returned to find out what had become of the vessel."

"I suppose David told you what I told him."

"Yes—although if I'd realized you were lying, I'd have dispensed with his services sooner."

"Dispensed with his services? Have you . . . murdered David, too?"

He smiled. "How do you think I got the chalice back?" He leaned close, his eyes so bright with pleasure that she recoiled. "I left him in the forest outside Carmarthen. I sacrificed him for the common good. Just as I sacrificed Lord Mansfield. And will sacrifice you, if you choose not to follow my rules."

Withdrawing the knife, he held the flat side of the blade against her cheek, then stroked it along her jawbone and down her neck. "Things can be . . . pleasant between us, Catrin, or painful. I'd prefer pleasant. Wouldn't you?"

Heavens, that was why he'd confessed his crimes to her. He wanted her to know exactly what he was capable of, so she wouldn't waste his time with attempts to avoid what he considered inevitable.

That knowledge horrified her most. She'd never met a man with no conscience, for whom reciting his crimes was merely a means to an end. A man like that might do anything.

"We shall make a potent child together, you and I," he said.

"What if I'm already bearing Evan Newcome's child?"

His face darkened. "Considering that you only met him a week ago, I'd find that hard to believe." He hesitated, searching her face. "I know you, Catrin. You aren't the sort of woman to leap into a man's bed without benefit of marriage. If you'd wanted to take a lover, you would have done so before now."

"And if I had?" she persisted, hoping it would make him release her.

"If I thought for one moment that you were no longer a virgin, I would kill you. I need a virgin for the sacrifice." The words hung between them, stark, cold, and sure. "But I know you are one, so this ploy of yours won't work."

Oh Lord, and she'd almost told him the truth. Not that lying to him had gained her much. If he ever did bed her, he'd find out she wasn't a virgin anyway.

He brought the knife down to her breasts and amused himself by running the tip over each swell, smiling to see how her breath quickened in fear, making her breasts shake beneath the blade. She leaned back to put some distance between her and the knife, but the movement nearly overset her.

As her bound hands scrabbled for purchase on the desktop, she felt something cold and metal. David's silver letter opener. She remembered seeing it on his desk. Closing her fingers around it, she wedged it up between her bonds, hoping to keep it hidden long enough to have the chance to use it.

Sir Reynald brought the tip of his knife down between her breasts and ran it along the hollow in a horrific caress. "It does no good to fight me. I always win. So any attempt to escape is foolish. In fact, now that you see what's planned for you, my dear, you should feel honored to be given the chance to bear a new race."

"You won't get away with this. Evan will come in search of me."

"I doubt it. And even if he does, he won't make it here before we're married. By then, I'll have you locked up tight and cozy at my estate." With a chilling smile, he brought the tip of the knife up her throat. "And we will already have begun the business of creating my heir."

Slipping the knife inside his waistcoat, he withdrew a handkerchief, which he used to gag her. "But for now, my dear, I'll content myself with dreaming of our wedding night. I still have to search Morys's office, then remove you from this too-public place so I can make preparations for the morn."

He left her side to rifle through David's desk, and she thought about sawing at her bonds with the letter opener. But he was at her back, where he'd notice any movement, and she dared not risk having her puny weapon taken away.

Panic seized her. She could only hope Evan found her, and that was a slim hope indeed. Even the letter opener would help her only a little; it wasn't exactly sharp.

The desk shuddered beneath her as Sir Reynald slammed drawer after drawer. Then he stopped. "That's done. Time to leave." There was an ominous silence before he added, "But I don't want to deal with your struggles in the meantime. Sorry, my dear, I'm afraid this will hurt."

Hurt?

Then something hit the back of her head and she fell into darkness.

22

Evan felt as if someone was clawing his heart out with a hook bit by bit. Catrin had disappeared, and no one knew where.

He and Rhys had ridden into Llanddeusant near midnight. They'd gone to Morys's house and the school, but no Catrin. And now they were at Plas Niwl and Bos was telling them he hadn't seen his mistress since she'd left for London with Evan.

Barely restraining the urge to grab the butler by the throat, Evan growled, "We know she's here somewhere. She left only a few hours before us. Surely you have an idea where she might be."

Bos pursed his lips. "Begging your pardon, sir, but if she left you, then perhaps she doesn't want to be found."

Only Rhys's hand on his shoulder prevented Evan from launching himself at the old man. "Damn it, she may be in danger! That chalice she went to London to buy was taken from her—from us—by David Morys, and his murdered body turned up outside Carmarthen yesterday."

As Bos paled, Rhys added, "We think Mr. Morys was killed for the chalice. Unfortunately, Mrs. Price doesn't know of his murder and came here to get it back from Morys."

Evan thrust out the note she'd left him. As Bos scanned it, he swallowed convulsively. "Truly, gentlemen, I have not seen my mistress. But I am happy to join you in a search for her."

"We don't know where to search!" Evan cried. "She's not at Morys's and she's not here, so where on God's green earth is she?"

Rhys frowned. "What if we try her father-in-law? You said he had cause to want to hurt her."

"That is an excellent suggestion," Bos put in. "Sir Huw has never hidden his unwarranted dislike for my mistress."

Evan nodded. "We'll go there next. It's the only possibility we haven't explored." As Rhys and Bos headed for the entrance, Evan said, "Bos, do you know where Catrin kept the diary that describes the curse?"

The butler nodded. "It is still in the safe where she kept the chalice. She left that open when you and she departed on your trip to Carmarthen."

"Good. I know it's unlikely, but perhaps something in it can give us an idea of why someone would kill for that chalice . . . or where Catrin might have gone to look for it."

"I shall fetch it." Bos strode off and returned moments later with an ancient-looking book. Evan took it and, after a cursory glance, stuffed it in his waistcoat.

"Shall you not peruse its contents?" Bos asked.

"Later. First we must get to Sir Huw's."

The next hour tried Evan sorely. It took them much too long to reach Sir Huw's estate, for although the moon was still full enough to give them ample light, the roads were bad. As they struggled along the last mile, Evan tried not to think about what danger Catrin might be in.

But he kept seeing Justin lying in a pool of blood. If that were Catrin—

He squelched the thought. He wouldn't let her be hurt. Somehow he'd find her . . . and the chalice, too, if that was what was needed to win her.

Once they reached Sir Huw's estate, it took several minutes to rouse anyone and several more to convince the servants to awaken their master. But when the baronet strode down the stairs still wearing his nightcap and belting a robe about his waist, Evan felt alarm set in. If Sir Huw had taken Catrin, he certainly hadn't let her presence deter him from sleep, had he?

"What is the meaning of this!" Sir Huw growled as he reached the bottom of the stairs. "To wrench a man from his bed at this hour is an outrage. I want you all out of my house. Now!"

To everyone's surprise, it was Bos who answered. "Begging your pardon, Sir Huw, but we are looking for Mrs. Price. It is a matter of some importance."

"Why the bloody hell would she be here?" He peered at Evan, then scowled when he recognized him. "Besides, I heard she'd run off to London with you, Mr. Newcome."

With an effort, Evan tamped down his dislike of the

man. "I'm afraid Catrin is in trouble, sir, and we thought you might be able to shed light on where she might be." In a few words, he told Sir Huw of the curse and what had happened with the chalice. He finished by asking if Sir Huw knew anything about the chalice or Catrin's whereabouts.

Sir Huw looked as if someone had just hit him over the head with a shovel. "Come into my study, all of you," he said hoarsely. "I want to hear more of this."

Impatient to be on with the search, Evan nearly refused, but Rhys's hand on his arm cautioned patience. So he followed the others into the study.

As soon as they were inside, Evan snapped, "Well? Do you know where she is? Or who might want the chalice?"

Sir Huw shook his head. "I assume you think I might have . . . done this thing. But I am innocent. Mr. Bos, you know I wouldn't steal or . . . or *murder* anyone."

Bos leveled him with a cold stare. "You must admit, sir, that you are not fond of my mistress. You have maligned her publicly."

"Only because I truly believed she caused my son's death."

"How?" Evan exploded. "By witchery? Spells and enchantments? What kind of man uses superstition to punish a woman for a tragedy that harmed her, too?"

Sir Huw's face crumbled. "'Tis not so strange to believe, is it? There *was* a curse upon my Willie, though I didn't understand until this night the nature of it."

"I don't believe in your bloody curse!" Evan cried. "But Catrin does. Have you any idea of the guilt she has lived with? She blames herself for your son's death because she didn't know about the curse. And she's in this mess because although she wants a life and a future, she's determined to make sure no one else dies!"

"Like Willie, you mean," Sir Huw persisted.

"Oh, for God's sake," Evan growled. "This is getting us nowhere." Clearly Sir Huw had known nothing of the curse and the chalice, which meant it was unlikely he'd had anything to do with Catrin's disappearance. "Come, Rhys, let's see if we can find another who might know where she is."

"Wait!" the baronet said. "I admit I was wrong to blame her. And I know that she has suffered for it."

"Your remorse is touching, Sir Huw," Evan bit out, "but it doesn't help us find her."

"Perhaps it is time to look at the diary, sir," Bos prodded. "Although I cannot imagine how it would be of any help, one never knows."

Evan nodded. He couldn't think of what else to do. Opening the leather-bound book, he scanned its fragile pages. Then he noticed that the book fell naturally open at one spot. "This is the part about the curse."

He read it aloud, but nothing in it was informative. A basic rendering of a typical myth, it nonetheless gave him shivers. The powerful words automatically invoked fear in the reader. No wonder Catrin had believed it. When he coupled it with what he knew of her family history, he could almost believe it himself.

"The chalice sounds ancient," Rhys said. "Perhaps it has intrinsic value."

"I don't think so," Evan said. "Believe me, if it had, Lady Mansfield would have sold it herself. Besides, I've seen the thing. It's ugly, and though it does have some sort of symbols on it . . . druidic, I think . . . it—"

Something nagged at his memory. He read the tale of the curse again. "'Ancient ways.' From the use of the word 'Saxon,' I'd guess this chronicles a medieval event. But 'ancient ways' might refer to the druids, mightn't it? I suppose there could still have been a few during the Middle Ages."

"There's a dolmen on Catrin's land," Sir Huw said.

"Yes, I know." Evan's heart pounded. "And there are practicing druids hereabouts. I learned that when I came upon Sir Reynald and Catrin's gamekeeper discussing how to deal with men who'd trespassed on Catrin's land to perform sacrifices at the dolmen."

"Sir Reynald?" Sir Huw scowled. "Now there's a man who's been wanting Catrin's land. It adjoins his. He's made her offer after offer, but she won't sell."

"I don't see how gaining the chalice would help him with that," Rhys said. "If she remarries, she'd be *more* likely to sell it to him than less, for she needs the property as long as she's unmarried."

Evan shook his head. "We're missing the point. Sir Reynald didn't take the chalice because he wants her land. He took it for the same reason he *wants* the land: because it's druidic . . . just as the dolmen on her land is druidic."

He clutched the diary. "That day when I saw them at the altar, they said it was Sir Reynald's bull that had been sacrificed. It was the *second* one." He shuddered, remembering the bull's mangled body. "Don't you find that odd? If someone were going to steal cattle to use for dastardly purposes, don't you think they'd steal from different people? Sir Reynald was furious, but I'll wager it was because his companions hadn't cleaned up the mess left from the previous night's ritual."

"Isn't that jumping to conclusions?" Rhys said.

"Perhaps. But I find it suspicious that it was Sir Reynald's bull butchered and it's Sir Reynald who wants the land with the altar on it."

"I hate to interrupt this intriguing discussion," said Bos, "but all this talk of druids has reminded me of something. Today is June twenty-first."

"The summer solstice," Evan whispered. "Oh God, we must get to that altar. I'll wager that's where we'll find both Catrin and the chalice."

Sir Huw rose as they headed for the door. "I'm coming with you. It sounds as if there may be more than one of these druid fellows, and you'll need help."

"Why do you care?" Evan ground out. "I thought you hated Catrin."

"If that chalice caused my son's death, then I wish to make sure it causes no one else's. It's the least I can do when my daughter-in-law has risked her life to do the same. Besides, you'll need weapons. And I can provide them."

In truth, Evan was glad to have another man on this mission, as well as the weapons. He had no idea what they'd be facing . . . a single madman or several. And given what he knew of druids and their bloody practices . . .

As Sir Huw hurried to gather his hunting weapons, Evan shuddered, trying not to think of Catrin lying atop that pagan altar. If anything happened to her, what would he do? How would he live the rest of his life without her, burdened by the knowledge that he had failed her . . . that he had come too late?

Sir Huw brought out an impressive array of flintlock rifles and hunting knives. As Evan stared at them, he made a decision. He drew off his shirt and coat, then unwrapped his sling.

"What are you doing?" Rhys hissed. "You need that."

"I need the arm more right now," Evan retorted. "I can't fight with my arm in a sling." He flexed the muscle, wincing when he felt it pull on his shoulder. But he wouldn't be much good to them otherwise.

Ignoring Rhys's scowl, he donned his shirt and coat, then chose two rifles and a sword. Fortunately, he'd dealt with plenty of physical pain in his life, thanks to his father. He could endure this, too. If he had to, he could endure the fires of hell to save her.

Because he could never endure losing Catrin.

~

When Catrin came to, she was still bound and gagged. She was sitting outdoors, propped against something cold. It was dark yet, but she could sense the changes that came before dawn . . . a far-off rooster crowing . . . birds chirping . . . the dimming of the stars.

There was a fire, but it gave only the faintest light. For a second she wondered where she was and why she was bound. Then Sir Reynald stepped in front of her, and everything came back to her.

"I see that my druid princess is awake." He'd changed his clothing and now wore a belted white robe with ancient symbols embroidered on its hem. A crown of greenery, probably mistletoe, ringed his balding head, making him look like a ludicrous impersonator of Caesar.

But there was nothing ludicrous about the knife tucked into his woven belt, nor the evil smile that crossed his face. "You know where you are, don't you, my dear? You should. It's on your land."

The dolmen. She peered around the dimly lit clearing and was just able to make out the towering shapes of trees.

Damp, cold air drove a chill into her bones. She flexed her fingers behind her, and that was when she felt the metal shaft wedged between her bound hands.

The letter opener. Thank heaven. She tried moving the shaft up and down against her bonds. Although the letter opener was dull, at least it had an edge. Maybe if she sawed at the cravat long enough, she could free herself.

Sir Reynald clapped his hands and she jumped, fearing he'd realized what she was doing. Then he called out, "Ifor! Where are you?"

A man materialized out of the darkness, dressed much as Sir Reynald was, without the circlet of mistletoe. She'd seen him before. He was a laborer on Sir Reynald's land.

"Have you posted a man at the road?" Sir Reynald asked.

"Yes. And we've got someone at each corner."

"Good." Sir Reynald scanned the clearing. "I don't expect encroachers, but we mustn't take chances. The others will arrive any minute." He paused. "I don't see the bull for the sacrifice."

"Dafydd is bringing it. 'Tis difficult since he can't follow the road."

"I don't care how difficult it is," Sir Reynald spat. "The bull must be here in time for the ceremony."

Thunder rumbled in the distance, and Ifor scowled. "There's a storm brewing. 'Tis a bad omen to have a storm on the morning of the solstice. Perhaps we should wait."

"No!" With a glance at Catrin, Sir Reynald added, "The Fates have already given her to me, which is a *good* omen. Besides, the storm is a symbol of power. I welcome the thunder and lightning: Someday my descendants will rule both."

She shivered at the thought of a race of Sir Reynalds. She'd kill herself before she let him make her part of that.

But she didn't intend to die yet. Feverishly, she worked the letter opener up and down in the same spot. It didn't seem to be doing much, but she couldn't sit here and do nothing.

The clearing filled with men, and her heart sank when a flash of lightning revealed twenty in all. Even if she did saw through her bonds, how on earth would she escape twenty men? Especially when she was at the center of this absurd ritual?

She studied their faces, but recognized only some farmers and a tradesman from Llanddeusant. The others were strangers.

One man approached Sir Reynald, and she recognized him as the priest from a neighboring parish. It startled her to see a man of the cloth among such scoundrels.

Everyone's eyes were on her now, and she shrank back against the stone. Despite being fully dressed, she felt naked. What would Sir Reynald do once he discovered she wasn't a virgin? Would he bring her here to sacrifice? Did he and his companions ever sacrifice humans? Were they such monsters?

The wind howled through the trees, the otherworldly sound fueling her fear. She lifted her face to the wind, trying not to think of what Sir Reynald planned for her. It would only make her weak, and she needed to be strong.

Sir Reynald gave a signal and two men stepped forward. One bent to untie her ankles; the other removed her gag. Then they caught her under the arms and jerked her up. As her wrists strained against the cravat, she felt the cloth give a fraction.

As soon as she was on her feet, they released her, but her legs had long ago lost all feeling, thanks to her bonds, and she fell to her knees. This time it was Sir Reynald who lifted her, holding her against him with one arm.

Her feet caught fire as they came awake, and she had to bite her tongue to keep from crying out. She wasn't sure she could anyway, for her mouth felt dry as dust after being stuffed with a handkerchief. How did they expect to force her to voice marriage vows? Or did they even care if she did?

Lightning streaked across the predawn sky as Sir Reynald began to speak of the wedding that "the gods had sanctioned" and the future that was to come of their "holy union." As he droned on, she moved her wrists and discovered that between the sawing she'd done and the pressure the men had put on her bonds, she'd torn the cravat just enough to loosen it.

Her hands were nearly free and she thought she could wriggle out, but she'd have to wait for the right moment.

23

Evan and his companions crouched in the woods around the dolmen. Lightning crackled overhead, and Evan groaned as it lit up the clearing. The druids had Catrin. He could see her leaning against the dolmen. In the storm-dulled light of dawn, her pink gown stood in marked contrast to the white-robed men around her.

She appeared unharmed, but it was hard to tell, for the wind whipped her hair about her face. Her legs seemed too weak to hold her up, and her hands were bound behind her back.

Rage surged through him, especially when Sir Reynald drew her close to plant a kiss on her lips. Evan leapt to his feet, but Rhys jerked him down again.

"Don't be a fool, man!" Rhys growled. "You won't save her that way." He surveyed the clearing. "There's near to twenty of them, and a nasty-looking lot, too."

Evan gritted his teeth. Right now, he could tear every one of them limb from limb.

"What's the bloody bastard planning to do with her?" Sir Huw hissed. "He's got a bull out there, so he can't be planning to sacrifice her. Wait! He's holding up that chalice you described! What's he saying?"

Evan couldn't make it out. Now Sir Reynald stepped away from Catrin to fill the chalice with what looked like red wine. Evan *hoped* it was red wine and not something more gruesome. "They've got men posted along the circumference. One . . . two . . . I think there's four."

"One for each of us," Rhys said grimly. "Perhaps we should take them first, while everyone is engrossed in this bizarre ritual." He glanced at Bos. "Do you think you could manage that?"

Bos scowled. "I assure you, sir, I am perfectly capable of doing whatever it takes to defend my mistress from skullduggery."

"Good," Evan said. "We need every man we can get." He assessed the scene. "The only way we'll get through this is by trickery. They outnumber us five to one. But we have the element of surprise, and we have rifles. Nothing alarms a man so quickly as the roar of a flintlock."

"How do you intend to keep Sir Reynald from harming her?" Bos asked.

"Leave him to me." Evan had a few ideas about how to manage this rescue. "Now here's what we should do . . ."

~

Relief surged through Catrin when Sir Reynald insisted that they stand on one side of the dolmen while the priest stood on the other. Thanks to Sir Reynald's belief in his own self-importance, the other men crowded behind the priest, leaving Catrin and Sir Reynald alone on the side closest to the trees.

If she could somehow distract the men long enough to run into the forest, she might lose them all, especially if the storm broke. It was her only chance for escape. Once Sir Reynald had her locked up on his estate, she'd be doomed.

But how to distract them? She wriggled the cravat off her hands, then clenched the letter opener between her fingers. There was one way. If she focused their concern on their leader, she might slip away in the confusion. It was worth the attempt.

Her hands grew clammy on the letter opener. The priest was already intoning the words of the wedding mass. Thunder cracked overhead, making everyone jump, but the priest went on.

She must seize the moment ... or face a future too grisly to consider. Swiftly, she stepped back and drove the letter opener toward Sir Reynald's back in what might have been a deadly stroke if he hadn't turned just as she thrust.

Instead, the letter opener drove into his shoulder. He let out an earsplitting scream. For a moment she stood there in shock, watching the blood course down the pristine white sleeve of his robe. Then she ran.

At first, she was so intent on escape that she didn't hear the sound of guns firing behind her. But when pandemonium ensued and she spotted Evan running toward her from the trees, she realized that more than her attack on their leader had occurred. Another volley of shots went off, sending the men in the clearing scattering into the woods around her.

"Evan!" she sobbed as he reached her and caught her in his arms. "Evan, you're here!"

"We've got to get you away." He hooked his good arm about her waist and pulled her toward the trees. "I told the others to aim above their heads, but a stray shot might still hit us."

Shots whistled past them, far too low. Evan dropped to the ground, taking her with him. Two of Sir Reynald's men were shooting back at whomever fired from the woods.

Sir Reynald leaned over the dolmen to shout, "Murder every one of the bastards," as he wrenched the letter opener from his arm.

"Deuce take it," Evan growled. "Someone should have told these bastards that druids don't carry pistols."

A brief silence hit the clearing, punctuated only by the whine of the wind and a roll of thunder. "We'll have to take our chances." Evan sprang to a crouch and tugged on her arm. But as they headed for the woods again, five men blocked their path.

Evan pushed her behind him and drew his sword, but Catrin could tell he would never win this fight. And when someone grabbed her from behind, put a knife to her neck, and called out to Evan, "Drop the sword!" she was almost relieved. She didn't want Evan to die in her defense.

With a cry of utter anguish, Evan whirled and dropped his sword at once, his face ash-white as his gaze fixed on the knife. The five men rushed up to restrain him. Only then did the man holding her take the knife from her throat.

Then other men filtered into the clearing, pushing Bos, Sir Huw, and Rhys Vaughan ahead of them. She wanted to cry. They'd come to her rescue, and they would die.

"You fools!" shouted a voice.

Everyone turned to see Sir Reynald standing atop the dolmen.

As Catrin caught sight of his bloody sleeve, she wondered how he'd managed to crawl up there. He didn't seem human anymore. Gone was any hint of age. His eyes were alight with fury, and in his white robe, he looked invincible.

Fear washed over her. This was the man who meant to make her the mother of his child . . . who would torture her if she didn't comply. If she'd had any doubt before that he could and would do it, it was gone.

Rain started to fall in fat drops, but Sir Reynald seemed oblivious to it, for he drew the dagger from his belt and pointed it at Evan.

"You, sir, have made a grave mistake. You shall be our sacrifice for this evening instead of that bull." He smiled, but to Catrin it looked more like a grimace. "But first you will watch me wed your love. And then take her here, on this very altar. I'd planned something more private, but this is better, is it not?"

Evan roared, straining against the men that held him. "You can't kill us all, Sir Reynald! How will you hide the murders of a baronet, a squire, and a Cambridge scholar? They'll hunt you down like the dog that you are and they'll hang you!"

Sir Reynald laughed. "You don't understand, you fool. I have power beyond your dreams. I've spent years studying the ways of the ancients, and when I couple my knowledge with the power of the chalice, no one will ever cross me!"

He held the chalice high. "As the legend says, marriage to Morgana's descendant will make the husband as strong and powerful as the warrior! When Catrin and I say our vows and drink from the chalice, we will both be as gods! Gods!"

Catrin's eyes went wide as she stared at the chalice. It had begun to glow, as if to confirm what Sir Reynald said about the power imbued in it. An orange light shimmered over the bronze, growing more intense as she stared. It was like nothing she'd ever seen. The other men were murmuring and pointing, and absolute terror gripped her. How could she fight such power from the beyond? She and Evan and the rest of them were nothing but ants in the face of the ancient legend of the chalice.

But as Sir Reynald held the glowing vessel high, his face contorted with his greed for power, a clap of thunder sounded, so loud that she and the man who held her staggered back.

Lightning struck the chalice and consumed Sir Reynald, pummeling him with stunning force. Catrin couldn't turn her face away, couldn't move, couldn't utter a sound. The only sound in the clearing was the crackling of nature's wrath at the center of the dolmen.

As suddenly as it had come, the lightning released Sir Reynald and he crumpled over, tumbling off the dolmen to the ground like a marionette tossed aside by its maker.

Catrin averted her gaze from his blackened body, but she couldn't keep out the smell of burned flesh.

The man holding her cried, "It's a bad omen!" and fled, as did the other druids.

In seconds, the only people left in the circle of trees were she and Evan and his companions. Evan rushed to her side, gathering her up in his arms with a cry.

She buried her face in his chest. "Oh my God, Evan . . ."

"Are you all right?" He clutched her tightly. "Did that monster hurt you or touch you or—"

"No . . . although he was planning to marry me and keep me prisoner . . . but you heard what he . . ." She broke off in a flurry of sobs.

He stroked her back. "You're safe now, love. He can't hurt you anymore."

"Is he dead?"

"I'm sure he is." He kissed her hair. "Did you see the chalice before the lightning struck?"

"I saw." She lifted her face to his. "What made it glow?"

"I don't know, love."

"Holy God in heaven!" exclaimed a voice behind them, and Catrin turned to see Sir Huw standing over the dolmen. "Would you look at this? The stone is split in two!"

Catrin shuddered as she hid her face in Evan's shirt. She'd never forget Sir Reynald's expression as the lightning hit him . . . a mix of horror and disbelief and shock. He'd wanted power . . . and he'd gotten it, more than anyone could withstand. Perhaps there were things men weren't meant to have.

"What about the chalice?" Evan called out to Sir Huw. "What happened to it?"

Catrin tensed.

Rhys answered, his voice full of awe. "Come see. You won't believe this."

They headed over, careful to avoid where Bos knelt beside Sir Reynald's body, examining it for signs of life.

When Catrin caught sight of the chalice—or what was left of it—she gasped. The lightning had melted the metal to a misshapen lump. Where the image of the raven had been was only a swirled surface of blackened bronze. But on the other side, the image of the maiden and warrior were perfectly intact.

"I don't suppose anyone will be drinking out of it now," she whispered.

"No, love, I don't think so."

"Someone needs to send for the constable in Carmarthen," Sir Huw said. "I'll see to that." He walked from the clearing.

Rhys murmured, "I'll make sure none of those bastards are lurking in the forest, though I think they were all frightened out of their wits. I know I was." He headed off toward the woods.

"With your permission, madam," Bos said, "I shall return to the house and inform the staff of what has occurred. They are all beside themselves with worry."

Catrin nodded, then watched as Bos, too, left, so that only she and Evan remained. Evan led her away from the dolmen. The storm seemed miraculously to have disappeared, as if Sir Reynald had created a disturbance in the elements that subsided the moment he died.

Now the first light of dawn was breaking over the tops of the trees, limning the ancient oaks with golds and reds and lavenders. Catrin paused in the center of the clearing to glance up at the sky, thinking of all that had occurred, all the damage Sir Reynald had wrought. Yet Nature passed over it as if it were only a ripple in the surface of eternity.

"I think you should know," she told Evan, "it was Sir Reynald who killed your friend Justin. He . . . he learned about the chalice through David, and he has been waiting ever since to take it . . . and to take me."

"Yes, I figured that," Evan murmured, tightening his arm about her waist. "He also murdered David Morys."

"Sir Reynald said as much." A tear slipped down her cheek. "So many men have died because of Morgana's wretched chalice. The men in my family. Willie. Your friend. And now David, poor man. I wonder if Morgana dreamed of the legacy of pain she would create in her petulance over her daughter's marriage."

Evan drew in a ragged breath. "I've never believed in magic or fairies or such. But then, I've never seen anything like what I saw today."

Her pulse racing, she left his side to look at the clouds that had gone from black and thundering to white and floating in a matter of moments. "So what do we do now? What is to happen to us?"

He came up to slip his arm about her waist. "We marry and we have children and we love each other for the rest of our lives."

"What about the curse?" she whispered in an aching voice.

"You can't be expected to drink from a chalice that no longer exists."

"But perhaps it was destroyed because I'm meant to be cursed forever."

He nuzzled her hair. "I believe it's the opposite. When Sir Reynald tried to tap the chalice's power for evil, Morgana put an end to it. That's why the symbol of death, the raven, has been obliterated, leaving only the image of the warrior and maiden." He kissed her ear. "Us, my love. I may not be much of a rescuer and you may not have hair down to your toes, but we're the warrior and maiden all the same. Morgana is giving us her blessing."

It made sense. Still, she'd lived so long in fear of the curse that to think of marrying without drinking from the chalice made her uneasy. "But what if—"

"Catrin." He turned her to face him. "I love you. I want to marry you. For once in your life, risk everything. Take hold of happiness with both hands and say, 'To hell with the curse and fear and death. I want to live. With Evan.'"

He lifted her chin with the tip of his finger. "Because if you don't, I swear I will hound you until the day you die all alone and pining after me in your great mansion. And then I shall lie down beside you and die, too, for life without you is no life at all."

She stared up at the face of the man she loved more than breath, the only man she'd ever wanted to risk anything for. The thought of losing him to some nameless force beyond her understanding terrified her, but the thought of losing him to her own fear terrified her more.

He was right. Even three years with the one she loved would be better than none. And no years with him would be like dying, so what would be the point?

"Will you risk it?" he asked. "Will you take the chance and be my wife?"

There really was no choice at all. Twining her arms about his neck, she smiled at him with all the love that warmed her soul. "Yes, my love. Forever and ever and ever."

And the sweet, searing kiss he gave her was the best foretaste of forever that a woman could ever want.

EPILOGUE

Catrin awakened before dawn on the day after the third anniversary of her and Evan's wedding. She lay there thinking of the lovely celebration they'd had the night before—both the sedate one in the dining room and the scandalous one later in the bedroom.

With a contented smile, she rolled over to face Evan, but the bed was empty, and her breathing stopped.

Three years. It had been three years and a day.

As she slipped out of bed and searched for her wrapper, she told herself she was being foolish. Evan was almost never in bed when she arose. He liked to watch the sun rise over the Carmarthen Fans before he began the work of the day—helping her run Plas Niwl and writing his books.

Still, she dressed hurriedly and rushed out of the bedchamber. She wouldn't feel secure until she'd seen him.

She padded down the hall past the open door to the nursery, then stopped when she heard a deep male voice coming from inside.

A rush of relief hit her as she entered to find Evan sitting in a chair by the window. Two-year-old Justine was curled up in his lap with her thumb stuck in her mouth, and both father and daughter stared out the east-facing window, awaiting the dawn that trembled on the edge of the horizon.

A lump stuck in her throat as she watched them. Although Justine had Catrin's coloring and features, it was Evan whom the little girl most emulated. She, too, could never sleep past dawn, and she was far braver than Catrin had ever been, getting into more scrapes than such a tiny girl should. Already she was bilingual, speaking both Welsh and English.

It was Welsh she spoke now. "Papa," she said in her lilting voice, "sing me about the maid in the garden."

"Yes, my sweet." In a low, rumbling voice he sang the first verse of an old Irish folk song that Justine had fallen in love with:

> There was a maid in her father's garden
> A gentleman then passing by
> He stood awhile and he gazed upon her
> Saying, "Fair young lady, will you marry me?"

Catrin stood motionless as he continued the tale of the woman whose long-lost love returns to claim her after seven years at sea. All the while, he stroked Justine's tousled curls, and Justine watched him with the trusting expression children reserve only for their parents.

Her throat tightened painfully. It was hard to believe

that Evan had ever worried about being a father, that he'd once feared he might do violence to any child of theirs. He was so good with Justine, so kind and patient. Sometimes *too* kind and patient, for Justine had him wrapped about her little finger.

But Catrin could never deny him the pleasure of spoiling their daughter. She knew what it meant to him to see Justine's face light up at his words of praise.

Catrin placed her hand on the faint swell of her stomach. And she would let him spoil the next child and the next and the next.

He finished the song and glanced up to see her standing there. A smile broke over his face. "You're up early this morning, my love. Have you come to watch the sunrise with us?"

His words reminded her of why she'd been searching for him, and her fears now felt foolish. He probably didn't even realize what day it was. Neither of them had spoken of the curse since that morning in the clearing.

"I woke up . . . and you weren't there and . . ." She trailed off, uncertain whether to mention what had made her hurry from their bed.

But as she moved to his side, he took her hand and squeezed it. "I'm here, my darling." His eyes were solemn as he stared up at her. "I'm alive and well and plan to remain so for the rest of our lives."

As always, he didn't belittle or chastise her for her fears. He simply showed them for what they were. Shadows. Misty shapes that couldn't bear up under the light of their all-consuming love.

She hadn't realized until now how much this particular fear had permeated her life—how terrified she'd been of waking to find at the end of three years that she was still accursed, doomed to lose him.

And as the sun broke over the mountains in a shower of pink and orange and lavender, dusting the greening hills with a shimmer of golden light, the last vestiges of worry and despair melted away from her like dew beneath the heat of the morning sun.

"Life is good, isn't it?" Evan said as he lifted his face to hers.

With a smile, she bent to kiss his lips. "Life is very, very good."

Will Niall Lindsey, the Earl of Margrave, and Brilliana Payne Trevor, the girl whose heart he broke seven years ago, be able to put their pasts behind them and work together to clear her father's name?

Keep reading for a sneak peek at the next sizzling installment in *New York Times* bestselling author Sabrina Jeffries's Sinful Suitors series!

The Pleasures of Passion

Coming Summer 2017 from Pocket Books!

PROLOGUE

London
1823

Seventeen-year-old Brilliana Payne shoved the note from Lord Margrave's heir—Niall Lindsey—into her pocket. Then she slipped into her mother's bedchamber. "Mama," she whispered. "Are you awake?"

Her mother jerked her head up from amid the feather pillows and satin covers like a startled deer. Brilliana winced to see her mother's lips drawn with pain and her eyes dulled by laudanum, even in mid-afternoon.

"What do you need, love?" Mama asked in her usual gentle voice.

Oh, how she loathed deceiving Mama. But until her suitor spoke to his parents about their marrying, she had to keep the association secret.

"I'm going for my walk in Green Park." *Where Niall, my love, will join me.* "Do you need anything?"

Despite her pain, Mama smiled. "Not now, my dear. You go enjoy yourself. And tell Gilly to make sure you don't stray near the woods."

"Of course."

What a lie. The woods were where she would meet Niall, where Gilly would keep watch to make sure no one saw him and Brilliana together. Thank heaven her maid was utterly loyal to her.

Brilliana started to leave, then paused. "Um. Papa said he won't be home until evening." Which meant he wouldn't be home until he'd lost all his money at whatever game he was playing tonight. "Are you *sure* you don't need me?"

She dearly hoped not. Niall's note had struck her with dread, partly because he rarely wrote to her. Usually he just met her at Green Park for her daily stroll when he could get away from friends or family. Something must be wrong.

Still, it shouldn't take more than an hour to find out what. And perhaps let him steal a kiss or two.

She blushed. Niall was very good at *that*.

Then again, he ought to be. He was rumored to be a rogue with the ladies, although Brilliana was convinced it was merely because of his wild cousin, Lord Knightford, with whom he spent far too much time. Or so she'd heard.

"I'll be fine," Mama said tightly. "I have my medicine right here."

Medicine, ha! It made Mama almost as ill as whatever mysterious disease had gripped her. The doctors still couldn't figure out what was wrong with Mama, but they continued to try everything—bleeding her, cupping her, giving her assorted potions. And every time a new treatment was attempted, Brilliana hoped it would work, would be worth Mama's pain.

Guilt swamped Brilliana. "If you're sure . . ."

"Go, dear girl! I'm just planning to sleep, anyway."

That was all the encouragement Brilliana needed to hurry out.

A short while later, she and Gilly were in Green Park, waiting at the big oak for Niall.

"Did he say why he wanted to meet, miss?" Gilly asked.

"No. Just that it was urgent. And it had to be today."

Gilly flashed her a knowing smile. "Perhaps he means to propose at last."

Her breath caught. "I doubt it. He would have approached Papa if that were the case."

"Not if he wanted your consent first." Gilly smoothed her skirts. "That's how all the gentlemen is doing things these days, I'm told. And just think what your mama will say when she hears you've snagged an heir to an earl!"

"I haven't snagged anyone yet." Besides, the word *snag* was too coarse for what she wanted from Niall—his mind, his heart, his soul. Since hers already belonged to him.

"There you are," said a masculine voice behind them. "Thank God you came."

Brilliana's heart leapt as she turned to see Niall striding up to them. At twenty-three, he was quite the handsomest man she'd ever known—lean-hipped and tall and possessed of the most gorgeous hazel eyes, which changed color from brown to green depending on the light. And his unruly mop of gold-streaked brown hair made her itch to set it to rights.

Though she didn't dare be so forward in front of Gilly. Not until she and Niall were formally betrothed. Assuming that ever happened.

Offering Brilliana his arm, he cast Gilly a pointed glance. "I'll need a few minutes alone with your mistress. Will you keep watch?"

Gilly curtsied deeply. "Of course, my lord."

Then, without any of his usual pleasantries, he led Brilliana into the woods to the little clearing where they usually talked.

Her feeling of dread increased. "You do realize how fortunate we are that Gilly is a romantic. Otherwise, she would never let us do these things."

"I know, Bree." Though he was the only one to call her that, she rather liked the nickname. It made her sound carefree, when she felt anything but.

He halted well out of earshot of Gilly. "And then I wouldn't get the chance to do *this*."

He drew her into his arms for a long, ardent kiss, and she melted. If he was kissing her, he obviously didn't mean to break with her. And as long as they had this between them . . .

But it was over far too soon. And when he drew back to stare at her with a haunted look, her dread returned.

"What's wrong?" she whispered.

Glancing away, he mumbled a decidedly ungentlemanly oath. "You are going to be furious with me."

She fought to ignore the alarm knotting her belly. "I could never be furious with you. What has happened? Just tell me."

"This morning I fought a duel."

"What?" Her heart dropped into her stomach. Good Lord. How could that be? "I-I don't understand." She must have heard him wrong. Surely the man she'd fallen in love with wasn't the violent sort.

"I killed a man, Bree. In a duel."

She hadn't misheard him, then. Still scarcely able to believe it, she roamed the little clearing, her blood like sludge in her veins. "What on earth would even make you do such a thing?"

"It doesn't matter." He threaded his fingers through his sun-kissed hair. "It's done, and now I risk being hanged."

Hanged? Why would he be—

Of course. Dueling was considered murder. Her heart stilled. Her love was a murderer. And now he could die, too!

"So I'm leaving England tonight," he went on. "For good."

The full ramifications of all he'd revealed hit her. "You . . . you're leaving England," she echoed hollowly. *And me.*

His gaze met hers. "Yes. And I want you to go with me."

That arrested her. "Wh-what do you mean?"

"I'm asking you to marry me." He seized her hands. "Well, to elope with me. We'll go by ship to Spain, and we'll wed there. Then my friends in Valencia will help us settle in."

She gaped at him. He was *serious*. He actually meant for her to leave her family and home and run away with him now that he'd gone off and *killed* a man.

But in a duel. Might it not have been done with good reason?

"Do you *have* to go abroad?" she asked. "Sometimes the courts will acquit a gentleman of the charges, assuming the duel was a just one—"

"It was." His face clouded over. "But I can't risk defending myself in court."

"What do you mean? Why not?"

His expression grew shuttered. "I can't say. It's . . . complicated."

"It can't be more complicated than running away to the Continent, for pity's sake."

A muscle worked in his jaw. "Look, I've made a vow to keep the reasons for the duel quiet. And I have to keep that vow."

"Even from me?" She couldn't hide the hurt in her voice. "Why? Who demanded such a thing of you?"

"I can't say, damn it!" When she flinched, he said, "It's not important."

"It certainly is to *me*. You want me to run off with you, but you won't even explain why you fought or even with whom you dueled?"

Letting out an oath, he stared past her into the woods. "I suppose I can reveal the other party in the duel, since that will get around soon enough. The man's name is Joseph Whiting."

She didn't know any Joseph Whiting, so that bit of information wasn't terribly helpful.

"But that's all I can reveal." He fixed her with a hard look. "You're simply going to have to trust me on this. Go with me, and I will take care of you."

"What about passports? How can you even be sure that we can marry in Spain?"

"There's no reason we can't. And I have a passport—we'll arrange for yours once we arrive."

She didn't know anything about international travel, but his plan sounded awfully havey-cavey. "If you're wanted for murder here, surely no British consulate—"

"I promise you, it will all turn out well in the end."

"You can't promise that."

"Deuce take it, I *love* you," he said, desperation in his tone. "Isn't that enough?"

"No! You're asking me to risk my entire future to go with you. To leave my family and my home, possibly never to see either again. So, no, it is *not* enough, drat you!"

He squeezed her hands. "Are you saying you don't share my feelings?"

"You know I do." Her heart lurched in her chest. "I'd follow you to the ends of the earth if I could, but I can't right now." Certainly not without some assurance that he truly meant to marry her and not just . . . well . . . carry her off to have his way with her.

Oh Lord, that was absurd. Just because he was heir to an earl and she the daughter of an impoverished knight didn't mean that Niall would stoop so low. Granted, she'd heard of women being fooled into thinking they were eloping when really they weren't, women who were discarded after they'd served their usefulness to some randy lord.

But Niall would never do such a thing. He was an honorable man.

Except for the fact that he fought a duel he won't tell me about.

She winced. It didn't matter. He would never hurt her that way. She couldn't believe it. And for a moment, the idea of being his forever, of traveling abroad and seeing the world without their families to make trouble—

Families. That brought reality crashing in. "You know I can't leave Mama." Regretfully, she tugged her hands from his. "She needs me."

"*I* need you." His lovely eyes were dark with entreaty. "Your mother has your father."

"The man who spends every waking moment at his club or in the hells, gambling away my future and Mama's," she said bitterly. "She could die, and he wouldn't even notice."

All right, so that was an exaggeration, but not much of one. Papa had never met a card game he didn't like. Unfortunately, he'd never met one he could win at, either. But he certainly spent all his time and money trying to find one.

And consequently, Mama spent much of *her* time alone with Brilliana or servants. Brilliana had hoped that when—*if*—Niall proposed marriage, she could persuade him to let her take Mama to live with them. But that was impossible if he meant to carry her off to the Continent.

"What about *your* family?"

He tensed. "What about them?"

"Do your parents know that you mean to flee London? Have you spoken to your father about . . . well . . . *us?*"

"He knows I'm leaving England. But no, he doesn't know about us, because I wanted to speak to you first. In case you . . . refused to go."

His reluctance to tell his parents about their courtship before approaching *her* parents had been a bone of contention between them.

She'd understood—really, she had. She probably wasn't lofty enough to suit his family, and Niall had been waiting until she had her come-out and his parents could meet her in a natural setting. Then he could ease them into the idea of his wanting to wed her.

But now . . . "You could still speak to *my* parents, gain their blessing and agreement to the marriage. Then you . . . you could get a special license, and we could marry before we leave here."

Though that didn't solve the problem of Mama.

"There's no time for that! Besides, it takes at least two days to acquire any kind of license. And my ship leaves to-night." He drew her close. "For once in your life, sweeting, throw caution to the wind. You love me. I love you. We belong together. I don't know how I'll bear it if you don't flee with me."

His words tore at her. She wanted *desperately* to go.

And apparently he could read the hesitation in her face, for he took advantage, clasping her head in his hands so he could plunder her mouth with breathtaking thoroughness.

Oh Lord, but the man could kiss. He made her heart soar, and her blood run fast and hot. Looping her arms about his neck, she gave herself up to the foretaste of what their lives could be like . . . if she would just give in.

But how could she? Reluctantly, she broke the kiss, even knowing it might be their last.

His eyes glittered with triumph, for he could always tell how easily he tempted her. "I know this isn't the ideal way for us to start out, Bree, but I'll make it up to you. Father will continue to send my allowance, and my friends will take care of us until we're settled. I might even find work in Spain."

She wavered. It sounded wonderful and exciting and oh, so tempting.

He cupped her cheek. "All we have to do is go. Tonight, with the tide. You and I, together for the rest of our lives. Trust me, you won't regret going."

Ah, but she would.

She could handle travel to a strange country and everything that such an upheaval entailed. She could live on a pittance. And yes, she would even risk ruin if it meant being with him.

But she couldn't leave Mama. Papa would never manage the doctors or sit wiping Mama's brow when she was feverish. Papa could hardly bear to be in the sickroom. He'd rather run off to his club. And with money short because of his gambling, they couldn't afford a servant to tend her mother night and day. Besides, she could never entrust Mama's care to a servant.

She pushed away from him. "I can't," she said. "I'm sorry."

Explore the history of desire with bestselling
historical romance from Pocket Books!

Pick up or download your copies today!

XOXOAfterDark.com

POCKET BOOKS
An Imprint of Simon & Schuster
A CBS COMPANY

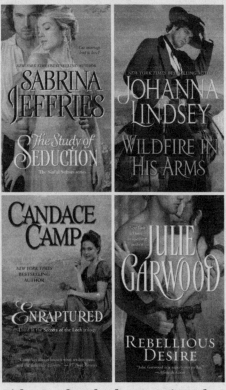